PENGUIN BOOKS

Judy Nunn's career has been long, illustrious and multifaceted. After combining her internationally successful acting career with scriptwriting for television and radio, Judy decided in the '90s to turn her hand to prose.

Her first three novels, *The Glitter Game*, *Centre Stage* and *Araluen*, set respectively in the worlds of television, theatre and film, became instant bestsellers, and the rest is history, quite literally, in fact. She has since developed a love of writing Australian historically based fiction and her fame as a novelist has spread rapidly throughout Europe, where she has been published in English, German, French, Dutch, Czech and Spanish.

Her subsequent bestsellers, *Kal*, *Beneath the Southern Cross*, *Territory*, *Pacific*, *Heritage*, *Floodtide*, *Maralinga*, *Tiger Men*, *Elianne*, *Spirits of the Ghan*, *Sanctuary* and *Khaki Town*, have confirmed Judy's position as one of Australia's leading fiction writers. She has now sold over one million books in Australia alone.

In 2015 Judy was made a Member of the Order of Australia for her 'significant service to the performing arts as a scriptwriter and actor of stage and screen, and to literature as an author'.

Visit Judy at judynunn.com.au or on
facebook.com/JudyNunnAuthor

T0363335

Books by Judy Nunn

The Glitter Game
Centre Stage
Araluen
Kal
Beneath the Southern Cross
Territory
Pacific
Heritage
Floodtide
Maralinga
Tiger Men
Elianne
Spirits of the Ghan
Sanctuary
Khaki Town

Children's fiction
Eye in the Storm
Eye in the City

Short stories (available in ebook)
The House on Hill Street
The Wardrobe
Just South of Rome
The Otto Bin Empire: Clive's Story
Oskar the Pole
Adam's Mum and Dad

JUDY NUNN

Spirits of the Ghan

PENGUIN BOOKS

PENGUIN BOOKS

UK | USA | Canada | Ireland | Australia
India | New Zealand | South Africa | China

Penguin Books is part of the Penguin Random House group of companies
whose addresses can be found at global.penguinrandomhouse.com.

Penguin
Random House
Australia

First published by William Heinemann, 2015
Published by Arrow, 2016
This edition published by Penguin Books, 2020

Cover design by Josh Durham/Design by Committee
Map by Ice Cold Publishing
Internal design and typesetting by Midland Typesetters, Australia

Printed and bound in Australia by Griffin Press, part of Ovato, an accredited
ISO AS/NZS 14001 Environmental Management Systems printer

A catalogue record for this
book is available from the
National Library of Australia

ISBN 978 1 76104 132 7

penguin.com.au

MIX
Paper from
responsible sources
FSC® C009448

There are more things in heaven and earth, Horatio,
Than are dreamt of in your philosophy.
William Shakespeare, *Hamlet*, Act I, Scene 5

AUTHOR'S NOTE

The anglicised spelling of Indigenous peoples, lands and languages varies immensely. This may well be dependent upon those who initially chose to translate a purely oral language to the written word, for example the German influence of Lutheran missionary Carl Strehlow in Hermannsburg during the early twentieth century.

There are several central desert groups mentioned in this book. These are the Arunta, the Western Arunta, Eastern Arunta, and the Anmatyerre a little further to the north.

These anglicised names are also recorded as Arrernte, Arrarnte, Arunda, Anmatjere and Anmatjerre. Indeed, there may well be many other ways to spell them, but I have chosen Arunta and Anmatyerre. In the first instance I followed the advice of a local Indigenous authority who adamantly favoured 'Arunta', mainly in order to clarify pronunciation as the emphasis should be on the first syllable, which I've found to be the case in the pronunciation of most groups.

The characters in this book are fictional and so are their names. In all instances I have changed the spelling of traditional names for my Aboriginal characters. If in doing so I have inadvertently used the real name of a deceased person, I humbly apologise.

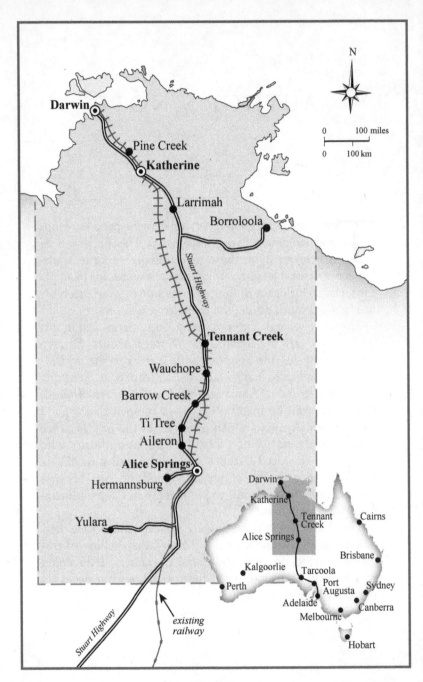

The Ghan

PROLOGUE

1876

James McQuillan knew he was a dead man. He knew the instant the snake struck. A large king brown, a good six feet in length. He didn't know how long his death would take or how much pain might accompany it, but he was aware the sight would not be pretty. 'Get back to the homestead, Emily, and fetch help,' he said. Quelling as best he could the fear that accompanied his awful knowledge, he kept his voice authoritative: 'Hurry along now, there's a good girl.' There was no point in her fetching help, he would be dead long before her return, but if his daughter were to witness his death she might panic and lose her way home. It was imperative he give her a sense of purpose.

Legs outstretched on the dusty red earth, he leant his burly frame back against the rock, the very rock with the very crevice from which the snake had darted its head. The very rock he'd steadied his hand upon while leading the way down to the rock pool. He'd so wanted to share with his daughter this oasis, this perfect gift of nature nestled in the desert. A place of such beauty, where white-trunked gums grew stark and ghostly out of ochre-red rocks that walled a pristine lagoon of blue. He cursed himself now. How could he have been such a fool? He was a dead man, and his daughter's life was in jeopardy. Emily should be safely home in Adelaide. He should never have brought her to this wilderness.

Sixteen-year-old Emily stared down at her father, dumb-struck with fear. She had seen the snake. Light brown in colour with a flat cobra-like head, it had struck with such speed and ferocity and then disappeared so quickly that she hadn't even screamed. Now, upon her father's instruc-tion, she was galvanised into action.

'No, Father, no,' she said, crouching beside him and urgently taking a hold of his arm. 'I can help you to your horse. We'll get you home together and Alfred will look after you.' Alfred was the property's overseer. A tough outback man, Alfred would know what to do. But even as she spoke, her father's arm began to shudder. The action was not deliberate, she knew, but a series of involuntary muscular spasms, and it frightened her.

'Do as you're told, Emily.' James tried once again to sound authoritative, but he was starting to convulse and his throat was swelling. His larynx restricted, his voice was only a painful rasp. Soon paralysis would set in and he would be unable to speak at all. 'Go home and fetch Alfred. Be quick now.' They had set out in the late after-noon to avoid the heat of the day, but she had a good hour of light still ahead of her, he told himself, and the homestead was only a two-mile ride away. So long as she doesn't get lost, James prayed, so long as she doesn't . . .

'Head east,' he said with the last few words he could push out, 'keep the sun behind you. Head east . . .' Then as his throat restricted further his voice failed him altogether.

Emily stood, her chest heaving, her breath coming in frantic, fevered gasps. Her father's body was starting to shake uncontrollably, but his eyes were still upon her, very much alive and ordering her to go.

Half blinded by tears of sheer terror, she turned from him and ran to where the horses were tethered twenty yards away. She must save her father. 'My daughter can ride like the wind!' She could hear his laughter and the proud boast to his friends; he delighted in her skill as a horsewoman. She tightened the girth strap and mounted the hardy little mare. She could hear him now, urging her on. 'Ride like the wind, Emily! Ride like the wind!' Well, she would ride as she had never ridden before. There was still time: there had to be. She must save her father's life.

James tried to watch her go, his eyes rolling in their sockets, but he couldn't see her. He couldn't move his head. He couldn't move any part of himself. Brain and body were disconnected, no longer his to command. All that remained was thought. And thought said, *There is no road to the homestead, not even a track, and I didn't think to teach her the landmarks.* Then a further thought ... *I should have told her to let the mare have her head – the mare will sense the way home.* Then all that was left as the venom overtook him was a terrible guilt and self-recrimination.

How could I have let this happen?

James Angus McQuillan, only son of Angus Donald McQuillan, gentleman, farmer and Director of the Bank of Scotland, was born in 1820 in Dundee, Scotland on 21 August, a birthday, he often remarked, that he shared with King William IV.

After migrating to Adelaide in 1854 to appraise and report on his father's already-established land-holdings in South Australia, James had formed a business partnership with lawyer and fellow Scot, Edwin Moss. The two presented an odd couple in appearance, James ginger-bearded and burly, Edwin moustachioed, lean and lanky, but a strong friendship developed between the Scotsmen, a friendship based on mutual respect, for they were similarly shrewd when it came to business.

In 1859 McQuillan, Moss & Co invested with Elder, Stirling & Co to finance the Wallaroo and Moonta

Copper Mines. After initial risks, the investment brought them a handsome return, and over the ensuing years James and Edwin went from strength to strength, acquiring vast tracts of land that spread further and further into the untouched wastes of South Australia and the territory to the north known as Alexandra Land. In tackling the problems presented by the outback, they spent thousands of pounds on fencing and the sinking of bores until finally their pastoral properties constituted a land mass far larger than the whole of their native Scotland. James McQuillan and Edwin Moss had become wealthy men.

James lived a happy, fulfilled life. He had fallen in love two years after his arrival in Adelaide, and became engaged to Eleanor Welles, a fair-haired, pretty young Englishwoman. Eleanor was the daughter of a prominent banker with whom James did a great deal of business and everyone agreed it was an ideal match. 'Convenient', some even said a little archly, which was an apt enough comment for the relationship did indeed benefit all parties concerned, but this happy fact did not make the love shared by the couple any the less real.

The two married and in 1860, after several unfortunate miscarriages, Eleanor finally bore James a daughter, Emily, who grew to be a replica of her mother. James, who could be surprisingly effusive when something delighted him, as Emily did, would happily declare to one and all in his rich Scottish brogue, 'She's the apple of my eye, that wee girl, the apple of my eye.'

The McQuillans lived in a gracious three-storey home that James had had specially designed in North Terrace, the very heart of Adelaide. A wide circular carriageway led up to the front of the house, where a series of impressive stone arches formed the ground floor facade, while the broad balconies above, encased by a lacework of ornate railings, offered excellent views of the surrounding township and countryside. The grounds were spacious and beautifully landscaped, with separate servants' quarters at the rear near stables housing James's beloved horses and a large barn sheltering a selection of vehicles – work-drays, traps, buggies and a covered carriage – together with the requisite harness tackle.

McQuillan House was a symbol of James's position in society and far larger than was necessary to meet the family's requirements, but it was not a deliberate show of ostentation. James and Eleanor intended to have many children, and their lifestyle obliged them to entertain. Along with the many philanthropic concerns both had embraced, Eleanor was a keen follower of the arts and nurtured budding writers and painters, while James, as a member of the Adelaide Legislative Council, took his civic duties very seriously.

Given the diversity of the couple's interests, McQuillan House saw numerous and eclectic social gatherings over the years. There were dinners with twenty to table in the formal dining room, gala charity concerts staged in the front salon, casual afternoon teas held on the balcony and huge garden parties each spring. But sadly, as time passed, the house did not see a growth in family numbers. After suffering another two miscarriages, both times well into her second trimester, Eleanor was warned that any further attempt to bear children could prove dangerous, perhaps even fatal.

'Oh James, I am so very, very sorry.' When the doctor had gone, Eleanor succumbed to the tears she'd been desperately fighting back. In her weakened state, they now flowed freely as her husband sat beside her on the bed. 'Oh my dearest, how I have let you down.'

'There, there, my dear, you have done nothing of the sort, don't talk such nonsense.' James drew his kerchief from his breast pocket and wiped the tears from her cheeks. His tone was brisk and business-like: indulging her in any maudlin sentiment would do her no good, he thought, though in truth his heart ached to see his normally vibrant wife so wretched and unhappy. 'Come along now, blow your nose,' he said as if to a child. 'No more tears, there's a good girl.'

She blew her nose obediently, but she could not stem the flow of tears. 'You married the wrong woman, James. You should have chosen a stronger wife, one who could give you the family you've always longed for.'

He took her hand in both of his and pressed it gently to his lips. 'I married exactly the right woman, my dear,' he said. 'I married the woman with whom I wish to spend the whole of my life. And we have a family. We have Emily.'

'But the sons you so craved . . .'

Disappointment ran deep, it was true; he would very much miss having sons. But he would teach Emily to ride like a man . . . He would imbue in Emily the thrill of adventure . . . 'Emily is family enough,' he said firmly, 'now go to sleep: we need you strong.'

Although his intention had been merely to placate his distraught wife, the years proved James right. All of the love he might have lavished on a large family he focused upon his daughter, who became the very centre of his existence. Emily was not mollycoddled or spoilt though, for that was not James's way. From a very early age she was treated as an adult and shared in his life, in his very dreams and expectations. Father and daughter quite simply adored each other.

To many, James McQuillan appeared a somewhat contradictory man. He was personally wealthy and lived a lavish lifestyle, yet the speeches he made at legislative council meetings were invariably in opposition to what he considered extravagant government spending. He was practical and conservative, his public addresses short and to the point, yet on social occasions, particularly as host in his own home, he was flamboyant and could wax lyrical with the best. But the most contradictory element

in James McQuillan's make-up was something that would
have been beyond the comprehension of his desk-bound
city colleagues. James McQuillan was an adventurer, a
man whose love of the outback was so fierce it bordered
on passion.

Even Edwin Moss, James's friend and business partner,
did not know the degree of passion he felt for the rugged
beauty of central Australia. Certainly the two had shared
excitement over their ventures into the wilderness of Alexandra Land. Certainly where others had seen nothing but
dry desert James and Edwin had seen endless possibility.
But Edwin had not bonded with the land as James had,
and James had not seen fit to share his feelings about
something he regarded as intensely personal. He did,
however, share them with his thirteen-year-old daughter,
painting vivid pictures of giant gorges and fiery-red escarpments and huge gum trees growing from the centre of
dusty, dry riverbeds.

'A primitive land, Emily,' he told her, 'a land so spiritual
you cannot help but feel at one with it. A person is closer
to God out there, I swear. You can feel His very presence.'

So enthralled was Emily with the images her father
painted of a landscape foreign to the green hills of Adelaide
that she made him promise to take her to see his newest
holding, a cattle station many days' journey from anywhere.

'I don't see why not,' James agreed, much to Eleanor's
consternation. 'Perhaps in a year or so when the homestead's living quarters are completed and the station is
running smoothly.'

'Not until she is sixteen, James,' Eleanor insisted. 'I will
not hear of it. Not until she has turned sixteen.'

'Very well,' James acquiesced good-naturedly, 'sixteen
it is. The homestead will be finished altogether by then.'

'And we'll travel up by camel?' Emily asked excitedly.

'We will indeed. You and I will be in a cart drawn by
a camel pair-in-hand, and a camel train will follow with

supplies. Splendid animals, splendid – this country would be lost without them.'

James McQuillan, like a number of adventurous businessmen, saw the camel as the answer to the transport problems of the outback. Recently, with the help of Thomas Elder, a fellow aficionado of the camel and first to introduce the animals to Australia, James had imported a batch of breeding dromedaries, together with Afghan cameleers to manage the beasts. He intended to breed sturdy stock at his pastoral property in Alexandra Land. An area of well over one thousand square miles, the property's border lay just twenty-five miles southwest of one of the newly established overland telegraph repeater stations, so an accessible track from Adelaide was already in existence.

The Overland Telegraph Line, traversing the continent from Adelaide in the south to the furthermost northern port of Palmerston, had been completed just the previous year, in 1872, and had very much followed the route of explorer John McDouall Stuart, who, a decade earlier, had led the first successful expedition north through central Australia. A massive undertaking, the Line had linked Australia by undersea cable to Java and therefore Great Britain. Two thousand miles of telegraph line had been painstakingly erected through the desert heart of the country and telegraph poles and materials for the construction of repeater stations had been transported into the barren wilderness. It was an extraordinary feat all round and, as James was wont to point out when enthusing about his new business venture, one that could only have been made possible by the camel.

'Couldn't have been done without the camel,' he would declare in a tone that defied argument. 'Not only is Australia now linked with the rest of the world, but the vast interior of this country is opened up for settlement, and all thanks to the camel! Just think of that! A splendid animal, splendid!'

The construction of the homestead on James's property was completed well before Emily's sixteenth birthday. The mud-brick and timber house consisting of five rooms with surrounding verandahs was modest, but comfortable; several smaller outbuildings and sheds housed employees and supplies; and there were corrals for the horses and camels. Already, within only three short years, Eleanor Downs Station was running smoothly, although yet to turn a profit, which was hardly to be expected at this early stage.

James had named the property in honour of his wife and Eleanor had accepted the tribute although they both knew it was doubtful she would ever travel there. The gentle foothills outside Adelaide were as far afield as Eleanor McQuillan wished to venture.

Now, as his daughter's sixteenth birthday approached, James intended to fulfil his promise. Indeed he couldn't wait. He was excited beyond measure by the prospect of showing Emily the glories of the outback.

'Oh James, must you?' Eleanor couldn't stop herself saying. 'Must you really?'

'Of course I must, my dear, a promise is a promise.'

Eleanor breathed a sigh of resignation, knowing any protest would go unheard by both her husband and daughter.

Several months later, final arrangements were made.

'No, Emily, of course you can't take Nell with you.' James laughed at the preposterousness of his daughter's suggestion. 'Nell's a city horse. She's not made for the bush.'

'But she's tough and she's spirited, Father – that's why I called her Nell Gwyn. My Nell's afraid of nothing. And she can go like the wind,' Emily added eagerly in the hope her father's favourite catchphrase might clinch the matter.

It didn't. 'There'll be plenty of outback ponies at Eleanor Downs,' James said firmly, 'I can assure you of that. And they'll be tough and spirited and fast enough even for you, my girl.'

Realising the response was a definite 'no', Emily didn't persist any further. But she would miss her Nell.

Now, as she urged the hardy little chestnut on to its very limits, Emily tried to keep her panic in check. Normally she would not work a horse so hard in such terrain; there were rocks and the mare could injure herself. But these were not normal circumstances. She must trust in the outback pony's sure-footedness and ability to avoid danger.

'Ride like the wind, Emily! Ride like the wind!' She kept hearing her father's voice in her head as she rode, little knowing that, a mile behind her at the rock pool, James McQuillan already lay dead.

She tried to recognise landmarks she might have passed on the ride out from the homestead. Was that red, rocky outcrop familiar? That clump of mulga over there? That ghostly white gum to the right? But there were so many rocky outcrops, so much mulga, so many white gums dotted about in the endless sea of spinifex and grasses – everything looked the same.

Then they were into slightly different terrain. The bush was becoming a little denser, more acacias, more casuarinas, more mulgas. A spindly dead tree lay on its side up ahead. The little chestnut sailed over it with ease. We must surely have travelled two miles by now, Emily thought. Once again, panic started to set in.

The horse had occasionally tried to veer to the right, but Emily forced it to stay on the course she had chosen, directly ahead. The animal now slowed its pace just a little, uncertain, indecisive, but Emily urged it on with her hands and her heels and her voice. In her terror-stricken state she had forgotten her father's one instruction, 'Head east, keep the sun behind you.' The sun, which was now setting, was no longer behind them. She was heading not east, but north, and had been for some time.

The mare, well trained, would have continued to obey instructions, but sensing her rider's panic she took the bit between her teeth and veered sharply off course. Emily kept her seat, but in fighting to regain control she jagged at the reins, dislodging the bit, which tore into the sensitive corner of the animal's mouth.

The mare too was in a state of panic. Ignoring the pain and the harsh metal bit, she wheeled sharply about, prepared to bolt in the direction that she sensed was home.

Emily was thrown from the saddle. She had been thrown from horses before and instinctively let go of the reins as she'd been taught, protecting herself with her hands and rolling with the fall to land bruised but unhurt among the desert grasses.

She sat up, winded and nursing a painful elbow, and, as she watched the horse gallop off she knew she'd taken the wrong action. She should have kept hold of the reins, even if in doing so she'd checked the animal's stride and risked an injury from its hooves.

Rising to her feet, she stood motionless, staring after the horse until she could barely see it in the surrounding scrublands, and as she stared there was strangely just one thought in her mind. Nell would never gallop off like that. Nell would never abandon me.

Then the horse was gone. Even the distant dust of its flight had settled, and she was alone. Alone in the gathering dusk, and soon darkness would fall.

The hours that followed were terrifying beyond Emily's wildest imaginings. Night crept around her, sinister and threatening, and in its black cloak she could hear sounds. Sounds from all directions – strange animal sounds, encircling her, closing in, bent on attack.

She ran, crashing, stumbling, falling in the darkness, scrambling to her feet and running desperately on, but she could not outdistance the sounds. They were not following her: they were everywhere. There was no escape.

Finally, exhausted and unable to run any further, she curled herself into a ball among the undergrowth and dried branches of dead trees and waited. Shivering with terror and on the border of madness, she waited for whatever fearful animal was about to devour her.

But as time passed no animal came, and in her fatigued state she drifted into a fitful sleep.

She awoke she didn't know how much later, perhaps minutes, perhaps hours, but still in darkness, still in the awful nightmare of her existence. Only there were no sounds, no noise at all, just a deathly silence. Had the sounds earlier been of her own making? Not able to tell, she stayed, curled up in a ball, not daring to move – the slightest rustle of the grasses could alert whatever might lie in wait out there in the night.

When next she awoke it was dawn, a radiant desert dawn, vibrant colours rising from the horizon to paint a cloudless sky and herald the sun. She uncurled her cramped body and stood stiffly, her bruised muscles aching, but feeling with the beauty of the dawn renewed hope. Surely the worst must be over. She had thought she was dead, but she was not and a new day was beginning.

Then as the first of the sun's rays appeared over the horizon, she again heard her father's voice, 'Head east ... head east ...', and she started towards the sunrise, walking now with purpose.

But the day, as it wore on, proved more horrific than the night. In only minutes the sun had made a mockery of the dawn. Dismissing all colour, even the very blueness of the sky itself, the sun glared down relentlessly, harsh and uncaring.

On and on Emily tramped towards the east. She knew it was far from midday for the sun was barely halfway up in the morning sky, and yet the heat was so intense. And she was so incredibly thirsty. Thinking of water, she involuntarily tried to swallow, but found she couldn't, her mouth was too dry, her throat too parched. Doggedly she continued, one foot after another, plodding in time to the mantra that rang in her brain, head east . . . head east . . .

Two hours later, she was dizzy and disoriented. The sun was directly overhead now and she no longer had any idea where east was. Through squinted eyes she could barely see for the glare. Her face was burning, her lips cracked, her breathing dry and laboured, but still she walked on, perhaps in the hope she might find water. In her dazed state she didn't know, just as she didn't know where she was going, but she was too afraid to stop. If she stopped, she would die.

As she walked, flies settled on her face, gathering around her mouth and her eyes and her nostrils, seeking her moisture, but she made no attempt to brush them away. All energy was preserved for walking. Even thought was banished as her mind simply planted one foot after another.

She started to stagger, several times nearly falling, but saving herself, pausing briefly and moving on. She was hallucinating now. In a shimmering world somewhere on the brink of death, she could see lakes of water and the shapes of people waving, beckoning. She even waved back as she struggled towards them, although something told her they weren't real.

Then she staggered a final time and couldn't save herself. She collapsed, first to her knees, then forwards onto the hot, red earth, knowing that she would never get up. The long walk was over.

She rolled onto her back, looked up at the blinding sky of white light and, closing her eyes to the sun, she surrendered.

Emily was to all purposes dead, beyond thought, beyond hope, when something stirred her back to consciousness. Strange sounds, harsh and discordant, registered in the hazy recesses of her brain as something akin to the human voice.

She opened her eyes to find the blinding light of the sun blocked out and in its place the faces of black men. They were leaning over her, three of them, peering down closely and speaking to each other in their strange language.

One of the men prodded her roughly in the side with his foot, as if to see what life was left in her.

She tried to scream, but no sound came out. The man barked an order at one of the others, who bent down and picked her up with ease, flinging her over his shoulder as he might a kangaroo he'd speared.

Then, as the men loped off into the afternoon with their catch, Emily once again lost consciousness.

PART ONE

CHAPTER ONE

J essica Manning was proud of her Aboriginality.

When people asked about her parentage, as they so often did, she would say, 'Aboriginal Irish,' then add with her irresistibly cheeky grin: 'An exotic mix.'

She was directly quoting her father.

'Exotic, that's what you are, Jess,' Toby Manning had told his daughter back in the seventies when she was tiny and he was preparing her for her first day at school. He doubted there'd be any other Aboriginal children in attendance at Balmain primary school and he was concerned she might cop some taunting from the white kids.

'A mix of the Dreamtime and the blarney,' he'd assured her with a wink. 'You don't get much more exotic than that.'

As it turned out, Toby had no cause for concern. Little Jess had encountered no taunting. To the contrary, her schoolmates had gravitated to her, as had her teachers. There was something magnetic about Jess. And as she grew from childhood to womanhood, her magnetism did not diminish, if anything it increased. It was difficult to say exactly why, but Jess attracted people.

In appearance, she was not really exotic, she was not even particularly beautiful, not in the conventional sense anyway, but when Jess walked into a room people noticed. Above average height, unruly black curls that bounced with an independence of their own, and fine, toffee-coloured skin that bore a satin-like sheen contributed to make her an arresting figure certainly, but it was her carriage and her manner that were most demanding of attention. She moved with an easy grace, at one with her body. She was confident without being cocky, opinionated without being arrogant. She looked people straight in the eye and said what she thought, and when she laughed she threw back her head and relished the moment. Jess was fun to be with.

Jessica Manning's self-assurance was no doubt inherent, but her comfort in being the product of an inter-racial marriage was directly attributable to her Irish father. Toby Manning had instilled in his daughter all the positivity he'd hoped to instil in his wife, the person he'd loved more than anyone in the world.

'Ah Rosie, my Rosie, you're magnificent,' he used to say in the good old days as he watched his wife dance and listened to her sing. Just for him. Rose would sing and dance, just for him: it was her gift. 'You have the music in you, girl, it's singing out through your very soul.' And it was, Toby thought. In all his years as a sound engineer, and a very successful one, he'd worked with many great musical talents, but he never met anyone quite like Rose. Music coursed through her veins: it was her connection with the world. But she had no wish to make a career of her gift – it was something she shared just with him. Music had been their bond, right from the start.

Rose Napangurrayi was a Western Arunta woman. She was born in 1950 at Hermannsburg in central Australia, but at the age of six she was taken from her parents by government agents and placed in the care of the Franklin family, wealthy owners of Eleanor Downs Station, one of the earliest established cattle properties in the Northern Territory.

According to the records, the station had been originally owned by James Angus McQuillan, one of the first developers of pastoral leases in central Australia, but McQuillan, his family and his estate had apparently relinquished all interest in Eleanor Downs late in the nineteenth century. Indeed, the McQuillan name featured only in the driest of texts relating purely to land acquisition. Eleanor Downs Station, a highly successful enterprise, had been the property of the Franklin family for several generations by the time Rose arrived there.

Rose had been educated to a minimal level and at ten started work as a housemaid, a position it was presumed she would serve at Eleanor Downs for an indefinite period, possibly the whole of her working life, as a number of the domestic help had over the years.

Shortly before her fifteenth birthday, Rose lost her virginity, not willingly, but knowing if she didn't acquiesce or if she made any complaint to the Big Boss, things would take a severe turn for the worse. Walter Franklin Jnr, the twenty-five-year-old son and heir to the Franklin estate, had a taste for 'black velvet', and he liked breaking in young virgins whom he would keep to himself for a year or so before moving on. Following her initiation, Rose, like the others, was expected to be available for their secret assignations whenever the Young Boss so desired, which he did with increasing regularity.

Rose's only escape was music. Without music she would have been lost. One of the other house girls, Betty, a year older than Rose and also taken as a child from a Western Arunta family, had a harmonica and would play while Rose sang. They'd perform the hit songs they'd heard on the wireless, Rose even perfecting the required American accent, or they'd make songs up, singing in their own language.

They often communicated in the Western Arunta tongue, but only when they were alone, for the white bosses forbade their servants to talk anything but English. Speaking Arunta was the girls' secret rebellion and music was their joint escape. They would play and sing their songs and they would dance together too, inventing the steps as they went along. Rose and Betty were best friends. More than best friends, Rose and Betty were family. Deprived of their parents and their siblings, Rose and Betty were the only family each had.

The highlight of Rose's station life came every second weekend, when she and Betty had Saturday off. They'd cadge a lift from one of the hands into Alice Springs, twenty-five miles away, and stand outside the pub listening to the music. There was always music playing on a Saturday arvo. If they knew the song, Betty would play her harmonica and Rose would sing along, and if they didn't know it they'd dance together to the tune. They were neither begging nor busking to start with, they were just having fun, but when people began chucking coins their way, they quickly developed a performance routine. They'd take a break and head off for ice creams and soft drinks or a pie with sauce then they'd return for more. They'd stay right through until the pub closed, getting a lift back with the station hands who were returning, by that time very much the worse for wear, to Eleanor Downs.

It was on one of these Saturday afternoons that sixteen-year-old Rose met Eddie Tjakamarra.

'You got a real good voice, you know that?'

She was pleased by the compliment, he was around twenty and very good looking, but she gave a noncommittal shrug.

'What's your name?' he asked.

'Rose.'

'I'm Eddie.'

She gave another noncommittal shrug as if she didn't care, but really to cover her self-consciousness. She wasn't accustomed to receiving such close attention from handsome young men.

Eddie was openly eyeing her up and down. 'You look real nice too,' he said.

Another shrug. Rose averted her eyes. Then Betty spoke up protectively. Being a year older and a bolder girl by nature, Betty was protective of Rose.

'Rose is shy.'

'Oh yeah?'

'Yeah.' Although he didn't seem particularly interested she introduced herself anyway, just to be polite. 'I'm Betty.'

Eddie gave Betty a nod and turned back to Rose. 'No need to be shy when you can sing like that. You could be real famous, I reckon. Crikey, looking the way you do and a voice like yours . . .' He shook his head in admiration. 'Real star material, you are.'

Rose smiled; she couldn't help herself. 'I like to sing.'

'And I like to listen.' He grinned disarmingly. 'Don't start again until I get back. I'm gonna grab a beer.' And he disappeared.

Eddie sat on the pub's verandah for the whole of the afternoon scoffing back beers and watching Rose, and for the whole of the afternoon she sang to him. That was all it took. By the end of the day Rose was in love.

When the pub closed she didn't go back to Eleanor Downs. She went off with Eddie instead.

'He's camped just out of town,' she'd told Betty mid-afternoon when Betty had returned with the pies. Rose hadn't been hungry, so she'd stayed and talked with Eddie, but Betty had brought a pie back for her anyway.

'He's got a ute,' Rose had said while Eddie was off getting himself another beer. 'He's heading for Sydney and I'm going with him.

Betty had been horrified. 'But you don't even know the bloke!'

'I know him good enough.'

There'd been an uncharacteristic touch of defiance in Rose's reply, so Betty hadn't pushed. She doesn't really mean it, she's just bunging on, Betty had thought, finishing the last of her pie and getting out her harmonica.

But apparently Rose had meant it.

'You can't, Rose! You can't do it!' As the pub was closing and they were preparing to leave, Betty spoke up openly, regardless of Eddie standing right next to her. 'Sydney! Heck, you can't let him take you to Sydney! You've never been to a big city in your life, Rose! Big cities are scary.' Not that Betty would know, she'd never been further than Alice Springs, but she'd heard things.

'Don't you worry about Rose, Betty,' Eddie said expansively, 'I'll look after her. I got mob living in Redfern. Blackfellas' paradise it is, right in the middle of Sydney, family just waiting to welcome us.' He put his arm around Rose and hauled her in close. 'And my Rose here's gunna be a star.'

He nuzzled his head into Rose's neck, to her delight. She didn't care about being a star. She didn't want any of that. She just wanted to be with Eddie.

Recognising the cause as a lost one, Betty gave up further argument. She knew Rose was unhappy at Eleanor Downs, hating the Young Boss the way she did, and why shouldn't she, the bastard pig! But this wasn't the way to escape – it was all wrong. Everything was moving too quick and Eddie was too smooth. Betty didn't trust him.

The girls hugged, holding each other closely and exchanging farewells in their own language.

'Travel safe, little sister,' Betty said. 'I'll miss you.'

'I'll miss you too, sister,' Rose said, 'but I take you with me in my heart.'

Betty's fears were justified. Eddie left Rose barely a year after their arrival in Sydney, and during that one short year he came close to breaking her spirit. He beat her regularly when he was drunk, which was often, and of a night when he wasn't out with his young hooligan mates, joy-riding in stolen cars or thieving to score money for grog, he forced her to drink with him at home.

'What's the matter with you, woman? Drink with your man, for Christ's sake! Where's the companionship? A woman drinks with her man.'

Rose gave in, developing a taste for alcohol she'd never had before, even allowing herself to believe it was a valid form of escape. He didn't bash her up as much when they got drunk together.

But it wasn't the answer. He left her anyway, disappearing one day with a pretty girl from out near Wagga Wagga who'd just arrived in the city in search of adventure, which Eddie was only too willing to provide. Eddie liked them young and innocent.

'We're heading north,' he announced, 'Surfers Paradise.'

And then he was gone, leaving Rose in the terrace house they'd been sharing in Eveleigh Street with a fluctuating population who came and went from the country and outback regions. The area on the western border of Redfern, known simply as 'the Block', offered low-cost housing that attracted Aboriginal people who'd gravitated to the city, many living on the poverty line and banding together to share accommodation, shacking up sometimes ten to a room.

Fortunately for Rose, there was a strong code of honour among the longer-standing residents of the Block who'd settled in to their city life. Rose was family to them now and Eddie had done the wrong thing in deserting her.

'You stay here with us, sister, we'll look after you,' Jimmy Gunnamurra and his wife, Bib, promised. And they stood by their promise, finding odd jobs for her via their many contacts and providing her with support. Rose's Redfern brothers and sisters were the only reason she survived.

Music continued to be the one pleasure in her life. She haunted the pubs around Redfern and Surry Hills where live bands were playing, standing out in the street if she didn't have enough money to buy a beer, ignoring disapproving glances from passers-by as she swayed to the music or tapped to the beat, sometimes whispering along with a harmony of her own.

Her favourite venue was the Labor Club. She wasn't looked down on there the way she was in some of the pubs. She was eighteen now, just, legal age, but in a couple of the pubs they still treated her as if she shouldn't be there. They didn't do that at the Labor Club.

The club was in Bourke Street, and had been established several years previously by the Surry Hills Branch of the Australian Labor Party. Ostensibly a venue where members could socialise and talk politics, in reality it served a far greater purpose opening its doors to the local constituents as it did. Surry Hills and the area's neighbouring suburbs were home to traditional, working-class, inner-city communities that suffered from overcrowding, poor housing, unemployment and in some cases sheer poverty. The Labor Club offered the locals a popular and affordable venue, a home away from home with good cheap meals and a live show on Saturday nights. You could drop in to the bar after work and have a game of billiards or play the poker machines or simply listen to the jukebox.

Rose didn't play billiards and she didn't play the pokies; she just stood in the corner by the jukebox, soaking up the music and singing along under her breath. She didn't even need to waste her precious coins – others did it for her. The jukebox was always playing.

Not as good as live music though, she thought wistfully, looking around at the posters on the walls. How she wished she could go to the concerts. They had real beaut entertainers at the Labor Club on a Saturday night, the very best. Crikey, Johnny O'Keefe had performed there just a while back! What Rose would have given to be in a room where JOK was performing. But live concerts cost money. So she just stuck to her corner by the jukebox.

That was where Toby met her, in the corner of the Labor Club right by the jukebox. It was a Friday, early afternoon, not many around as yet, and he'd arrived to set up for his gig the following night. He'd only been in the country for a year, but he'd quickly found his feet. There were a lot of live performance venues around Sydney and he did quite a bit of work for the Labor Club. Good space, good gigs, good performers – he enjoyed his jobs there.

Toby himself was as yet unaware, but it was through the musicians and entertainers at the Labor Club that word was spreading fast. The Irishman was a bloody good sound engineer, they all agreed.

He saw the Aboriginal girl the moment he entered the club. She was standing all alone by the jukebox grooving to 'The Green, Green Grass of Home' and singing along with Tom Jones. Not loudly, in fact he couldn't hear her at all, but she was clearly mouthing the words. Her head was back, her eyes closed and she was pulsing to the rhythm of the song. Some might have presumed she was drunk, but Toby knew better. She was in another place altogether, giving herself up to the music.

He put down his gear and quietly crossed to her. Lost in her world, she didn't notice him though he stood right beside her. He leant in closely and listened, and as he listened, he was amazed. She was not only pitch perfect, she was singing a harmony, but not the obvious harmony line most would choose. This was something quite different, something that enriched the song, adding a poignancy and depth to both the melody and the lyric. She has to be a back-up singer, surely, he thought, and a bloody good one at that.

As the song came to an end, Rose opened her eyes and gave a startled gasp to find a man standing close beside her.

'Sorry, sorry,' Toby said, stepping back a pace. 'Didn't mean to crowd you – just having a listen. You're a singer, I take it?'

Rose shook her head, mortified, wondering how loud she'd been singing. There'd been no-one nearby, so she hadn't thought for one minute anyone would hear her.

'Don't worry, love,' the man assured her, 'nobody else was listening, just me, and if you're not a professional singer then by God you should be. I'm Toby, by the way,' he held out his hand, 'Toby Manning. I'm the sound engineer around here. Well, on Saturdays when there's a gig, anyway.'

She shook his hand self-consciously, still unsure of herself. 'I'm Rose, Rose Napangurrayi.'

'Right you are.' He winked. 'I'll just stick to the Rose part. You sure can sing, Rose. That was a grand piece of harmony that was.'

The lilt of his accent was pleasing and his easy manner reassuring and Rose felt herself relax. He looks like someone from the music business, she thought, intrigued. She'd never met anyone from the music business herself, but she'd seen plenty of pictures. A bit on the skinny side and hair too long – He looks like one of the Beatles, she thought, John Lennon without the glasses or George Harrison, only not so good-looking.

'Where're you from?' Toby asked. He too was intrigued. She was the first Aboriginal person he'd ever met.

'A long way away,' she said. 'The grasses aren't green where I come from.' They shared a smile. 'Who's singing tomorrow night?' she couldn't help asking.

'Col Joye.'

'Oh . . .' Her expulsion of breath said everything.

'You want to come? I can get you in for free.'

Col Joye! Was he joking? Rose was speechless. She just nodded.

She didn't want to sit at a table down the front with people she didn't know and where she obviously felt she'd be conspicuous, preferring instead to stand up the back against the far wall, which to Toby's mind only made her all the more conspicuous. He couldn't take his eyes off her the entire night. He could see her lips moving imperceptibly throughout each song. She knows every melody, he thought, and she knows every lyric. There's a voice in her head that's singing harmony with Col. Toby was riveted.

The following week it was Judy Stone, another favourite performer of Rose's, and things developed from there. Toby took Rose to every gig he worked on after that, not just at the Labor Club, but all over Sydney. Before long they were sleeping together. And then she moved in with him, into the old ramshackle house in Glebe that he shared with several musicians. And then they were inseparable.

It was a bohemian existence. The Glebe house regularly served as Sydney lodgings for performers on tour and there were always people coming and going, smoking dope and downing beer and cheap wine. It reminded Rose of Redfern, but with one difference: there was always music in the house.

Rose was happier than she remembered being in the whole of her life. The partying was fun certainly and she joined Toby and the others, smoking and drinking at times with abandon, but there was far more to her newfound happiness than partying. Never before had Rose felt more loved or more useful. She was Toby's assistant these days, his 'roadie' he called her. She helped him set up before each gig and she helped him with the bump out after each show, and during rehearsals she fetched take-away coffees or made cups of tea for the singers and musicians.

'You're a Godsend, love, truly you are,' Toby would tell her time and again, 'don't know how I ever managed without you, and that's a fact.' All shite of course, but something she needed to hear. Rose's self-confidence had taken a beating somewhere down the track, Toby had sensed it right from the start. Poor Rosie's damaged, he thought, anyone can see that.

Over the ensuing months, in bits and pieces Toby teased Rose's story from her, and the more he learnt of her past the more protective he became. He found it rather amusing that their relationship raised eyebrows. 'My, my,' he would say to people's faces when he sensed a nudge or a whisper, 'black girl, white man, tut tut, how shocking,' and then he'd laugh at their embarrassment and the fact he'd caught them out. But if he sensed Rose was the specific target of their disapproval, he quickly sprang into action. 'C'mon Rosie love, let's go,' he'd say, and taking her arm he'd whisk her away. He would far rather have challenged the offender, but knowing how Rose hated any form of confrontation he understood that a scene would only have added to her discomfort.

Toby shielded Rose in every way he could, but there was one time when he made a rather bad mistake. It had, however, taught him a serious lesson about the woman he loved.

They were in a rehearsal studio with a six-piece band called The Real Goodes, a group that Toby knew well and with whom he worked regularly. The band members were rehearsing for an upcoming gig at a popular venue in Paddo where they often performed, principally covers, but always throwing in a few numbers of their own. The three Goodes brothers, who'd started the band over two years previously, were talented, hard-working and ambitious. They recorded their songs and feted every radio disc jockey in town, determined to get a hit up and going, and Toby had no doubt they would. 'It's only a matter of time, fellas,' he'd say encouragingly, 'only a matter of time.'

The atmosphere in the rehearsal studio was friendly and relaxed but unbeknownst to Rose a plan had been set in place. The band's lead vocalist, Ray, the youngest of the Goodes, was normally backed up by two female singers as well as his brothers, but one of the girls had just quit. Toby had suggested they give Rose a try without her knowing she was being auditioned.

'Don't want to put any pressure on her,' he'd said to the brothers. 'She'll be fine if she thinks she's only helping out at rehearsal. And just you wait till you hear her!'

Ray and his brothers and the other band members were only too happy to oblige – they all liked Rose, and if Toby said she was good then that was enough for them.

'Rose'll sing back-up, she knows all the covers,' Toby suggested, apparently struck by sudden inspiration at the next rehearsal.

Rose stared blankly at him.

'Go on, Rosie love.' He ushered her over to the microphone where the other back-up singer was waiting. 'Take your lead from Evelyn, you'll be fine.' She'll hardly need any lead, he thought. Rose'd leave Evelyn for dead any day.

Evelyn gave an obliging smile and as the band struck up the opening chords of 'Big Girls Don't Cry', she started clicking her fingers and nodding rhythmically at Rose in the obvious assumption that Rose needed counting in, which Toby found vaguely amusing.

But seconds later, when it came time for the vocals, Rose wasn't there. She wasn't even making any attempt to be there. She was somewhere else, staring into another time, another place, and Toby knew immediately he'd done the wrong thing. It wasn't that she didn't know the song. Hell, Rosie knew every popular song on the charts. How many times had they performed 'Big Girls Don't Cry', along with every other Four Seasons hit, him on guitar, her singing the lyrics directly to him as if there were no-one else in the world, as if the song belonged purely to them? Rosie had a way of making every song special. And that was when the truth hit Toby: the truth that music, to Rose, was a private thing. He realised then and there that Rose sang for him, no-one else, just him.

Rose herself was in a strangely distant state. Her thoughts had drifted off, but oddly enough they were not altogether dissimilar to Toby's. She was remembering those times when she'd sung in public. First it had been with Betty, outside the pub in Alice Springs – but they'd been performing for each other really, hadn't they? Music had been what kept them going, her and Betty. Then there'd been Eddie. She'd never forget that afternoon they first met. Geez how she'd sung her heart out for Eddie! She'd sung for him during the early days in Sydney too; they'd been happy for a while, her and Eddie. She'd hated the way he'd made her sing in the streets with an empty ice-cream carton for people to throw money in though. 'It's not begging,' he'd said, 'it's busking,' but she'd still felt humiliated. Hadn't he realised she didn't want to be on show? She didn't want to sing for strangers: she wanted to sing for him. And he always chose the tourist areas, Circular Quay or the Town Hall or the Strand Arcade, where she knew that the passing parade of white people looked down on her. But those days were over – there was Toby now. She sang for Toby now. And they shared the music, her and Toby. The music was something special . . .

That was as far as Rose's thoughts got, standing there beside Evelyn, who was clicking her fingers like a castanet and nodding with furious intensity, trying to shake the girl out of what was presumably stage fright.

'Come on, love.'

Rose felt Toby's arm around her.

'Sorry,' he whispered as he shepherded her away from the microphone, 'didn't mean to be pushy.'

He gave Ray and the brothers a wave. 'Don't worry, boys, I'll have a back-up singer within the hour, there're heaps of good ones just queuing up for a job.'

As if the boys didn't know that. 'No worries, mate,' Ray said.

Toby and Rose left, and the incident never once came up for discussion between them. Both knew there was no need.

Barely eighteen months later, in mid-1970, two major events occurred more or less simultaneously, or at least they appeared to. The Real Goodes rocketed to fame, apparently overnight, and Rose discovered she was pregnant.

The Goodes brothers, after working their guts out around the pubs and clubs of Sydney for well over three years and releasing several singles that had gone relatively unnoticed, finally had a hit on radio that was picked up nationally, and quickly followed by another. 'Flash Annie' and 'Once is Not Enough' took Australia by storm, and with two hits in the Top Ten the Real Goodes were heralded as the hottest new popular-rock sound in the country. At least they were by Lenny Benson, their astute new business manager.

'Australia's own Beatles and Four Seasons all wrapped up in one,' Brian Henderson enthused when introducing The Real Goodes on Channel Nine's 'Bandstand'. The quote had come directly from Lenny's publicity release, which had accompanied the band's hastily produced brand new album.

A 'National Spring Tour' was mounted with equal haste and heralded far and wide in order to cash in on the success of the band's hit singles and promote the new album. The Real Goodes were to take to the road and perform all around the country for their growing legion of fans. Concerts and club gigs were arranged in every capital city and every major regional town where Lenny had managed to score a venue at relatively short notice, and he'd managed to score many. Some venues had even cancelled previous bookings, Lenny having convinced them they'd be missing out on the chance of a lifetime if they didn't. Lenny was the consummate entrepreneur, pushy, persuasive and difficult to say no to.

The prospect of the tour filled Rose with apprehension. She dreaded what would happen when Toby went out on the road with the band. He'd accepted the news of her pregnancy with surprising calm. She'd been nervous when she'd told him, unsure of herself, wondering what his reaction might be, for they'd never talked of a baby. He might well be angry and she reckoned he had every right to be because she was always forgetting to take her contraceptive pill. She'd thought he might insist she get rid of the baby, but she really didn't want to. She hadn't forgotten to take the pill on purpose, she would never do that to him, but now she was pregnant she didn't want to get rid of it. She would like to have Toby's baby.

'Don't you worry, love,' he'd said, 'a baby will fit into our lives quite nicely. Don't go fretting now.' Toby could see all the fears that were circling like demons in Rose's head. He could always see Rose's demons. He hadn't planned on a child, certainly, but they'd get around it all right. Who knows? he thought in his typically laid-back fashion. It might be rather fun being a dad.

As the tour date grew ever nearer, Rose's misgivings loomed larger and larger with every passing day. Toby would be leaving to travel around the country with a famous rock band. He'd be surrounded by the band's adoring fans and all the trappings of success. He'd be living a life of reflected glory. Why would he bother coming back to her? What place could there be in that new life of his for a black woman who didn't fit into his circle and a child he'd never asked for and couldn't really want?

Again, although Rose kept her fears to herself, Toby could see the demons circling.

'Let's get married,' he said, the week before he was due to leave.

'What?' She was struck virtually dumb.

'We'll get married and you'll come on tour with the band. The boys won't mind – you can work your way, you're a damn fine roadie.'

'Married,' she repeated, sounding foolish, but unable to think of anything else to say.

'Sure, I'm not having a child of mine born a bastard.' Toby hadn't actually given the matter much thought, but now, in allaying Rose's fears, it occurred to him that marriage was a rather good idea. He loved her and she was having his baby. Why not? he asked himself. Why not get married? It's what people do, isn't it?

They married at the Registry Office the following week and spent their honeymoon on the road with the band.

The tour was as hectic as had been expected and as madly fan-fuelled as Lenny's promotional drive had dictated it should be. Television crews, photographers and journalists were lined up at every stop along the way and crowds were whipped into a frenzy of adulation.

For Toby the work was gruelling. The endless setting up and bumping out of one-night stands was relentless and he was grateful not only for Rose's company, but for her practical assistance. Despite her pregnancy, Rose worked as hard as any of the three roadies who followed the bus in their beaten-up Holden.

Rose loved every minute of the tour. She'd been well past the morning sickness phase when they left, having suffered little discomfort in any event, and she revelled in her usefulness.

By the time they returned to Sydney, her pregnancy was patently obvious and over the next couple of months as the New Year crept in and January slipped by, the larger she grew the more they both basked in the sight.

'This is what they mean by "huge with child", Toby said as they sat naked together in bed, Rose propped up on pillows. He ran the palms of his hands over her taut black skin, his fingers tracing the impressive globe of her belly.

'*Huuuge with child*,' he repeated, chanting the words, milking them for all they were worth and enjoying the sound, '*huuuuge with child*. It makes a man feel humble, it truly does.'

Rose laughed. He'd just smoked a joint. 'You and your Irish blarney,' she said, but she delighted in his admiration, knowing it wasn't just the dope and that he was only half joking.

She gave birth in early March, a relatively easy delivery, and when they returned home from the hospital with their little brown bundle, Toby remained lost in awe.

'Look at her now,' he said, gazing down at the baby in its cradle, studying the tiny hand clutching his little finger with such surprising strength even in sleep. 'Was there ever a more perfect baby?'

'No. Never.' Rose savoured the moment, holding it close, knowing that this was the happiest moment in her life, simply because no human being could possibly be happier.

With the proceeds of the tour, which had paid well, Toby put a deposit down on a modest one-storey terrace house in the neighbouring suburb of Balmain, not far from the harbour.

'I'll not have my daughter raised amongst a horde of doped-up, drunken musicians,' he said with mock severity, 'oh dear me, no, it's the straight and narrow for our Jess.'

Rose smiled. Toby would always be surrounded by musicians wherever he lived, but once again she knew that he was only half joking and that their days of heavy partying were probably over.

'It's ours, Rosie,' he said as they wandered around the house, Toby running his hands over walls that were badly in need of a fresh coat of paint. He addressed the baby asleep in her arms: 'What do you think, Jess? Our very own home, every brick of it, all ours. Well, no,' he corrected himself, 'not all ours – all the bank's actually, but it'll be ours soon enough.'

They stepped out into the backyard, which was surprisingly large, particularly given the size of the house. The backyard was the reason Toby had chosen the property.

'And here's where the recording studio will go,' he said, arms outstretched, encompassing the entire yard, 'right here.' A recording studio of his own had always been Toby's dream. A state-of-the-art affair with plenty of space for the band to set up, a huge dividing double plate-glass window, a sixteen-channel mixing desk and big JBL speakers for perfect playback: he could see it all.

He put his arm around Rose and together they surveyed the tangled mess of weeds and debris over-run by morning glory vines. A crumbling home-made brick barbecue, once someone's pride and joy, sat on one side, lantana bushes did battle with the morning glory on the other, an umbrella tree and a rubber plant vied for supremacy down the back and in pride of place stood the metal skeleton of a Hills Hoist clothesline, ubiquitous symbol of suburban Australia.

'It'll take a few more tours I reckon,' Toby said, sensing as he did that might be something of an understatement.

Three years, three tours and three albums later, The Real Goodes had faded from the charts to be replaced by other bands with a hotter, newer sound and Ray and his brothers were back playing the clubs and the pubs, although now they performed their own songs and for a far higher fee. But by then Toby's house was paid off and renovated, and he had his dream studio. He also had a burgeoning reputation as one of the finest sound engineers in the local music industry.

In a further two short years, Balmain Sound had become *the* studio for aspiring rock bands and hard-nosed entrepreneurs with an eye for the main chance. Toby Manning's services were eagerly sought, his clients ranked among the best, he was on the road to success and the timing was perfect. His daughter had just reached school age.

CHAPTER TWO

'Exotic, that's what you are, Jess.' Toby hoisted the five-year-old up into his arms. 'A mix of the Dreamtime and the blarney,' he added with a wink. He gave another wink to his wife, who was standing beside them. Rose had refused to come to the school even though it was only a walk away. She believed her presence would cause added problems for the child. 'You don't get much more exotic than that,' he said to them both, the reassurance intended as much for his wife as for his daughter.

He put the girl down and Rose knelt to hug her.

Jess flung her arms around her mother's neck. *'I wish you would come with us, Mumayee,'* she whispered in Rose's ear.

'No, no,' Rose hissed urgently, breaking free of the embrace, 'you mustn't speak like that at school. You must *never, never* speak like that at school.' The child had said the words in Arunta.

Jess looked confused. The edge of panic in her mother's voice had sounded like anger and she didn't know what she'd done wrong.

Toby quickly jumped in. 'She won't, Rose, she won't,' he insisted. 'Why would she, for God's sake? No-one would understand her.'

Rose stood, bowing her head and staring guiltily at the floor as she always did when she sensed something she perceived as criticism or disapproval.

'Don't, Rosie,' Toby said, 'please, please don't.' He
gently lifted her chin, forcing her to look at him. 'No criticism was intended, love. You have nothing to feel guilty
about, nothing at all. It's good that you teach Jess your
language. Arunta is something special that you share, it's
her language too.'

He kissed her tenderly. Then he bent down and took
Jess by the hand. 'And now we're off to school,' he said
brightly, skipping towards the door, the child laughing
and skipping with him.

Jess had no problems at all with school. In fact for a
while Jess's schooling was something mother and daughter
took delight in sharing.

There were some initial difficulties when, after the first
week, Toby insisted Rose accompany him and meet the
other mothers. 'It'll be good for you, love,' he said firmly,
'and it'll be good for Jess.' He refused to take no for an
answer. 'Besides, they're a nice bunch. Well, for squares
anyway,' he added with a smile intended to put her at
ease. 'I doubt they've ever smoked a joint in their collective
lives, but we can't hold that against them.'

Toby was aware that Rose, shy at the best of times,
was bound to feel uncomfortable. There were no other
Aboriginal women among the mothers, who were a
conservative bunch, and she might well get some odd
looks to start with. But he'd decided Rose needed to
mingle with people other than the bohemian circle of
musicians and performers in whose presence she'd become
comfortable. If not for her own sake, he thought, then for
her daughter's. Rose needed to mingle without him. Even
when they visited the recently created Black Theatre Arts
and Cultural Centre in Redfern it was always at his insti-
gation, and she always stuck by his side.

Toby was a strong supporter of the cultural centre in
Botany Street, where an old warehouse, once a printing
factory, had been converted into a theatre and studio.

There, Aboriginal artworks were on display and dance, music and theatre works were performed, an expression of Indigenous culture not previously witnessed in Sydney. Toby, like many, saw it as a breaking down of barriers, but above all he liked to watch little Jess happily mingling with other Aboriginal children, even though that made Rose's shyness all the more obvious.

A week or so later, when the women at Balmain Public had become acquainted with his wife and he could see that she was accepted as a fellow mother rather than being held apart as something alien, he went a step further. He persuaded Rose to walk Jess to and from school on her own. Or rather, he blackmailed her.

'I'm busy recording, love,' he said. 'I can't just keep the fellas hanging around now, can I?' Of course he could. He wouldn't charge for the extra time and the band would be quite happy rehearsing for twenty minutes while he popped out to collect his kid, but that was hardly the aim of the exercise, was it?

His ruse succeeded. Much as she dreaded the prospect, Rose was so riddled with guilt that she instantly agreed to undertake the trips to and from school. It's the least I can do, she told herself. I must be more useful, I must pull my weight. More and more these days, with Toby locked away in his studio, she felt she served little purpose. He always made it quite clear she was welcome to come and sit up the back during the recording sessions, but when she did, much as she loved the live music, it only made her feel more useless. She was far better off listening to her own music on the stereo while she did the housework.

Rose never became comfortable with her trips to the school, despite the fact her social exchange with the other mothers was brief and even though several of the women went out of their way to be friendly. She remained painfully self-conscious and so lacking in confidence that she couldn't wait to get away.

Jess loved school with a passion and each day as they walked home together hand in hand she would skip along the pavement beside her mother, chattering non-stop about every fresh experience and every new thing she'd learnt. Little Jess's happiness was so infectious that Rose would laugh out loud.

When they arrived home, they'd sprawl out on the open-plan living-room floor surrounded by the equipment necessary for whatever project had been the highlight of the day. Rose, who was creative and inventive, had an endless supply of drawing paper, crayons, pencils, paints and plasticine, together with a miscellany of fabrics and felts and glitter that a child might like to glue onto something. Between the two of them they created works of art that Toby declared masterpieces and stuck up all over the walls of the house.

Before long they segued from finger painting and plasticine to the alphabet, painstakingly printing out each letter and making up words together, starting from the beginning and working their way through. '*Ant*, *bat*, *cat*, *dog* . . .' Jess would recite out loud, and when they got to '*x*, *y*, *z*' they would call Toby in. Next they were reading to each other about cats on mats and dogs called Spot, and then they progressed to little picture books about everything from fairies to fire engines, all of which they both loved.

One day it was decided that Jess was old enough to go to school on her own. A lot of the other kids did, she said, and she was eight years old, she wanted to be grown up. Toby agreed. She was a big girl now, he said. But the relief the decision occasioned Rose, who was still uncomfortable mingling with the mothers, was outweighed by a fresh horror that had by then presented itself.

Even though over the years she had educated herself further to a certain degree, Rose's formal schooling to the age of ten only had left her semi-literate. Jess, an eager and clever pupil, was already showing signs of outstripping her at just eight years of age. In the past, Rose had not seen her limited education as a particular obstacle in life. Having always managed somehow, she'd given the matter little thought. But she did now. Now she was so haunted by the prospect of exposure she could think of nothing else. All she could see was the horror that loomed ahead. She was about to be humiliated in the eyes of her daughter.

'No, no, Jessie love, I'm busy with dinner,' she'd call from the island bench at the kitchen end of the living room, 'come and read to me while I cook.' Or: 'I think it's best if you read out loud on your own, Jess. The teachers would want you to – you'll learn quicker that way.'

Rose came up with endless evasion tactics, all of which Jess accepted at face value, suspecting nothing. But Toby knew. Toby recognised the problem in an instant.

As a rule he was in the studio all afternoon, but one day he came inside early to fetch some charts that had been delivered to the house that morning.

'No, we can't take it in turns, Jessie love, I'm peeling the spuds. You bring the book over here and read out loud to me, there's a good girl.'

The moment he heard Rose calling to her daughter across the living room, he knew what the problem was. And the moment he challenged Rose, she knew that he knew.

'How long's this been going on?' he asked quietly.

She stared at the floor, saying nothing, just shaking her head helplessly.

Toby gathered her in his arms. 'You don't have to live a lie, love,' he whispered. 'Jess loves you the way you are – we both do.'

But she continued to shake her head and he could tell by the way she was gulping air into her lungs that she was desperately fighting back the need to sob her distress out loud.

'There, there,' he said stroking her gently, 'there, there. Everything'll be all right, Rosie love. Everything'll be all right.'

She broke free, quickly wiping away the tears so the child wouldn't see. 'Come along, Jess,' she called briskly, 'bring the book over and read to me while I do the spuds.'

Toby collected his charts and went back to the studio. But that night, when Jess was safely tucked up in bed, he confronted Rose.

'Shall we have some wine?' he said, although it wasn't really a question: he was already opening a bottle of red. 'Take a seat, love.' He poured two glasses, and they sat opposite each other at the dining table.

'We need to talk, Rosie,' he said. And talk they did. Or rather, Toby talked. Rose listened. And the longer she listened the more the questions began to whirl around in her brain.

'You mustn't feel threatened by Jess's education, love,' he said, getting straight to the point. 'Leave that side of her life to the school, it's what they're there for. Hell, leave it to the *university*,' he added with a bold wave of his glass. 'She's way out of my league that one, so bloody smart she'll probably end up a nuclear physicist.'

He took a swig of his wine and leant forwards in all seriousness. 'You can be of so much value to Jess, Rosie, can't you see that? There's so much she can learn from you and you only, so much you can teach her. With or without the academic side of things, love, you're the most valuable education she could possibly have.'

Toby could see Rose was hanging on his every word, and he could only hope he was getting it right.

'You've taught her your language – what better start could there be? They sure as hell don't teach Western Arunta at school.'

Rose nodded in solemn agreement, a sign Toby found most encouraging.

'Teach her all you can, Rosie,' he urged. 'Teach her about where you come from. Teach her about your people. Tell her their stories. They're her people too . . .' Then he stopped, halted by the utter hopelessness he saw in her eyes. He'd lost her, all of a sudden, just like that. Why?

'What is it, love?' he asked.

'I don't know my people,' she said, 'I don't know their stories.' She shook her head, again helplessly, and Toby thought he had never seen a soul more lost. 'I grew up in a white man's world.'

What could he say? He reached out and took her hand, caressing the silky softness of her skin and they remained silent for a moment or so. 'Then you must teach her about you, Rosie,' he said finally. 'You must teach her who you are.'

She stared down at their hands entwined, the black and the white, and the questions whirled anew. But who am I? How can I teach her who I am when I don't know myself? Don't you see I am nothing? Don't you see I belong nowhere? I am a person of no significance. What can I possibly teach my daughter?

He could see the familiar demons circling. Her lack of self-confidence was always so heartbreakingly painful to watch. 'Tell her your feelings, love,' he said gently but firmly. 'Speak from your heart. Share as much of the past with her as you can. Tell her about where you come from. Tell her how you were taken as a little girl. Jess will learn about herself through you, Rosie, I know she will.' He prayed he was right. He also prayed that he hadn't made matters worse: she looked so bewildered.

He stood and circled the table. Then easing her to her feet he kissed her. 'Now come along, girl. It's bedtime and I'm in need of a cuddle.'

They left the wine virtually untouched and went to bed, where they made love. Afterwards, as Toby lay gently snoring, Rose gazed into the darkness, pondering the past. What was she to teach her daughter? What could she remember from the past that would be of any value? All she'd known was Eleanor Downs, a cruel, white world that brought back memories she'd long put behind her. But she did still feel the call of the desert. It was in her blood, that land. And the more she thought about it, the more she felt it in her very heartbeat, throbbing through her body. Is that who I am? she wondered.

The following morning, when Jess had left for school and Toby was in the studio, Rose took out the drawing paper, the pencils and crayons, the paints and the brushes and settled down to work. Memories flooded back. She was devoured by images of giant eagles soaring over rocky wooded hills, of rugged escarpments towering into cloudless skies, of vast plains of spinifex and endless dry riverbeds where red gums thrived . . .

When Toby came in for his scheduled lunch break he found no sandwich waiting, no tea brewing in the pot. He always took a break on the dot of one and Rose always had a sandwich and a pot of tea ready, but not today. Instead, the dining table was covered with vivid paintings and bold, crayon drawings, and all were of central Australia.

She jumped up when she saw him. 'Oh!' She glanced at the clock on the wall, startled. 'I'm sorry, I didn't realise it was so late.'

'Well, well, what do we have here?' Toby said, picking up one of the drawings. 'A wedge-tailed eagle, am I right?'

'Yes. It's not very good.'

'It's bloody fantastic, that's what it is!' He picked up another, and then another. 'Oh Rosie, just wait till Jess sees these.'

But Rose had disappeared to the kitchen end of the room and was ferretting in the refrigerator. 'Lunch won't be too long, I promise,' she called apologetically.

'Take your time, love, take your time.' Toby breathed a sigh of relief as he sat and continued leafing through the drawings and paintings. Last night's chat had apparently served a purpose after all.

Toby was right. Rose's artwork stimulated endless questions from Jess and in fielding them, Rose painted pictures as vividly with words as she had with her brushes and crayons. She had spoken before of the desert area she came from, but always dispassionately.

'I was born in central Australia,' she'd told her daughter when Jess, ever inquisitive, had asked, 'at a place called Hermannsburg, not far from Alice Springs. It's desert country. I'll show you in the atlas.' And she'd looked up the atlas, the way Toby had taught her many years previously when they'd talked of her past, and she'd pointed out to Jess the region she came from and the nearby towns of importance.

In those days, Rose had considered it her duty to impart only the facts in order to contribute to the child's education. She saw things differently now. Now, she took her husband's advice, speaking from her heart and with a passion that surprised even Toby. Also acting on her husband's advice, she told her daughter of her childhood. Previously, when Jess had asked she'd kept her answers brief and evasive.

'I grew up on a cattle station,' she'd said. 'It was run by white people.' She never gave the station's name, not wanting to say the words out loud. 'A great big cattle station in the middle of the desert. The properties have to be big out there, so the cattle can roam a long way for food.'

Now she told Jess the truth of her past, or at least of the early years, and they talked together in Arunta.

'I was taken from my family when I was six years old,' she said. *'I was the youngest. I had two brothers and a sister, May. I don't really remember my brothers. They didn't take much interest in me; I was too little. But I remember May – we played together. I remember Mum*

screaming when they took me too. Screaming her lungs out, she was. Didn't do her any good. They took me off to the cattle station and I never saw her again. I was brought up by the whitefellas there.'

'Why?' Jess asked, mystified. She'd often wondered why her mother's parents were never mentioned, why her mother's childhood was always just 'the cattle station'. Jess had come to the conclusion that her mother's parents must be dead and that was why the white people had looked after her. *'Why did they take you away from your family, Mumayee?'* She was mystified and horrified equally.

'I don't know. That happened to a lot of our people.'

Toby stood silently by, observing them as they spoke. He loved seeing his wife and daughter speak their language; and he understood the conversation. He spoke passable Arunta himself, having insisted Rose teach him in their early years together. He'd considered it important she have someone to communicate with in her native tongue. 'It's like us Irish and our songs, Rosie,' he'd said, 'it's who we are, love. A person must never lose sight of that.' Now, of even greater importance, Jess was discovering who she was, and she was doing so, as Toby had hoped she would, through her mother.

And always there were the paintings, the paintings and the drawings that so fired the child's imagination.

Toby lounged against the island bench one wet Sunday morning, mug of tea in hand, watching Jess watching Rose. Rose was painting and Jess was hunched over, elbows on the table, following her every action. Both were totally absorbed: he might as well not have been there. Normally all three of them would have taken a ferry ride to Manly, one of their favourite Sunday outings. Or else they would simply have wandered down to nearby Ewenton Park where Jess would play and Toby and Rose would wander along the foreshore, looking out over the neat pocket of the bay and across the harbour waters to the city skyline.

It was a beautiful spot. But outside the rain was bucketing down and showed no sign of easing so the girls had settled themselves at the dining table.

'Are the rocks really that red?' Jess asked as her mother, having mixed the colours on the palette, applied a vivid slash of paint to the paper.

'Oh yes, they're that red all right,' Rose gazed down critically, 'but they're a different kind of red – deeper, richer somehow. There's no paint here that'll do them justice, Jessie love.' She shrugged. 'Or else I just can't get the mix right.'

'We'll go there one day.' Toby made the announcement unexpectedly. It came from right out of the blue, surprising them all.

His wife and daughter turned to stare at him. Neither had even been aware of his presence.

'Will we really, Daddy?' Jess asked after a breathless moment. Her eyes gleamed with unbearable anticipation: surely it couldn't be true.

'Yes, we will.'

'When? When will we go?'

'When you're twelve and you've finished primary school. That's a promise.'

'Oh.' Instant deflation as she'd only just turned nine. Twelve seemed so far away it didn't warrant thinking about.

His statement appeared to have had a similar effect upon Rose, for the two of them returned their attention to the painting.

Toby was not in the least bothered. His promise had not been an idle one. Already in his mind he was planning the trip. We'll take off the moment she's finished at Balmain Primary, he thought. We'll go for the whole of the summer holidays and come home in time for her to start at SCEGGS. He'd had Jess booked into the elite Sydney Church of England Girls Grammar School for some time now. Only the best for his daughter, he'd decided.

Summer in central Australia, he thought, it'll be bloody hot, but who cares? It'll be the making of Jess. And it'll be the making of Rosie too. Oh yes, he had such plans for his girls.

Toby put his plans into action in the late spring of 1983. He made all the necessary arrangements and then one night, after Jess had gone to bed, he sat Rose down at the dining table and told her about it over a fresh bottle of wine.

'The three of us, Rosie love, you and me and Jess, for the whole of the school holidays, just like I promised.'

Rose looked at him blankly. She couldn't remember any promise. When had they talked about this? She was taken completely by surprise.

'I've already booked the flights,' he went on enthusiastically. 'We'll hire a four-wheel drive in Alice Springs and we'll camp out under the stars. We'll show Jess the red centre, Rosie, where her mob comes from, the very heart of Australia. All the stuff you've been painting and drawing for years.'

He skolled his wine, knowing he was getting a bit drunk. He'd knocked back close to a bottle already during dinner, trying to curb his excitement, wanting to spill his plans out to them both, but aware he should discuss things with Rose first.

'And we'll go to Hermannsburg, love,' this was the most exciting prospect of all, 'and we'll find your family, Rosie. If they're no longer there, others are bound to know where they've gone – we'll find them, Rosie love, make no mistake about that, we'll find them.' He finally drew breath, poured himself another glass, and waited for her reaction.

There was none. She was simply staring at him.

Toby was nonplussed. He'd expected at least some enthusiasm, if not downright excitement. But then he'd sprung it on her pretty quickly, hadn't he, and Rose was not one for surprises. He should probably have taken things a little slower. 'Oh, sorry, love. I've rushed you a bit, haven't I, taken you by surprise . . .'

Then, to his utter dismay, she started shaking her head in the way he'd come to recognise, the awful way that signified defeat.

'What is it, Rosie? What's the matter?'

'I can't,' she whispered. 'I can't go back.'

'But you wouldn't be going back to Eleanor Downs, love,' he assured her. 'We wouldn't go near the cattle station, I promise.' He stroked her bare arm gently, soothingly. 'Don't you want to show Jess your country, Rosie, all the pictures you've painted, all the things you've described to her? Don't you want her to see them for herself?'

Rose nodded.

'Of course you do. And that's what'll happen. Don't you worry about things, love. I just rushed you, that's all, and I'm sorry. We'll talk about it tomorrow, eh?'

She nodded again and they left it at that, but Rose didn't sleep for the whole of that night. She lay awake trying for her child's sake to summon up the last vestige of courage she might once have possessed. Why did she feel so threatened? I belong to that land, she thought. Why should I fear returning to my country? But voices in her brain taunted her. *You don't belong there*, they said. *It's not your country. You have no country.* She tried to force the voices aside. I must find my family, she told herself. I must unite my daughter with her people. Again the voices mocked her. *You have no family*, they said. *You have no people. You belong nowhere.* The harder Rose tried to persuade herself, the louder the voices in her brain whispered and the more her fear grew. She didn't know why she was afraid, but the more she tried to reason with herself the more panic-stricken she became until the fear that consumed her bordered on terror and she thought she might be going mad.

Toby awoke to discover the bed beside him empty, which was not unusual – quite often Rose went for an early-morning walk down by the harbour.

He wandered out to the living room in his pyjamas. Jess was getting herself breakfast before heading off for school.

'Mum's gone to the park,' she said, cereal packet poised. 'Is everything all right?' Her eyes searched his for an answer. 'She didn't look too good, I have to say, and she wouldn't let me go with her.'

'No, no, nothing to worry about, Jess, you just get yourself off to school.'

He quickly changed and strode down Grafton Street to Ewenton Park.

She was there, seated on the grass, her knees scrunched up to her chest, staring out across the bay and over the harbour waters at the city, but even before he joined her he could tell she wasn't really seeing the view.

He sat beside her and she acknowledged him with a quick glance and a tremulous smile before returning her gaze to the harbour. He sensed she was gathering herself together to make some sort of announcement so he said nothing.

After a moment's silence, Rose opened her mouth and took a deep breath, but the words wouldn't come out. She was incapable of speech. All that issued from her was a low, keening sound and she started to rock slowly back and forth, shaking her head.

He put his arm around her and drew her close. 'Shush, shush, love, don't let things get to you like this, there's no need,' he said, trying desperately to stem her anguish. 'You mustn't worry about the trip, Rosie love. There's no rush, no rush at all. We'll leave it for some other time further down the track.'

Toby knew there would be no other time further down the track. Rose's demons were as visible as ever, but these were not just the demons of self-doubt that he'd come to recognise over the years. These were demons he didn't understand and from which he could not save her.

He cancelled the flights later that same day, thankful that he hadn't told Jess. At least he was off the hook there, he thought. But he wasn't.

'Final term ends next week.' It was a fortnight later when Jess confronted him.

'So?'

'So I've been twelve for ages now and in one week I'll have finished primary school. When do we leave?'

'Oh.'

'You thought I'd forgotten, didn't you?' She gave him that challenging look that was so disconcertingly adult. At times he could swear the girl was going on thirty. 'A promise is a promise, you know.'

'Yes, Jess, I do know.' He was relieved that she'd sought him out alone in the studio and that he didn't have to explain in front of Rose. 'But I'm afraid we have to postpone the Northern Territory for a while, love: your mum's not quite up to it right now.'

Jess held his gaze boldly for a moment or so then nodded. 'Fair enough,' she said. She'd expected as much, it's why she'd fronted him on his own. Her mother had been in the strangest mood lately, fragile and withdrawn. Jess had no idea why and she didn't expect her parents to tell her, but something was wrong.

'I've booked us a holiday apartment up the central coast for a month,' he said, 'Terrigal.'

She raised a wry eyebrow. 'Terrigal for the Territory, eh?' Then she shrugged and gave one of her irrepressible grins. 'Seems a fair exchange.'

'Hey, Jess,' he said as she turned to go. God but he loved the girl. 'A promise *is* a promise, and we *will* go to the Territory one day. You do know that, don't you?' He'd take her there on his own if needs be, but he couldn't leave Rose in her current condition.

'Yes, Dad. I do know that.'

Rose's condition did not improve – if anything it worsened, particularly during the holidays. Toby knew she felt guilty for having deprived her daughter of the promised trip to the Northern Territory, but whenever he tried to assure her that she mustn't she withdrew even further, locking herself away somewhere beyond his reach, so he gave up trying.

There were times when Rose detested Toby. She hated the way he said 'You mustn't feel guilty, love.' Why would she not feel guilty? She'd deprived her daughter of her heritage. She'd transferred her own ghastly curse to Jess: the curse of belonging nowhere, of having no people. Rose suffered far more than guilt. Remorse and shame ate away at her like a cancer.

Toby worried endlessly about his wife's fragile state, but he knew he was powerless and the end of the holidays came as something of a relief. With Jess off to school at SCEGGS he dived into the backlog of work that awaited him in the studio. Surely now things could get back to normal.

Rose, too, was glad the holidays were over. But she was lonely, very lonely. Jess was at school and Toby was locked away in his studio, so near and yet so far, even at lunchtime now he collected his sandwich and tea and then disappeared. The days were empty and she longed for distraction from the thoughts that plagued her.

One fine autumn afternoon in March, not long after Jess's birthday, Rose decided to pay a visit to her old stamping ground. Although not far from where she lived, it might have been a world away, she hadn't revisited the Block for over fifteen years. She had often attended the Black Theatre and Cultural Centre in Redfern, it was true, but the Black Theatre was hardly the Block, was it? Besides, the Black Theatre had long since closed through lack of funding.

Perhaps some of the old gang are still there, she now thought. In any event, she needed black faces around her, even black faces she didn't know. She needed to be with people she could pretend were her own.

The Block had undergone many changes since Rose's time in the late sixties. Local landlords had tried to have the Aboriginal residents evicted in the early 1970s, but Indigenous leaders and supporters had successfully lobbied the Whitlam government to prevent such action. The Aboriginal Housing Company had been formed and offered a grant to purchase their first six houses, with many further acquisitions to follow over the ensuing years. The Block was an innovative, pioneering urban experiment in Aboriginal-run housing, and as such attracted much media attention.

Now a decade on, the Block had become far more than the affordable rental area for disadvantaged Aborigines it had been in the past. Now run by its own, the Block was viewed by many outback and rural Indigenous as a spiritual home in the very heart of Sydney. The Block was special to Aboriginal people.

To non-Aboriginal people, however, this clearly defined area of Redfern represented something quite different. Over the years, the Block had earned a reputation as a ghetto notorious for crime and violence. White people didn't feel safe walking the streets of the Block.

Rose felt no threat at all as she walked down Eveleigh Street towards the house where she'd lived a lifetime ago. It even seemed to her that for the first time in many years she was somewhere she belonged.

As it turned out, Jimmy Gunnamurra was still there, Jimmy and his wife, Bib, who'd been so good to her when Eddie had run off. But Jimmy and Bib were old now, or at least they looked it, particularly Jimmy. He couldn't have been any more than fifty, but he was in the grip of the drink, lolling around, brain-addled, making no sense.

Bib looked old too, Rose thought, but probably because she'd worn herself out looking after Jimmy and the kids. The kids were grown up now of course, in their twenties, Bib told her as they sat around downing beers with some of the other mob who shared the house. Mavis was no problem, Bib said, in fact Mavis was being courted by a most acceptable young man from down the street, but the boys? Well the boys were always trouble.

'Nicking cars, thieving, break and enter when they reckon there's no-one there,' Bib said with a shrug, 'you know, same old thing. What do you do? Boys, they're more trouble than they're worth.'

No wonder poor Bib looks old, Rose thought.

As they chatted, more people kept arriving and settling in for a drink and a chat, which Rose found most companionable. They were a younger set than Jimmy and Bib and when the grog ran out they moved on to someone else's house where there was a fresh supply. Rose went with them, and when they took up a collection from whoever had money, which Rose did, she forked out and a couple of the blokes went off to the pub, returning with another slab of beer and two cardboard casks of wine. She knew she was getting drunk, but it didn't seem to matter: she was having a good time.

Common sense kicked in at around five o'clock. Crikey, is that the time? she thought, glancing at her watch. Jess'll be well and truly home from school by now.

She made her hasty farewells and took off, walking a little unsteadily she knew. When she got on the bus, she hoped the other passengers weren't judging her, but she had a definite feeling they were. Looking around at the white faces, she was quite sure she could hear their thoughts. *Drunken Abo – they're all the same.*

She'd more or less sobered up by the time she got home, but it wouldn't have mattered anyway. There was no-one there when she arrived. Toby was still in his studio and

Jess was in her room applying herself to her homework at the desk Toby had set up for her.

Rose poured herself a large tumbler full of water, downed it quickly and set about preparing the dinner. When Toby and Jess finally surfaced half an hour or so later she was relieved to note that neither suspected a thing.

They sat down to their chops and vegetables and she listened to her husband and daughter as they chatted about school, Toby demanding a blow-by-blow account of Jess's day and Jess good-naturedly obliging.

Then from out of the blue came a comment that rather took her by surprise.

'Did you go out this afternoon, Rosie love?'

She started guiltily. *Why did he want to know?* 'Yes, for a while. Why?'

'Oh, no reason,' he answered with a shrug, 'just that when I came inside to fetch something you weren't here is all.'

It was a lie. He'd been locked away in the studio with a rock band for the whole of the afternoon, but he could tell she'd been drinking. He'd read the signs immediately, the glazed eyes and the way she followed the conversation between him and Jess in slow motion like an observer at a tennis match who was always a second or so behind each shot. He'd found it endearingly funny in their partying days of old. 'You're a two-pot screamer, love, that's what you are,' he used to say. Rose had never been able to handle the drink well. She wasn't one to drink alone though, and he wondered where she'd been. More importantly, he wondered why she was keeping the matter to herself.

'Go shopping, did you?' He concentrated on the huge forkful of mashed potato he was shovelling together and tried to make the question appear as casual as possible. He wasn't trying to catch her out. He didn't care in the least that she was drunk, but he fervently hoped she wouldn't lie to him.

It would have been so easy for her to answer 'Yes, I went shopping,' but some sixth sense warned Rose not to. 'No,' she said, 'I went to see some old friends in Redfern.' Then she added, with a slightly defiant air. 'I had a real nice afternoon actually.'

'That's good, love.' Toby grinned and gave her a nod. 'I'm glad,' he said, tucking into his mashed potato. He *was* glad. It was a healthy sign, he thought.

He wasn't so glad several weeks later, however, when the 'real nice afternoons' had become a habit and Rose was regularly rolling home drunk. That was not a healthy sign at all. Jess was also aware of the problem by now and Toby knew it was time to read the riot act.

'You don't have to go out to drink, Rosie,' he said one late afternoon when she arrived to discover him sitting in the living room waiting for her. Jess, just back from school, was again in her bedroom doing her homework.

He rose to meet her. 'You can drink right here in your own home you know.' He knew that she already did drink at home, he'd seen the empty bottles hidden behind the bin, but he'd decided that a bit of cupboard drinking was the least of their worries. It was the drunken excursions that needed to be addressed.

Rose had been expecting him to confront her for some time. In fact she'd been wondering why he hadn't. Twice now she'd got back from Redfern so drunk she'd just collapsed on the bed and they'd had to get their own dinner.

'I want to be with my friends.' She glared accusingly at him. 'You're out there in that studio surrounded by people and I'm supposed to stay stuck in here all day on my own. I don't reckon that's fair.'

She was swaying unsteadily on her feet. God, he thought, she's well and truly hammered this time. How the hell did she get home? It's a wonder she wasn't arrested.

'You're welcome in the studio any time,' he said patiently, 'you know that. You can spend the whole day in there with us if you like. The bands always love an audience.'

But she wasn't listening. 'You don't like me having friends – that's it, isn't it?' she said, her words slurring. 'You don't want me to have friends! You've never wanted me to have friends!'

'Of course I want you to have friends, Rosie.' He refused to be goaded into an argument; it was the mixture of guilt and grog that was making her belligerent. 'Why don't you bring your friends home? You can drink here.'

'My friends wouldn't like it here. My friends wouldn't like *you*,' she gave a scornful wave of her hand, tottering as she did so, 'and you wouldn't like my friends.'

'Give it a try, Rosie, that's all I ask, just give it a try. Now come on, girl, let's get you to bed.' God how he hated seeing her like this, this wasn't his Rose.

The following morning, Rose had only the vaguest memory of the confrontation. But she knew there'd been one and she felt thoroughly ashamed.

'I'm sorry,' she whispered over and over. 'I'm sorry, I'm sorry, I'm sorry . . .'

'Shush, shush, love,' he said comfortingly, 'don't go upsetting yourself now. But like I said, if you want to have an afternoon on the turps, bring your friends home here. At least that way you won't get yourself arrested.'

He tried to make it sound amusing, but Toby knew they had a problem, a very serious problem. What exactly was it though? Why was Rose drinking? What was she trying to escape from? Did she even know?

Rose didn't invite her Redfern drinking mates to the house, she felt too ashamed, but the problem didn't go away. For a while she managed to moderate her drinking, but it was still a daily habit. She avoided the Block, drinking at home instead, not to excess but enough to suitably dull the senses.

Toby, relieved that his wife wasn't wandering the streets in a stupor, kept an ample supply of wine in the house and even joined her, drinking more than he normally would in order that she shouldn't feel guilty. And on the weekends they'd leave Jess with friends and go to pub band sessions and party as they had in the old days, but Toby knew it wasn't solving the issue, that he was only buying time.

A year or so later, the binge sessions reoccurred, the Block beckoned, and the cycle of shame and remorse followed, particularly when, on two occasions in just three short months, Toby was called down to the police station to collect Rose, who'd been picked up for being drunk and disorderly.

'For God's sake, Rose, what the fuck are you doing to yourself? What the fuck are you doing to *all* of us?' There was the odd occasion when Toby lashed out, frustrated beyond endurance, unable to contain his temper any longer. 'Things can't go on like this, woman! God in heaven can't you give it a fucking rest?' But of course she couldn't. His anger only made matters worse.

Both Toby and Jess were at a loss as to what they could possibly do to address the issue. Toby tried to convince Rose to seek help. She should go to Alcoholics Anonymous, he said, but she closed off completely. She could just see that, couldn't she? All those white people looking down on the drunken Abo.

On the bad days that followed a binge, when Rose could vaguely recall her mortification, the memory of the police cell, her husband virtually carrying her stumbling through the front doors of the house, the look of alarm on her daughter's face, she would be overcome with shame.

On such days fourteen-year-old Jess would do all she could to comfort her mother. She would cuddle Rose in her arms as she sobbed and begged for forgiveness. '*It's all right, Mumayee,*' she would whisper in Arunta, rocking her back and forth like a child, '*it's all right,*' and Rose, overwhelmed by guilt, would sob all the more. *It isn't all right*, the voices in her brain whispered accusingly, *it's all wrong, and you know it. It's all wrong, and it's all your fault.*

Toby and Jess discussed the problem endlessly, but it continued to appear insoluble. Then shortly before the summer holidays Jess came up with a suggestion.

'Got an idea,' she said, fronting him when he was alone in the studio.

'Fire away.'

'We have to get one thing straight though,' she held up her hands in a gesture of solemn declaration, 'I am not motivated by self-interest here.'

'I believe you.' He nodded back with equal solemnity. Fourteen going on thirty, he thought as usual.

'What say we do that trip to the Northern Territory this summer? You reckon it'd help Mum?'

Oh dear, he thought. 'Unfortunately no, Jess. In fact I think that's how this whole problem got started. Well no,' he said with a shake of his head, 'it got started way before that. Sit down, love.' He patted the chair beside him and she sat. 'There are a lot of things about her past that your mum hasn't told you, but you're nearly fifteen, old enough now, and I think it's time you knew.'

He proceeded to tell her about Rose's systematic rape from the age of fourteen. 'Same age as you, Jess,' he said bluntly, 'and it went on for over two years.' Then he told her about Eddie, and the beatings, and the Block and those lost years when Rose had been rudderless.

'I don't know why she doesn't want to go back to the Territory,' he concluded, 'truly I don't. But she's frightened. Perhaps she sees it as some new form of threat, I don't know. I'm not sure if Rose knows either. She's so lost I'm not sure if she even knows who she is.' Toby had told his story matter-of-factly, but there was a wealth of sadness in him as he added, 'We're all she's got, you and me, Jess love, and I'm afraid right now we don't seem to be quite enough.'

Jess was saddened by how defeated her father looked. She took his hand. Mum isn't the only one in need of comfort, she thought.

'I'm glad you told me all that,' she said. 'It's right I should know.'

'Yes. Yes it is.'

The terrible day came early in 1988. Jess was sixteen and shortly to start her final year at school. Then on this terrible day Rose didn't come home. Toby waited for the call from the police station and when there wasn't one he went down to check, but she wasn't there. He drove around the streets of Balmain and Redfern in the deepening dusk, headlights on high beam, frantically searching the laneways and alleys, while Jess walked down to Ewenton Park in the hope of finding her mother passed out on a park bench. She searched every other park in the area too, calling out for her mother, but to no avail.

They found Rose the next day, or rather the police did. An early-morning jogger reported a body washed up around the point. Apparently, when Jess had been searching Ewenton Park the previous dusk, her mother had been there after all. But she hadn't been in the park. She'd been in the water.

Autopsy reports showed the deceased had been heavily intoxicated and the death was officially recorded as accidental.

Whether Rose had died as the result of a terrible drunken mishap or whether she had simply walked into the water and taken her own life, Toby would never know, but for his daughter's sake he chose to believe the official version and no alternative was ever discussed.

In the awful months that followed, however, he couldn't help but be nagged by secret doubts, and he vowed that

Jess's confidence would never be undermined as Rose's had. She must not go down her mother's path. Jess must be strong. Jess must know who she was and be proud of it.

Any fears he may have had were, fortunately, unfounded. Jess already knew who she was. Jess had always known. But strangely enough, it was Rose herself who was to ultimately prove the greatest influence upon young Jess's life.

'I've been discussing my uni choices with the counsellor, Dad,' she announced a year after the death of her mother. Despite her grief, or most probably because of it, Jess had thrown herself into her studies and now, after passing her HSC with flying colours, had been accepted into Sydney University. 'I'll do an arts course, majoring in anthropology, and then I'll go on to study Indigenous languages.'

From his stunned reaction she judged he was impressed, but she could also tell he was a little confused.

'There's a way I can do it, you know,' she continued enthusiastically, 'even though it's not a set course. After an honours year, if I end up doing a PhD in English, which I certainly intend to, I'll get a choice of Language or Literature, and if I go the Language I can focus on what I like. And that'll be Indigenous languages,' she concluded with a ring of triumph, 'particularly those of the central desert people. Let's face it, Mum gave me a walk-up start.'

'Wow, pretty impressive, Jess,' he said. To Toby it was all so much double-dutch, but he could feel a pall slowly starting to lift. 'Looks like you've got everything worked out, love.'

'Yep, but before I start uni, we're going on that trip to the Territory, you and me, just like you promised.'

'We are that.'

'I need to meet up with some of the Western Arunta mob,' she said, 'learn a bit about them. And maybe we'll find some of Mum's family while we're at it, eh?'

'Maybe we will, love. Maybe we will.'

Toby felt happier than he had for the whole of the past year. Rose lived on in her daughter, but this was a different Rose: one who was strong. It was as if his Rosie was somehow still here, alive and well.

CHAPTER THREE

Upon first meeting, Matthew Witherton appeared something of a mystery. He was good-looking enough in a rugged sort of way. Early thirties, tall, sandy-haired and hazel-eyed with the weathered skin of one who worked outdoors under an Australian sun: the image was commanding. But Matthew's manner belied his appearance. He tended to watch from the sidelines, seemingly uninterested in making any form of impact. Was he by nature a sullen man? Was he in a bad mood for some specific reason? Or was he perhaps simply shy? To those who didn't know him, Matthew was difficult to fathom.

To those who did know him, and particularly to those well acquainted with his family, the answer was simple. Matthew was a product of his parents not only biologically, but also behaviourally.

Young Matt had learnt from his father to take a back seat to his mother at all times and to feign indifference, because there was no point in attempting to compete for centre stage. David Witherton had never competed with his wife, who had declined to take his name upon their marriage, remaining Lilian Birch, much as Dave had expected. Dave had not taught his son to emulate him, however; the boy had taken on the mantle of indifference more through a form of osmosis. He may have been imitating his father to begin with, but after observing his parents over the years, young Matt had finally come to appreciate the symbiotic relationship that existed between these two people who appeared to have come from quite different planets. His father was not feigning indifference at all, Matt realised. His mother needed centre stage and his father did not; it was that simple. David Witherton's acquiescence was not a sign of weakness, but rather one of strength. Granting his wife the freedom of expression she demanded was a gift of love, a gift that Lilian returned with equal fervour, for David was the calm in her stormy existence.

Matthew hadn't always realised this fact. As a child he had secretly agreed with his grandmother, although of course he hadn't dared say so.

'You are selfish, Liliana,' Svetlana declared in her imperious Russian manner, she was an imposing woman. 'You were a selfish child and you have become a selfish woman.'

The family, all four, Lilian, Dave, little Matt and Babushka 'Lana' were gathered in the main downstairs lounge of their two-storey bluestone house in Wakefield Street not far from Adelaide's city centre. The house had been built in the late nineteenth century and everything about it was grand as befitted its owner, Svetlana Bircher, nee Morozova, including the antique furniture that filled every room to the point of clutter, courtesy of her late husband, who had been a highly successful antique dealer. In the decade since Frank Bircher's death, Svetlana, an astute businesswoman, had taken over her husband's enterprise, building even further upon its success, and the house reflected her passion. Each room bore a different theme and the main lounge was pure Louis XV.

Now, enthroned upon her Louis Quinze armchair, with her vividly kaftan-clad daughter and gangly son-in-law seated opposite on a matching sofa, both very much at odds with the piece, Svetlana's steel-grey eyes bored into Lilian's. 'You have an eight-year-old son you have not seen for months,' her eyes flickered to young Matt where he was perched uncomfortably on an ornate hardback, 'and now you announce you are once more deserting him?' Svetlana's voice rose in pitch. 'Furthermore you insist David go with you to these Godforsaken places that so attract your interest.' Her angry gaze took in Dave who, accustomed to the family dramas, remained silent. He saw little point in explaining that he was contracted to work in remote locations; Lana would only say, 'Then why don't you seek contracts closer to home.'

'What sort of mother are you?' Svetlana demanded.

'The sort of mother who knows her son's education must not suffer, Mama.' Lilian didn't flinch for one second, coolly meeting her mother's attack head-on. 'I would far rather take Mattie with us, but he's much better off staying here with you and going to school.'

'You could always stay here with him yourself, has that thought not occurred?' Svetlana was outraged. 'Where is your shame? Where is your guilt? How can you be so selfish?'

Lilian felt neither shame nor guilt. 'It's an artist's duty to be selfish,' she replied – an answer that appeared glib, but was actually made in all seriousness. 'In fact it's essential. Artists need to be selfish in order to devote themselves to their art. George Bernard Shaw was very much of that opinion and I agree with him entirely. Besides, in creating works of beauty I'm contributing to the world. I would hardly call that selfish.' Arrogant as the statement sounded, it was not merely ego speaking. Lilian's paintings hung in galleries throughout Australia and she had recently received acclaim overseas, but Svetlana refused to accept this as any form of argument.

'God will strike you dead for such a sentiment that excuses the desertion of your child,' she declared. 'How could I have given birth to such an unnatural creature? You are a disgrace to womanhood!'

But Lilian was impervious to both threats and insults. She was an atheist anyway so God was immaterial and, having been born in Adelaide, she considered herself thoroughly Australian, with no time for the Russian melodramatics of her mother. It was why she'd long ago dropped two syllables from her name, transforming herself at the age of fifteen from Liliana Bircher to Lilian Birch, a change which Svetlana had steadfastly refused to acknowledge.

'Come along now, Mama.' Lilian rose, intending to put an end to the scene, which she considered completely unnecessary, and bending down to kiss her mother's cheek. 'You won't miss us for a minute. You adore having Matthew all to yourself, you know you do.' She held her arms out to her son, her kaftan becoming the brilliantly coloured wings of a giant bird. 'Mattie, darling, let's go for a lovely long walk in the park. You can play on the swings.'

Matthew glanced uncertainly at his grandmother, who gave a brisk nod and, jumping from his chair, he took his mother's hand.

Lilian tossed her silken scarf around her neck and sailed out the door with her son in tow, without a backward glance.

Dave rose. 'Shall I have Olga bring you some tea?' he asked. Such theatrical displays were nothing new to Dave who took it all in his stride. Much as Lilian might deny it, she had a flair for the dramatic that could equal her mother's.

'Please,' Svetlana replied tightly.

David Witherton and Lilian Birch had met in 1966. They swore for ever after that it was the Tea and Sugar Train that had brought them together. He was a twenty-five-year-old surveyor, employed at the time by the Surveyor-General's Department, and she was a twenty-eight-year-old artist whose work was beginning to attract the attention of

Adelaide's art gallery curators. It was Divine Providence, they both later agreed, somewhat tongue in cheek as neither were true believers, that the Tea and Sugar Train should prove the catalyst for their meeting.

Initially a supply train for workers constructing the Trans-Australian Railway, the Tea and Sugar Train, as it later became known, had begun regular operation in 1917 after the line was completed. Settlements had quickly grown up all along the route where once there had been only fettlers' camps, and the delivery of supplies from luxury items to the most basic of requirements was essential. For decades now the Tea and Sugar Train, which ran the sixteen-hundred-kilometre route between Port Augusta and Kalgoorlie, had been a lifeline to the outback residents it served, a welcome sight on its weekly trips along the lonely stretch of track that traversed the vast Nullarbor Plain. The train was not only a travelling shop with a provisions car displaying everything a corner store could offer and a butcher's van where fresh meat could be expertly cut to order, it also provided medical services and entertainment. A nurse travelled on board once a month to give children their necessary injections and check on the townspeople's health, and most exciting of all once a month there was a 'film car'. An outing to the pictures was an eagerly awaited treat. There was even an annual 'Christmas car' with a Santa who provided presents for children at every town along the track. Little wonder the Tea and Sugar Train had become such an outback institution, running close to fifty years now and destined to run for many years to come.

Dave often travelled aboard the Tea and Sugar Train, particularly when contracted by the government to work with the military at a restricted area in the outback regions of South Australia. He loved the outback and always put his hand up for jobs that took him to remote locations, which meant he travelled a great deal. He rarely had competition for the faraway tasks: most of his colleagues preferred the comforts of home.

He'd first noticed the young woman in Port Augusta when he'd arrived to board the train; he was off to work on the military's new town-planning development for Woomera village. As he walked towards the railway station, he could hardly fail to notice her. A statuesque figure, focused and confident, multi-coloured full-length skirt billowing about her legs, she strode purposefully down the main street, huge cloth bag slung over one shoulder, auburn hair held back by a bright yellow headband. Not exactly your run-of-the-mill Port Augusta resident, he thought, she's probably a hippy. He didn't much care for hippies, they always struck him as poseurs, but he couldn't help being intrigued.

He noticed her again a fortnight later upon his return. The timing was nothing short of astonishing. He'd just stepped off the Tea and Sugar Train and out of the station and there she was. But she wasn't striding down the street this time. This time she was driving right past him in an aging Land Rover that had seen a fair bit of wear and was so covered in red dust you could barely make out the green paint beneath. The vehicle's windows were down and she was clearly recognisable, the same strong face, the same auburn hair, but this time the headband was orange. Dave decided that despite appearances she must be a local after all.

The third time he saw her, around six weeks later, was in such unexpected circumstances it appeared somehow surreal. He was actually aboard the Tea and Sugar Train at the time. Once again under contract to work with the military, he was bound for Watson and the restricted site of Maralinga where, after a decade of experimentation, the nuclear testing ground was finally nearing closure. It was one of those jobs Dave referred to as 'hush-hush'; in fact he'd been required to sign the Official Secrets Act.

As was customary he was travelling in the sleeper van at the rear of the train, sharing on this occasion with three railway workers who were joining a track maintenance crew at Hughes near the Western Australian border.

Since leaving Port Augusta, he'd spent the entire time gazing out the open carriage window at the sea of saltbush plain, shimmering grey-green-silver in the ever-changing play of light between the sun and the clouds; he never tired of the desert panorama. They'd even passed a herd of wild camels. Then, a hundred and eighty kilometres from Adelaide, when the landscape had dramatically changed to a crusty blanket of red earth and the train was travelling directly alongside the saltpan of Lake Hart, he saw her. Or rather, he saw the Land Rover.

The sight of the vehicle, of any vehicle, flying across the dried face of a salt lake in the middle of nowhere would have been arresting, but the fact that it was this particular vehicle struck Dave as bizarre. Surely he was mistaken.

But he wasn't. The Land Rover was barely fifty metres away and once again she was driving with the windows down, so he could see her quite clearly. Her hair was tied up in a bright green scarf and she was looking out through the passenger window at the train as she kept pace with it, the Land Rover kicking up great clouds of white dust in its wake.

Travelling directly opposite his carriage as she was, Dave could swear she was staring right at him, and he suddenly found himself waving. To his amazement her arm appeared through the driver's window and she waved back across the roof of the vehicle. Good God, he thought, how extraordinary. They kept waving intermittently to each other until the salt lake ran out and the Land Rover slowed down, finally coming to a halt while the train sped relentlessly on its way.

Although no longer able to see the woman herself, Dave continued to lean from the window peering back at the receding salt pan until both the lake and the vehicle became lost amid the surrounding wilderness.

His three sightings seemed so coincidental that he came to associate the woman with the Tea and Sugar Train, as if the two were somehow connected, and each time he travelled to and from Port Augusta he looked out for her.

Then one day, sure enough, there she was in the flesh. It was a Wednesday, the train always departed on a Wednesday, and he'd arrived at the station early as he normally did. They were still loading, so the platform bustled with activity, teams of men carting furniture and crates of fresh produce, sacks of flour and grain and whole sides of beef slung over shoulders, a colourful sight. The woman was seated on a bench, a large sketchpad in hand; she was busily drawing the whole process, or so it appeared, her eyes, a startling grey-blue, darting about taking everything in.

He stood to one side barely ten paces from her, watching, fascinated. There was nothing delicate in the way she approached her work. Her glance flickered up and down from the workers to the sketchpad and her strokes were bold, the pencil swooping across the page without hesitation as if her hand was emulating the action her eyes were observing. He longed to see the result and considered creeping up behind her and trying to sneak a peek, but he didn't want to break her concentration.

Lilian sensed she was being watched, which was nothing unusual. People always wanted to see what an artist was drawing or painting, but they invariably crept up behind to sneak a peek, which broke her focus in a most irritating way. The tall, gangly young man in the battered Akubra hat whom she could see in her peripheral vision was standing deathly still, which she found most respectful. She lowered the pad and turned to gaze directly at him.

Dave started guiltily. 'Sorry,' he said, 'didn't mean to stare.'

'Come and take a look,' she offered with a jerk of her head, 'and tell me if you approve.'

He crossed to the bench and looked down at the sketch-pad she held out before him. 'That's amazing,' he said. It was. With the simplest of strokes she had created the chaos before them, the hustle and the bustle and even the weight of the men's burdens. He was lost in admiration. 'That's truly amazing.'

'No it's not,' she gazed critically at the drawing, 'but it's got the feel I'm after at this stage and that's the main thing.'

'It's got the feel all right.' He wanted to introduce himself and say that he'd seen her before, but it seemed wrong to interfere with her work. 'Well I'll leave you to it, didn't mean to interrupt.'

'You haven't,' she closed the sketch pad, 'I've finished for the day.' Lillian had been at the station all morning drawing far more detailed images of the train itself and of individual workers. 'That's my last sketch for now, just an overall feel and the sort of layout I'm after.' She'd been planning the painting for some time; *The Loading of the Tea and Sugar Train* would be a large work, oil on canvas. 'I'm Lilian Birch by the way.' She held out her hand.

'Dave Witherton,' he said, taking off his hat as they shook. She seemed to be inviting him to join her so he dumped his swag on the ground and sat, resting his Akubra on his knees. 'I've seen you before actually.'

'You have?'

'Yes, about a month back. You were racing the Tea and Sugar Train across a salt pan.' The expression she returned him was rather blank; she must remember surely, he thought. 'Well you and the Land Rover were on the salt pan,' he corrected himself, 'the train wasn't of course, but we were waving to each other, don't you remember?'

'Oh I always wave at the Tea and Sugar Train,' she said airily, 'and people always wave back.'

Dave was instantly deflated. Foolish of him to have expected recognition, he supposed, but he felt a stab of disappointment that she found the incident itself inconsequential when to him it had been so significant.

Lilian, however, did not find the incident at all inconsequential. 'But you were actually aboard, were you?' she carried on without drawing breath. 'You were actually travelling on the Tea and Sugar Train?'

'Yes.' Why was that remarkable? 'I quite often do. In fact I'm travelling aboard today; that's why I'm here.'

'How come?' She openly appraised him, her sharp eyes taking everything in, from his khaki shorts and open-necked shirt to his well-worn boots and the battered Akubra in his lap. Customary outback garb, she thought, but he doesn't seem like a farmer and he's certainly not a labourer. 'You don't look like a railway man,' she said, just a touch critically, 'and the Tea and Sugar Train doesn't carry passengers.'

'It does if you work for the government,' he explained. 'I'm a surveyor.'

'Ah,' she nodded, 'so that's it. Well I envy you.' She turned away to gaze at the delivery men loading the last of the provisions. 'There's something rather noble about the Tea and Sugar Train, isn't there?' she said thoughtfully, 'something that somehow symbolises this country.'

'Yes, I agree.'

A moment's silence followed as they both stared at the train then Lilian looked back at him. 'So where are you off to today?'

'Watson. It's a pretty remote spot, just a siding really.' He was headed back to Maralinga to complete his work with the military there, but he was not at liberty to tell her even that much.

He didn't need to. Lilian knew every stop along the route of the Tea and Sugar Train and although Watson was indeed little more than a siding, it was a siding of considerable importance, serving the nuclear testing ground of Maralinga as it did.

'Bloody disgraceful in my opinion,' she said. 'We'll end up paying a price for it, you know.'

'For what?'

'Maralinga. You can't blow up atomic bombs in the middle of the desert and expect to get off scot free,' she said scathingly. 'What was the government thinking, offering us up to the British like sacrificial lambs to the slaughter, poisoning the people, the animals, the bloody country itself? Downright outrageous!'

She's certainly forthright, Dave thought. Once again he agreed with her, but he didn't say anything.

'So you're part of the clean-up process, I take it?' she queried. 'The government *is* still trying to decontaminate the area, isn't it?'

He shrugged apologetically. 'Can't really say, I'm afraid, all a bit hush-hush.'

'Oh.' She halted in her tirade. 'I'm sorry. I do go on at the mouth, don't I? I'm probably not even supposed to know you're going to Maralinga, right?'

'Right.'

'Sorry,' she said again.

'No worries. Just between you and me I agree with every word you said.'

'Oh good.' She smiled and they changed the subject, discovering they both came from Adelaide, a fact that Dave found most encouraging as he certainly wanted to see Lilian again. They discovered also that they shared a passion for the outback and desert regions of Australia.

'Oh yes,' she agreed fervently, 'the desert light is so extraordinary, isn't it, and so variable! The way it creates a sense of movement, you could swear sometimes the land's actually breathing. And the people! Weathered like the country itself. No wonder Drysdale loves the outback, what an endless source of inspiration . . .'

Dave studied her as she chatted away enthusiastically, first about Russell Drysdale's brilliance and then about her own love of painting the outback. A handsome woman with a strong-boned face and a dramatic arch to the brow, she didn't look like the average Australian of Celtish or English background, and he wondered about her antecedents. But it was her vitality that most attracted him. She was stimulating and yet at the same time strangely relaxing to be with, as if they were old friends.

'You travel a great deal then?' It only took one question and off she went again while he sat back and continued to study her. Yes, she travelled a great deal, she said, but her studio was in the city at her mother's house.

'Until I'm rich and famous it's cheaper that way,' she added with a smile, although he gathered from her tone that she wasn't really joking, more predicting a certain future. 'Besides, Mama has a disgustingly huge house with tons of room for a studio out the back so it's very convenient. We had a country property too, in the Adelaide Hills near Hahndorf, but Mama sold it recently. Papa died last year and she didn't want to go back there without him.'

'That's sad,' he said.

'Sad yes, but expected,' she replied with a philosophical shrug. 'He'd been ill for a long time. I think he worked himself to death, poor Papa.'

He'd never heard a local girl call her parents 'Papa' and 'Mama' before; how intriguing. Her voice was pleasant, but distinctly Australian, as was her manner, and once again he wondered about her background. 'Where are you from?' he asked bluntly: she didn't strike him as the type who would take offence. 'You don't look Australian.'

'Well I am,' she declared vehemently, 'born and bred,' then she went on to explain. Her father was German, she said, German Jewish and her mother Russian.

'They met in Berlin in the early thirties. Not a good time or place to be Jewish,' she added dryly. 'They could see the threat Hitler's Nazi party posed so they moved permanently to Australia. Papa had an antique exports business to the UK and here,' she explained, 'so he already had contacts.'

'I see.' The briefest of pauses followed while he wondered what question to ask next – he didn't want her to stop – but she got in first.

'I don't always talk this much, you know.'

He made no reply although something in his eyes said 'Really?'

'Well yes all right, I do,' she admitted, a touch on the defensive, 'but only if I like someone.'

He grinned. 'I'll take that as a compliment.'

The tables had turned now, and it was she who was studying him. 'You did that deliberately, didn't you,' she said with an air of accusation.

'Did what?' he queried in all innocence.

'Got me to talk all about myself and deliberately offered nothing in return.'

'There's nothing to offer really.'

'How about a bit of family history?' she demanded. 'Come on, fair's fair.'

'Sure,' he gave a shrug. 'No siblings, my mother died of cancer two years ago and I never knew my father because he died as a prisoner of war on the Burma Railway.'

'Oh.' For the first time during their entire exchange Lilian appeared to have run out of words.

He realised he'd sounded overly abrupt. He hadn't intended to be rude, just succinct, and he hoped she wasn't offended.

'Sorry,' he said, another shrug. 'No family to speak of; there was only ever Mum and me.'

A whistle sounded. 'All aboard,' the guard called. The huge sliding doors of cargo vans slammed shut, carriage doors opened and closed, the Tea and Sugar Train was about to depart.

'I see,' she answered. She wasn't in the least offended, only intrigued. 'So you intend to remain a man of mystery, Dave.'

'I sincerely hope not.' His eyes locked into hers. 'I get back in a fortnight –' He was going to say he'd like to see her again and to ask for her address and phone number, but she cut him off.

'I'll be here,' she said, 'right here on this bench.'

Their eyes remained locked. She has to be joking, he thought.

'I know exactly when the Tea and Sugar Train gets in,' she said, 'and I'll be here. I need to do a lot more sketches before I start on the actual painting.'

'All aboard,' the guard called again.

'Right.' He stood, picking up his swag and donning his Akubra. 'I'll see you here then.'

She nodded.

He boarded the train, wondering if she'd meant what she'd said, wondering if he'd ever see her again, but on his return, true to her word she was there seated on the same bench, sketchpad in hand.

Within a year they'd married. Their very differences were their strengths. Mad had met sane, wild had met calm and, somewhere in the mix, soul had met soul.

When Matt did finally recognise the bond between his parents, it created a further bond that was equally special: a bond between father and son. Dave and Matt were observers both, solitary men, possibly as a result of their solitary childhoods. They shared much that was unspoken, not least being their recognition of Lilian's eccentricities. Quite often they found her funny, sometimes when she didn't mean to be, and their response infuriated her.

'Why are you both smirking?' she'd demand in the middle of a tantrum as she whirled about, a blur of colour and movement, a sort of demented peacock, usually because a piece of work was not going to her satisfaction. 'I fail to see what's so frightfully amusing.'

But she was unable to ruffle the feathers of either husband or son. Matthew, like his father, was implacable. Indeed implacability was where young Matt's strength lay, for like his father he had no need of centre stage. Matt was quite happy to sit, observing others, taking action only when and how he deemed necessary, which more often than not proved highly effective.

For all her indulgent behaviour and egocentricity, Lilian stayed true to herself over the years, always brutally honest and, to those she loved, always fiercely loyal. She became rich and famous, just as she'd predicted, but she did not desert her mother. Having no desire for the trappings she could have afforded, she and therefore Dave and Matt remained ensconced in the bluestone in Wakefield Street with its studio out the back. They remained not only because it served their purpose, but because Svetlana needed them. Svetlana, cantankerous as she was, would have been lost without them, particularly the grandson to whom she had become so devoted. Lilian had no wish to deprive young Matt, too, of his babushka, the woman who had been more of a mother to him than she had herself.

Dave didn't mind. He quite happily went along with the arrangement, the family downstairs, the old lady upstairs. He was away half the time anyway and, as usual, very little bothered Dave.

Lilian's loyalty was never more evident than in the spring of 1989 when, not yet fifty, she was at the height of her career. Twenty years of dedication had brought critical acclaim worldwide and in her native country the status of national icon. She'd been awarded an Order of Australia; her work hung in galleries and private collections around the globe; and she was feted by the international art world. But all was put on hold as Svetlana, who had suffered a series of heart attacks and a crippling bout of pneumonia, succumbed to old age.

Determined that her mother should not languish in a hospice, but rather die in the comfort of her own home surrounded by her precious antique collection and the people she loved, Lilian hired a live-in nurse to help her and the long-suffering Olga with Lana's care. Then she cancelled her London exhibition, scheduled for early the following year, along with her many other commitments, including a long-awaited return to the outback with Dave. Their trips had become less frequent over the past several years, Dave opting for contracts closer to home as more and more demands were made on his wife's time. Now everything was put on hold so that Lillian could remain by Svetlana's bedside until the end came.

Eighty-year-old Lana, in typically tetchy fashion, did not appear to appreciate her daughter's display of devotion. Propped up like a queen, albeit a withered one, in her massive Georgian four-poster, Lana managed to find something to complain about or something with which to find fault on a daily basis.

'I do think it's time you started dressing your age, Liliana.' The voice, although frail like the body, still carried an imperious edge.

Lilian put the customary mid-morning pot of tea on the bedside table, plumped up the pillows and straightened the bed's coverlet. 'And how exactly should I dress my age, Mama?' She wasn't remotely interested in the answer, but was willing to humour her mother.

'Something less gaudy for a start.' Svetlana looked her daughter up and down critically. 'Something in muted colours and of more stylish cut, you're a middle-aged woman for goodness' sake.'

'I dress for comfort and I like bright colours,' Lilian replied simply. She left it at that and started pouring the tea.

Then later the same day . . .

'It's a little late, don't you think?' Svetlana grumbled as her daughter fed her the soup that Olga prepared fresh each morning.

'Eat up, you need your strength.' Ignoring the complaint, Lilian continued to spoon chicken soup into the shrunken mouth; her once-imposing mother was skeletal.

'A little late in the day, isn't it?'

'Rubbish. It's right on lunchtime.'

'I mean a little late to be showing you care.' Lana waved the chicken soup aside. 'You never cared in the past.'

'You never needed me in the past.' Lilian remained patiently poised with the soup bowl; Lana always waved it away and always came back for more. 'Besides I left you with Mattie. Mattie was far more important to you than I was.' She intended no drama in the remark, just a simple statement of fact.

'Selfish,' Lana shook her head disapprovingly, 'selfish woman, selfish mother,' and she opened her mouth for more chicken soup.

'Yes, yes, you're quite right.' Lilian spooned in the soup, mopping with a linen napkin the dribble that trickled down her mother's chin, 'but a selfish woman and a selfish mother who cares, Mama. I've always cared, you know I have.'

'Is Matthew home from university yet?' Lana asked.

'No, it's only lunch time.'

'You will make sure he comes to see me as soon as he returns, won't you?'

'Of course – he always does, doesn't he?'

The conversation took a similar turn each day, in fact was almost routine. Svetlana was far more interested in her grandson than she was in her daughter, which Lilian found perfectly understandable. She respected the relationship between her mother and her son. It was to be expected given her years of 'desertion' or 'dereliction of duty' as Lana was wont to say, but she suffered no guilt, nor did she envy the bond the two shared: it was just the way things were.

'Ah *mily moy*.' Svetlana greeted her grandson in Russian as she always did. 'My darling,' she repeated, beckoning with her hands that she wanted a hug. In the old days she would have held her arms out wide, but she no longer had the strength.

'Babushka.' Nineteen-year-old Matt, now tall and sturdily built, bent down and embraced the stick-like body of his grandmother with infinitesimal care. She was so fragile he felt she might break. It saddened him immensely when he recalled the ample bosom to which, as a child, he'd been clasped with such proprietorial strength. His grandmother's embraces had always embarrassed him, but now he would give anything to feel his head buried once more in that bosom.

He pulled the chair up beside the four-poster, preferring not to sit on the bed itself for fear of jarring her.

'How was university? Tell me all about your day,' she insisted.

He did, filling her in on every single detail, although this day had hardly differed from the previous day or the one before that. He knew she just wanted to hear the sound of his voice.

Young Matthew was in the second year of his science degree at the University of Adelaide and intended to become a surveyor. During his early teenage years many a school holiday had seen him accompany his parents on their travels and not unsurprisingly he had inherited their joint passion for the country's remote regions. As a result he'd chosen to follow his father's career, deciding at the age of fifteen that he would become a Licensed Surveyor and travel the outback. To Matt, his father's seemed the ideal life.

'So you feel confident?' Lana asked. He'd mentioned his forthcoming exams, which would see him either progressing to third year or failing altogether, a nerve-wracking time for university students.

'Yes I do,' he said without hesitation. Then he smiled self-deprecatingly. 'I hope that doesn't sound complacent and I hope I'm not asking to be shot down in flames, but yes I do feel confident.'

'That is good. There is nothing wrong with confidence, Matthew; confidence is not complacency.' Lana's stern expression, which seemed perennial these days, softened into one of her rare smiles and for a fleeting moment the handsome woman she'd once been was discernable. 'Ah *mily moy*, your father will be so proud. It is good that a father should be proud of his son, just as one day you will be proud of your son.'

Svetlana spoke often to her grandson of family. She had made a point of doing so over the years, telling him stories of her childhood in Russia, of her siblings and her parents. She had read out loud to him her brother's and her sister's letters, and she'd shown him photographs of his great-uncle and great-aunt and his great-grandparents. Her motives had not been self-interested, although she had enjoyed very much sharing her memories, even with a small boy. She had wished to give the child a sense of personal history, a sense of where he belonged. He had no family at all on his father's side, no grandparents, no aunts and uncles, no cousins, which to her seemed so very wrong. Fond as she was of her son-in-law, Svetlana considered it inexcusable that David was unable to provide even a family tree.

'My mother never knew her natural parents,' he'd explained when she pushed him for answers. 'She didn't keep in touch with her adopted parents, and my father died as a prisoner of war, so I never met him. That's all I can tell you I'm afraid.'

She'd been able to get no more out of him, and her daughter had been no help whatsoever. 'Stop badgering him, Mama,' Lilian had said, which had infuriated Lana.

Didn't the woman care that her son had no paternal family history? Further proof surely that she was an unnatural mother.

So Svetlana had decided it was she who must provide her grandson with a family history and she'd taken her task very seriously, even teaching the child Russian, or at least attempting to.

'Ah *mily moy*,' she would say, clapping her hands in delight when he repeated a phrase to her satisfaction, 'that is excellent: we must continue with these lessons until you are fluent.' The boy would never achieve fluency – she'd known that from the beginning. He didn't have his mother's natural linguistic skills.

'When your mother was a little girl she spoke Russian with me,' she would tell him. 'She spoke German too, she was very gifted linguistically, but then your mother was gifted in so many areas. A child prodigy, your grandfather and I were told. Such a brilliant pianist! She could have had a splendid career as a classical performer, that's what her tutors said.'

And just look at her now, Svetlana would think, denying her heritage, even changing her name, gallivanting off to paint pictures of the Australian outback. What sort of a career is that?

'But she has become selfish,' she would conclude dismissively, 'very, very selfish.'

Little Matt's early views of his mother had been influenced by Svetlana, certainly, but even as a small child he had been aware of his grandmother's inordinate pride in her daughter. He often wondered why Babushka never told his mother that she was proud of her.

Babushka eventually did, but she left her declaration until the very last minute, just as she'd planned.

It was towards the end of November, Matt's exams were over and Lilian had turned fifty, momentous occasions both, and cause for celebration. But things quickly returned to normal, and this particular evening started out the same as any other.

The nurse had delivered Lana's medication ground up in juice as usual, and when she'd gone Lilian sat on the edge of the bed, small paper cup in hand. She fed her mother her medicine, then took away several of the pillows that were propping her up, easing her carefully back on the bed.

'There you go, Mama, are you comfy?' No answer. 'Would you like me to read to you?' Again no answer, but the faded blue eyes were appraising her, and Lilian waited for whatever complaint or criticism was about to issue forth.

'*I am proud of you, Liliana.*'

The words took Lilian by surprise, not only their sentiment, but the fact that her mother had said them in Russian. They had not spoken Russian to each other for years.

'*I know you are, Mama.*' She responded in kind, rewarded by the instant gratification she could see in her mother's eyes.

'*Ya lublu tebya,*' Svetlana said.

'*I know that also,*' Lilian replied in Russian. '*I have always known that, Mama.*' She leant forward and very gently kissed her mother on the lips. '*I love you too.*'

Svetlana smiled. 'I shall sleep now,' she said, reverting to English.

'Would you like me to read to you?'

'No, no, I shall sleep. I am very tired.'

She did not wake up. The nurse discovered her dead early the following morning. She'd suffered a heart attack during the night, a mild one, but enough to take her in her sleep.

'Mama willed herself to die,' Lilian said as the family gathered in the bedroom to pay their respects to the frail little body lying in state like royalty in the vast four-poster bed. 'I didn't realise it, but she was saying goodbye to me last night.' She studied her mother's face, which in death was serene and somehow ageless. The deep furrows had disappeared and the texture of the skin seemed to glow afresh. Lilian was fascinated. 'Doesn't she look beautiful?' she whispered.

'Yes,' Dave agreed, 'yes, she does.'

Beside them, Matthew nodded. Tears were running down his face, and he didn't trust himself to speak.

Despite the selfless dedication she'd displayed during her mother's lingering months, it was not long before Lilian's ruthless ego resurfaced. Less than six weeks after Svetlana's death she set about radically re-designing the home in Wakefield Street to suit her purposes, starting with her mother's beloved antiques, all of which were to be sold as soon as possible.

'If Leonard can't display them at the showrooms,' she said, referring to her mother's manager and partner, who now ran the business, 'then he'll just have to put them in storage until he can find buyers. This place has become a veritable museum. I need space! And I need light, lots and lots of light!'

She intended to convert the upper floor to a massive studio. The upper floor had always been her mother's exclusive quarters, with master bedroom, dressing room, bathroom, sitting room and the spare bedroom that had recently housed the live-in nurse.

'I'll keep the spare bedroom and the bathroom intact,' she said to Dave as they toured upstairs together discussing the renovations, or rather as Lilian unveiled her plans, 'and all the rest will be gutted. I'll have the walls ripped out and huge skylights built into the roof: the light will be amazing.'

Dave wasn't sure how the Heritage Council would feel about the gutting of a hundred-year-old home.

'Pretty structural stuff,' he pointed out. 'You might have trouble getting permission and I don't think they'll like you chopping holes in the slate roof.'

'Rubbish,' she declared, 'I'm not altering the facade of the place. It's none of their business what goes on inside and who the hell ever sees a roof anyway?'

Dave didn't pursue the subject. The property was hers after all and he had his comfortable study downstairs. He rarely came up to the top floor anyway.

'What about the studio out the back?' he asked. 'What do you plan to do with that?'

'That'll be Mattie's,' Lilian had everything worked out, 'his very own quarters. There's tons of space and it already has a kitchen. I shall have it converted to a self-contained flat.'

'Good idea.' Dave very much approved. Matt had had two girlfriends in the past and although he didn't appear to be on the kind of rampage many sex-obsessed males his age indulged in, he was certainly not a virgin. 'A young man should have his privacy,' he said.

'Of course he should. You never know when he might want to bring a girl home and this way he doesn't have to run her by the parents.'

'Right.' Dave smiled. Lilian always had to state the obvious. He wondered if she'd be as blunt with Matt. Yes, he thought, she probably would.

She was. 'You'll have your very own place, Mattie,' she said as she told him her plans. 'You can bring girls home whenever you like and we won't even know.'

Father and son exchanged a whimsical glance. Was she merely being forthright or did she intend to be funny? No matter: she was just being Lilian.

Two and a half years later, however, when Matt *did* bring a girl home, and not just to his flat, but in order to meet his parents, Lilian was the one who was flabbergasted.

'Mum, Dad, this is Angie . . .'

They'd been waiting to meet Angie. He'd talked about her a lot and was obviously very keen. The two had met at university. Angie was doing an arts course. She was very pretty, he'd said. Then he'd corrected himself.

'She's good-looking actually,' he'd admitted, 'really good-looking. I don't know what she could possibly see in me.'

'Why so bloody humble?' Lilian had castigated him roundly. 'Don't put yourself down like that.'

'. . . Angela Marsdon,' Matt completed the introduction. 'Angie this is my mum, Lilian, and my dad, Dave.'

'How do you do?' the girl said and they shook hands all round.

Lilian remained uncharacteristically silent and let Dave do the talking, which he quite happily did. They were gathered in the main sitting room and he told Angie to take a seat and offered her a drink.

Lilian automatically sat herself while Matt fetched her a glass of wine and as she did so she openly stared at the girl.

Very pretty? Really good-looking? How utterly inadequate. Young Angie was neither 'pretty' nor 'good-looking': she was flawlessly beautiful. And not only was she flawlessly beautiful, she oozed sex appeal. She's a siren, Lilian thought, aghast. She's the kind of woman who lures men to their doom. Oh my God, Mattie, what sort of trouble have you let yourself in for?

CHAPTER FOUR

Matt and Angie had met at that year's O-Ball. It hadn't really been a meeting as such, more a challenge, or so it seemed to Matt. At the time he'd been rather swept off his feet.

'Want to dance?'

Pitching her voice above the cacophony, she hadn't even said 'hello', this glorious sex goddess in a bright red mini-dress standing before him.

'Sure,' he yelled back and they weaved their way through the throng.

Hundreds were gathered in the open quadrangle, the rock band was thumping out 'When Love Comes to Town', and in the corner reserved as a dance floor bodies were gyrating to the beat in a youthful frenzy.

Matt and Angie joined them. They made no attempt to communicate with each other, but just hurled themselves around like everyone else, which was after all the purpose of the exercise. Orientation week was promoted by the staff as a welcome to new students, an opportunity for them to 'explore the campuses, make new friends, and acquaint themselves with university life' they were told, but the students themselves, freshmen and seasoned alike, knew better. Orientation week was an excuse to party, particu-larly the culminating event of the O-Ball.

The O-Ball was held in the huge, open courtyard of Union House known simply as the Cloisters, a lovely rectangle surrounded by verandahs and stone-arched walkways. A stage was set up and the live entertainment was non-stop, rock bands and pop groups belting out their stuff, solo performers braving an audience vocal in its criticism if they were found wanting and loud in voicing its approval if they were not. Licensed areas provided alcohol, also non-stop, and hundreds upon hundreds of revellers partied through the night, spilling out into the grounds and onto the lawns, flooding the campus. These were not only Adelaide University students, but many others who'd come to know the O-Ball as one of the events of the season.

The band's choice of music proved relentless and after throwing their bodies around to 'All I Want is You' and 'Angel of Harlem', Matt and Angie retired from the madness of the dance floor.

They each grabbed a beer and headed out to the lawn where people were mingling. Then, finding a spare piece of grass some distance from the crowd, they plonked themselves down to recover, Angie kicking off her evening sandals and stretching out her legs, the mini dress exposing a healthy expanse of bare, tanned thigh.

'You're Matt Witherton, aren't you?' she said. Still panting from her exertions, she tossed back her mane of honey-blonde hair and took a healthy swig of beer.

'That's right.' He was surprised she knew his name.

'I'm Angie Marsdon.'

'I know.' Everyone knew Angie Marsdon's name. The moment she walked past you could hear the whispers of 'Who the hell's that?' as heads turned. He doubted there was anyone at uni who didn't know Angie's name and hadn't for the past twelve months. 'You're doing second year arts, aren't you?' he said. He'd made no enquiries, this was just another piece of information offered up by the whispers, 'Angie Marsdon, she's in arts.'

'Yep.' Angie nodded, unsurprised that he knew about her, everyone did. 'And you've finished your BSc and your honours and you're in your final post-grad year.' Her voice had a 'so there' ring to it and her glorious sapphire-blue eyes gleamed, triumphant. Angie's own enquiries had been very thorough. 'And when you've completed your MSc I believe you'll be known in the trade as a Master Surveyor,' she added smugly.

'Where the hell did you hear that?' Matt was amazed. He got on well enough with his fellow students, but tended to keep fairly much to himself and certainly never talked about his plans.

'I asked one of the tutors of course.' Her shrug seemed to say 'simple', and it had been. The male tutors, like the male students, were only too eager to oblige Angie. She held up her beer: 'Nice to meet you, Matt Witherton.'

'Nice to meet you too, Angie Marsdon.' They toasted each other.

Matt was flattered that she'd singled him out for attention, but he couldn't help wondering why she had. He'd seen her around on campus over the past year of course, who hadn't, but not once had it crossed his mind to introduce himself. Why bother? She was way out of his league, probably a spoilt princess, and he had no wish to compete. The prize of wearing the best-looking girl at uni on his arm was one that didn't interest him enough to enter the contest.

All of which made him highly intriguing in Angie's eyes. So much so that she'd had him in her sights for the past several months. There was an air of mystery about Matt Witherton that was extremely attractive. Why hadn't he made a play for her? He wasn't one of the shy ones who ogled from a distance, too scared to come near her; he wasn't one of the smartarses who made showy passes and after being knocked back badmouthed her to his mates; he simply appeared disinterested. Why? She wondered if perhaps he was gay. He certainly doesn't look gay, she thought, but of course it's sometimes so hard to tell.

She'd decided to put him to the test. Unaccustomed as she was to going unnoticed, Angie couldn't resist a challenge.

'Ready to return to the fray?' she asked, polishing off her beer.

'I'm up for it if you are,' he replied.

They returned to the dance floor two more times and they drank two more beers, then . . .

'Do you want to come back to my place?'

He was astonished, both by the offer and the timing. It was only ten o'clock – she wasn't propositioning him surely.

She most certainly was. 'I share a house in Richmond with three other students,' she said, 'they'll be partying on here for hours. If we go now we'll have the place all to ourselves.'

'Right. Great. Good idea.' He was being railroaded, but how could he resist such an offer?

They drove there in her Corolla, which had been parked several blocks away. Matt drove a Land Rover himself, but had walked to the university as he always did.

The house in Brooker Terrace was a modest three-bedroom brick-and-wood dwelling, probably built in the late 1950s or early 60s, with a shabby front hedge and an even shabbier front garden.

'None of us is keen on gardening,' she said as she turned on the porch light to reveal the ill-kempt patch of grass and the weeds that had overtaken what had once been flower beds. She unlocked the front door. 'It's a bit better inside.'

They stepped into an old-fashioned lounge room with big comfortable sofas and armchairs: a cosy room, but decidedly drab, the colours being predominantly brown and beige. Hardly the setting Matt would have associated with a glamorous young woman of the nineties like Angie, or for that matter with university students in general. Everything was so dull.

'The place came furnished,' she explained, dumping her small evening bag on the coffee table. 'Actually it belonged to Jane's godmother, who died a couple of years ago. Ena was a bit of an eccentric apparently, never married, no kids of her own, doted on Jane and left the place to her in her will.'

Jane must be one of the flatmates, Matt thought as he followed her through to the kitchen where a mottled-green Laminex-topped table stood opposite an ancient Kooka-burra stove and an enormous, equally ancient Kelvinator refrigerator. He felt he'd stepped onto the set of a movie based in the fifties.

'Jane has a theory about Ena. Ena was her mother's best friend –' Angie interrupted herself as she opened the fridge door '– wine or beer?'

'Oh.' The offer took him by surprise: she hadn't halted for breath. 'Whatever you feel like, I'm not fussy.'

'Time for a change I think.' She lifted out a bottle of white wine, put it on the table and handed him a cork-screw. 'You do the honours.'

He started opening the bottle.

'She thinks Ena was a lesbian,' Angie continued, taking the glasses from the cupboard and setting them on the table. 'She's convinced that Ena was in love with her mother for the whole of their lives, but never declared herself. Hence Jane sees herself as the symbol of "the love that dare not speak its name".' Angie gave a suitably melodramatic ring to the Wildean quote and smiled as she watched him pour the wine. 'Jane has a decidedly romantic streak.'

She returned the bottle to the refrigerator and they took their glasses into the lounge room where she threw off her sandals and rather pointedly elected to sit on the sofa.

'I take it Jane's one of your flatmates,' he said as he joined her.

'Yes. She's a lesbian herself, which probably explains why she romanticises poor old Ena, who probably wasn't a lesbian at all. Cheers.' They clinked glasses and drank. 'Or perhaps Jane's right. Perhaps Ena saw in her best friend's daughter a younger version of herself, who knows?' She gave a careless shrug. 'Either way we win with the house. It's fantastically cheap living here.'

Matt enjoyed the uninhibited way she chatted. She's very easy company, he thought, no spoilt princess at all. Assured, yes, but nicely so.

'Jane shares the master bedroom with her girlfriend,' Angie explained, 'and Helen and I have the two spare rooms. We split all the bills, and the rent we three pay sees Jane through uni, so everyone's happy and we get along fine.'

'Sounds ideal.'

They conversed comfortably for the next fifteen minutes and Matt, upon enquiry, discovered that her family had a farming property a hundred kilometres or so north west of Adelaide ... 'Too far to commute,' she said, 'but easy enough to get home on weekends if I want to.'

'What sort of property?' he asked.

'Wheat and sheep mainly, but they've recently converted a sizeable acreage to vines – they're not far from Clare so the country's ideal. I love vineyards, don't you?'

'Sure.' He raised his glass as if to prove the fact. 'What sort of wines do they intend to produce?'

Like his father, Matt had a talent for encouraging others to talk while revealing little of himself. In any event, he had no wish to speed up proceedings. The prospect of sex with Angie was certainly arousing, but he'd let her call the tune. She'd done so from the outset and they were on her home ground after all.

He didn't have to wait long. 'I don't think we want another wine, do we?' she said meaningfully as she placed her empty glass on the coffee table.

'No, we don't.' He put down his own glass, which was still half full, and followed her into the hallway that led to the bedrooms.

Hers was the door to the right at the far end, and as she turned on the light and ushered him inside he was surprised to discover how vastly the room differed from the rest of the house.

She was aware of his reaction. 'You can take only so much of Ena,' she said, closing the door behind them. 'We're happy to live in her time warp, it's cheaper that way, but our rooms are our own to do with as we please.'

The furnishings certainly reflected her personality, smart, modern and for the most part red, which appeared to be Angie's favourite colour. But the most dominant feature of all was the prints that covered every inch of wall space. There were several that were attractively mounted and framed, probably limited editions and of some value, including a very impressive Brett Whiteley, but every other inch of wall was given over to cheap poster prints stuck up with sticky tape. Matt recognised the distinctive styles of Charles Blackman and Robert Dickerson among them.

'I rotate the posters to match what I'm studying at the time,' she explained. 'If you'd been here a while back it would have been the Impressionists.' She gazed about at the collection. 'My history tutor told me this week we'll be looking at The Antipodeans Group of the late fifties, so I hunted around for these and stuck them up just yesterday. I find it an inspirational way to study.'

'How clever . . .' he said. He hadn't known she was so focused on art. The BA course was a flexible one and could be used as a springboard for many a career. He wondered what path she intended to pursue, but they weren't here to talk about art. 'That's a really clever idea,' he murmured, drawing her to him and moving in for the kiss. It was time to take the initiative.

Given the anticipation that had been building up over the past hour or so, they were both quickly aroused and without breaking free from the kiss they started undressing themselves, fumbling with buttons and hooks and zips while their mouths continued to explore.

They made love with the overhead light on, neither of them self-conscious, each revelling in the sight and the sound and the touch of the other.

Matt was unsurprised to discover that her body was as flawless as the rest of her, the mini dress had left little to the imagination, but he had not anticipated her total lack of inhibition. Angie clearly enjoyed sex, giving herself whole-heartedly to the exercise, which he found so exciting that at one stage he was close to losing control. He managed, through sheer force of will, to restrain himself, however, and having safely regained command of his body he basked in the reckless abandonment of their lovemaking. The crescendos of her moans were so unrestrained, the muscular spasms that undulated wave after renewed wave so gripping he felt he could have gone on forever. It was only when he sensed she was utterly spent that he finally allowed himself to let go, by which time his own climax was a merciful release.

Angie flopped back in an exhausted heap, hair splayed messily about on a pillow wet with the sweat of her labours. Well he's not gay, she thought.

It was evident to all from the very start of first term that Matt Witherton and Angie Marsdon were 'an item'. Reactions were varied, particularly amongst the male students. *Why him?* thought the studs who'd been rebuffed; *Lucky bastard,* thought the merely envious and more generous of spirit. The female students were less taken aback by what appeared a mismatch, for many found Matt Witherton attractive, but they were nonetheless surprised that Angie, who could have had her pick, hadn't settled on one of the real high-flyers.

Angie and Matt were perhaps in love, it was a little early to tell, particularly with sex consuming them as it did.

But Matt had never in his life felt this way about a girl, and Angie was happier than she'd been during the whole of her time at university.

In truth, it had never been easy being Angie. The curse of beauty was ever-present. She had a healthy libido and enjoyed sex, but a casual fling often resulted in a boastful claim to fame and 'I scored with Angie Marsdon' joined the whispers around campus. Then there were those she rejected, many of whom, considering themselves scorned, were quick to deride her. 'Angie Marsdon's up herself,' was a particularly common whisper. It had been a no-win situation right from the start.

Being in a steady relationship solved a lot of things for Angie, but Matt was far more than a convenient way to scotch the whispers. He was a lover who excited her and even more than that a constant source of intrigue, retaining as he did such inscrutability. In fact there was so much Matt held back that sometimes Angie felt she didn't know him at all. Does he do it deliberately? she wondered. Like the very first time he'd taken her home to his flat on that Saturday afternoon. They'd been going out together for a whole month by then and he'd never once said a word! Why hadn't he told her?

'These are originals.' She hadn't even looked around at the flat itself, a beautifully renovated studio with perfect natural light that flooded in through huge skylights and windows, all of which would normally have thrilled her. She'd been immediately transfixed by the paintings that adorned the walls of the open-plan living room: there must have been a dozen at least.

'Yep,' he replied, 'they're originals.'

Matt had brought several girls back to the flat over the past two years, often a girl he'd met that same evening, fleeting dalliances only, understood by both parties to be a casual one-night stand. There was always a reasonable chance his parents would see the girl leaving the following morning via the side pathway that led to the street, which was of little concern and should really have presented no cause for comment. When an exchange student from Germany had progressed to a three-week affair, however, Lilian had been unable to resist.

'Good God, Mattie darling, if she's going to become a regular girlfriend why not ask her in to meet us?' she'd blithely suggested. Matt, feeling his privacy thoroughly invaded, had flashed a murderous glance at his father, but Dave had just returned a shake of his head and a why-bother? shrug.

Matt was far too serious about Angie to let such snooping happen again. He had not invited her to the flat until his parents were safely away in London for the long-overdue opening of Lilian's exhibition. The first time Angie would meet his parents would be when he introduced them face to face in the main house, he'd decided, because Angie was the woman with whom he was in love. Of that fact Matt was now certain.

Angie wandered around, studying each work closely. She'd recognised the artist the moment she'd entered the room; she didn't need to look at the signature on the paintings. 'But these are Lilian Birches,' she said incredulously.

'That's right.'

She continued from one painting to the next. How come I haven't seen these works before, she wondered, or at least reproductions of them? And what are they doing *here* of all places?

'I've never seen any of these before,' she muttered more to herself than to him. She was utterly mystified.

'No, these are the ones she thinks aren't quite up to scratch,' he said, 'but she doesn't want to get rid of them either. They seem to sit somewhere in between.'

'So how come *you* have them?' She turned to him in amazement. 'How come you have an entire collection of *Lilian Birch*?'

'She's my mother.'

If a young woman as beautiful as Angela Marsdon could look comical then that was the moment.

'She's what?' she said, jaw agape.

'Lilian Birch is my mother.'

There was a pause while Angie absorbed the news. 'Why didn't you tell me?'

'I don't know.' He didn't. 'It didn't occur to me I suppose.' It hadn't.

'But I've never heard anyone mention the fact at uni. You've been there over four years – surely they know.'

'I doubt it. I've never told anyone.' His shrug was careless. 'Why would I?'

Angie didn't understand Matt at all. Every single person she knew would have dined out on the fact that their mother was one of Australia's most famous artists.

'Well you should have told me!' she exploded after a moment of speechlessness. 'I'm studying art! You know my passion for painters – why would you keep a thing like that to yourself?'

'I don't know.' It was something he honestly couldn't answer. The omission hadn't been deliberate; he was simply unaccustomed to talking about himself on any personal level or in any great detail. When the topic of childhood had come up between them he'd simply told her his parents had been away a lot and he'd been brought up by his grandmother. He supposed now upon reflection that it had been rather thoughtless. He looked at her with a woebegone, hangdog expression, hoping it would raise a smile. 'Perhaps I just wanted you to love me for who I am?'

Angie fortunately found the act amusing. 'Bastard,' she said.

'Sorry.' He kissed her and she responded immediately as she always did. 'Let's go to bed,' he murmured.

After they'd made love they lolled back naked on the rumpled sheets, regaining their breath, her head cradled against his shoulder, both gazing up through the skylight at the grey clouds that gathered. Soon it would rain.

'So when do I get to meet her?' she asked.

'Exactly one month,' he replied, 'first thing after Mum and Dad get back, I promise.' In the meantime, he thought, we have a whole four weeks of freedom. He delighted in the knowledge that Angie could visit the flat safe from Lilian's prying eyes.

Following the introduction to his parents, Matt had no compunctions at all about Angie staying at the flat and being seen coming and going by Lilian. Now that she was accepted as his steady girlfriend it didn't matter in the least. He wondered why he'd felt the need to observe convention in such a way. Had he been protecting Angie? Had he been protecting his own privacy? Or was his conventionalism a form of rebellion against an unconventional mother? There were occasions when Matt was a mystery even to himself.

Over the ensuing months, the relationship intensified: things were clearly becoming serious. Angie invited Matt home to the farm for the weekend in order to meet her parents, a pleasant country couple who appeared vaguely bewildered as to how they'd managed to produce such a ravishing creature, and an older brother, Murray, big, beefy and born to take over the property. Matt very much met with Barbara and Bob Marsdon's approval and they weren't shy in showing it. 'Don't you be a stranger now,' Barb insisted as they made their farewells, Angie doing an eyeballs-to-heaven act behind her mother's back. 'That's right, son,' Bob, also insistent, pumped Matt's hand vigorously, 'you come back and see us any time – you're most welcome.' Monthly trips to the country appeared set to become something of a routine.

Angie also became a regular visitor to the main house in Wakefield Street, particularly on the weekends when she didn't go home. Sunday lunches were a favourite. Dave would cook a roast or a stew, his two winter specialities. During the summer months he made hearty salads to accompany seafood he purchased at the markets. Dave very much enjoyed the preparation of food; he found it relaxing. Lilian never cooked. Apart from toast in the morning or sandwiches when Dave wasn't home, Lilian was a stranger to the kitchen. 'One can be only so creative,' she would say, but the fact was cooking bored her.

When Matt had told his mother of Angie's passion for the world of art, Lilian had been quite astounded. But surely with looks like that the girl should concentrate on the performing arts, she'd thought. Young Angie should set her sights on Hollywood, or if she couldn't act, which didn't appear essential these days anyway, perhaps a career as a catwalk model. Or she could become 'the face of something-or-other' like gorgeous girls did, skin creams and fragrances and things like that.

Lilian's initial misgivings had been put to rest: Angie was not a femme fatale out to lure her son to his doom, but actually a rather nice girl. Nonetheless she found it difficult to take someone as beautiful as Angela Marsdon seriously. Angie was a crush that Matt would get over, she'd decided. Once the girl's beauty lost its novelty and he felt himself in need of stimulating company he'd look elsewhere. She sincerely hoped he would anyway. She didn't say so of course. But then she didn't have to. Lilian was very readable on occasions, particularly to her son.

'Good God no, Mattie,' she said, 'why on earth would I want to paint Angela?' She was considering entering a portrait for next year's Archibald Prize and he'd suggested Angie would be a good subject.

Matt was puzzled; surely it was obvious. 'Because Angie's beautiful,' he replied, 'she's a beautiful person.'

'Exactly! Beautiful is boring! Who wants to paint perfection? It's the flaws that inspire, my darling – they reveal the character within. Your Angie offers no depth, I'm afraid,' she added with a dismissive shrug.

She hadn't intended to be cruel, she never did, but she had a habit of wounding nevertheless. She saw the flicker in her son's eyes, a mixture of hurt and anger that she should be so contemptuous of a girl she didn't even know, a girl with whom he happened to be in love.

Damn, she thought, I was only talking about art, doesn't he realise that? But she knew she'd unwittingly displayed her true feelings and she cursed herself. Damn, damn, damn. Mattie being Mattie, he won't say anything, he'll just close off as he always does. Lilian resolved then and there that she must be nice to Angela. If she didn't show some interest in the girl she risked alienating her son.

'So tell me, Angie dear, what particular period or artists are you studying at the moment?' She put her plan into practice two weeks later on a wintry August Sunday, after lunch when the four of them remained cosily gathered around the table sipping red wine, having consumed huge bowls of Dave's lamb shank stew.

'We're looking at conceptualism,' Angie said eagerly, thrilled that Lilian was finally showing an interest in her studies. She'd never once brought up the subject of art herself. She was aware the woman must get tired of being fawned over by admirers and those seeking her opinion. 'The theory that concept takes precedence over execution, that the idea itself is the most important element of the piece . . .'

'Yes, yes,' Lilian replied, rather wishing she hadn't asked, 'a bit like joining the dots in my opinion; I've never been a great fan of conceptual art.' She smiled, however, determined to remain 'nice', and nodded for Angie to go on.

'During first term this year we studied the Antipodeans and their manifesto of 1959 . . .' Angie quickly dropped conceptualism and moved on to an area that was bound to be of interest to Lilian. She'd been longing to bring up the subject for months now, but hadn't dared. 'You would have known all seven artists involved, wouldn't you, and Bernard Smith, the art historian who was catalyst to the movement?' Even as she asked, Angie could see from the corner of her eye the quick glance exchanged between Matt and his father and she wondered if, in touching upon the personal, she was overstepping the mark.

Under normal circumstances Lilian would certainly have ended the conversation there, but she stuck to her resolve. 'Well I knew *of* them,' she said pleasantly, 'I was only twenty when they wrote the manifesto, but I grew to know them all quite well over the years. Indeed I still do, except for Clifton of course,' she added, referring to Clifton Pugh. 'He died only two years ago, heart attack, sixty-six poor dear, far too young. Sad that this country should lose such a talent so prematurely.'

Angie nodded, breathless with anticipation as she waited for Lilian to continue. This was far more exciting than lectures at university. This was living history, straight from the mouth of one of Australia's greatest painters.

'They were all terrified that the new wave of American abstract expressionism was taking over the world,' Lilian said with her usual nonchalance and her at times irritating tendency to generalise. 'In hindsight a bit of an over-reaction, at least that's what I thought and still do: there's room for all schools of art, so long as it's *good* art.'

'But they were fighting to preserve the national identity of Australian figurative painting,' Angie said, thrilled beyond measure to be discussing art with none other than Lilian Birch. 'You don't agree that the image, the recognisable shape, was the basic unit of the artist's language?' She waited for some input from Lilian, who was bound to subscribe to the Antipodeans' concept since she was a figurative artist herself.

But Lilian merely shrugged and took a healthy swig of wine.

'The manifesto claimed that the image communicated itself through the shared experience of artist and audience,' Angie continued. 'It even went so far as to say that abstract expressionism was not an art for living men.'

'Yes, yes . . .' Lilian tried not to sound terse. Having bits and pieces of the Antipodean Manifesto haphazardly quoted at her was annoying, but the girl was a student, and students were always intense. 'Bernard was certainly conservative,' she said drily, 'but it was a bit tough on the Australian abstractionists who were struggling to make a name for themselves, wouldn't you say?' The question obviously rhetorical, she continued, 'The Antipodean group were all rather successful at the time, it seemed a little unfair to me.'

'So you don't agree with the stance they took in defending tradition and preserving the cultural identity of Australia?' Angie was surprised by the contradictory nature of Lilian's response. Not only was Lilian Birch a figurative artist, her paintings very much mirrored the Australian landscape and its people.

'I don't agree with anyone dictating what art should or should not be,' Lilian replied abruptly: she'd had quite enough by now. But she smiled brightly about at the table in general, still determined to be nice. 'You're obviously an excellent student, Angie,' she said, 'I admire your commitment.'

Matt and Dave exchanged another brief glance, this time of amusement. Dave was a little mystified as to why Lilian was working so hard to be charming, it was unlike her, but Matt, aware his mother was doing her best to make amends, flashed her a grateful smile.

'So upon completion of your degree what particular path do you intend to follow, dear?' Lilian asked. 'Given your commitment, obviously something connected to art! I'm most interested to hear of your plans.' She wasn't at all, but she wanted to call a halt to the current discussion.

'A teacher perhaps? Art historian? Gallery curator? What is your aim in life?'

'My aim in life is to be an artist. I want to paint.'

'Oh . . .' The reply was so unexpected that Lilian came to a momentary halt. 'Really,' she said. 'Well, well, how very interesting. Are you receiving any form of practical tuition?'

'Oh yes, I've been doing evening classes in life drawing for the past year, and I've also studied still-life composition.' Angie's magnificent eyes were ablaze. 'My life-class tutor is wonderful,' she enthused. 'He says drawing is the key that opens all doors.'

'And he's quite right.' Lilian beamed, this certainly put a different complexion upon things. 'The most important talent an artist must possess is the ability to *draw*,' she said adamantly. 'Once the principle of drawing is mastered, the artist can then branch into whatever form he or she wishes. Just look at Picasso, the perfect example.' She drained the last of the wine from her glass. 'Mind you, Picasso was a child prodigy,' she said, reaching for the bottle and pouring herself another, 'a born genius, the true Mozart of the art world. He could draw better at the age of eight than most trained artists of today . . .'

Matt took the bottle his mother had plonked down on the table and topped up Angie's glass.

'And then there's the *language* of art, Angie,' Lilian continued, 'the experience shared between artist and audience . . .'

'Absolutely,' Angie agreed with fervour, 'the painting must speak, it must have a voice.'

'Exactly!' Lilian was enjoying herself immensely: she liked Angie now. The discussion of theory and history she found boring, but to share one's passion was something else altogether. 'The very paint itself must speak,' she said. 'Someone who thinks they can become an artist without learning the language of paint is like a writer attempting to write a novel without command of their given language.'

'We might need another one of those,' Dave said, gesturing to the now-empty bottle. Matt rose from the table and went off to the wine cellar, his exit and return a few moments later barely noticed by the women.

'So after you graduate next year,' Lilian continued, 'where do you intend to study? Will you go overseas? Slades perhaps?' Lilian herself, after completing her BA, had gone to London at the age of twenty-two, where she'd studied for two years at the Slade School of Fine Art.

'I'm afraid I haven't really given it much thought,' Angie admitted.

'Well whatever you decide, you really must go to Europe at some stage or other,' Lilian said. 'After Slades I took off to Paris for a year and just painted and painted and painted, mostly horrible stuff, but there's a lot to be said for starving in a garret and devoting oneself to one's art. Both the artist and the art mature through hardship – at least that's my belief and I'm sticking to it.'

She raised her glass, Angie raised hers, and they drank in unison, whether to each other, whether to starving in a garret or whether to art in general was difficult to say, but Matt and Dave shared a smile. It would appear that Angie, despite her beauty, had finally been granted the Lilian Birch seal of approval.

'Your mother's wonderful,' Angie said later that night as she and Matt lay snugly curled up under the quilt, a strenuous bout of sex having left them both deliriously sated. 'She's the most exciting woman I've ever met.'

'Yes,' Matt agreed drowsily, already on the brink of sleep, 'she's extraordinary all right.' Lilian was mercurial at the best of times and he wondered, with a sense of trepidation, how long the honeymoon would last.

Not long, as it turned out. But to give Lilian her credit she did her utmost best to disguise her disenchantment and offer encouragement.

'Very interesting, dear,' she said when, upon request, Angie arrived at the house with a folio of her work. 'You certainly have an eye for composition.'

Then later to Dave, 'The girl's all talk,' she said accusingly. 'She has no particular artistic talent at all.'

'Ah well,' Dave's reply was jovial, 'beauty and brains, you can't have it all.'

But Lilian wasn't prepared to dismiss things so easily. 'She's superficial, that's what worries me. There's something lacking in the girl. I don't know what it is, and I don't think she's aware of it herself, she certainly seems genuine enough, but Mattie needs someone with more depth, someone –'

'Leave it, Lilian.' Dave cut her off right there. 'Leave it alone. Angela's a nice girl. She can't help being gorgeous. Furthermore, Matt's deadly serious about her. You need to back off.'

For once Lilian did as she was told. She remained always pleasant to Angie, even dredging up a warmness she didn't feel for Matt's sake, but she couldn't muster any interest in the girl herself; she couldn't play that game.

'Your mother didn't like my work, did she?' Angie made the rather confronting remark to Matt one day when they'd returned to the flat after an extended Sunday lunch, seafood and salad now that summer was upon them.

'Rubbish,' he replied. 'Mum said she found your work interesting, didn't she? She said you had a great eye for composition. That's big praise from Lilian, believe me.'

'Perhaps,' Angie remained suspicious, 'but she doesn't discuss art with me these days. She asks how I'm going at uni and when I bring up a topic for discussion she changes the subject. I don't think she respects my opinion.'

'Oh that's just Lilian being Lilian, Ange, take no notice, she runs hot and cold all the time.' Matt was fully aware his mother had dismissed Angie as ungifted, but then his mother was the most shocking talent snob, as many artists were. He rather wished she could pretend, or at least try to, but then he also respected the fact that she couldn't and didn't. Matt had decided not to let the matter bother him. He did not need his mother's unequivocal endorsement of the woman with whom he intended to spend the rest of his life. He hoped Angie didn't need it either.

When the results of his final exams came through Matt discovered to his delight, although not to the surprise of his tutors for he was an excellent student, that he'd passed with flying colours.

'You are now looking at a Master Surveyor,' he proudly announced to his parents, who gave him a hearty round of applause.

The further announcement that followed not long after, early in the New Year, however, received an altogether different reaction.

'I've asked Angie to marry me.'

He'd called into the main house at breakfast time, knowing he'd catch them at the table over their toast and coffee before Lilian disappeared upstairs to her studio and Dave left for work.

'She said yes, by the way,' he added in the shocked pause that followed. His statement was brazenly directed at his mother. He didn't expect either of his parents to wholeheartedly embrace the notion, but the most volatile reaction was bound to be Lilian's.

'That's a bloody ridiculous idea and you know it!' Lilian did not disappoint. 'You haven't even turned twenty-three. Angela's only twenty-one. You're children!'

'No we're not.' Matt glanced at his father, expecting if not approval at least a saner voice.

'You are a bit young, mate,' Dave said mildly.

'We'll wait until Angie finishes uni the end of this year,' Matt directed his response at his father, 'but we're going to get engaged straight away. We want to make it official. Well at least I do; I don't think Ange cares either way.'

Once again Matt had wondered at the intensity of his desire to observe convention. Did it have something to do with his mother? Was he rebelling? He truly didn't know.

Dave nodded. There wasn't much else to be said. Matt's made his decision, he thought. He's a man now, and his life is his own to lead as he chooses.

'But you've known each other less than a year.' Lilian hadn't finished. Her manner was no longer belligerent though – she was desperate more than anything now, desperate to buy time. 'Why the rush?' she queried. 'This is the nineties, young people live together these days, don't they? They live together for years before they get married – it's a good way to test the waters, make sure you're compatible.'

'Yes, that's what Angie says.'

'Good for her. How very sensible. And you've agreed?'

'Yep.'

'So Angie will move into the flat with you?' There was a definite note of hope in Lilian's query. Perhaps things weren't quite as drastic as they appeared.

Matt grinned. He loved her transparency. 'Bit close to home, Mum.' Then, as disappointment clouded his mother's face, he softened the blow. 'But yes, Ange'll move in for a couple of months till we find a place,' and Lilian had to be content with that.

As she joined her husband in bed that night, however, she continued to bemoan the situation. 'I only hope we're not going to lose him,' she said.

She'd been going on for quite some time already, but Dave hadn't yet bothered offering an opinion: best to let her get it off her chest.

'We won't.' He waited for her to switch off the bedside lamp and snuggle up beside him as she always did, but she remained sitting bolt upright, staring ahead, her mind somewhere else.

'Lana was right,' she said.

'Lana was right about what?'

She turned to him. 'I'm not a good mother, am I?'

'What's a good mother?' He left the comment hanging for a moment's consideration. 'You're certainly not a *bad* mother.' She continued to look at him, apparently uncertain, and he thought how rare it was to see her unsure of herself. 'You are who you are, Lilian; you can't be somebody you're not. And there's no point in pretending because you're no good at it. Matt respects you for that.'

'Does he?'

'Yes, now turn out the light.'

She switched off the bedside lamp and snuggled up against him. 'Thank you,' her voice whispered from out of the darkness.

A month or so after Angie moved into the flat there was a change of plans. Matt received a job offer from the recently created outback mining town of Roxby Downs, over five hundred and fifty kilometres north of Adelaide. He'd applied for several jobs and had received two offers, but the Roxby Downs contract was the most financially lucrative, as he would be working directly for the Western Mining Corporation, which was extending its road works and general infrastructure just north of the town.

'The mining sector pays big money,' he told Angie. 'I'd have a deposit for a house by the end of the year. Only trouble is if I take the job I'll be gone for three months on the trot – do you reckon you could cope with that?'

'A whole three months,' she said, pouting sulkily. 'I suppose I'll have to if it's what you really want.'

'This'd set us up financially, Ange, and it'd be great for the future. Once I've worked for WMC offers will follow from other mining companies. The big guys favour those who have experience working in remote locations.'

'All right ...' The sulky pout having been pretence only, she smiled her glorious smile, 'I'll live without you if I must.' She kissed him. 'No more than three months though,' she said, holding up her hand and waggling the finger that bore the brand-new engagement ring. 'Any longer and I'll run off with someone else.'

'I promise.' They kissed again, a lingering kiss that became progressively urgent, leading them directly to the bedroom.

On the day of Matt's departure Angie skipped morning lectures in order to drive him to the airport. He insisted she drop him off out the front of the terminal: he didn't want her to come inside.

'Saying goodbye's hard enough,' he said, 'no point in dragging it out.'

She alighted from the car as he hauled his case and backpack from the boot and they stood together on the pavement, at a loss for words. Angie didn't trust herself to speak at all, but she didn't need to. The embrace and the kiss they shared said everything.

'I'll miss you,' he whispered as they parted and she nodded, managing to whisper 'Me too' in reply. He shouldered his backpack. 'Mum and Dad'll look after you while I'm gone,' he said, cheerily trying to lighten the mood.

She nodded again and as he set off with his suitcase she watched until the last minute when, at the doors, he turned back to wave to her. She returned the wave, tearful now, a forlornly exquisite figure unaware of the admiring glances she drew from passers-by.

During the drive home Angie thought about Matt's parting remark, which seemed somehow ludicrous. She doubted Lilian was capable of looking after anyone.

But strangely enough, Lilian did try. She tapped on the door of the flat that very same day, late in the afternoon when Angie had returned home from university.

'I thought you might be lonely, dear,' she said, 'would you like to come over to the house for dinner? Dave has said he'll cook something special – I've no idea what.'

'That's very kind of you, Lilian, but no thanks. Matt'll be ringing. He's promised he'll ring every weeknight. And besides I want to do some reading up for tomorrow's theory lecture.'

'Sunday lunch then, yes?'

'I'm going home this weekend. Actually I'll be going home most weekends, I told Mum and Dad I would, that's why Matt's going to call during the week.'

'Yes, of course, dear.' Lilian was relieved to be let off the hook. She'd promised Matt she'd look after Angie, but she was glad the girl was proving independent. 'Do give my very best to your parents, won't you . . .?'

She and Dave had met the Marsdons when they'd come into town for a joint family gathering in recognition of the official engagement of their respective offspring. The six of them had shared a very pleasant night dining out together, although Lilian had spent most of the evening studying Barbara and Bob and their daughter and pondering the contrariness of genetics.

'And don't forget I'm right next door if you need company. Just ring the house beforehand in case I'm in the studio.'

'I will, thank you, Lilian.'

Angie didn't give the offer much consideration, aware that it had been made out of a sense of duty, but several weeks later, a thought occurred. Did she dare? Yes, she decided, why not? She needed an answer. She deserved an answer.

'Hello, Lilian.' She telephoned late in the afternoon upon her return to the flat. The phone had rung for quite a long time before Lilian answered. 'It's Angie.'

'Yes of course,' Lilian was distracted. She'd been working in her studio and had forgotten to switch the answer machine on. Dave switched it on as a rule, but he was out of town for a fortnight. 'How are you getting along, dear? Is everything all right?' She did her best to sound pleasant.

'Fine, thank you. I've decided not to go home this weekend and I wondered if I could pop over to the house for a moment, Saturday or Sunday, whichever you'd prefer.'

'Of course, dear, let's make it Sunday lunch as usual, shall we? Dave's away on a job I'm afraid so it'll just be sandwiches. I'm not very good in the kitchen.'

'No I won't come for lunch, thanks all the same. I just want to have a chat. How about three o'clock?'

'Three o'clock Sunday it is then. I look forward to seeing you.' Lilian hung up wondering what on earth the girl could possibly want to chat about. Only one thought came to mind. Good God, she's pregnant!

Angie arrived with a portfolio under her arm. 'I've brought some more of my work to show you,' she said bravely as Lilian ushered her inside.

Oh dear, not again, Lilian thought. But she was so relieved a pregnancy announcement was not the cause for the visit that she found it quite easy to be nice. 'Lovely. Come into the kitchen and I'll make us a cup of tea.'

'No thanks. I don't want any tea, just an opinion, that's all.' Having steeled herself for this moment, Angie wanted it over and done with as soon as possible. 'I'd like your honest assessment, Lilian.' She wasn't prepared to be fobbed off this time.

Lilian looked into the splendid sapphire-blue eyes that held her gaze so boldly and thought, the girl's got guts, I'll give her that much.

'All right then. Let's go into the dining room.'

Angie spread the contents of the portfolio out onto the large dining-room table and Lilian sifted through them. The selection was different, but not dissimilar to the work she'd seen on the previous occasion. There were life drawings in pencil and charcoals and there were still-life watercolours, insipid bowls of fruit for the most part, and vases of flowers, the sorts of arrangements concocted by art teachers who were neither talented nor imaginative. The paintings themselves could have been attractive enough if well executed, but they weren't. She ignored the life studies altogether. Flat and characterless: there was no flesh to them, no muscle, no sinew or form – the girl's drawing skills were sadly lacking. Among the still-life compositions, however, were several rather interesting arrangements just as there had been previously, some drawings in crayon and some paintings in acrylic, the subject matter imaginative, the colours vivid.

She picked up one of the paintings. An old-fashioned earthenware pot with *Flour* drawn roughly on the side was crammed with modern kitchen utensils, their handles down, their purpose exposed; brightly coloured serving spoons, tongs flashing silver, heavy soup ladles and potato mashers, stylish whisks and pastry brushes.

'This is effective,' she said. 'Your art teacher didn't set up this arrangement, I take it? This is your own invention?'

'Yes, that's right.'

'Interesting,' Lilian said and she started methodically gathering up the drawings and paintings. 'As I said before, Angie, you have a definite eye for composition.'

'Composition, but not much else, that's what you mean, isn't it?'

Lilian knew there was no way out. The girl wanted a straight answer.

'I think you should concentrate on the academic, dear,' she said, handing the portfolio back to Angie. 'Why not continue with your history and theory studies? Given your passion for art, you'd make an excellent historian or gallery curator.' There was silence. Angie appeared to be waiting for more. Lilian wasn't quite sure about the next step, but she dived in anyway, determined to do her best. 'Of course if you're bent on a practical application of your studies, you could always turn to design – you have a certain flair. There's a wonderful career to be had in design. Fabrics and ceramics and . . .' she didn't dare say wallpaper '. . . and things like that . . . or so I believe.'

Angie paused before replying. She wasn't sure if this was exactly the answer she'd expected, but she'd come prepared in any event.

'I'm going to concentrate on Pop art, actually,' she said with a rebellious flick of her blonde mane. 'I've met a highly successful entrepreneur, Josh Bradley, you may have heard of him?' She'd been introduced to Josh Bradley at a rock concert she'd gone to with a girlfriend. 'He's mounting a major retrospective exhibition of Andy Warhol's work next year and wants to showcase some local modern artists too. He intends to launch a "Pop art renaissance",' she lent the term the same gravitas Bradley had, 'and he's interested in including some pieces of mine.' Josh Bradley hadn't even seen her work yet, but he'd certainly been interested when he'd heard she was a fledgling artist.

'Really? That's excellent.' Lilian had heard of Josh Bradley; who hadn't? The man imported extravaganzas, anything from the Russian Ballet and the Welsh Choir to the latest rock bands and circus spectaculars: he was a showman. So Pop art had garnered his interest, had it, and a 'Pop art renaissance' no less. How pretentious, she thought, but not altogether surprising. Although a product of the sixties, Pop art remained eminently sellable to the masses as anything from that era did. But Angie's work was hardly up to exhibition level. The girl's salvaging her pride, Lilian thought, she can't be serious.

Angie, however, appeared deadly serious. 'Yes, a whole new career is about to open up for me,' she said, 'I'm very much looking forward to the opportunity.' And tucking the portfolio under her arm she set off briskly towards the front door.

'Good for you, dear.' Lilian followed and opened the door for her. 'I'm sure you'll do very well.'

And if you're not spinning a load of bullshit you just might, she thought. Pop art was principally design anyway and even more to the point it thrived on celebrity. Young Angie was an extremely marketable product, a fact that someone like Josh Bradley could hardly fail to recognise.

'Thank you for your advice, Lilian,' Angie said, 'but as you can see I don't intend to follow the academic path.' Then head held high, dignity intact, she sailed out the door.

Lilian admired the girl's spirit, but she felt sorry for Angie. Looks and sex appeal might well open doors, but on a superficial level only and then only fleetingly. The girl would never be accepted into the art world as she so longed to be. You poor little thing, Lilian thought. When the first signs of age lay claim you'll be destined for obscurity; your work won't stand the test of time. There's no easy way, dear, not in the long run.

It very soon became evident that Angie *had* chosen what she presumed to be the easy way.

'That's Angie,' Dave said, pointing at the television screen.

They were watching the ABC news several weeks later, which concluded with a brief report on a red-carpet event, a charity fundraising extravaganza at the entertainment centre. Lilian had no idea what it was – she hadn't been paying attention. She did now, leaning forward in her armchair, eyes glued to the TV screen.

Sure enough, there was Angie, looking very glamorous on the arm of a stylishly trendy man probably in his mid-forties but posing as mid-thirties, Armani-suited, highlighted hair pulled back in a pony-tail. He was shepherding her along the red carpet as flashbulbs popped and fresh limousines pulled up behind them, fans squealing at each new arrival. Off-camera a female reporter's voice kept up a running commentary, tone hushed and deferential, lending an ABC gravitas to the proceedings.

'And now here's well-known entrepreneur, Josh Bradley, one of the co-producers of tonight's AIDS Gala concert . . .'

Once level with the camera, Josh paused, putting his arm around Angie's waist, an obvious signal, and together they smiled down the barrel.

'. . . And with him his protégée, young up-and-coming artist Angela Marsdon, who is to figurehead the Bradley Andy Warhol retrospective next year . . .' The reporter read directly from notes sent to her by Bradley's publicist.

Josh gave Angie's waist a quick squeeze, they shared a smile and a brief wave to camera and moved off as the reporter turned her attention to the arrival of the major guest star whose limousine had just pulled up.

'Looks like you were right,' Dave said. Lilian had told him all about her exchange with Angie and her own feelings on the subject. 'She's certainly opted for the celebrity path.'

'Yes,' Lilian replied, staring distractedly at the screen, where Mel Gibson was climbing out of the limo to the delighted shrieks of young women. She pressed the remote's mute button.

Dave sensed her concern. 'Ah well, love, you can't begrudge the girl her moment in the sun. Even if it doesn't last, it's exciting and she's young.'

'Of course.' Lilian returned a smile, not daring to mention what was uppermost in her mind. She wasn't concerned about Angie at all: she was concerned about her son. Josh Bradley's manner had been rather intimate – was he just training his protégée in celebrity behaviour as it had appeared or was there possibly more to the relationship?

The nagging thought remained with Lilian for the next day or so. She said nothing to Dave and she naturally did not bring up the subject with Angie, although she did mention that they'd seen her on television.

'Yes, isn't it wonderful?' Angie responded enthusiastically. 'Josh is going to promote me as the centre of the exhibition's local content. He says I'll represent a whole new generation of Australian Pop artists. It's the opportunity of a lifetime.'

'It certainly is,' Lilian said. So the girl has become the face of something after all, she thought, no different from a skin cream or fragrance really.

'Matt's so proud of me, Lilian,' Angie's face was radiant, 'you should have heard his voice when I told him.' She laughed with delight. 'He was even more excited than I was. He's so happy for me!'

Nobody's that good an actress, Lilian thought. Relief brought with it an unexpected wave of affection. 'And so am I, dear,' she said, 'so am I.' She hadn't wanted this marriage to go ahead, she'd hoped her son would get over his 'crush', but she knew now it wasn't a crush, that Matt deeply loved this girl. If Angie's love for him is equally deep, Lilian thought, and it certainly appears to be, then surely that's all that matters.

Over the ensuing weeks, however, as Josh Bradley continued to promote his protégée and as Angie's celebrity status grew, Lilian found it difficult to remain unconcerned. Apparently there was innuendo in the gossip pages of tabloids and popular magazines. They were publications she never read and she might not have heard of the fact had it not been for Angie herself.

'They're actually suggesting we might be an item.' Angie had been filling them in on the latest developments over Dave's Sunday roast. She'd decided not to go home that weekend. 'It really is wicked of Josh,' she continued, 'he always says he's my mentor or patron, and that we're just good friends, but I think he plants the gossip himself. He's a shameless publicity monger.'

'Which is why he's so successful, no doubt,' Dave said, spearing another potato and reaching for the gravy boat.

'Absolutely.'

Lilian looked from one to the other. Suspicion was obviously the farthest thing from Dave's mind, but then Dave always took people at their face value and he'd liked Angie right from the start. Lilian couldn't help feeling a stab of concern. Is the girl perhaps covering her back? Matt's due home in three weeks.

'I wonder how Matt will react,' she said.

'Oh he thinks it's funny,' Angie replied airily. 'I've told him all about it. I read the gossip columns out to him and we have a good laugh.'

There were smiles all around and Dave refilled the glasses of red.

Lilian found it difficult to believe that Angie was anything other than genuine: she appeared so guileless, so incapable of duplicity. But if I'm wrong, she thought, disaster is looming. If Angie betrays Matt it will break his heart. Lilian hoped fervently that the girl was above suspicion and that nothing terrible was about to happen.

But something terrible did happen.

It was just five days later, early on a Friday evening.

Dusk had fallen. The road was gloomy and deserted and the Porsche was travelling at a hundred and twenty kilometres an hour, not fast at all by European standards, he said, and besides, in a Porsche 911 you're only cruising at one-twenty clicks. He promised her he wouldn't go any faster, though. He appeared to be driving responsibly and they were both enjoying the ride, but he was talking in the vigorous, animated way he so often did and that was perhaps why he didn't see the semi-trailer until it was virtually upon them.

She'd been vaguely aware of lights in the distance, but she'd been listening to him so avidly she hadn't realised that the Porsche had slowly crept over to the other side of the road. Then she saw the truck bearing down on them and screamed.

The truck saw them also, directly in its path. The driver leaned on the horn and there was the awful bellow of air brakes, but the truck couldn't stop. Nor could the Porsche change direction in time. Seconds before impact it veered, but not enough to get clear. The truck caught the driver's side directly, crunching through the metal and sending the Porsche spinning like a toy, over and over, to land a hundred metres away.

Josh Bradley and Angela Marsdon were killed instantly. The force of the impact left Josh virtually unrecognisable, but Angela, with a cleanly broken neck, remained in death as beautiful as ever. Autopsy reports would later show a considerable presence of cocaine and Dexedrine in Josh's body. Angela's body was drug free.

It was, not unexpectedly, headline news for weeks. A spokesperson for Josh Bradley's production company said the pair were travelling to Canberra in order to visit the modern art exhibition at the National Gallery the following day. Josh's decision had been a last-minute one, the publicist said, and separate hotel rooms had been booked at the Hyatt, a fact which the hotel verified. There was nevertheless endless conjecture in the press about the personal relationship shared between Josh Bradley and his protégée, which inevitably led to discussion at dinner tables and parties. Were they sleeping together or weren't they? The general consensus of opinion seemed to be in the affirmative.

'Nothing was going on between them, Matt.' Lilian didn't know what to say to her son, who seemed to have disappeared into himself. She loathed the press for adding the suspicion of betrayal to his burden of grief. 'Their relationship was purely professional, nothing more . . .'

Matt slowly turned to look at her, his expression unfathomable. What was it she could see in his eyes? Contempt? Amazement? Disbelief? Then she realised it was all three. He didn't for one minute believe the press reports and he didn't care in the least what was being said. He was simply amazed that she should bring up the subject.

Lilian had no words of comfort. She longed to offer some show of support, to be of some practical assistance, but she felt utterly inept in the face of her son's grief. He was far better off alone with his father. Dave who said and did nothing seemed able to reach out simply with his company. The two, so alike, had always shared a connection that didn't need words.

She was grateful for one thing though. Matt's memory of Angie would remain unsullied. She would always be his and his alone. But in Lilian's mind there was an element of uncertainty. Had the girl been faithful? No-one would ever really know.

لسلام

1879

Emily is called Akarletye now. She has forgotten she was once Emily. That name is of no importance. Distant memories of her father and her mother and her previous life remain buried in the recesses of her mind, but they no longer come to the fore as they once did. That life belongs to another person, another person who existed in another time.

'Akarletye' is the Arunta name for the pretty white blossom of the bush orange tree that grows on the river flats. The family named her so for the whiteness of her skin, and they fondly refer to her as Letye for short. But there are times when they are careful to cover Letye's whiteness. The singing string that now stretches across their desert land and the lands of others, its poles humming a high-pitched baleful song, is linked here and there by the houses of white men. When the family's travels take them near one of these houses they cover Letye in mud, or if there is no water to make mud they cover her in charcoal dust mixed with kangaroo fat from the cooking fire. If the white men see her they will steal her back as one of their own. But Letye is no longer theirs. Letye belongs to the family now.

Letye runs her hands over the bare skin of her swollen belly, feeling the movement of the child within. She glances at Nyapi, sensing he is watching her from where he sits by the fire's embers some distance away. Their eyes meet and they share a smile before Nyapi returns to his work. He is making a new spear, melting a portion of the spinifex gum that he carries with him at all times. With the softened resin he will attach a shard of quartz, hard and sharp, to the slender acacia tree limb he has selected with care and straightened after heating over the embers. He has been working on his spear for some time now and is fully focused upon the task, just as his father and his grandfather are when making weapons and tools, for it is a laborious business that requires intricate skill. But unlike his father, Tjumuru, and his grandfather, Atanum, young Nyapi finds himself occasionally distracted. He cannot help his eyes flickering over to where his wife sits with the other three women.

In their wooden dishes they are winnowing and panning the grass seeds they have collected. When they have separated and discarded the chaff they will grind the seeds into flour with their grinding stones and the flour will be mixed with water to form seed cakes to bake in the hot ashes of the fire. The women's work, too, is laborious, but their full focus is not essential and they chatter together as they toil. The current object of their attention is three-year-old Kwala, who is playing with the dingo pup. Or perhaps the dingo pup is playing with Kwala, it is difficult to tell, but the two infant creatures rolling around in the red dust of the dried creek bed where the family has set up camp are a source of amusement to the women.

Letye laughs at the sight and her pleasure so

delights Nyapi that he wants to laugh with her. He is proud as he watches her caress her belly, knowing she is feeling their child. When they are alone he puts his hands on her belly and presses his ear against the tight skin and he can hear his baby. He whispers to the child he will soon hold in his arms.

He resists the urge now to laugh along with Letye. Instead he pretends indifference to the women and their chatter. Not far away Atanum is butchering the kangaroo that Tjumuru speared that afternoon; it would be unseemly to laugh. But Nyapi is secretly bursting with pride. He is two years younger than Letye and had only recently been initiated into manhood when he and his father and grandfather had found her, close to death. Now three years later and barely nine months after their marriage, his wife is about to give birth. Having sired a child so soon after wedlock is proof of his virility. Now he is truly a man.

In truth Nyapi is bursting with something far greater than pride. He is bursting with a love so fierce he finds it difficult to disguise.

Letye tips a portion of the now separated seeds from her wooden dish onto her flat base stone. Then, taking up her round hand stone, she starts grinding the seeds into flour. The two stones are her personal tools that travel with her, carried in the wooden dishes and bowls she bears, like the other women do theirs, on her head, the weight cushioned by emu feathers.

Her eyes remain on Nyapi as she works. She is amused by the way he concentrates so studiously on his spear, for she knows what he is thinking. She knows, too, that he feels her eyes upon him, and each time he glances at her she offers a teasing smile. When he guiltily returns to his spear she wants to laugh, but out of respect she does not. They will laugh together when they are alone. This is a game she often plays. Letye's love equals her husband's.

It was Nyapi's love that saved Letye from the all-consuming terror she knew in the long ago days when she was still Emily.

At first she had recoiled from the touch of the boy-man, convinced of his intention to defile her. She had recoiled from everything back then: the black faces that surrounded her, the harsh, jabbering tongue, the strange foods and potions she was forced to eat, but most of all she had recoiled from the nakedness. She had never seen a man unclothed and she found the sight shocking. The women shocked her also for apart from a pubic covering that hung like a small apron from a string around their waists they too were naked, and the youngest of the three, little more than a girl herself, openly suckled a child. But the most shocking thing of all to Emily had been her own nakedness.

The women had stripped her while she was unconscious, coating her sunburnt face and limbs with a foul-smelling lotion and placing small stones on various parts of her body. She had tried to cover herself, but they had not allowed her to do so and she'd not had the strength to fight them. She had been forced to lie there in a state of unbearable humiliation, aware that all, including the men, could see her nakedness. She had wished at that moment that they had left her to die.

They had never returned her clothes to her. Discarding them somewhere along the path of their travels, the women had provided her with a pubic covering instead. Clothes were obviously of no importance.

Those early days with the family had all followed a similar pattern. In the mornings when the men had set off on their hunt the women, together with the two children, travelled slowly towards the next campsite, taking their time in order that Emily in her weakened state might keep up.

Nangala was Atanum's wife and the matriarch of the family, a lean, strong-boned woman in her early fifties. The other two women, Ngita and young Macanti, were Tjumuru's wives. They would gather fruits and berries and seeds as they went, and painstakingly extract grubs from the roots and trunks of trees. Ngita's nine-year-old daughter Tama would keep up a running monologue pointing things out to Emily in eager detail. Little Tama, Nyapi's younger sister, was excited to be teaching the strange white girl their ways.

Later in the day the group would meet up with the men at the pre-arranged campsite. The family's knowledge of their people's land was intimate. Even Tama carried a map in her head of all the choice campsites. And if by chance the family were travelling the less familiar lands of others, as they sometimes did in order to attend ceremonial occasions, the women would follow the signs their men had left. Little Tama knew how to read all the signs too.

It had been Nangala who had named Akarletye. Ever-observant and always wise in her decisions, the matriarch had noted the white girl's innate fear of the men and decided that a family name would help salve that fear. The white girl would be called Akarletye, she had announced, and the women and young Tama had immediately adopted the diminutive 'Letye'.

Emily had been grateful to the women for saving her life and for welcoming her into their midst as they had, but the adoption of her new name had done little to alleviate the awful trepidation that visited her daily. The men had remained fearsome figures, arousing in her a sense of terror whenever they came near. At the campsite she would keep her eyes averted from their nakedness, feeling herself start to shake, expecting at any moment the unspeakable. So when the boy-man, whom she had thought the least fearful of the three, had sat on the ground beside her and touched her arm, she had started violently, sure that this was to be the moment of her defilement.

She had been wrong. Nyapi had shuffled away on his bare backside, hands in the air in a placating gesture. His intention had been to comfort the white girl, who was clearly terrified. He'd had no wish to further alarm her.

From that moment on Nyapi had taken care never to touch Letye, but he had made it his mission to welcome her into their group as the women had done, and he had determined to teach her that he and his father and grandfather meant her no harm. At the end of each day he would bring her the collection of small prey he had caught, bandicoots and various sorts of lizards and goannas. They would be dangling by their necks from the woven string band about his waist. Each of the men wore such a string band in order to carry smaller prey while keeping their hands free for the hunting of larger game.

Nyapi would lay his catch on the ground before Letye, placing them down with care one by one, and as he did so naming each slowly and distinctly.

At first Emily had thought the boy-man, whose name she had come to know was Nyapi, was merely trying to impress her, but then she had realised that Nyapi was teaching her his language. When little

Tama and the women pointed things out, explaining their food sources and methods of gathering, their voices were no more than discordant gabble to Emily. She had never understood the words themselves, but she understood Nyapi's lessons.

Nyapi had continued the process day after day. And when he had taught her the Arunta names of the creatures he had presented, he would point at parts of his body, his hand, his arm, his shoulder, his leg, and with infinite patience he would say each word, waiting for her to repeat it after him, which she obediently did, pointing in turn at the relevant parts of her own body, no longer conscious of her nakedness, nor even of his.

Their focus upon each other had not gone unnoticed. Atanum and Tjumuru had shared meaningful nudges and muttered asides. It was clear to them that Nyapi found the white girl desirable. They could not understand why themselves: they found her pallid and uninteresting.

Nyapi's mother, Ngita, and his grandmother, Nangala, had also noted Nyapi's attraction to Letye. But Nangala had sensed something else. Nangala had sensed that the feeling was mutual. She awaited the outcome with interest.

Then there had finally come the day when Nyapi had declared himself. There had been no words. The dance had been declaration enough.

Emily had watched in spellbound silence as Nyapi performed his love dance. The ritual was primitive, the steps unerringly animal-like, the clicking of the sticks insistent and primal. The dance was something she had never seen, something she could never have expected to witness in the whole of her life, but its message was abundantly clear. She was being wooed. Mesmerised by the sight of Nyapi and the intensity of his dance, her body had responded. Suddenly she had longed for him to touch her.

Nangala had granted permission for the two to marry and a traditional ceremony had been conducted to confirm the union. Akarletye had now become a true member of the family.

Letye feels the baby kick again, hard this time, and again her hand instinctively goes to her belly, making contact with the child.

Seated cross-legged beside her, Nangala notices. But then Nangala has noticed the entire exchange between Letye and Nyapi too. Nothing escapes Nangala's eagle eye. Nangala is glad that despite her initial misgivings she allowed the union, for it is clear the pair love each other deeply. When the child is born she will teach Letye the women's dance. They will dance awelye, all of them, she thinks; they will have their own ceremony, they will dance in turn, taking over from one another throughout the entire night from evening star to morning star, and they will rejoice. As women do. Nangala watches Letye watching Nyapi and she is happy for them.

Unaware that she is being observed by the woman she fondly calls 'Nyanye', the woman who has become her grandmother, Letye studies her husband. Nyapi is now absorbed in binding the kangaroo sinew firmly around his spearhead, reinforcing the strength of the glue. It is the final process in his spear-making. Letye, watching him, remembers the love dance. She will never forget that day. That was the day she stopped being Emily. Soon her child will be born and Emily will cease to exist altogether.

PART TWO

CHAPTER FIVE

2000

The new millennium saw Australia about to embark upon one of the largest civil engineering projects ever undertaken in the country. A mighty railway line traversing the nation from Adelaide through the arid heart of the continent to Darwin had been the dream of settlers and the ambition of governments ever since the completion of the Overland Telegraph Line. Now, over a hundred and twenty years later, that dream and ambition was about to become a reality.

The narrow-gauge railway track that ran as far north as Alice Springs had started operation in 1929 and was unofficially known as 'the Ghan', an abbreviation of The Afghan Express, a nickname aptly coined by one of its crew as a tribute to the Afghan cameleers whose teams of beasts had been essential to the opening of the hinterland. The plan had always been to extend the line through to Darwin, but by the time the connection to Alice Springs was completed, the costs had become prohibitive. The Ghan was running at a financial loss, too, so plans to extend further north were put on hold indefinitely.

The original southern Ghan track roughly paralleled that of the Overland Telegraph Line, which in turn followed the route of John McDouall Stuart's 1862 crossing of Australia. Stuart had blazoned the trail for the Ghan, as his route to Alice Springs was the only one that provided a reliable water supply and steam locomotives needed large quantities of water. This very fact, however, led to difficulties, discomfort and added expense as the flood-prone track was notorious for washouts. Spare railway sleepers and equipment were carried in a separate flat-car and, upon encountering a washout, crew and passengers would alight to work together as a railway gang in order to repair the line. Travelling the Ghan could be quite an adventure for those from the city who might have presumed they were simply 'catching a train'.

When the track was laid for the new southern Ghan, the advent of diesel locomotives needing far less water proved more comfortable for all concerned, as the track could then be altered to follow a much drier route from Tarcoola to Alice Springs.

The change of the Ghan's track from the old narrow gauge to the new standard gauge in 1980 reignited hope in the hearts of the frustrated Territorian 'Top-Enders'. After years of political discussion and endless broken promises, the federal government finally committed ten million dollars for preliminary work and design in extending the new standard-gauge line all the way to Darwin.

There followed a flurry of excitement that waxed and waned over the ensuing decade as teams of surveyors and engineers examined the terrain and professional negotiators met with Indigenous landowners to discuss the proposed route. But as time passed, the grand scheme once again languished due to the varying and often lackadaisical degree of support received from successive federal governments, who sadly did not share the passion and commitment of the Territorians and South Australians.

Finally, as the stalemate crept further and further into the nineties, the Northern Territory and South Australian governments took matters into their own hands, establishing the AustralAsia Railway Corporation in 1997 and calling for tenders to build the line between Alice Springs and Darwin. A BOOT (Build, Own, Operate and Transfer) scheme was proposed, meaning the private sector would build, own and operate the project for fifty years before ultimately transferring it back to the respective governments.

In June 1999 the Asia Pacific Transport (APT) consortium was awarded the commercial tender to design, construct and operate the railway. ADrail was to be the design and construction contractor and FreightLink the operator.

Less than two years later financial settlement was reached between all parties to fund the one point four billion dollar project, which would see the construction of fourteen hundred and twenty kilometres of standard-gauge railway line, together with all its attendant bridges and culverts, between Alice Springs and Darwin. The great dream was at last to be realised. The mighty Ghan would link the north and south of the land, traversing the vast red centre and forming the very spine of Australia.

An official ceremony was held at Alice Springs Railway Station on 17 July 2001. There, in the presence of South Australian premier John Olsen and Northern Territory chief minister Denis Burke, Prime Minister John Howard symbolically turned the first sod of red earth, delighting the throngs in attendance including hundreds of flag-waving schoolchildren.

From then on, as if to compensate for more than a century in the doldrums, everything started to move at mind-boggling speed. Factories and quarries sprang up in the country's scorched heartland; sleepy desert hamlets that in bygone days had been no more than relaying stations for the Overland Telegraph Line became centres of industry; and temporary workers' townships appeared like magic; slick, modern and completely at odds with the primitive landscape.

Production of crushed rock ballast for track reinforcement began at the Warrego Quarry in Tennant Creek and at Witte Quarry north of Katherine, and in both townships factories started pouring concrete sleepers. Thousands of tonnes of rail were delivered from the steel plant at Whyalla to Roe Creek just south of Alice Springs. An armada of heavy machinery, bulldozers, graders, excavators, haulage trucks and the like arrived in the outback to begin the laborious job of creating the rail corridor preparatory to the laying of track, and workers' donga townships sprang into being every hundred kilometres along the proposed line, readily erected and dismantled within weeks as work progressed.

The plan, for time- and money-saving purposes, was to build the line in four sectors simultaneously, teams working north and south from Katherine and north and south from Tennant Creek. The final track to be laid would be that at the Port of Darwin in the north and that which would join the southern and northern Ghan at Alice Springs in the country's desert centre. It was a plan that seemed not only efficient but symbolically satisfying.

A period of roughly twelve months had been allowed for the preparation of the corridor before track-laying could commence. Preparation included not only heavy earthworks, but the construction of bridges and culverts and level crossings, all hopefully to be completed before rail construction began. The route itself, however, which like the southern Ghan for the most part followed that of the Overland Telegraph Line, had long been decided. Negotiators had been working with Indigenous communities throughout the Northern Territory for well over a decade, confirming where the track could or could not go. Much of the land being under the freehold ownership of Aboriginal people, permission was needed and payment required, but most importantly, sacred sites were to be avoided at all costs. Anthropologists and linguists had been hired by the Northern and Central Land Councils and lengthy, complicated negotiations held with the local people of each area. All communication had been documented and legal agreements drawn up to the point where surveyors could set about mapping the course.

A further complication presented itself, however. Many Aboriginal elders who had met with negotiators in the early years of discussion, before the AustralAsia contract was proposed, had died. Fresh negotiation was now required to reassure new Indigenous leaders that everything was in place as previously agreed.

Nearly three years later, early in 2001, full agreement was reached and a total of twenty-two million dollars was paid for all land purchased or leased for the corridor.

Jess loved her job. It was 2002 and now, aged thirty, she'd been jointly employed by APT and the Central Lands Council, which was based in Alice Springs, for close on three years. Jess loved her job and she loved Alice. She returned regularly to Sydney to see her father, and he in turn visited her – whenever time allowed anyway, for Toby Manning's recording studio remained as busy as ever. But Alice had become home to Jess and would continue to be home until the completion of the railway line, a fact for which she was profoundly thankful. Her work there with the outback communities she'd come to know so well had brought to her life a sense of purpose that had for some time been lost.

The purpose Jess served was certainly vital. She was quite possibly the best negotiator the Central Lands Council had ever encountered, and there had been many over the years, highly skilled experts in their field. Jessica Manning had every necessary academic qualification, she was an anthropologist with knowledge of the central desert people and a linguist fluent in many Indigenous languages, but of far greater importance she was accepted by the people as one of their own. Indeed, to the Western Arunta she was direct family. And what's more, she really cared! Jessica Manning's value, as agreed by all, was inestimable.

Jess had reverted to her maiden name when applying for the position of negotiator. She'd been determined to put behind her the marriage that had so undermined her confidence, the marriage that would most certainly have destroyed her had she not escaped its confines. Now these several years later, she was relieved to discover that she was well on the road to recovery. She no longer thought of Roger. Or if she did, she brushed his image aside. She was no longer Jessica Macready and Roger was no longer important. She could not afford him to be.

Jess pulled the four-wheel drive up at the end of the dirt track where, in the dry creek bed twenty metres away, the three women were waiting. They were sitting cross-legged in a circle chatting and drawing patterns in the dusty ground they'd brushed clear between them. She was surprised the aunties had arrived before her. She was even a little surprised they'd arrived at all. She'd offered to drive them out from town but they'd said no, no, Pam's son Donny would give them a lift because Donny had to go to Ti Tree for a job that morning. Jess had half-expected that Donny would change his mind, or that the aunties themselves would: anything was possible. She was usually kept waiting at least an hour for a pre-arranged meeting like this and even then, on occasions, no-one turned up. Time meant little to the locals.

She jumped from the Toyota, which was a dull pink in colour, unrecognisable from its original white, melding with the landscape as most outback vehicles did.

'*Werte.*' Calling a greeting in Arunta she strode over towards the women and they smiled as they returned the greeting, teeth gleaming in black faces. Jess was a favourite with the aunties.

'*Narlaanama,*' Pam said, gesturing for her to sit with them.

Boot-clad and in shorts, Jess did so, plonking herself down beside the women to feel the earth soft and warm against her bare legs; it was a fine day in mid-April. 'You been here long time?' She knew that when the aunties were representing their people on official business they chose to open the proceedings in English.

'Yeh, been here long time,' Pam answered, Jill and Molly nodding and adding, 'yeh, long time,' although none of the three appeared in the least bothered.

Jess didn't ask for specifics, but 'long time' probably meant hours. 'How come long time?'

Pam explained that Donny had wanted to leave early in order to reach Ti Tree and report for the new labouring job he was to start that day. 'He got a month contract up Ti Tree way,' she said, 'working for the railway.'

'That's good,' Jess said, 'that's good news.'

'Yeh, real good,' Pam agreed.

They smiled at each other, but they both had their doubts. Donny had a big problem with the grog. He'd tried now and then to hold down a job – when there was one to be had anyway, employment for locals was scarce around Alice – but he'd rarely lasted more than a week. Jess sincerely hoped that with the railway providing a whole field of fresh work opportunities Donny might find a way to fight his addiction. Just as she hoped many others like him might. Donny's problem was an all too common one.

Having settled themselves down for a chat, the customary niceties followed and, reverting to Arunta, Jess asked after Pam's family. Then she asked after Jill's family and then Molly's, in order of the women's seniority as a show of respect. Pam was in her early fifties, Jill and Molly, two years apart, in their late forties. All three were not only elders but grandmothers and as such the matriarchal position they held within their respective families was of immense significance, both practically and traditionally.

The recognition of family was imperative to any meeting. When Jess visited outback communities in her role as negotiator, she was prepared for endless greetings with elders and their families. Often she would sit talking with them all day and always when she took her departure there would be ceremonial farewells. Getting down to business could prove a lengthy affair.

She wasn't meeting the aunties that day as negotiator, but rather as peacekeeper, which was the part she now principally played, assuring people that all was as it should be and that no undue desecration was about to take place. The endless arrival of heavy machinery throughout the desert was unnerving to some, threatening untold defilement of the land, and a particularly frightening aspect was the talk of explosives. Today was an example of such concern. Word had got around that at some stage there were plans for rock cuttings to be blasted just north of Alice Springs, massive explosions that would rip the earth apart, hurling boulders and debris vast distances. This would surely affect the surrounding landscape, which was of particular worry to the women.

Pam, Jill and Molly, as elders, had approached Jess on behalf of the women of their community. There was a sacred site not far north of Alice Springs that was of great significance, playing an important part in secret women's business. They needed a guarantee that this site would be safe and they wanted Jess to visit it with them. Once they had been there in her presence and once they had had her personal assurance, they could feel at ease and they could ease the minds of others. There was no-one else to whom the aunties would have made such a request and no-one else in whom they would have placed such trust. But despite their anxiety, first, as always, there must be discussion about family.

Jess listened to the talk of grandchildren, allowing things to take their natural course, for it would not be right to speed up the procedure. They were on to Molly's family now anyway so there wasn't long to go. Gazing at the aunties, her mind wandered a little. She thought what fine women they were, strong women with a deep commitment to their people. But for all their strength of character their physical condition was another matter altogether. All three were overweight, and their faces seemed to have lost their bones. Handsome faces that should have been lean were bloated. Pam, Jill and Molly all suffered from diabetes, a disease that along with alcoholism was rampant in the central desert communities. Jess's own Western Arunta community at Hermannsburg was beset by the same problems. The issue aroused in her a fiercely mixed reaction: one of anger, frustration and despair. Surely there was more that could be done . . .

Her thoughts were interrupted by Pam who was now keen to move things along. Being the senior aunty, Pam considered it her job to do so: Molly had had her chat, the niceties had been observed.

'Righto,' she said, reverting to English, 'time to go,' and she hauled herself to her feet with a grace that belied her considerable size.

Jill and Molly rose with equal ease. They could sit or squat on the ground for hours and experience no stiffness or discomfort upon rising. The three walked from the creek bed, Jess by their side, and out into the open scrubland. Unlike Jess, who had work boots on, the women wore rubber thongs, but again their movement was graceful, their thin strong legs at odds with the bulk of their bodies, as they strode across the rough terrain, languid and assured.

They walked for several kilometres until they reached their destination, a formation of rocks with a clearing in the centre that might well have been part of a dried creek course, for several white-limbed coolabah trees stood there and coolabah trees like water. The setting was pretty, but nothing remarkable – such settings abounded.

The women had chatted while they'd walked. Now they were silent. From the moment they entered the clearing not a word was spoken.

Moving slowly about the site, Pam, Jill and Molly paid their respects to the spirit beings that dwelt there. Hands were run reverently over rocks, fingers lingered on the smooth trunks of coolabah trees, outstretched arms brushed foliage in passing, all fond, familiar actions like the sharing of a caress with something unseen.

Jess had witnessed similar practices before. Sometimes those paying homage talked or chanted, sometimes they were silent, but always deeply respectful. On several such occasions she had experienced the strangest of sensations. At first she'd been alarmed, even fearful, sensing the unknown so close at hand.

Now, standing in the centre of the clearing, she was visited by the same sensation, but she was no longer alarmed, no longer fearful. Instead, she gave herself up to the touch that was not really a touch, to the breath that was not really a breath. How could she possibly describe the presence she felt? Something unseen was making contact with her skin, something unseen was breathing on her. But this 'something' was not frightening. This 'something' wished her well.

She had no idea how long she'd been standing there communicating with whatever force was present, or perhaps allowing whatever force was present to communicate with her. It might have been minutes, it might have been hours, but feeling a human touch on her arm she was startled.

She turned to see Pam, Jill and Molly lined up beside her. The women were ready to go.

They left in silence, but once clear of the site, the aunties chatted, leaving Jess to reflect upon her experience. For all her academic knowledge of Indigenous culture and mythology, there was no denying the desert had changed her. Or perhaps it had merely made her aware of who she really was and who she always had been. Either way, it doesn't matter, she told herself. It doesn't matter at all. The connection has been made.

Jess was to drive the aunties back to town, but before getting into the car, Pam spoke on behalf of all three and on behalf of the women of their community.

'*You know our place now.*' Despite the fact that she was discussing official business, Pam chose this time to speak in Arunta. '*You have felt this place.*'

'*Yes, I have felt this place,*' Jess replied.

Pam glanced at Jill and Molly, who both nodded. Each of the women knew that the spirit beings had made themselves known to Jess.

'*You will look after this place? You will make sure it is safe?*

'*I will make sure it is safe.*' Jess was already quite sure that the site was safe, for it was well clear of the rock cuttings that were to be blasted, but the aunties would no doubt like assurance from a higher authority. '*I will meet with the surveyor boss tomorrow,*' she said, '*I will check with him the effects of the explosives and make sure that this place will not be harmed.*'

'*Good. That is what we wish.*'

More nods all around and the women smiled, clapping Jess on the back before piling into the car, Pam in the front, Jill and Molly in the back. Problem now solved, they talked happily throughout the twenty-kilometre drive back to town. They had been right to approach young Jessica Manning. She was one of them and a true champion of their cause.

Looking at Pam beside her and the other two women in the rear-vision mirror, Jess felt an overwhelming wave of affection. She could have been looking at her very own aunty. Aunty May, like these women, was an elder who held the official title of 'aunty' to her people, whether directly related or not. Like these women, Aunty May was also a grandmother who played an invaluable role in her family and community. The only unfortunate similarity was that Aunty May, too, suffered from diabetes.

Jess had met her mother Rose's older sister twelve years previously, during the trip she'd made to the Northern Territory just before starting university. She and her father had travelled to Alice Springs together and it had been a cathartic time for both, Toby Manning taking his daughter on the journey he'd longed to make with his wife, and Jess bent on learning of her mother's people, if possible even discovering members of their family.

Finding the family hadn't proved difficult, but then Toby had never really expected it would. They'd headed for Hermannsburg, the Aboriginal community roughly a hundred and thirty kilometres southwest of Alice Springs, and once there they'd asked around. As it turned out the Napangurrayi family hadn't moved out of the area at all. Old Mum and Dad Napangurrayi had passed on a long time ago, they'd been told by a man they'd met in the local shop, but members of their family were still there and well known around town. 'Anyone who's been here that long is,' he'd said. 'Hermannsburg's a pretty small place.' He'd directed them towards Aunty May's house. 'Aunty May was a Napangurrayi,' he'd told them, 'course she's Tjeni-mana now since she married Ken, but the Napangurrayis always stay at her place. Keeps them out of trouble; she's well respected in town.'

How easy it would have been, Toby had thought, for Rose to trace her family. But he'd shrugged off the thought – no sense going down that road. There was his daughter to think of now.

He'd waited outside in the four-wheel drive hire car watching as Jess knocked on the door of the tin-roofed shack that was no better or worse than others in the little township's broad, dusty streets. It was a stiflingly hot afternoon in January, still and breezeless, and there was a desultory feel to the place. Everything seemed to move in slow motion, as if time itself were baking in the heat, here and there people lolling under the shade of scrawny trees, the dogs beside them equally languid, here and there people ambling down the road in silence, speech seemingly too much of an effort.

Hermannsburg, established by two Lutheran priests as an Aboriginal mission in 1877, had a colourful history. Pastor Carl Strehlow, who had taken over the settlement in the 1890s, had been credited with translating sections of the Bible into the local language. His son, TGH (Ted) Strehlow, had become a noted anthropologist and linguist and had undergone a ritual adoption by the Western Arunta people. The renowned landscape artist, Albert Namatjira, born at Hermannsburg in 1902, had created a unique style that over following generations had become known as the Hermannsburg School of Painting. The town had a great deal to be proud of, but somewhere along the line pride seemed to have taken a bit of a beating.

Toby had been thinking exactly that as he'd watched Jess knock on the door of the tin-roofed shack, then again more loudly when there was no answer. He'd done his homework well in advance, and he knew of Hermannsburg's proud past, just as he knew of its recent history. The community had a severe alcohol problem and a reputation for violence that kept the police busy. Lazy and languorous as the township appeared on this blistering afternoon, he'd nonetheless kept the car door open, ready to run to his daughter's aid should she need him. Jess had been insistent she introduce herself to the family alone and he'd respected her argument, agreeing that the presence of a white man could prove a hindrance, but it hadn't allayed his concern.

The shack's door had been opened by a boy of around ten with a football nonchalantly tucked under his arm.

There was a brief exchange, then Jess had stepped inside, the door had closed, and Toby had waited.

'*She's out the back doing the washing,*' the boy said as he closed the door. He let the football drop into his hand and started tossing it up and down with a quick flick of his wrist, not intending to be rude, but keen to return to his footy practice. '*Do you want me to get her?*'

'*No, I'll go out the back – you lead the way.*'

They communicated in the local language, Jess having asked for Aunty May in the Western Arunta dialect.

He led the way through the house, which was a shambles. Jess took in everything as they went. The front room was a mess of sleeping bags and, as she followed the boy down a short hallway, she saw much the same disarray past the open doors of two more bedrooms. One room had several two-level bunks, the other a double bed with two single mattresses on the floor. A lot of people were obviously housed in this modest weatherboard, which meant the next room came as something of a surprise. It was the kitchen and it too was crammed with the evidence of many residents. Benches were piled high with pots and pans, shelves were stacked with dishes and mugs, and walls were adorned with all manner of cooking utensils hanging from nails driven into the timber. But despite the endless activity it must have seen on a daily basis, the kitchen was spotless. Aunty May runs a tight ship, Jess thought.

'*Hey, Gran,*' the boy called in Arunta as he stepped through the open door and into the yard, Jess close behind him, '*someone wants to see you.*' Then, kicking the football to the back fence forty metres away, where another boy of around his own age was waiting, he scarpered off leaving her standing there.

A woman was hanging washing on two clotheslines that stretched from the side of the house to a pole with a crossbar at the rear of the yard. She turned, a boy's

T-shirt in one hand, clothes pegs in the other. She was a large woman in her mid-forties, her broad face framed by a handsome head of silver-grey hair, the light cotton shift she wore accentuating the lean arms and legs at odds with her body. Beside her a pretty girl of around twelve was cradling a plastic laundry basket and she too turned. Both were clearly surprised to see Jess.

'Hello,' the woman said. 'What can I do for you?'

Jess took a deep breath and embarked upon the opening lines she'd rehearsed in her mind. *'I have been told you are May Tjenimana and that you were May Napangurrayi before you married, is that right?'*

May was surprised to hear the girl speak her language. The girl was black, certainly, but you could tell at a glance she was a city girl – smartly dressed, slick: she wasn't one of them.

'Yes, that is right,' she replied. Confused though she was by the bluntness of the question, her response was nonetheless polite, for the girl's tone had been respectful. *'I am May Tjenimana and I was May Napangurrayi before I married.'* There was a pause as she waited for the girl to explain herself, but the girl, for all her initial confidence, seemed unsure of what to say next. *'Who are you?'* She was still polite, but she stepped up the authority in her voice. *'What do you want?'*

Jess had rehearsed in her mind the next line too and she had no idea why it had become momentarily stuck. Now the words came out clearly and boldly, but in something of a rush, as if they had been imprisoned too long and needed to escape.

'My name is Jessica Manning. I am the daughter of your sister, Rose.'

They stared at each other across the twenty metres or so of dusty yard that separated them. The scene remained frozen for what seemed to Jess an agonisingly long time as she waited for a reaction, but nothing was said, no movement was made. Then finally May, eyes still trained upon this stranger who professed to be kin, placed the T-shirt and pegs into the laundry basket her granddaughter Millie held and slowly, as if mesmerised, crossed to where Jess stood.

Young Millie hadn't moved a muscle all the while. Now she watched the ongoing proceedings with wide-eyed fascination. Gran's in a trance, she thought. Millie had witnessed her gran's trances in the past. And is it really true? she wondered. Is this city girl really one of our mob?

Jess stood very still, feeling May's fingers trace their way around her face, feeling the touch of May's fingers upon her hair and upon her shoulders and stroking a path down her bare arms in some strange, silent ritual. She could see the wonderment in the woman's eyes as they roamed about her, taking in the very essence of who she was. It was some time before May spoke.

'*You are our Rose's girl. You are our little Rose's daughter.*'

Jess made no answer; she didn't even nod. There was no need. May was not asking a question.

'*I see her in you,*' May said. '*I feel her in you. She is here, my little sister Rose.*' She smiled, once again stroking Jess's face with fond familiarity, as if she were stroking the face of her sister. Then her smile faded and the tone of her voice changed. May could also feel the truth and she needed an answer. '*But she is with the ancestors now. She is gone, is this true? Our Rose is no longer with us in this world?*'

Jess did nod this time, and this time she spoke in English. 'Yes, she's gone,' she said, trying to keep her voice firm like May's, doing her best to fight off the embarrassing threat of tears. 'Mum died just over a year ago.'

Then, suddenly finding herself engulfed in May's huge embrace, Jess could no longer stem the tears, hard as she tried.

They clung wordlessly to each other for a while and when they parted Jess saw that May's face too was streaked with tears. But May wasn't in the least embarrassed.

'Bit of a cry does you good,' she said. 'Come inside and I'll get us some tissues.' She turned back to the children, to Millie who was still standing transfixed with her laundry basket and to the two boys who were kicking the football up and down the yard, oblivious to the drama.

'Hey there, Jack, Bobby,' she yelled to the boys. 'Clean yourselves up and give Millie a hand hanging out the washing. Then come inside the three of you and meet your new aunty.'

May took Jess into the kitchen where she fetched a box of tissues and made them mugs of tea. Then they sat at the small table in the corner.

'The front room's too messy and outside's too hot,' she said, not by way of apology, but simply explanation. 'When the mob's here that's where they eat, the front room or outside: they're not allowed in my kitchen. Do you want some biscuits? Jessica you said, that right?'

'I'm called Jess, and no thank you, no biscuits ...' Having just met her aunt, Jess was unsure how familiar she should be in her address, but noting the hesitation May quickly set her straight.

'Right, no biscuits, and I'm Aunty May,' her face cracked into a smile, 'your real Aunty May – we're blood you and me. Now, Jess, tell me about Rose. Was Rose happy? Did she have a good life?' May's smile broadened into an infectious grin. 'She must have had a good life to produce a daughter like you. You're something to be proud of, you are.'

Accepting the compliment with a smile, Jess proceeded to tell May all she could about the sister who had been so long lost to her. Out of respect for her mother, she omitted the alcoholism that had brought about Rose's demise, concentrating instead upon the happiness of her marriage.

'My dad's Irish,' she said, 'and he and Mum met in Sydney. It was a wonderful marriage. They loved each other very much.'

She did not hold back, however, about Rose's unhappiness as a girl working at Eleanor Downs Station, although, again out of respect for her mother, she did not mention the systematic rape that had taken place.

'It wasn't a happy time for my mother,' Jess said. 'She never spoke of it to me, but Dad believes that being taken from her family to Eleanor Downs brought a sadness that stayed with her the whole of her life.'

May's expression was troubled. She'd been only eight years old when Rose was taken, but hearing her sister's story aroused in her a terrible guilt.

'It's because of me Mum didn't try to trace Rose,' she said, staring down at the mug of tea though it was no longer of interest. 'Dad wanted to go to the authorities, but Mum wouldn't let him. "Rose will have a good home where she'll be looked after and well educated," she told us all a week after it happened. "That's what the government agents promised and that's what I believe." Mum probably talked herself into believing them: the truth is she was too scared to go to the authorities. She was too scared to even try to find out where Rose had been taken – none of us knew – it could have been anywhere. Mum was terrified they'd take me too, see. She'd hide me whenever the government agents came around. She'd hide me when there were *any* whitefellas around the place and she didn't stop hiding me until I was fifteen. They lose interest after that: it's the real young ones they're after, see.'

May continued to stare distractedly down at her mug of tea on the table, turning it around and around with her fingers, agitated. She shook her head, wretched at the thought. *'Poor Rose,'* she murmured in her own language, *'poor little Rose. It was all my fault.'*

Jess felt riddled with guilt herself now for having spoken so openly. *'No it was not, Aunty May,'* she said and leaning across the table she took both of May's hands in her own. *'It was not your fault and it was not your mother's fault. It was a terrible thing that happened to far too many of our people, but it will not happen again. We will make sure of that.'*

May felt the reassuring pressure of the girl's hands and heard the force of her words, and she looked up to meet the determination in Jess's eyes. She was impressed by this show of strength and maturity in one so young. Jess can't be more than eighteen, she thought. Where does this strength come from?

'Tell me about your brothers, Aunty May,' Jess urged, keen to learn of her mother's family, but keen also to distract May from her turmoil. 'Mum said she had two brothers who were a lot older.'

'Yeah, that's right, Archie and Leo, gone now, both of them.' Successfully distracted, May's tone was again practical. It served no purpose to dwell upon the past, not now when her niece needed information. I'll think about Rose later, she told herself. Yes, that's it. I'll think about Rose and she'll come to me and we'll talk and I'll tell her I'm sorry.

Buoyed by the thought, she continued. 'Leo died as a young man, an accidental death, racing with a mate in revved-up cars. He was a wild one, Leo. Archie died a few years back, fifty he was, same age as my husband, Ken, who went around the same time. That was sad, losing a brother and a husband in just one year. Good men, Archie and Ken, too young to go.' She gave a shake of her head then brightened considerably as she added, 'But Archie's son and family live here, and my son and his lot, so that's good. And my daughter and her mob stay whenever they're in town, she and her husband live up Katherine way, so there's always a crowd, lots of grandkids. I like that.'

They were interrupted as if on cue by the arrival of Millie and the boys, who lined up to be introduced.

'These are my grandchildren, Millie and Jack,' May said, 'and this is one of my brother's grandsons, Bobby.'

Jess proffered her hand and as they shook all around May made the official announcement with pride. 'This is my sister Rose's daughter, Jessica. Say hello to your Aunty Jess.'

'Hello, Aunty Jess,' all three chorused and Millie gave a sort of bob as if to royalty.

'All right, you can go now.'

The boys charged off to return to their footy practice, but Millie dawdled away, casting lingering looks over her shoulder, praying she'd be asked to stay.

'Next time, Millie,' May said, 'next time your Aunty Jess comes to visit you can stay and talk, but not now.'

Millie cast a regretful glance at her aunty from the city, obviously doubting she'd ever see her again.

'I'll come back, Millie,' Jess said. 'I'll come back, I promise and when I do we'll talk you and me, a very special talk, just the two of us.'

Millie smiled the prettiest of smiles, she was a very pretty girl, and there was a skip in her step as she went happily on her way.

'She's a good girl,' May said. 'They're all good. I got six grandkids living here and they don't cause trouble, even the boys. Not out there sniffing petrol or paint stripper or whatever they can get their hands on like some of the others. My lot go to school,' she said with inordinate pride. 'I make sure they do, take them there myself every day. Their own parents don't bother, too busy drinking.' Her face hardened. 'Not fair on the kids, they'll end up going the same way. Not fair.'

May's stern expression was confronting and Jess wasn't sure what she should say.

'Where are the rest of the family?' she asked.

'Gone into Alice for the day,' May gave a shrug, pretending she didn't care, 'probably on the grog. Soon as the government money comes in it goes on the drink.' Her mood remained stern. 'Trouble is it's the school holidays and they've taken the rest of the kids with them. Jack and Bobby only stayed home cos they wanted to muck about with the football: they're both footy mad. I won't have it,' she said, a ferocious gleam in her eyes. May could be fearsome. 'If that lot come home drunk the kids can stay, but I won't have the parents here in this house, not with the grog in them. They can sleep in the streets and get picked up by the police, I don't care . . .'

May's tirade continued, but Jess sensed the sadness that lurked beneath the woman's rage. Eventually May herself conceded that her anger was born of despair.

'Archie and Ken were good men,' she went on to explain when her anger had abated to be replaced by frustration, 'proud men, fine examples to their sons. But their sons don't have the same pride. Their sons are broken men and their sons' women aren't much better. I feel a bit sorry for the women,' she admitted in a rare moment of honesty – as a rule she had little time for her daughter-in-law and her nephew's wife, both of whom she considered weak. 'They should have stood up for themselves, but they didn't. They thought the easy way out was to get drunk with their men, but it only brings on the fights and then they get bashed.'

May downed her tea, which was thoroughly cold by now, but having someone intelligent with whom to discuss her predicament so distracted her that she didn't notice.

'Things should have got better when the rights to our land were handed over,' she continued. 'That was a proud time for us all. But things didn't get better. Things seemed to go even more wrong after that. People didn't care the way they should have, not around here anyway. They were greedy, only wanting whatever they could get out of the government. This is a sad place, Jess, so many lost people. No pride left, nothing to live for but the grog, what sort of life's that?' May was well and truly warming to her theme now. 'And that's the problem, see, they don't know what they want out of life. They don't know what's on offer.'

She gave the table an alarmingly loud thump, startling Jess. 'That's why my lot go to school,' she announced. 'My lot go to school because school's the answer. Education,' she declared triumphantly as if unveiling a great hidden truth. 'Education!' she repeated, daring Jess to differ. 'That's the answer.'

Jess smiled. May was clearly accustomed to haranguing others on the subject. 'I can't argue with you there,' she said.

Her niece's agreement would have pleased May immensely had she heard it, but she was so wound up again that she didn't. 'You don't have to be educated yourself to know it's the answer for the new generation,' she went on passionately. 'I'm not educated – I left school when I was thirteen and even I know.'

'Yes, but you're wise, Aunty May.'

May stopped abruptly, realising she'd been on her soapbox, as she so often was, and it occurred to her that Jess was the last person she needed to lecture about education. Jess was from the city. She's probably had a real good schooling, May thought, past thirteen, I'll bet. 'How far did you go with your education, Jess?'

'I'm only just about to begin really.'

'Eh?' May was confused.

'I start uni next month.'

'Uni? University, you mean?'

'That's right.'

'You got to be joking.' May's incredulity was bordering on comical. '*Rose's* girl going to *university*?'

Jess laughed. 'Yes, Rose's girl going to university.' There was a lengthy pause, May successfully rendered speechless. 'Don't you want to know what I'll be studying?'

'Yeh, course I do.' Does it matter? May wondered as she relished what was surely the proudest moment of her life. Rose's girl is going to university – does it matter what she's studying?

'I'm going to study *us*, Aunty May. I'm going to study our people. And when I've graduated I'm going to use my studies to help our people.' It was Jess who was now passionate: May had lent her inspiration. 'I'm not sure exactly how I'll help, perhaps I'll become a teacher, I don't know, but I'll work with our people.'

'How do you mean you'll study us?' May was still pondering the words, mystified. Reading and writing and arithmetic, she could understand, but how did you study people?

'I'll learn about our history from way, way back,' Jess explained, 'and I'll learn our languages . . .'

'You already speak our language.'

'Only one of them,' Jess said. 'Only Western Arunta, and I don't even speak that particularly well.'

'You speak it good enough for me,' May said firmly, then she smiled, gladdened by the sudden realisation. 'So even living in the city with a whitefella husband Rose brought you up speaking our lingo. That's real good, that is.'

'Yes. Dad wanted her to teach me, he even speaks a bit himself –' Jess came to a halt. 'Oh hell,' she said, suddenly reminded of the fact that her father was waiting outside in the car. 'I have to go, Aunty May.' She stood.

'What's the matter?' May also stood. 'What's wrong?'

'Dad. He's waiting outside.'

'What?!' May was appalled. 'You left him out there all this time?'

'I forgot,' Jess admitted sheepishly.

'God, girl, it's a hundred and ten in the shade out there!' May had never converted to the metric system. For practical purposes she recognised dollars and cents, but when it came to the rest, particularly measurements and temperatures, she was intransigent. A mile was a mile and a hundred and ten degrees was hot. 'You can't leave a white-fella from the city hanging around in that sort of heat!'

'He's in the car and it's got air-con,' Jess countered hopefully, but her aunt was already heading for the front door. She followed.

Outside, May made a beeline for the four-wheel drive, where the white man was sitting behind the wheel, the door open, but the engine running and the air-conditioning turned on.

Toby saw the large black woman charging towards him, Jess in her wake. He turned off the engine and got out of the car.

Coming to a halt in front of the white man, May didn't wait for Jess to join them and make the introduction. 'I'm Rose's sister, May,' she said, offering her hand.

'I'm Rose's husband, Toby,' he said, and they shook.

But the handshake wasn't enough for May. She gathered him in her bear-like embrace and Toby returned the hug with a wink to Jess. The meeting had obviously gone well.

Upon parting, May's eyes remained linked with Toby's and her hands retained a firm grip on his shoulders, refusing to relinquish contact. 'You got a fine daughter here, brother,' she said.

'You are right, sister. I am proud for father such a daughter.'

His mispronunciation didn't bother May in the least. She was delighted by her brother-in-law's use of her language. 'That's pretty good,' she said, 'I'm impressed,' and she hugged him all over again.

Watching the two on that day all those years ago, Jess had had the distinct feeling she knew what her father was thinking, and that it wasn't of her at all, but rather of Rose. She'd been quite sure he was thinking that Rose, through her daughter, was finally being reunited with her family. Later, when they'd conferred, Toby had told her she was right.

Jess dropped the aunties off in town at the northern end of Todd Mall as requested.

'I'll be in touch in a few days after I've seen the surveyor boss,' she promised. She was to travel north to Ti Tree the following day to meet the team that was working on the southern leg of the railway corridor from Tennant Creek to Alice Springs; it had recently arrived with all its attendant heavy machinery. She would allay any fears the local community might have and check on the welfare of newly employed Aboriginal workers.

After waving goodbye to the aunties through the open car window she continued along Wills Terrace, down the slope of the riverbank, across the dry bed and up the other bank to the eastern side of the Todd where the terrace then became Undoolya Road. Needless to say, on those rare occasions when the Todd River was in full flood and a raging torrent, the Wills Terrace crossing was non-existent. Pedestrians could avail themselves of the footbridge certainly, but vehicles could cross the river only via the main bridge at the other end of town.

As she drove Jess's mind was still on Aunty May, recalling another visit she'd made to Hermannsburg a whole six years later and how different it had been. Well of course it was different, she thought, I was with Roger. There'd been no relationship between them at the time other than that of tutor and student, heaven forbid! The mere thought that there might be one day would have shocked her back then. But she'd certainly idolised him. Professor Roger Macready was idolised by all his students.

She recalled how she'd felt embarrassed when Roger had insisted on taking photographs of her with her family. She hadn't known exactly why she'd felt embarrassed,

Roger was only doing what anthropologists did, surely, she'd told herself, but it had felt wrong somehow.

That visit to Aunty May's should have warned me, she thought, I should have read the signs, how naive I was . . . Then the cautionary voice in her brain activated and she forced Roger's image aside the way she regularly had over these past several years. I really must go and see Aunty May, she told herself, her thoughts having served as a timely reminder, it's been a whole two months and she's not getting any younger.

She turned into the driveway of the block of flats where she lived, a pleasant collection of single-storey apartments, old-fashioned in style, strung out in a row rather like a country motel, hers the one at the western end. She drove around the back to the parking area and, pulling up at the bay reserved for her, gave Roger one last thought. Oh well, I must certainly thank him for the flat.

The provision of the flat had been very generous given the short duration of their marriage. She hadn't asked for a thing from the divorce, but when Roger had discovered that she'd accepted a long-term contract requiring a move to Alice Springs, he'd arranged the purchase of the flat, sight unseen, via one of his many contacts there. She had to acknowledge now that she was grateful

Jess was very fond of her modest little two-bedroom apartment. It was attractive and, being a short walk over the footbridge into town, conveniently situated, but most of all it was a safe haven a long way away from Roger Macready.

She unlocked the front door and stepped inside to a pleasant open-plan sitting room and kitchenette. The window above the sink looked out over the street and its acacia trees, and the ones to the side offered glimpses of the red gums that towered majestically over the river. Only glimpses indeed, but so very Alice.

Dumping her backpack on the sofa, she poured herself a glass of water, downing it as she went through to the bedroom. She started stripping off her gear: a shower first, then she'd walk over the footbridge and meet up with whichever group of mates was having a drink at the Todd Tavern. There was always a bunch of them there after work, an eclectic mix. They might be colleagues from the Central Lands Council or from the temporary office that had been set up by APT, or they might be others who were in local business. Jess had a wide circle of friends in Alice Springs, both black and white.

But she wouldn't go on to dinner as she often did. Just one drink with the gang, she decided, then she'd come home, have a snack and get an early night. She'd have to be up at the crack of dawn. Ti Tree, close to two hundred kilometres north, was not considered a long drive at all by desert standards, but she wanted to be there early. Meeting with the community elders was always a lengthy procedure and after checking on the locally employed Aboriginal workers, she'd need to chase up the surveyor as she'd promised the aunties she would. The surveying team was bound to be somewhere south of Ti Tree, blazing a trail well ahead of the workers and their heavy machinery. She would have to seek the surveyor out separately and that would take extra time.

Tomorrow promises to be a big day, Jess thought, as she stepped into the shower.

CHAPTER SIX

Matt Witherton had been steadily working his way south for the past eight months. As Senior Surveyor employed on the construction of the railway corridor from Tennant Creek to Alice Springs, he led a four-man team comprising Assistant Surveyor, two junior assistants and a machine operator for land-clearing purposes where necessary. A new machine operator together with the bulldozer was recruited from each donga township – generator-driven and with all modern facilities – that sprang up every hundred kilometres or so along the route in order to house the workers and teams of experts required to create the massive corridor with its bridges, culverts and roadworks. The reconnaissance surveying team, although operating well in advance of the rest of the workers, was also housed at the donga camp, the men returning at the end of each day's work.

For the past decade or more Matt had chosen to work in remote locations and was an acknowledged expert in his field, but the Ghan was undoubtedly the most stimulating challenge he'd yet encountered. Other experts had quickly come to the same conclusion. In fact the teams of surveyors, engineers and designers employed on the various sections of the corridor had encountered such ever-changing conditions and in such remote terrain that inventiveness had become essential. From the outset they'd adopted a pioneering approach. This was the Northern

Territory after all: wild, uncharted land. Surely better to use what was available and make decisions on the spot than to rely upon supplies and solutions from far-distant sources unfamiliar with the topography. This laissez-faire attitude infuriated the bureaucratic superiors in the city, often arousing friction and causing trouble for those who chose to 'bend the rules'.

Matt enjoyed both the challenge and the freedom his work on the Ghan offered. Coupled with his love of the desert, he had to admit that this was possibly the most stimulating and enjoyable job he'd ever had – until a fortnight back anyway. A fortnight back trouble had arrived in the form of Gavin Johnstone.

Gavin Johnstone was the new machine operator recruited from the donga camp that had recently been set up not far from the small outback town of Ti Tree. Gav had been surly and uncooperative from the start and Matt had at first assumed it was because he didn't wish to be assigned to the surveying team, but would have preferred instead to remain one of the crew involved with the heavy earthworks. Having always considered a harmonious relationship between his team members essential, Matt had been quite happy to offer the man an escape route.

'S'cuse me, Gav. Mind if I have a word?'

He'd sought Gav out back at camp at the end of the work day. Better to front him alone, he'd decided, rather than on the job and in the company of the other members of the team. He'd put up with the man's surliness for three days now, but had said nothing, avoiding confrontation as he always did. Matt disliked confrontation by nature, and as a leadership method avoided it whenever possible, rarely asserting his authority. He preferred to respect each man's contribution to the team rather than play 'boss'. In a remote location, and particularly when a small group was working far from the company of others, mutual respect, he'd discovered, was vital.

Gav gave a shrug as if he couldn't care less, which was no doubt the case. He was sitting on the front step of his donga, can of beer in hand, a dark-haired man in his early thirties with the burly build of the rugby league player he'd once been and clearly wished he still was. He was chatting to another worker sitting on the step of the donga opposite, also with beer in hand. The transportable units, four dongas a piece, were twelve metres long and three metres wide; set out in rows they formed a barracks that could house over two hundred.

'Sorry to interrupt.' Matt smiled an apology to the other man.

'No worries, mate.' The man saluted him with his beer.

'Want to come for a bit of a walk?' Matt suggested.

Another shrug and Gav stood.

They walked on past the ablutions block and laundry, where men were showering and washing clothes; on past the kitchen where cooks and kitchen hands were preparing the many dishes that would constitute the evening meal – workers needed variety as well as substance; and on past the prefabricated building of the canteen that stood adjacent, men already milling, helping themselves to coffee and tea as they waited for the food to be delivered to the serving tubs. The camp was always busy at this time of day, when the final shift was over.

When he felt they were far enough away from the others, Matt decided to get straight to the point.

'Do you want me to have a chat with your boss, Gav?' He kept his voice friendly and the suggestion casual.

'What about?' There was no denying the edginess in Gav's reply.

'About putting you back on the workers team. We can get another machine operator appointed to us. I don't mind in the least.'

'You going to make a complaint about me, are you? Why would you do that? What's wrong with my work?' Matt was met by a barrage of belligerence.

'There's nothing wrong with your work, mate,' he replied pleasantly; the man's antagonism was bewildering. 'I'm not being critical, I can assure you. It's just that you don't seem to be happy with us and I thought . . .'

'You want to get me the sack, do you? You want to get me busted, is that it?' Gav's fury was growing by the second. It was true he didn't particularly like being part of the surveying team, he was a man's man and he wanted to work with men, not university smartarses. But there was no way he was going to have a wimp like Matt Witherton complain to his boss and say his work wasn't up to scratch. That'd be fucking humiliating. 'If you reckon my work's no good then you say so to my face, you don't go ratting to my boss.'

The man's more than antagonistic, Matt thought, he's downright hostile. There could be only one conclusion. The reason was personal. Gav simply didn't like him. Ah well, he decided, I can live with that. Pity the rest of the team has to though.

'Rightio then, we'll leave things as they are.'

'We're stuck with him I'm afraid, Pottsy,' he said over dinner an hour or so later. He and Craig Potts, Assistant Surveyor, were good mates. They'd met in the Pilbara eight years previously and since then had worked together as a team on many a project all over the country. Matt would put in a request for Craig Potts as his assistant whenever possible – that is, if Pottsy was available. Many others were also aware that Pottsy was very good at his job.

'He won't bother us,' Pottsy replied with a shrug and a glance at Gav, who was holding court with a gang of his mates a number of tables away. Gav made a point of distancing himself from the surveying team back at camp. 'We'll just ignore him.'

An amiable Western Australian, Pottsy was the type who should never work in the desert. Of Scottish heritage on his mother's side, ginger-haired and freckle-skinned, the sun was not kind to him and he looked ten years older than his thirty-four years, but he didn't care. Like Matt, he couldn't help himself. Pottsy was lost without his regular dose of the desert.

'Don't give him a second thought, Withers,' he said, 'Gav's a ratbag, not worth the worry.' Pottsy was aware as always of Matt Witherton's genuine concern for the welfare of his team. The boys are too, he thought, inexperienced though they are. Baz and Mitch, newly qualified and on their first job, couldn't have copped a better boss than Withers. He'd told them so. 'This job's the best field experience you boys could have landed,' he'd said, 'you'll learn more working with Withers on the Ghan than you have in the past three years at Tech.'

'The boys won't care either, mate,' he said, watching Baz and Mitch, who were wending their way over to the table, plates piled ludicrously high. 'Gav'll become invisible – we'll pretend he's not there.'

That had been over a week back and they'd successfully ignored Gav since. Even on the occasions when he'd openly goaded Matt, daring him to lose his temper, the others had followed the example of Withers himself and simply ignored the man.

But the previous night things had come to a head.

'I think you've got trouble on your hands, Withers,' Pottsy had said, seeking Matt out back at camp an hour or so after they'd returned from their day's work.

'Gav I take it?' Matt had been waiting for the moment when Gav would go that step too far. The man seemed determined to force a confrontation.

'Yep. He's pissed off to Aileron, left just after we got back. Made a big song and dance about it to young Baz and Mitch; said, "Tell your mate Withers to come and get me if he's got the guts.'"

'Oh shit.'

The Aileron Roadhouse on the Stuart Highway fifty kilometres from the donga camp was supposedly out of bounds to the workers, but a rough dirt track had been carved through the scrub and the bosses turned a blind eye to the obvious action the bar saw during the weekends when the various shift workers were allocated an afternoon off. Weekdays were a different matter, however. Any worker daring to pay a visit to Aileron during the week did so covertly. He did not announce his intention.

'Bugger the man,' Matt said, frustration bordering on anger. Today was a Wednesday. 'What the hell's he playing at?'

'He's out to rile you, that's for sure.'

'Ah well, nothing for it I suppose: I'll just have to play boss.' He set off purposefully if reluctantly towards the Land Rover.

'I'll come with you,' Pottsy said, falling in beside him.

'If you like,' Matt was glad for the company, but firm in his instruction nonetheless. 'No interference, though, I need to handle him on my own.'

'Sure, mate. I'm only coming along in case someone needs to pick up the pieces – let's face it, the bloke's built like a brick shithouse.' Pottsy grinned to show he was joking, but Matt didn't appear to hear. His focus was elsewhere.

It was dusk when they arrived, the air turning chill and promising a cold night as the desert in April could. Aileron was little more than a roadhouse and petrol station, but attractive nonetheless. A tin-roofed building with surrounding verandahs sprawled amongst acacia trees in the middle of nowhere, it was atmospheric, boasting a bar that was sizeable and welcoming and food that was tasty and substantial. Aileron was a popular stopping-off place for travellers.

Matt pulled the Land Rover up in the large parking lot, which was virtually empty but for a few vehicles including a conspicuous AdRail company four-wheel drive. He and Pottsy climbed out and together they headed through the main doors that led directly to the bar.

Gav was there, propped on a stool at the far end. Having settled himself in for the past hour or so, he was chatting animatedly to the young barman, who appeared to find him riveting. The place was pretty much deserted, as it usually was mid-week. Beyond where Gav sat, in the open dining room adjoining the bar, two men were tucking into their sausages with mash and gravy and a middle-aged couple, teenage son in tow, were dining at a table near the windows. In the bar itself, however, Gav was the only customer.

'Well, well, look who's here,' he said jeeringly the moment Matt and Pottsy stepped inside. From his position he had a clear view of the main doors and had obviously been waiting. 'Come to tick me off, have you, *Boss*?'

With a wink to the barman, who was all of twenty, he downed the remains of his drink and dumped his glass on the table. 'Fill her up, Harry mate, same again.' Gav was drinking double Bundaberg rums with coke in short glasses and downing them quickly to make up for lost time; they didn't allow hard liquor back at camp.

Young Harry was quick to oblige. This'd be the fifth double Bundy and coke he'd served Gav in an hour, but the bloke could obviously handle it. Hell, he'd been a professional rugby league player! Still would be too if his injuries hadn't caught up with him. They were as tough as all get out those blokes. Harry wasn't from New South Wales and didn't follow NRL closely, being South Australian Aussie Rules was his code of choice, but he admired the toughness of League and those who played it.

'Brought Ginger Meggs with you, I see.' Gav looked Pottsy up and down: Another university smartarse, he thought, weak as piss. 'Needed a bit of back-up, did you, *Boss*?' he sneered. 'Well I don't reckon old Meggsy here'd be much use.' Gav had no time for uni blokes. Up themselves the lot of them, thought they were superior – well they could go and get fucked.

Harry placed the rum and coke on the counter, a little tentative now. Gav's tone was insulting and he hoped there wouldn't be trouble. Should he get the manager? The manager was out the back having dinner with his missus and wouldn't like being disturbed unless it was necessary.

Matt crossed to the bar where Gav sat and Pottsy remained at the door, knowing that's what Withers wanted.

'Time to go, Gav,' Matt said calmly but firmly.

'Is that so, *Boss*?' Gav swigged back the Bundy and coke in several hefty gulps, slammed the glass down on the counter and stood. 'That an order, is it?' The bloke was a wimp and Gav didn't take orders from wimps.

'Yes, you're right on both counts: I'm your boss and that's an order. While you're on my team you do as I say and I'm ordering you back to camp.'

'Oh yeah?' Gav's sneer turned to a threat as he threw down the challenge. 'You're gunna make me, are you?' He glanced over to where Pottsy remained at the front door. 'You and what army? Meggsy here?'

'No. Just me.'

'Right, you weak prick.' He put up his fists, this was just what he wanted, he'd been spoiling for a fight with the smartarse surveyor, who he knew looked down on him. 'Come on then: give it your best shot.'

Young Harry, alarmed, was about to dash out the back for the manager, but catching Matt's glance, which clearly said 'don't bother', he suddenly realised who was in command and that it wasn't the rugby league player. This bloke really was the boss.

'You don't want to fight, Gav,' Matt said.

'Oh yeah, and why's that?' Gav's fists remained raised.

'You're drunk. You'd lose.'

'Try me, you bastard.'

A brief pause followed, Matt considering further negotiation, then, 'All right,' he said, 'outside.' No point, any
further negotiation would have been futile.

Pottsy held the door open and Matt strode past without
a glance, Gav hot on his heels.

Gav was fuming, he'd murder the bastard – he wasn't
drunk. Christ, he could drink a bottle of Bundy straight.
Who did the prick think he was saying he couldn't
hold his liquor? It was typical of uni shits like him who
looked down on everyone else just because they had
an education.

The door swung closed behind the three, Pottsy also
stepping outside to stand on the verandah and observe
the proceedings. As instructed, he had no intention of
intervening, whatever the outcome. Young Harry stared
after them, wide-eyed. Crikey, he thought, there's going
to be a fight. He was no longer concerned about fetching
the manager, the men couldn't do any damage outside,
but he might get into trouble if he deserted his post and
he wanted to watch. What the hell? he thought after a
moment or so. I can see the bar from the door.

Circling the counter, he crossed to the door and opened
it to look out at the car park where, in the lights from the
petrol station, he was just in time to see Gav hurl himself
at his adversary.

Matt blocked the man's punch and stepped aside,
allowing the impetus of Gav's attack to hurtle him uselessly forwards, then turning he waited, studying the man's
every movement as Gav also turned, marshalling his forces
to attack again. The same thing happened, only this time
after blocking the punch Matt landed a hefty blow to the
solar plexus before stepping aside.

Gav grunted and staggered, but kept his feet, and now
enraged came at Matt like a battering ram, head down,

fists pumping like pistons – anything to land a blow that would cripple the bastard.

Watching from the verandah, Pottsy thought that by physical appearances it should have been an equal match. Both men were fit and of a similar age, Matt the taller of the two giving him the advantage of reach, Gav the more powerful in build and obviously the stronger. But it wasn't an equal match. Pottsy had suspected it might not be. He'd seen Matt in action before, particularly in the Pilbara all those years ago when they'd been working for Woodside. There'd been some tough boys around then, and Matt had more than held his own with those who'd goaded or bullied or those who'd needed, for whatever reason, to pit themselves against someone who'd earned a bit of a reputation as Matt by that time had, albeit reluctantly.

Pottsy had often wondered whether anger played any part in the physical conflict Matt Witherton was at times driven to confront. If so, you'd never know it. To Withers, doing battle seemed devoid of anything personal. He fought only when there was no alternative, but when he did his commitment was total and he didn't stop until the fight was unequivocally decided, be it himself reduced to a bloodied mess or the other man acknowledging defeat. There was never a draw, always a decisive victory, and in the past more often than not the victor had been Withers.

He watched now as the familiar pattern unfolded, Matt nimble and focused, anticipating every facet of Gav's attack like a chess player several moves ahead of his opponent, dodging, landing blows when it was safe to do so, Gav all the while increasingly frustrated, becoming clumsy in his fatigue.

Matt was thankful for Gav's anger and also for the fact that the man had had too much to drink: the power of his punches, had they connected, would have done a good deal of damage. But Gav's clumsiness was easy to read and Matt was quite prepared to stay on the defensive, allowing the time it would take to wear the man down to a state of exhaustion and capitulation.

Then out of the blue Gav scored a lucky punch. Matt, in deflecting a heavy blow to the ribs, was caught briefly off-balance and didn't manage to avoid the fist that connected with his left cheekbone. His head whipped to the side and, disoriented, he staggered back a pace or so.

The blow, forceful as it had been, lent Gav new vigour. He'd scored a hit! Just one more punch, a voice in his brain screamed triumphant. One more punch! Make it a killer and murder the bastard! Re-energised and snarling like the all-powerful bull he now felt himself to be, he again hurled himself at his opponent.

Time to finish it, Matt thought. He met the attack head on, blocking Gav's clumsy punches, landing blow after blow, each perfectly timed and placed, methodical, almost machine-like. Gav became a punching bag. Matt took no pleasure in the exercise. It was simply time to wrap things up. It was over. It had been over from the start.

Gav's one lucky hit had expended the last of his energy and staggering back under the force of the blows, he collided against the petrol bowser and slithered to the ground, not unconscious, but exhausted.

Matt nursed the aching knuckles of his right hand and took a handkerchief from his pocket to dab at the cut that was starting to bleed above his left eye. He watched as Gav tried to haul himself to his feet and continue the fight.

'Give it a rest, man,' he said. 'You're drunk. You can't go on.'

Pottsy, crossing to the petrol bowser to lend some help now that the fight was over, thought drunk or sober would have made little difference. Gav would have lost in any event.

Gav had made it to one knee. As he struggled to stand Matt offered his hand by way of assistance, but the offer was angrily waved aside, an action which only served to throw Gav off balance. He crashed back against the petrol bowser and slid to the ground, where he lay, barely able to move and forced to cede defeat. There was no more fight in him.

Matt gave a nod to Pottsy and bending down they grabbed Gav under his shoulders and hauled the man to his feet.

'I'll drive him back to camp,' Matt instructed. 'You take the Land Rover.'

'Right.'

Supporting Gav between them, they half-dragged, half-carried him to the AdRail four-wheel drive and piled him into the passenger seat.

'Keys, mate,' Matt said with outstretched hand. It was an order, brisk but not peremptory. He might even have been doing a favour, driving a drunken mate home.

Gav, sullen but unprotesting, dug the car's keys from his pocket and handed them over while Matt tossed the Land Rover's keys to Pottsy.

'I'll see you back at camp,' he said and climbed into the driver's seat.

Pottsy watched the vehicle pull out of the car park. Despite the years of their friendship, he felt on occasions that he really didn't understand Matt Witherton. There was a remoteness about him, something so detached that it was easy to understand why people sometimes considered him unfeeling, even though Pottsy knew him to be the most caring of men.

Oh well, he gave a shrug as he walked off to the Land Rover; he'd given up trying to figure out what it was about Matt Witherton.

'What's your problem, Gav?' Matt asked when they'd driven in silence for ten minutes or so. 'Why the chip on the shoulder?'

Further silence as Gav continued to stare morosely through the closed window at the desert night speeding by.

'Come on, mate, spit it out.' Matt was determined to push for answers even at the risk of alienating the man further, indeed perhaps hoping that further alienation might reveal the truth. 'Why are you taking your unhappiness out on the rest of the team? If you're having a crook life, and you appear to be, it's hardly their fault.'

The goading tactic worked. Gav turned to him glowering, one eye already closing, bloodied nose and split lip congealing: not a pretty sight. 'Yeah, it's all right for you isn't it, *mate*?' he said derisively, his voice husky and rasping from the pounding he'd taken, 'your life's never been crook, has it? You and your lot, you've got it made. Money no problem, posh schools, university, cushy jobs: you pricks have never had to do it hard.'

So it's that simple, Matt thought, I represent everything he envies, no wonder he's taken a personal dislike. There really isn't much I can do to change an attitude like that. He maintained silence and let the man rant on further.

'Think you're better than us lot, don't you,' Gav said accusingly. 'You're not, you bastards.' He wanted to call the bloke a wimp, he wanted to call them all bloody wimps, but how could he after the thrashing he'd just received? Gav had never felt so humiliated. 'You're not better than me, you smartarse bastard,' he ended weakly. 'You're bloody well not.'

'Of course I'm not. I never said I was.'

'Course you fucking did. You say it every fucking day. You've been pissing on me right from the start, you and your bloody cronies.'

'No we haven't, mate.' Matt couldn't let that one go past and he couldn't be bothered talking any further. 'Why would we waste our time? You're too busy pissing on yourself.'

End of conversation. Matt focused solely on the track ahead and Gav turned again to gaze morosely through the window at the desert night, but he wasn't seeing the passing spinifex and acacias lit up briefly by the car's headlights. He was thinking of the words that had really hit home. 'If you're having a crook life', the prick had said. Well of course he was having a crook fucking life. He'd been having a crook fucking life ever since they'd dropped him from the club list, and that was a whole five years back. A career in Rugby League was all he'd ever wanted, to be one of the boys, a man among men, a real somebody, and he'd worked bloody hard – Christ, no-one had trained harder. But they'd dropped him from the reserves after only two bloody seasons. He'd never played first grade, not even one game: hell, he hadn't even sat on the bench! He'd come up with the injury story over the years, sure, but he hadn't suffered injuries: he just hadn't been good enough. And now he was a shit kicker like everyone else. Everyone except those university pricks who'd had it all handed to them on a platter.

A crook life, Gav thought, my oath it's a crook life, and it's about to get a fucking sight crooker. I'll be on report for tonight, I'll probably get the sack, but worst of all when the boys hear the bloody surveyor belted my lights out I'll be a fucking laughing stock!

Gav's perennial bitterness had finally been overshadowed: humiliation outweighed insignificance.

The following morning Gav didn't join his mates for breakfast in the canteen, grabbing an egg sandwich and a coffee to take back to his donga instead, but even then despite the dark glasses he couldn't avoid the odd comment. 'Walk into a door did you, Gav?' and from those who knew him as the tough NRL bloke he was, 'Shit, mate, is the other fella still on his feet?'

He shrugged off the comments and headed back to his donga where he sat on the step eating his sandwich and waiting to be called to the AdRail site office for dismissal, or at the very least a whopping great lecture and a warning.

'G'day, Gav, ready to go?'

The surveyor was standing right in front of him. Apart from the small square of Elastoplast above his slightly puffy left eye, it was if nothing had happened: his manner, his appearance, everything was as normal. Gav stared up from the step of his donga, egg sandwich forgotten.

'Got your crib?' Matt knew Gav had expected his whole life would change, but it wouldn't, not unless he wanted it to. Either way, Matt didn't particularly care. The man needed to get his act together, nobody could do it for him.

Gav shook his head. He didn't have his crib. He hadn't even considered making up his lunch box at the canteen. He hadn't expected to be out in the scrub with the others, not today of all days.

'Hurry it up then, you've got ten minutes.'

As it turned out, bizarrely, the day went much like any other. There was some initial commentary from Baz and Mitch – 'Been in a bit of a punch-up, mate,' Baz said sympathetically, and Mitch, always one for a laugh, added 'Bet the other bloke looks like a Mack truck hit him' – to which Gav returned his customary grunt, but after that not a word. Withers and Pottsy made no mention of the fight and young Baz and Mitch clearly didn't link his battle scars with the small square of Elastoplast on their boss's face. They didn't seem to notice the grazed knuckles of their boss's right hand either, or if they did they made no connection. Why would they? Their hero Withers never got into fights. Their hero Withers was the sort who always turned the other cheek.

Gav couldn't believe his luck: he was off the hook. He'd obviously not been put on report, he was not going to lose his job and, most important of all, it looked like he had escaped the unspeakable horror of public humiliation.

All this and more was whirling around in Gav's mind as he looked on from the sidelines at the surveyors going about their work. They were an efficient bunch, he had to give them that much. Withers had his eye to the theodolite set up on a tripod, Pottsy some distance away was holding the pole with its prism that reflected the telescope's laser beam, and Baz, standing beside Withers, was marking down details as instructed, for although the electronic measurements were sent straight to a data recorder Matt Witherton always chose to record his mathematical definitions on paper. Mitch, like Gav himself, was standing by awaiting orders; areas would shortly need to be cleared and boundary pegs set up some distance from the centre line, marking the necessary allowances for firebreaks and service roads.

They're more than just 'an efficient bunch', Gav thought, watching them. The reason they worked so well together was because they liked one another and because each bloke was proud of his place in the team. And that was due to just one man. A team always reflected the bloke at the top.

When they broke for lunch he joined the others, which was unusual. In the past he'd made a point of taking his crib several yards away, considering it a statement, disassociating himself from the wimpy boss and his wanker mates. He didn't say anything as he ate, but listened to the others chatting. Well he listened to Mitch anyway: Mitch was a real talker about all and everything from sport to movies to politics, at the moment it was the American Academy Awards of a month or so back. The others for the most part found Mitch a source of interest or amusement or both, a fact that Gav had always taken as further evidence of the wankers they were. Certainly if he went on too much Pottsy or Baz would tell him to give it a rest, but Withers never said anything, which had of course revealed him as the wimp Gav had believed him to be.

Withers wasn't saying anything now. Gav's gaze had been drawn to him again, as it had been repeatedly since they'd all sat down and the man's focus was principally on his meal, as it usually was. His aloofness had always seemed proof he considered himself superior.

Then suddenly their eyes met: Withers had obviously sensed he was being looked at. Gav wondered what he should say or do. Apology did not come easily to him. In fact he couldn't quite recall having apologised to anyone. Perhaps he never had.

Their eyes remained momentarily locked, Withers appearing curious, aware that Gav wanted to say something. Then as Mitch continued his spiel about the injustice of Russell Crowe not receiving Best Actor for *A Beautiful Mind*, Gav heard his own voice.

'Thanks,' he said. He doubted the others heard him because Mitch didn't let up for a second, but Withers certainly had, and that's all that mattered. He struggled briefly with the next words, 'I'm sorry', which he intended to add, but he was too late, Withers had turned away to pick up his Thermos flask. Not that an apology appeared necessary, Gav realised, for before he'd turned away he'd given the merest of shrugs that said 'no worries'.

Matt poured himself a mug of coffee. He was pleased. No, he was more than pleased: he was thankful. The fight he'd been trying so hard to avoid had served a purpose after all. Good, he thought, problem solved.

Back at the donga camp, Jess was about to join a group of Aboriginal workers who were tucking into their well-earned lunch.

She'd seen Donny the moment she'd entered the canteen. They'd exchanged a wave and when he'd beckoned her to join him and his mates she'd returned a nod. Then she'd headed off to the self-serve counter and helped herself to a plate of ham and a variety of salads, avoiding the heavy stews and steaks and roast dinners so favoured by the men. Donny and his mates were downing huge meals, as were the dozens of other labourers who'd just returned from the gruelling dawn shift.

The mammoth job of creating the rail corridor was relentless at all times, but particularly so further to the north, with the Dry season now upon them. The earthworks crews progressed at an average rate of one to one point five kilometres a day and their schedule needed to be strictly maintained if not bettered. Delays might well be encountered later in the year during the Wet, when flooding could hinder the building of bridges and culverts. At the moment, however, each of the four sections of the railway's construction was progressing remarkably to plan. With much of the corridor now created, the first track had been laid at Katherine just the previous week, a momentous occasion accorded great celebration by the locals, and track-laying was shortly to commence north from Tennant Creek. Already the mighty Ghan was starting to snake its way across the vast Northern Territory.

Jess's meeting with the local community leaders at Ti Tree that morning had gone extremely well. This was Anmatyerre land and the Anmatyerre elders were pleased that a number of their young men had been employed to work on the railway. Indeed most of the talk had been about the job opportunities on offer and the new work camp that had been set up just south of town. The railway was keeping their boys out of trouble and earning them good money, the elders agreed.

Now, having arrived at the camp, Jess had decided that lunch in the canteen would be an excellent opportunity to chat to some of the young men themselves. She'd politely declined the invitation to dine with the AdRail site office team and two visiting APT executives. She was there to do a job after all.

'Thanks, Donny.' Donny had pulled a spare chair up to the table for her. 'Saw your mum yesterday,' she said sitting beside him, 'and Aunty Jill and Aunty Molly.'

'Yeh I know, I dropped them off early on the way up here.'

'That's right. Course you did. I forgot.' Jess hadn't forgotten at all; she'd deliberately mentioned Donny's mum in order to give him face with his new mates.

The ploy worked. Donny beamed broadly as he introduced her around, his mum's real good friend, he said. Donny was proud as punch – crikey, who wouldn't be, introducing the good-looking negotiator employed by the head honchos? He was winning points like there was no tomorrow. He could tell the boys were impressed.

There were eight Aboriginal workers at the table: Donny and two others were Arunta men and the rest were Anmatyerre. All were speaking English, which Jess thought was probably in deference to her. They no doubt assumed she was from a city mob down south and had little knowledge of their desert language, but she was accustomed to such a reception upon first meeting. In any event they were very friendly and welcoming.

She was pleased to see Donny off the grog and so happy and healthy, tucking into his food with a labourer's appetite. This was only his second day, of course, but the hard work, the camaraderie and above all the sense of purpose the job offered would surely keep him on the straight and narrow. She certainly hoped so.

'So how's it going,' she asked the table in general, 'everyone good?'

'Yeh, yeh, real good,' they agreed with grins all around. 'Good tucker,' one said and the others nodded, jaws pumping vigorously.

Only one of the men seemed quiet and lacking his mates' enthusiasm, the young one seated opposite her, the youngest of them all – barely twenty, Jess guessed. He'd been introduced as Laurence and this was his first day on the job. Laurence was withdrawn. More than withdrawn, she thought, Laurence was angry. He was not eating, but glowering at the hearty bowl of casserole on the table in front of him as if he found it offensive.

'What's the matter, Laurence,' she asked, 'your tucker no good?'

His black eyes shot up to meet hers, but before he could reply one of his mates answered for him.

'A whitefella told him it was emu,' Kevin said, pointing at the casserole. Kevin, around thirty, was another Anmatyerre man and knew young Laurence well. 'The bloke was only joking, didn't mean any harm, but Laurence believed him . . .' Kevin gave a shrug that said it all. 'Made him feel crook,' he added.

'I see.' So the white worker knew the locals never ate emu, Jess thought – a joke maybe, but insensitive, whether or not he knew why. Emu was one of the totems of an Anmatyerre man. To eat a totem creature was against traditional law and strictly forbidden.

'It's chook, you dumb bastard,' one of the men said with a huge grin, 'how many times we have to tell you, it's bloody chook, mate.'

A couple of the others laughed, not maliciously, but certainly having a bit of fun at Laurence's expense. Laurence, however, was not in the mood to be the butt of anyone's joke. He stared down at the bowl of casserole, the sight sickening him, his guts still in a state of turmoil. He'd been the first to arrive at the table, the others still at the servery, and ravenous, he'd dived into the stew only to hear the white bastard behind him.

'Good tucker emu, eh mate?'

He'd looked up at the bloke, a big jovial man with a sweaty bald head. 'It's chicken,' he'd said. 'That's what they told me at the counter. It's chicken.'

'Course that's what they told you,' the man had informed him in all apparent seriousness. Baldy just loved playing this joke on the new boys. 'That's what they tell you fellas in order to keep you happy, but the chef's real proud of his emu stew.'

The white bastard had walked off leaving Laurence sick to the guts. He'd been on the point of spewing until a few of the others had arrived at the table with their own meals and explained the 'joke' to him. What joke? That was no joke, he'd thought. He still felt bilious as he looked at the bowl. He felt angry too, angry at the white bastard's lack of respect, angry at his own gullibility, angry that he was being laughed at. He couldn't take his eyes off that fucking bowl of stew.

'Would you mind if we exchanged meals, Laurence?'

He looked up. She'd spoken to him in the Anmatyerre tongue. He didn't know she could speak his language, this city girl.

'I would very much like some chicken,' she said and when he made no reply, she pushed her plate of ham and salad across the table, exchanging it for the bowl of stew. *'The ham's very good,'* she added with a smile, *'the potato is too.'*

Laurence remained at a loss for words. She's bloody gorgeous, he thought. He'd been so angry he hadn't noticed what a top sort she was. Jeez, and that smile was directed right at him. He wondered if he might stand a chance: perhaps she fancied him. He liked older women himself and she had to be at least thirty. He flashed her one of his sexiest grins and tucked into the ham and potato salad.

Around the table the men shared smiles of their own. It was pretty obvious Laurence didn't feel crook any more.

Jess made a point of eating every mouthful of the stew and pretending to relish it although she was not at all in the mood for a heavy meal. Young Laurence needs toughening up, she thought. The men will see to that. Working on the railway will do him the world of good.

Following lunch, she made enquiries at the AdRail site office about the whereabouts of the surveyor and his team.

'About twenty Ks south,' she was told, 'stick to the track and you can't miss them. I'll radio ahead and tell them to keep an eye out for you.'

She met up with the team about a half an hour later.

'Matt Witherton,' the surveyor said by way of introduction, and he offered his hand, a rangy, fit man she took to be in his early thirties although he could have been older, his face interestingly weathered like the faces of most white men who worked in the outback.

'Hello, Matt, I'm Jess Manning,' she replied as they shook. He blinked as if startled. Had she squeezed his hand too hard? She'd noted the grazed knuckles of the hand he offered and, linking it with the Elastoplast sitting above an eye that looked puffy, she wondered if the surveyor had been in a fight.

He introduced her to the members of his team, an older man with ginger hair, two younger ones who looked fresh out of uni or TAFE and a beefy machine operator with a bashed-up face. She wondered if perhaps the fight had been with that one. If so the surveyor had certainly come out on top. Hardly appropriate behaviour for a person in authority, she thought, and hardly what she would have expected of the man she'd been told was such an expert in his field.

Jess was not in the habit of judging others, but she couldn't help feeling a little critical: she abhorred violence.

He offered her a cup of tea or coffee, iced water or soft drink – they carried ample supplies, he said.

She declined the offer, explaining she'd had lunch back at the camp and, leaving the others to carry on with their work, the two seated themselves on the ground under the sparse shade of a desert oak and got straight down to business.

'Not a boundary problem surely,' Matt said, curious as to the reason for the negotiator's visit. 'We've stuck rigidly to all native title alignments. There's been no deviation from the originally agreed route.'

'No, no, not at all,' she assured him, 'no problem with boundaries.' Then she told him of the concern circulating in the Indigenous community at Alice Springs since the locals heard about the intended use of explosives just north of the town. 'They didn't know this until recently,' she said, 'they've never been told. Word only just got around. I don't know exactly how,' she added with a shrug, 'but it's out on the grapevine now and the locals want reassurance.'

'Yes,' he agreed, 'I can only presume the powers that be considered a general announcement might give cause for alarm,' he knew she was thinking along the same lines, 'but it's true there will be rock cuttings blasted north of Alice Springs. The use of explosives will be quite extensive, but I'm told the blasting will be contained and well-monitored, and that there's no cause for concern.'

She appreciated the direct, no-nonsense response to her query, but found his business-like manner a little off-putting. He was addressing her as he might a journalist. Why the formality? It was so out of place. They weren't at a press conference. They were sitting in the dust just the two of them in the middle of a desert.

'So when do you reckon the blasting will be, Matt?' she asked, deliberately laid-back, perhaps as a hint for him to unwind a bit.

'Not for some time,' he replied briskly. 'It'll be the last major earthwork in the creation of the rail corridor. I'd estimate probably early in the New Year.'

'Right.' Well he obviously hadn't registered the hint. 'I'll let it be known there's no cause for worry then,' she said and she smiled to show she wasn't really having a dig as she added, 'not that there'd be much they could do about it if there was.'

He finally returned the vestige of a smile, albeit a rueful one. 'Which is why the announcement wasn't broadcast in the first place, I'd say. But there really won't be a problem, I can assure you. I know the engineer, and he and his team are experts.'

'Good.' He was so obviously sincere that she decided he wasn't a bad bloke after all, just a bit stitched up. Oh well, he can't help it, she thought. 'There's one other assurance I'm after, Matt,' she said, 'but I'm afraid it involves a personal favour.' She went on to tell him about the aunties and the secret site that was so important to the women of the community.

'How far north of town?' he asked.

'Just under twenty Ks, I clocked it.'

'The radius of the blast won't reach anywhere near that distance,' he said with a shake of his head. 'The rock cuttings are less than seven kilometres from Alice. The site will be perfectly safe.'

'Yes, that's what I thought. But any chance you could tell the elders yourself?' she asked hopefully. 'I mean if it's at all possible? It'd put them at ease to have some assurance from a higher authority.' Jess's tone was apologetic as she realised she was probably pushing things too far. 'I sort of promised you'd meet with them.' A brief pause followed. 'And it's very good for public relations,' she added hastily.

This time the barrier was lowered, only fractionally, but the surveyor appeared faintly amused. 'You're wheedling, aren't you?'

'Yes,' she agreed, 'although I would have called it grovelling myself. Is it working? Will you come into town and meet the aunties?'

'Sure. How about Saturday afternoon, would that suit?'

'Absolutely,' she agreed, delighted.

'Let's say three o'clock.' He stood and she quickly scrambled to her feet to join him. 'Whereabouts?' he asked.

'Why don't we meet at my place and I'll take you to the community.' She gave him her address in Undoolya Road. 'I'll be waiting out the front,' she said.

'Right you are. Three o'clock your place it is.'

'Thanks, Matt. I'm most grateful, really I am.' This time it was she who offered her hand. He accepted it and once again they shook.

He pulled his hand back smartly. 'See you Saturday,' he said then he turned abruptly and walked off, the barrier well and truly back in place.

She looked after him for a second or so. What a strange man, she thought, not exactly hostile, but apart from that one brief exchange completely withdrawn. And not once did he call me by name, she realised as she crossed to the Toyota.

He didn't watch her drive away, but returned to his work, appearing not to give the negotiator a second thought.

'What did she want?' Pottsy asked. 'Any problems?'

'Nup, just a meeting with some elders in Alice on Saturday.'

Pottsy waited for a little more information, but none was forthcoming, which was not unusual for Withers, so he didn't push any further. The negotiator's visit had clearly been of no importance.

But the negotiator's visit had been of vast importance. Jess Manning had had an extraordinary impact upon Matt. What had happened? Both times as they'd shaken hands it had seemed as though an electric current had run from her fingers into his. Hadn't she felt it? She certainly hadn't appeared to. He'd tried to fob it off as a normal reaction, just some form of static electricity, but through-out the whole of their meeting he'd continued to feel an inexplicable connection to the woman. So much so that he'd found it necessary to put up a wall. Stick strictly to business, he'd told himself, don't let your guard down whatever you do. But why? he'd wondered. Why did he feel vulnerable? What was going on?

The more Matt pondered the question, the less he could come up with an answer. Jess Manning was an attractive young woman, certainly, but the compulsion of his feeling toward her had not been sexual. It had been something magnetic, a force, a field of energy he'd felt himself being drawn to. And when they'd shaken hands that last time, the connection between them had extended well beyond the touch of their fingers. A tingling sensation had run right up his arm, yet she'd appeared to notice nothing. What the hell was going on?

He wondered if the same thing would happen when he saw her on Saturday, and the more he wondered, the more he looked forward to finding out.

CHAPTER SEVEN

Matt slept fitfully that night, which was unusual. He was a good sleeper as a rule and not given to dreams, not ones he was particularly aware of anyway, just vague images that faded shortly after waking. But he dreamt that night. And the images, vivid as they were, stayed with him long after waking.

In his dream he saw, as if from far above, a long line of surveyors' pegs hammered into the ground, but the ground was not the dried red earth of the Northern Territory: the ground was mud, thick, black mud. And the flora was not the flora of the Northern Territory. In place of spinifex and acacias and groves of mulga were ferns and giant teak trees and thick stands of bamboo. This was not desert country: this was jungle.

Men were working in this jungle, hundreds upon hundreds, possibly thousands of men, it appeared from on high where he soared with his eagle's-eye view. Emaciated and half naked, the teams of men slaved with the most basic of tools – axes and ropes and bars – grubbing out giant teak trees and breaking up rock, following the endless line of surveyors' pegs. They were being beaten as they laboured, their persecutors mercilessly whipping them on despite the seeming impossibility of their task. Here and there a man succumbed to the beatings and fell into the mud, but his companions hauled him to his feet and side by side they continued to work on down the line. These men, Matt realised, were building a rail corridor.

The images were disturbing and remained with him throughout the day as he pondered their meaning. He could come up with only one conclusion: he'd been dreaming of his grandfather. The men in his dream had been working on the Death Railway, he decided, the infamous line over four hundred kilometres long that the Japanese had built from Siam to Burma during World War II. Prisoners of war had been used as slave labour to build the railway and thousands upon thousands of lives had been lost in the process. His grandfather's had been one of them.

Matt could see the connection: it made sense. His father's stories about the heroism and mateship of those men who had suffered so terribly had made a deep impression upon him as a child.

'I never knew my dad, but his name was Charles Matthew Witherton and they called him Charlie,' Dave had said. 'Mum didn't know she was pregnant when Charlie went off to war. She reckoned I was probably around a year old when he died on the Burma Railway, but she couldn't be sure. My God, Matt, you've only got to read about the hell those men went through . . .'

Here he was working on the Ghan and his grandfather had worked on the Burma Railway. It would appear his subconscious mind had associated the two, but why now? He'd been working on the Ghan for well over eight months – why hadn't he made the subconscious connection earlier?

The mystery deepened that night when he was visited by a further dream, and this time the images were far more than disturbing, this time they were horrendous. No longer floating safely above the scene: he was now in the thick of the horror, moving down the line, an invisible spectator walking with the men. He could hear the wheeze of breath in throats and the rattle of lungs in chests as weakened, emaciated bodies were forced to perform feats far beyond their capacity, yet amazingly enough and through sheer will succeeding in their tasks.

Here men were clearing jungle, there men breaking rock, and further back down the line, like beasts of burden, were men carting sleepers and iron rails on hunched, bony shoulders. And every last one had the look of death. Cadaverous bodies with skull-like faces, jaundiced eyes that bulged from sockets, ulcerated flesh rotting through to the bone, yet still these men worked on. And still where they could they helped those of their comrades who had fallen under the frenzied clubs of Japanese guards – the guards themselves driven by the fanatical order of their Emperor. It seemed master and slave shared one common obsession: the line must keep moving forwards.

There were some though unable to move at all, men beyond help who lay dead or dying in the monsoon mud, their mates forced to leave them where they had fallen.

Matt wondered which of the soldiers might be Charlie and moving unseen among them he started his search. Was Charlie one of those still clinging to life or had he suc- cumbed to the mud? The dream, already horrific, quickly reached nightmare proportions as he peered desperately into men's faces, seeing close-up the pus of their sores, smelling the foetid breath from their rotting guts, seeking somewhere among them a likeness to the one faded photo- graph he'd seen of his grandfather.

No answer was revealed and, after another fitful night, Saturday morning found him as tired as if he'd not slept at all; the images of his dream were still etched in his mind. He was annoyed that they should remain to haunt him and did his best to dismiss them – what purpose was served by dwelling upon the hell those soldiers had experienced? Nothing could be gained except sleepless nights. Why was this happening to him?

The weekends were layoff time for Matt and his team, and while the others drove over to Aileron for a day at the roadhouse, he spent the morning doing paperwork. Then after lunch in the canteen he set off for Alice Springs, as had been his intention even before he'd agreed to meet Jess and the aunties. He would book into the Heavitree Gap Hotel for the night as he always did during his brief visits to Alice. The hotel was cheap and comfortable and, situated at the base of the MacDonnell Ranges beside the Gap after which it was named, only a few minutes from the town's centre. Heavitree Gap itself, a natural breach in the MacDonnell Ranges, formed the impressive gateway to Alice Springs, allowing entry through the mighty rock edifices that protected the south of the town like a fortress.

Matt planned his day as he drove. He'd book into the hotel first, then after his meeting with Jess and the women elders, he'd have a drink at the Todd Tavern followed by dinner at a restaurant. It was good to get away from the donga camps now and then.

She was waiting outside the block of flats in Undoolya Road dressed again in khaki shorts, sleeveless shirt and boots much the same as his. Regardless of gender, theirs was the uniform of the outback worker.

He pulled the Land Rover up and jumped from the driver's seat. 'G'day, Jess,' he said, circling the car and extending his hand, interested to discover whether there would be another frisson upon contact. There wasn't, just the pleasurable experience of a strong firm handshake.

'Hello, Matt.' Jess was a little surprised by the handshake, it seemed unnecessary, but was pleased they were now on a mutual first-name footing. She noted the Elastoplast had gone and the eye was no longer puffy – just a small nick below the eyebrow remained. Perhaps the fight was the reason he was so uptight, she thought, he's certainly more relaxed today. 'Your car or mine?' she asked.

'Mine,' he said, opening the passenger door for her. 'Hop in and show me the way.'

She directed him to the Aboriginal community on the outskirts of town, a cluster of cottages and shacks for the most part, village-like, with a communal open area in the centre. There was junk littered about and bombed-out cars here and there and the houses were in various states of disrepair, but Aunty Pam's where they were to meet was tidy and trim and complete with front garden. Even the most delinquent of youths did not dare desecrate Aunty Pam's property.

The meeting with the aunties was a resounding success. Pam, Jill and Molly were pleased that the surveyor boss had seen fit to pay them a personal visit and welcomed him with open arms, making cups of tea, and introducing him to the various grandchildren they were babysitting before getting down to business.

Then two hours later ... 'We appreciate you going to all this trouble,' Pam said formally at the conclusion of the meeting. She was speaking for the three of them, Jill and Molly equally formal nodding their agreement, 'and we'd like to thank you on behalf of the women of our community.'

Pam was the first to offer her hand then vigorous hand-shakes ensued all around. The aunties were far more than pleased. The aunties were proud, very proud, that the surveyor boss had paid them a personal visit, and on their home ground, where his arrival had been witnessed by all. It showed great respect.

Following the handshakes, Jess was embraced by each of the women in turn.

'You done good bringing Matt here, Jess,' Pam said, sharing a broad grin with the surveyor boss now that the formalities were over, 'you done real good.'

During the drive back to Undoolya Road, Jess offered her own vote of thanks. 'Well I scored a big win there,' she said. 'I owe you one, Matt. It really was good of you, thanks a lot.'

'All part of the service,' he said and he added with a smile that was genuine, 'they're a great bunch, your aunties.'

'Yes, they are, aren't they?' She was glad he'd noticed.

They pulled up outside the flat. 'Want to have a drink at the Todd Tavern?' he asked.

'Sure.' She didn't hesitate for a moment. 'Hang on, I'll just grab a jumper.' It was approaching dusk and soon the cold would set in.

Jess dashed into the flat and reappeared seconds later with a woollen sweater. She was pleased he'd suggested the tavern. She'd thought that by way of thanks she should really invite him in for a drink, but she hadn't wanted him to get the wrong idea. Not that he appeared the type who would, but she remained wary nonetheless. She was always wary these days.

They drove back across the river into town. They could have left the car outside her place and walked across the footbridge as she normally did, but she didn't suggest it as an option for the same wary reason – she wanted to avoid the need to return to her place.

'So where do you come from, Jess? Are you a local?' Seated in the front bar with the beers he'd bought them, Matt opened the conversation. As usual he was far more interested in talking about others rather than himself, and he found Jess Manning a most intriguing young woman.

'Yep,' she said, 'but I didn't grow up here. My mum was Western Arunta, my dad's Irish ...' He noted the tense and wondered whether her mother was dead or simply not around. '... which makes me Aboriginal-Irish.' She grinned as she added the catch-phrase from her childhood: 'An exotic mix, as Dad likes to say.'

'Dad's right. You are.'

'Hardly exotic.' She gave a derisive snort.

'Intriguing though,' he said, 'very intriguing.'

She wondered what the comment signified and searched for a hidden implication. She'd been doing that a lot lately, well, ever since Roger: she no longer took people at face value as she once had. Was Matt Witherton flattering her or was he patronising her? Neither, she realised, watching him as he calmly sipped at his beer. He was just saying what he thought.

'Thank you,' she replied. 'Intriguing's much better than exotic.'

'Where did you study, Jess?' Matt was equally intrigued by her academic background. He'd met professional negotiators before when he'd been working on mining operations in Western Australia, and as a rule they'd been white and male, highly qualified anthropologists and linguists employed by government and private enterprise to conduct Aboriginal site surveys and confer with Indigenous landowners. A female negotiator was rare in Matt's experience and an Aboriginal female negotiator unheard of. He was both intrigued and impressed.

'Sydney Uni,' she replied. 'I was born in Sydney, grew up there.'

'And what was your major? Anthropology, I presume?'

'Yep. Then after a PhD in English I focused on Indigenous languages, particularly those of the central desert. I had a bit of a head start there because I'd grown up speaking Arunta with Mum.'

'That's really impressive,' he said admiringly. 'I bet your parents were proud.'

'Dad was. Mum never got to see me graduate, she never even saw me go to uni. She died when I was sixteen.' Jess's manner was business-like; she was just stating the facts.

'Oh, what a pity, how sad.' He was neither confronted by the disclosure nor compelled to offer sympathy, she noted, but his reaction could not have been more genuine. 'How very, very sad,' he said.

'Yes it was,' she admitted, 'it was terribly sad. Mum died under tragic circumstances. She was a beautiful woman, but a lost soul in many ways, not knowing who she was, a black woman in a white world. That's why Dad was so keen for me to embrace both cultures.'

'A wise man obviously.'

'Yes,' Jess gave a light laugh, 'he's not at all bad for an Irish muso.' She felt self-conscious that she'd shared such intimacies with a virtual stranger, but Matt's sincerity had demanded an honest response. 'My round,' she said and polishing off the last of her beer she rose and crossed to the bar.

She was back five minutes later.

'So what about you, Matt?' she said, determined to change the subject. 'What's your story?' And placing the beers on the table she sat expectantly.

'Not much of a story at all,' he replied with a shrug. 'Adelaide boy, following in father's footsteps, dad a surveyor, that sort of thing . . .' He was about to fob her off in his customary manner when he felt the strangest compulsion. I must tell her about my dream, he thought, and even as he wondered why he would consider such a thing, a voice started urging him on. *Tell her*, the voice said, *tell her, tell her*, over and over, insistent, demanding, and he found himself unable to resist. 'There is something I'd like to share with you actually. I don't know why, but . . .' He halted, unsure how to begin.

'Go on, Matt,' she said encouragingly. It was Jess who was now intrigued. This bewildering man who fluctuated from remote to caring, but who appeared at all times supremely confident, seemed suddenly unsure of himself.

'I had a dream last night,' Matt heard himself say, 'as a matter of fact I've had a similar dream for the past two nights and I believe it has something to do with my grandfather . . .'

Why am I telling her this, he wondered, why? But he'd started now and he couldn't stop. The normally detached

Matt Witherton, who made a habit of revealing nothing of himself to others, now could not stop talking. He told her about the dreams he'd had, recounting them to her in their every horrific detail. He told her about the grandfather he'd never known who had died working on the Burma Railway.

'His name was Charlie,' he said, 'he was around twenty-seven years old when he died and he never knew he had a son. He didn't even know his wife was pregnant when he went to war. My father was born after Charlie was taken prisoner.'

Why am I pouring out the whole family history? he thought. But still he couldn't stop. He told her of his desperate search for Charlie in the dream that had become a nightmare, and he told her of his conclusion that there must be some connection between his grandfather working on the Burma Railway and him working on the Ghan.

'I suppose there's some parallel that can be drawn between the two,' he said, fumbling desperately to make sense of it all, 'but why my subconscious mind would choose to make the connection now and with such force, I really don't know.'

Then the words stopped tumbling out and he came to a halt. 'I'm sorry,' he said after a moment or so. 'I can't imagine why on earth I told you all that. I just felt some insane need to –' He broke off, convinced he must appear quite ridiculous. 'Something seemed to demand I share my dream with you and . . .' He shook his head confused. 'I'm sorry, really sorry. I don't know what got in to me. I don't know what's going on.'

She could see he was lost, perplexed. Even in the very short time of their acquaintance it had become clear to Jess that this was not a man accustomed to experiencing confusion, and in the face of his obvious discomfort she couldn't help feeling sympathetic. She was relieved – when he'd started to speak so personally, she'd wondered for one brief moment whether he might be coming on to her. She was quite sure now that he was not. She was quite sure now that she knew exactly what was going on.

'Do you believe in an afterlife, Matt?' she asked abruptly.

'A what?' He was taken aback by the non sequitur.

'The spirit world,' she said, 'do you believe in the spirit world?'

'No.' Where the hell is this going? he wondered.

'I didn't think so.' She gave a brisk nod, which only mystified him further. 'I do,' she said, 'I believe implicitly in the spirit world, which means that I find all of this quite simple. Your grandfather is making contact with you.' She ignored the dumbfounded stare that greeted her remark. 'I don't know what Charlie's trying to tell you, but he's out to make contact – of that I'm quite sure. He's sending those images so you'll know who he is.'

Matt made no reply, remaining agog at the mere thought of such a possibility, so she continued. 'It wasn't just *something* demanding you share your dream with me, Matt, it was your grandfather.' She smiled. His expression of sheer disbelief amused her. 'Charlie knows you're a non-believer and he wants me to convince you he's around so that you'll listen to what he has to tell you. Am I making any sense at all?'

'Ah ... I'm not really sure.' He gave a noncommittal shrug, not wishing to offend, but finding the whole idea utterly fanciful.

Jess laughed, aware she'd made no inroads. 'Who knows, perhaps Charlie's even channelling himself through me,' she said jokingly. 'I must say I've never thought of myself as a spiritual medium, but anything's possible.'

Matt decided not to tell her of the weird sensation he'd experienced when they'd first shaken hands and the connection he'd felt upon their meeting, God only knew what she'd come up with if he did.

Jess's smile faded as she made one last serious attempt to convince him. 'You really should give this some thought, Matt. We blackfellas believe the link with our ancestors is strong, very strong and that when they visit us it's usually for a reason, perhaps to ask something of us, or perhaps to give us a warning. If your grandfather is trying to communicate with you, and I'm quite sure he is, you must make yourself accessible, you mustn't put up walls.'

She leant back, beer in hand. 'End of lecture,' she announced, lightening the moment, 'but don't be alarmed if the dreams re-occur; just go with the flow and see what happens.'

He picked up his own glass. 'I'll do my best,' he said. They acknowledged a brief salute and took a swig of their beers. 'Thanks, Jess,' he added, 'and I really mean that.' It was doubtful she would ever convert him, but he was grateful for the attempt. And he felt strangely unburdened by the recounting of his dream. They had shared something. That much he could not deny. 'You've been a great help. I'm not sure exactly how,' he admitted, 'but you have.'

'Good, I'm very glad to hear it.' Then she added glibly, 'I was a bit worried at first, I thought you might be coming on to me.' The words slipped out with ease, but she was aware that she meant them as a gentle warning.

'Good God no,' his response was so immediate that he hoped he hadn't offended. 'Not that you're not extremely attractive,' he added with a grin, and she certainly was, 'but a relationship is the last thing I'm after.' He'd recognised from the outset that Jess Manning was not the sort to be briefly bedded, and one-night stands interspersed with the odd casual fling was the only sex Matt was interested in. He hadn't had a serious relationship for close on a decade, not since Angie's death. He doubted he ever would. Even after all these years the memory of Angie and the love they'd shared remained so strongly with him that he couldn't encompass the thought of commitment to another woman.

'The last thing I'm after too,' Jess said agreeably. 'Once bitten twice shy as far as I'm concerned. Here's to friendship,' and they clinked glasses.

They had one more beer after that and then parted company, Jess saying three was her limit. They'd exchanged phone numbers and he was enjoying her company so much he would have liked to have asked her to join him for dinner, or at least arrange to meet up again, but he didn't, sensing for the first time that there was something vulnerable beneath this young woman's confident exterior. 'Once bitten twice shy,' she'd said, and he hadn't pursued the topic – it was none of his business.

She refused his offer of a lift home, she liked walking over the footbridge, and they said their good nights outside the Tavern.

'Let me know if Charlie pays another visit,' she said in such a casual manner that he really couldn't tell whether or not she was joking. 'I'm quite sure he will and I'm dying to find out what he's so keen to impart.'

They were both aware that a genuine friendship had been established and in Jess's case it came as a great relief. Friendships with white men she was happy to embrace, relationships with white men she was not. She did not want a relationship of any kind, not now while her wounds were still healing, but most particularly she did not want a relationship with a white man. Never again, she thought, her mind on Roger as she walked across the footbridge.

Professor Roger Macready had been Jess's mentor during her PhD days. He'd also been her hero, but then he'd been the hero of every student fortunate enough to experience the one-on-one tutorials he conducted in his private office at Sydney University. A charismatic man who flaunted convention, he was the antithesis of the crusty academics whose lectures they were accustomed to sitting through day after day. Even his appearance set him apart from the norm; wiry, athletic, brown hair flecking attractively and prematurely grey, a beard that was neatly clipped as a rule, but on occasions wild and unkempt, signalling he'd just returned from a field trip to some remote region.

Roger Macready had come to the fore as a young anthropologist in the early eighties when he was contracted to supervise a series of Aboriginal site surveys in Western Australia. The Burrup Peninsula was being opened up for mining and the offer of employment had come, strangely enough, from the WA Museum. The Museum Board was the vested authority for Aboriginal sites under the *Aboriginal Heritage Act 1972*, and therefore responsible for employing the necessary experts to survey the project area. Given the times, it was hardly surprising that the Anthropology department was undergoing a boom at the University of Western Australia, but as yet there had been no fully qualified anthropologists in the state, so the museum had hired a number of undergraduate and Honours students and a job offer had been put out to the eastern states for an expert to lead the team. Roger's application had been accepted and, aged twenty-seven, he'd found himself at the vanguard of career opportunities previously not available to the average anthropologist, whose path was destined to follow more conventional academic lines. The controversial mix of petroleum drilling rights, mining leases and Aboriginal heritage sites was opening up a whole new world for those anthropologists prepared to 'go bush'.

It wasn't long before Roger Macready's services were called upon throughout the country in areas where mining and other outback development projects were proposed, and the experience gained from his field trips readily served the further pursuit of his academic studies. Roger had the best of both worlds. He was an acknowledged authority in the practical field of Aboriginal site surveys and an academically respected anthropologist specialising in Indigenous culture, most particularly ancient artworks, which he'd embraced with a passion. From the petroglyphs of the Burrup Peninsula, where all Aboriginal art was in the form of rock carvings, to the ochre and kaolin paintings of the central desert people, Roger, now Professor Macready, was a recognised expert.

By the time Jess had come into Roger's life he'd carved out a very tidy niche for himself. At thirty-seven he enjoyed the freedom of field trips that took him away from the world of academia while basking also in the respect accorded him upon his return to Sydney University. Most particularly he enjoyed sharing the passion of his work with the eager young students who attended his private tutorials. Roger loved firing up his students. The enflaming of youthful minds kept him young himself and lent vibrancy to his life.

But he hadn't been prepared for Jess. She'd taken him by surprise. He'd looked forward to tutoring his first Aboriginal student, certainly. The irony of teaching a young Indigenous woman the history and culture of her own people was not lost on him and he'd anticipated the exercise would prove both interesting and stimulating. But he hadn't taken into account the young woman herself. She was far more than an educated city version of the Aboriginal people he'd come to know during his outback travels. She was quite simply mesmeric. At least, she was to him. Everything about Jessica Manning, her personality, her complete lack of pretension, her intelligence, and not least of all her looks had captivated him right from the start. That grace, so assured, so unconsciously sensual – he'd found her irresistible. Well, not exactly irresistible for he *had* resisted, of course he had, he always did. He'd been confronted by any number of highly attractive students over the years, many of whom had made it obvious they would like to push the boundaries of the student–tutor relationship, but never once had he faltered. It was a tantalisingly enjoyable, albeit frustrating, element of his job to be in the presence of desirable young women yet maintain distance at all times. Jessica Manning, however, was pushing the boundaries to their limit. He'd found it extremely difficult to disassociate himself from the physical effect she had upon him.

Twenty-three-year-old Jess had felt much the same way, although she hadn't analysed her reaction with the same objectivity, probably due to her lack of experience. She'd presumed she was suffering a severe case of hero worship like every other student who took private tutorials with Professor Macready.

'Christ alive, there should be more around like Roger,' Ben, a fellow Anthrop student, had said when she'd told him she'd signed up for one-on-one sessions. 'It'd make study a damn sight easier and a hell of a lot more fun.'

The female students were equally vociferous in their praise, but offered an additional comment. 'You'll adore Roger,' Vivian had said, 'he's drop-dead gorgeous.' Professor Macready was always 'Roger' to his students.

Jess had accepted the fact that she was just another of the loyal followers worshipping in Roger Macready's wake and she'd given herself up to the cerebral love affair he appeared to have with all his students. In any event his tutorials were certainly assisting her with her PhD study.

Then came the field trip to Alice Springs. It was late in the year during the Christmas holidays of 1995. Roger was to conduct some surveys of Aboriginal heritage sites that could be affected by the proposed extension of the Ghan railway line from Alice Springs to Darwin. Government money was funding the exercise, just as it was funding everything else that related to the Ghan project: the land surveys, the mapping of the route, the negotiations with Indigenous landowners, the whole process had been going on for years and in all likelihood would go on for many more before the enterprise would be given the green light. By now the exercise appeared futile to many, but not to Roger, whose purposes were being excellently served. Here was yet another perfect opportunity to conduct research. He would visit sites and take photographs and collate material for the next paper he proposed to present to the Australian Anthropological Society.

'Would you like to accompany me on a field trip?' he'd asked casually toward the end of an afternoon tutorial. 'I depart for your neck of the woods in a month or so – I'll be heading for Alice Springs.' He knew Jess was Western Arunta and that her mother had come from Hermannsburg; there had been avid discussion about her ancestry. 'I'll be camping out rough for a good month or so, but you might like to tag along for the first few days when I'm based in Alice. Could be interesting to visit some sites together,' he'd added, 'and perhaps we might call in on your family. I'd very much like to meet them.'

The prospect had thrilled Jess immeasurably. Other students had accompanied Roger on field trips from time to time and they'd always come back raving about the experience. Jess herself had made several research trips to central Australia and another could only serve her well at this stage of her studies; she was hoping to complete her PhD by the end of the following year.

'When do we leave?' she'd asked eagerly.

Although she was to pay her own expenses, Roger had been only too happy to make all the arrangements. He'd booked the flights and car hire and accommodation in advance, everything strictly above board, a very respectable motel even ensuring their rooms were well apart, a factor he took into account whenever accompanied by a student in order to avoid any possible innuendo. He had no intention of taking advantage, it was more than his job and his reputation were worth, but Roger was very much looking forward to Jess's company.

Toby had happily provided the funds for his daughter's excursion, although he hadn't been able to resist a passing remark.

'Off with the Prof for a long weekend,' he'd said with raised eyebrow, 'sounds a bit suss to me.'

'Don't be ridiculous, Dad.' Her response had been flippant. 'He's my tutor for God's sake.'

'Oh well, well, well now,' he'd said, his Irish lilt adding weight to the mockery of his remark, 'that makes everything all right, doesn't it? You need to read more novels, girl. Tutors? They're the worst kind.'

At which she'd just laughed.

But something *had* happened on that trip, something that should have been trivial, summarily dismissed by them both, but hadn't been. Jess would never forget that day.

They'd visited her family at Hermannsburg. Aunty May had been warm and welcoming, as had the other members of the family, all pleasantly well-behaved. It was a Tuesday morning and 'pay-cheques' were over a week away, so they weren't on the drink. Young Millie hadn't been there because young Millie, now nineteen and her grandmother's pride and joy, was in Darwin studying to be a teacher.

'All your doing, Jess,' Aunty May had said. 'Millie wants to be like you, wants to learn and give back to her people. She's smart that girl, real smart.'

Jess had visited her family twice during her research trips to the Centre, the first time being again in the company of her father. Both occasions had been joyful affairs and she'd wondered why this particular visit had ended up feeling a little awkward. Perhaps it was Roger's insistence upon photographs, although why that should bother her she wasn't sure – he'd asked permission politely enough. Or perhaps she'd simply felt self-conscious about having arrived with a stranger and a white man at that. She'd never felt self-conscious arriving with her father, but then her father was family, which she supposed made things different. She couldn't figure it out, but she'd felt a vague sense of relief when they'd left.

Upon their return to town, Roger had driven out along the Ross Road to Emily Gap in the Heavitree Range of the East MacDonnells ten kilometres from Alice Springs. Anthwerrke, as Emily Gap was known to the Eastern Arunta, was a site of great spiritual importance, and he'd wanted to share with her the ancient rock paintings of the Caterpillar Dreaming.

Jess had visited the site during a previous trip, but had been unable to view the paintings themselves as the creek that ran through the Gap had been flowing, rendering them inaccessible. She was glad now to be seeing the ancient works for the very first time in the company of Roger. The rock paintings of the Caterpillar Dreaming were of immense significance to the people born in the region of Alice Springs and it seemed right she should view them with an expert respectful of their true meaning.

There was no-one else around, no vehicle in sight, no adventurous tourist wandering off the beaten track, and the silence was total as they crossed the sandy creek bed towards the towering rocks that formed the walls of the Gap.

To Jess the mighty rock faces, fiery red in the afternoon light, seemed alive, sentinels ready to spring into action should the treasure they guarded come under threat. She was in awe of the life she felt in everything around her. The very land itself seemed to throb, pulse-like, a living, breathing entity. Little wonder Anthwerrke is a sacred site to the people of Mparntwe, she thought, here in this home of their ancestral beings the spiritual presence is palpable.

Upon reaching the paintings, which sat side by side at the base of the massive rock face, they examined each closely, a series of stylised images painted in red ochre and white lime, large, bold and perfectly preserved over the millennia.

'Amazing, aren't they?' Roger's voice was hushed. 'Quite, quite amazing.'

She simply nodded.

The paintings were sharply delineated horizontal lines that ran parallel to each other. Each line was drawn with precision and each painting differed slightly from its companions, here several dots added, here a line at odds with the symmetry. The impression was one of a series of tracks punctuated by landmarks as was no doubt the artist's intention.

'Yeperenye, Ntyarlke, Utnjerrengatye . . .' Roger named the Caterpillars of the Dreamtime Story, the three ancestral beings who had formed Anthwerrke itself, and much of the topography surrounding Mparntwe. 'The Caterpillar Dreaming trail started from here at this very site,' he said as he gazed at the paintings. 'You wonder just how old these are, don't you?' he mused as much to himself as to Jess. 'You wonder exactly how many millennia.'

They sat themselves down in the sand and remained gazing at the paintings, Roger marvelling at their antiquity, Jess in a state of sheer wonderment at the mystical presence she felt surrounding her. She had never experienced such a sensation before, and she had never in her life expected to. She could feel the softest touch on her skin, as tactile as anything human, yet no person was there. A spiritual being is welcoming me to this place, she told herself, enraptured by the thought.

Several minutes must have passed as the two sat in silence, and by now Jess was unaware that Roger was no longer studying the paintings, Roger was studying her.

Roger had been lost the moment he'd glanced at her. He'd been about to suggest it was time they were going, but he hadn't said a word, he'd just stared at her instead, her expression, one of rapture, holding him spellbound. She's transported, he thought, she's in a state of euphoria.

He knew he was intruding as he leaned in to kiss her. He knew he should break the spell and bring them both back to reality. But he couldn't help himself. He wanted to share that euphoria.

Jess was not shocked by the kiss, nor was her reverie shattered, but rather enhanced. As their lips met, she wondered whether Roger, too, had felt the spiritual presence, but if not, no matter. For this brief moment and in this sacred place they were sharing something intensely special.

The kiss was lingering, sensual, but he did not gather her to him, he did not even place a hand upon her. There was no contact between them but the touch of their lips.

They pulled back and Roger rose to his feet. He'd shocked himself. He'd never transgressed with a student before.

'Time to go,' he said as if the incident had not happened at all.

Jess stood, also making no comment, but knowing that things between them would never be the same. Her feeling for Roger Macready was not a severe case of hero worship as she'd persuaded herself it was. She was in love with the man. Perhaps she always had been.

Much as Roger might have wished to delude himself, he too recognised the change in the status quo. Jessica Manning was no longer a tempting distraction to be admired from a distance. He wanted her now, and not just physically: he wanted to make her his, to possess her totally. He was prepared to wait however. It would prove difficult he was sure, but he sensed very strongly that his feelings were reciprocated.

It proved difficult for them both. Not a word was said about that day in the desert and they pretended to ignore the unspoken promise that hovered in the air. Jess took her lead from Roger. If he'd made the slightest overture she would have succumbed, but he didn't. They both knew they were biding their time until she had finished her PhD. They both knew that the moment she was no longer a student they would become lovers. The future held no surprise for either, only exquisite anticipation.

But a little over a year later, in early 1997 when Jess had received her doctorate, it turned out there was a surprise.

'Marry me, Jess.' Roger's original intention had not been to propose, but the torturous, tantalising existence of the past year had convinced him he wanted nothing less than marriage to Jess. She was young, a whole fourteen years his junior – how else could he ensure she would remain his? And he'd decided to make his proposal before they slept together as a declaration of his serious intent.

Jess had been amazed. A marriage proposal was the last thing she'd expected. It had taken her by such surprise that she'd actually laughed. 'Don't you think you should sample the goods first?' she'd said, already knowing her answer was yes.

They'd made love that same night in Roger's attractive Double Bay flat overlooking the water, and the sex had been every bit as exciting as each had anticipated. In fact it had been the best sex either had experienced, although in Jess's case she'd had little by way of comparison. She'd had only one previous lover, Payu, a talented young musician she'd met through a band whose album was being recorded at her father's studio. Payungka McPherson was Aboriginal-Scottish and they'd had a great deal in common, at least that's what Payu had maintained. He'd been a nice young man and they'd had a good time, but she'd not been 'in love' as such. In truth she'd only embarked upon the affair because she'd thought at the age of twenty-two the loss of her virginity was well overdue. She'd been left feeling more than a little guilty six months later when Payu, very much in love, had wanted to marry her.

Jess had found sex with Payu a highly pleasurable experience, but with Roger it was something else altogether. Being passionately in love was a powerful aphrodisiac.

Roger Macready had been her hero and mentor for the past three years and now he was her lover. Both in and out of bed he was the most exciting man she'd ever known.

As for Roger, all his erotic fantasies had come to fruition. The girl who'd captivated him the moment she'd first walked into his office, the girl he'd found so irresistible, was everything he'd imagined she might be, and more. She was uninhibited in bed, but above all it was the feel of her that drove him to untold heights. Her skin was like satin, exquisite to the touch. He'd never slept with an Aboriginal girl, and the outback phrase he'd heard bandied about by white cattle men came instantly to mind. 'Black velvet, mate,' he recalled one saying, 'you won't want another white woman after you've had a taste of black velvet.' Offensive as most might find the remark Roger secretly couldn't help but agree.

They'd married only two months later in a low-key civil ceremony – Roger's idea, but Jess hadn't minded in the least.

Toby, however, had had a few words to say on the subject. 'Don't you want a bit of fanfare?' he'd queried disapprovingly. 'A wedding should be a big day in a young woman's life.'

Jess had grinned and turned the moment into a joke, knowing the criticism was directed at Roger. 'You reckon I should have a white wedding, do you, Dad?'

But Toby hadn't responded to the joke. 'You know exactly what I mean,' he'd said tartly.

'You and Mum didn't have any fanfare,' she'd replied with an air of one-upmanship, 'you married at the Registry Office and then went straight out on tour; you told me so yourself.'

'Altogether different. Your mother and I couldn't afford to do anything else,' the inference clearly being that Roger could, 'and as father of the bride I'm more than happy to foot the bill, you both know that,' another dig at Roger.

Jess hadn't bothered arguing further. She was aware her father didn't particularly like Roger and she sensed the feeling might be mutual. On the several occasions of their meeting Roger had always been pleasant to Toby, as indeed had Toby to him, but it was evident that the two didn't really gel somehow. A pity, she thought. Both white men who'd chosen to marry black women, they could have shared a great deal.

After gaining her doctorate Jess had accepted an appointment to the lecturing staff of the University of New South Wales. She could have applied to Sydney University, but Roger had suggested it might be better for their respective careers if they observed a little distance, and she'd agreed. Personally she would have preferred to apply for a job that took her to remote regions and allowed her to deal with Indigenous concerns, but as Roger had said there was time enough for that. They could perhaps look at hiring themselves out as a team a little further down the track, he'd suggested. The idea was so appealing to Jess that she'd been more than happy to bide her time and lead an academic existence for a year or so.

Following their marriage, life became far more hectic than she'd expected. She hadn't realised what a broad circle of friends Roger had. Not many were particularly close, they were colleagues for the most part, but the various cliques, academic and corporate and even political with whom he mingled were all highly social. There seemed to be a continuous round of conferences and dinners and fundraising functions of some kind or other.

'Who would have guessed you'd turn out to be such a social butterfly?' she'd complained one night as they dressed for yet another cocktail party. 'I might not have married you if I'd known.' The comment was made jokingly, but her criticism was genuine. This was the third function they'd attended in a week and she would far rather have stayed home.

'Got to keep everyone on side, my love,' he'd replied with a smile, 'they're the bread and butter after all.' He'd kissed her, running his fingers over her shoulders and arms. 'Besides, I like to show off my beautiful, intelligent, talented young wife,' he'd said as he unzipped the dress he'd only just zipped up. They'd been late for the cocktail party that night.

The first major sign of trouble came barely a month later at an event held in the Sydney Town Hall to welcome the American National Geographic team. A four-part series of television specials was to be filmed all around Australia, one in a number of such series the Americans were making on the flora and fauna of ancient regions of the world, and the project, huge as it was, had attracted attention from all quarters. The several hundred guests milling about the grand ballroom of the Town Hall was a veritable potpourri of the academic, artistic and commercial, with a number of politicians thrown in.

Upon arrival, Roger and Jess accepted a glass of wine each and started to mingle. Within only minutes Roger was introduced by a colleague to several of the National Geographic team, including Professor Neil Hemsley, the American scientist who was to host the series. Hemsley, a highly qualified and much respected naturalist, had become a familiar face to television viewers worldwide via the documentaries he'd co-produced and hosted over recent years.

Roger in turn introduced Jess.

'And this is my wife, Jess Macready,' he said to the company in general, 'Doctor Macready, actually,' he added.

Jess always felt self-conscious when he referred to her as 'Doctor', which he often did, particularly in academic circles. She never used the title herself. 'People think you're a GP and start telling you their medical problems,' she'd say, 'it's too confusing. I'm not a real doctor at all.'

'Of course you are,' he'd insist, 'don't be so self-deprecating: you worked hard for your doctorate, you deserve it and I'm very, very proud of you.'

Professor Hemsley shook Jess's hand. He was a pleasantly innocuous-looking man. Middle-aged and on the beefy side, he could have seemed commonplace had it not been for the fiercely intelligent glint in his eyes.

'So what's your background, Dr Macready?' he asked with a curiosity that was disarmingly genuine. 'Where exactly are you from?'

Jess was accustomed to people asking about her antecedents, they so often did, some directly, some indirectly. She preferred the direct approach and, as always, was more than happy to supply the answer.

'My mother was Western Arunta from the central desert of Australia ...' she replied, gaining immediate interest from the American and a nod of approval from Roger, then she added '... and my Dad's Irish.' Hemsley's attention remained focused upon her, so she continued. 'He's a muso actually –' She was going to explain that the two had met in Sydney, but she didn't get any further.

'He's not exactly a *musician*, darling,' Roger interrupted, correcting her good-humouredly, 'your father's a sound engineer. It's not quite the same thing.'

'He's a sound engineer who just happens to be one of the best in the country,' she responded, trying not to sound brittle.

'Indeed he is,' Roger agreed, and he turned back to the group of Americans. 'Toby operates a very successful recording studio in Balmain,' he said with a smile, 'and his work is highly recognised in the rock industry.' It should have sounded like a compliment to her father but it didn't. Roger's tone was that of a parent indulging a child.

Jess hadn't pursued the matter, but she'd fumed throughout the evening. And later that night when they arrived home she confronted him.

'Why did you do that?' she demanded.

'Do what?' His response was the personification of innocence.

'Why did you put Dad down the way you did?'

'What on earth are you talking about?' He still appeared mystified.

'When we met Hemsley,' she reminded him and this time her voice really was brittle, 'you said Dad wasn't a muso.'

'Oh that.' He shrugged off the matter as if it was of no consequence.

'Yes *that*,' she said emphatically.

'Do you know what you sounded like, my love?' He shook his head and she was astonished by the fact that he actually appeared amused. 'Couldn't you hear yourself? "My dad's Irish, he's a muso" – do you know how that sounds?'

She was confounded. 'So? What's wrong with the way it sounds? You've heard it before. I've said it often enough.'

'Not to people like Hemsley, Jess, not in academic circles – it's a ridiculously juvenile turn of phrase. You've moved on from there, my darling, truly you have.'

That same tone, Jess thought, patronising and somehow indulgent, as if I'm a child. And what the hell does he mean? I've moved on from *where*? I've moved on *from* where, *to* where? She was bewildered. Roger had always loved her lack of pretension. He'd been fascinated by the fact that despite years of academic study she'd remained essentially unchanged: he'd told her so. 'Intellectuals tend to lose their ability to respond instinctively,' he'd said, 'or rather they tend to distrust intuition in their need to over-analyse anything and everything they encounter. But not you, Jess, you've always remained true to yourself, true to who you really are. It's extremely refreshing.' He'd said that. He'd actually said that! She remembered every word.

'What about remaining true to myself, Roger.' It was an accusation not a query. 'What about remaining who I really am.'

He recognised his own words were being thrown back at him. And out of context what's more, which under normal circumstances he would have found really irritating. But he refused to take umbrage, giving a light laugh instead.

'Come along now, my love, you're over-reacting.' He took her in his arms. 'I'm just offering you a little lesson, Jess, that's all,' he said. 'As if I would ever change you.' And he kissed her.

But that's exactly what you're doing, she thought, or that's what you're attempting to do. Then she felt the straps of her dress eased over her shoulders, silk fabric sliding across her skin to the ground, hands caressing her body, and moments later she was responding with an immediacy that matched his.

Their lovemaking was as fulfilling as always and the next day the incident appeared forgotten to Roger. But it wasn't to Jess. The night of the National Geographic party had opened her eyes to a pattern that would slowly unfold during the months that followed, a pattern over which it seemed she had no control.

'Jess was a student of mine,' she would hear him say. 'I'm extremely proud of her achievements.' And on another occasion, 'Jess has a wonderful brain. She was by far and away my brightest student.'

It was impossible to confront him on the subject. A stalemate was reached whenever she tried. 'Of course I boast about you, my darling, I'm extraordinarily proud of you. Why shouldn't I boast?'

'Because it sounds condescending, that's why. You're patronising me.'

'Don't be ridiculous,' he was dismissive every time, 'I'm championing you.' And when she pushed him further he would laugh. 'You're becoming paranoid, Jess; now stop being silly and come to bed.'

Sex was always the great leveller to Roger. On the odd occasion when he found her 'paranoia' irritating and couldn't resist snapping back, sex wiped the slate clean and the next day was a fresh new start. At least it was for Roger. Things weren't quite the same for Jess. Their sexual congress continued to excite her, she could not alter the dictates of her body, but there was never a fresh start the next day.

More and more she felt demeaned when she heard him boast of her accomplishments to others, and he continued to do so openly even knowing she wished that he wouldn't. He's not proud of me at all, she would think, he's proud of his achievement. Insecurity started to creep in. Roger seemed to be taking credit for her success as if she was something of his personal making. Could he be right? Was she nothing without him?

But whenever she attempted to voice her misgivings, the words always came out the wrong way. Or perhaps they sounded wrong because of the way he twisted them back on her, she really couldn't tell.

'For God's sake, woman, what's the matter with you?' he'd rant in frustration, 'I am your greatest champion. I laud you to the skies! You should be *proud* of the pride I take in you.'

The terrible realisation slowly dawned on Jess that, apart from the sex they shared, she was really no more to Roger Macready than a symbol of his success. As they embarked upon the second year of their marriage she was plagued by the notion and then other thoughts piled on top, jumbling her mind into a sea of insecurity. Roger didn't love her at all, he never had. She'd been a case study to him all along. She remembered the day they'd visited Aunty May at Hermannsburg, the pictures he'd taken of the fresh-faced young Aboriginal student with her uneducated outback family. Had those photos accompanied the papers he'd presented to the Anthropological Society? Was she like a butterfly to an entomologist, a specimen pinned on a card and filed away for study?

Jess knew she was driving herself mad, but she couldn't stop. Her marriage was a sham in every conceivable way. And then, as their hectic social life continued and she was whirled about from cocktail party to dinner to conference with pride, she recognised the most insidious aspect of all. She was Roger's personal badge of honour, the symbol he wore on his sleeve that gave him credibility. The charismatic, non-conformist professor, remaining true to form, had outrageously married a young black woman.

For the first time in her life Jess's confidence was shattered. And for the first time in her life, she felt as her mother must have felt: a nothing, a no-one, a black woman in a white man's world.

She left her marriage and she left Sydney. Had she stayed any longer, Roger Macready would have destroyed her.

She made her exit the coward's way, without confrontation, just a letter. By that time she was so deeply in Roger's clutches she didn't dare do anything else. The lawyer will be in touch, she informed him. She wished for a divorce and would agree to whichever path was the most expedient. Their marriage had lasted just eighteen months.

Jess had put that time behind her now. Sometimes when it threatened to revisit she would tell herself she was grateful to Roger for awakening her to the nightmare of her mother's existence. Rose, despite the depth of her husband's love and compassion, had always considered herself inferior, a second-class person. Perhaps, Jess thought, I should even thank Roger for making me aware of a plight so common among our people.

Upon returning home from the Todd Tavern and her pleasant evening with Matt Witherton, Jess made herself a light meal and watched television for a while. She wasn't sure exactly what it was she watched, perhaps because the programme was boring or perhaps because Roger remained inexplicably on her mind.

Later when she took herself off to bed she switched her thoughts to something else. Experience had taught her that dwelling upon the past in any form was an open invitation to a sleepless night.

Instead she thought about Matt. She wondered if Charlie would visit him tonight. And, only minutes later, as she felt herself drifting off to a blissful sleep, she wondered what exactly it was that Charlie was trying to tell his grandson.

CHAPTER EIGHT

In his little single room at the Heavitree Gap Hotel, Matt did dream that night. But he didn't dream about Charlie. And the landscape this time was not that of the Burmese jungle, but rather the central Australian desert. Once again the view was detached and from on high. He was gliding, looking down at the familiar terrain of dry flood plains and rocky outcrops and parched, red earth, and every now and then he found himself zooming in for a closer inspection, like an eagle in search of its prey. The images were as vivid as those of his previous dreams and as before they remained with him long after waking, but this time he did not question them. He supposed that as far as dreams went they were normal enough. Why he should be soaring about in the sky like an eagle was beyond him, but at least he'd been dreaming of something familiar. At least he was not about to be haunted throughout the day by the skeletal faces of dying men.

He gave the matter no further thought, dismissing the images from his mind as he took himself into town for a pleasant breakfast at an outdoor café in the mall and a read of the Sunday newspaper. Then he drove back to camp.

That night he was visited by a similar dream, and then again the next night, and on both occasions he dismissed them from his mind throughout the following day. He had no doubt that Jess would say his grandfather was trying to tell him something, but he refused to ponder any possible hidden meaning. It was annoying enough that his normally peaceful sleep was being disrupted without wasting further time worrying about why. He put the dreams aside and concentrated on his work, and after the three consecutive nights of their recurrence they disappeared altogether.

Late the following Saturday afternoon a bunch of young apprentice workers returned to camp from Aileron a little the worse for wear. They were happy and harmless, but an arvo's drinking at the tavern had left the half dozen or so in the mood for a bit of diversion, so when young Batty careered out of his donga screaming 'Snake! Snake!' at the top of his lungs, it was destined to arouse interest.

Batty was the youngest of the bunch, only nineteen, and an apprentice diesel mechanic. His nickname could have been perceived by some as cruel for he did indeed have ears like a fruit bat, but as any outback worker knew if you didn't have a nickname it was quite possible you weren't popular, so once this had been explained to Batty he'd happily relinquished 'George' and embraced his new identity.

Snakes were objects of terror to Batty, growing up as he had in the suburbs of Adelaide, so having, upon arriving back from the pub with his mates, practically trodden on one curled up asleep in a cosy corner of his donga he'd been horrified. 'Snake! Snake!' he'd yelled.

The others quickly followed Batty back to his donga, which was at the far end of the row twenty metres or so from the scrub, and gathered at the open doorway to peer in at the snake. It was a brown, around a metre and a half long and, having been disturbed from its slumber, it now sat coiled with its head raised high. The fact that the one avenue of escape open to it was suddenly barred only agitated the creature further and it started to hiss and wave its head from side to side.

'How the hell did it get in there?' Batty demanded with a touch of hysteria. 'I closed the door when I left.'

'You couldn't have, mate,' one of the men said.

'I did, I did, I know I did, and it was closed when I got back, what's more!'

'Must have swung open, I suppose,' another commented, 'and somebody closed it for you.'

'Or else the snake's been living there all along without you knowing,' came a further laconic comment.

Batty blanched at the mere thought.

'Who gives a shit how the thing got in there?' a fourth man countered. 'How the hell are you going to get it out?'

The group remained gathered at the door studying the snake, discussing what action should be taken and soon others joined them, beers in hand. Some of the seasoned workers sensed a bit of fun could be had at the expense of the young apprentices, all of whom were city boys.

'We need a snake wrangler,' Baldy said, 'anyone up for it? Come on, boys, I dare you.' Big Baldy just loved a good stir. 'Twenty bucks to whoever can get the fucking thing out of there.' He wouldn't go near it himself – a bloody king brown? No way, you'd have to be mad.

One of the apprentices, 'Fish' Whiting, bolstered by a few too many beers and keen to achieve hero status in his mates' eyes, was sorely tempted.

'Is it poisonous?' he asked, looking into the donga where the snake, now in a state of extreme agitation, was hissing louder than ever and threshing its head wildly from side to side. The sight was daunting certainly, but Christ he'd be a hero if he could pull it off. Perhaps he could throw a tarp over the thing and drag it out. Fish was giving the matter serious consideration.

Baldy threw back his massive domed head and laughed out loud. 'Course it's venomous, you stupid bastard, every snake around here is.' He raised his can of beer encouragingly. 'But don't let that put you off, son, if we get you to the hospital in time for the anti-venom to kick in you'll live.'

Young Fish wisely decided hero status wasn't worth the price.

A voice said from behind them: 'Only one way to get rid of that fella.' It was Donny. 'You got to sing him out blackfella way, isn't that right, Laurence?'

'Yeah, that's right, mate.'

Donny and young Laurence had drifted over to watch the proceedings, Laurence, upon Donny's instructions, bringing with him a good-sized stick. They'd shared a muttered conversation and Donny had devised a plan.

'I'll sing him out for you if you like.' He addressed the group in general, but his eyes came to rest upon Baldy for it was Baldy who'd made the offer. 'Twenty bucks, right?'

Baldy looked him up and down suspiciously: was the prick having him on? But Donny appeared deadly serious as did the other blackfella and you just never knew with these blokes. Baldy, deciding in the name of amusement to give it a go, took his wallet from his hip pocket and held it up to show the offer was genuine. Then he gave the nod to proceed. Clearly no money was to change hands until the mission was accomplished.

Donny immediately took charge, displaying an authority that was impressive. 'Got to clear the place,' he ordered, arms wide, ushering the men to one side, 'get back, right back now, snake can't see me with you fellas in the way.'

Laurence, too, waved his arms urging the men aside and they obediently backed clear, chattering among themselves about whether or not they should lay bets: the Aboriginal blokes appeared to know what they were doing.

'Quiet now,' Donny ordered, 'bit of shush; snake can't hear me sing with you fellas natterin'.'

There was instant silence and the men watched as Donny and Laurence seated themselves side by side on the step of the donga opposite Batty's and Donny started very softly to sing his song. It was a chant more than a song really, nasal, monotone and strangely compelling.

All eyes remained focused on the open door, waiting for the snake to appear. The men had been ushered well to one side and Donny and Laurence were the only two who could actually see inside the donga, but not a man moved, each mesmerised by the haunting sound of Donny's snake song and the image of the open door.

The song went on for several minutes, but there was no sign of the snake and the men were starting to grow restless.

'This is fucking stupid,' Baldy muttered, with the distinct feeling they'd been taken for a ride.

'Yeh, he's not doing much,' Donny agreed in all seriousness, eyes still trained upon the snake. 'Maybe this fella snake don't know my song.' He turned to Laurence. 'Maybe this fella snake don't know Arunta – what do you reckon?' Laurence gave a nod that said 'it's possible'. 'You give 'im a try, mate,' Donny suggested and Laurence started a song of his own, which was presumably Anmatyerre, but which sounded very similar to Donny's.

'You're having us on,' Baldy growled, 'this is a load of fucking bullshit.'

Donny gave a shrug and nudged Laurence, who stopped singing. The songs were certainly bullshit, but they hadn't been having the men on altogether. Donny had decided that if he and Laurence could get everyone out of sight and keep them quiet, thus clearing an avenue of escape for the snake, it might come out of its own volition. The songs had just been a bit of a joke. If it had worked it would have been downright funny.

'Righto,' he said, rising to his feet and taking the stick from Laurence, 'we'll do it the other way,' and to the amazement of everyone except Laurence he disappeared into the donga.

'Shit,' Baldy said, and there were audible gasps from the others.

Seconds later, Donny reappeared, holding the snake by its tail, high and at arm's length, while keeping its head clear from his body with the stick. Without traction the animal was unable to strike, but could only squirm help-lessly, seeking a target.

'What do you want me to do with him, eh?' he asked as he stepped down from the donga and thrust the writhing creature towards the others, who recoiled to a man. 'Oops, maybe I'll drop him, he's pretty heavy this fella.' A gasp went up as he pretended to lose his grip on the snake.

'Get rid of it, you mad bastard,' Baldy said.

'Okay,' Donny said with an amiable grin, 'I'll take him back where he lives, but I reckon that's worth more than a twenty, Baldy. How about fifty, what do you say?'

He waved the snake about, but by now Baldy knew there was no cause for alarm, that Donny had the situation under total control. He respected the bloke for it, just as he respected the joke. They'd been played for mugs, but the entertainment had been worthwhile and Donny deserved fifty. Baldy was a fair man. 'Fifty it is,' he said, taking a note from his wallet.

'Collect our money, will you, mate?' Donny called over his shoulder to Laurence as he set off for the scrub, the snake still writhing powerlessly. 'They were good snake songs we sung.' He gave a little skip as he went and started singing the same tuneless chant, the others bursting into a spontaneous round of applause.

Laurence relished the moment as he collected the fifty-dollar note from Baldy.

Donny achieved cult hero status that day, word spread-ing quickly around the camp. Some who'd known him as a drunk back in Alice were surprised, but Laurence wasn't. Donny had been a hero to Laurence right from the start.

Donny had taken young Laurence under his wing. He could see the problem: the kid was over-sensitive and needed toughening up, sure, but most important of all the kid needed to develop a sense of humour. Laurence took life too seriously, that was his trouble. And so Donny had stepped in. Donny was a funny man.

The relationship that had quickly developed between the two had been of great benefit to them both, but most particularly to Donny. He hadn't been drunk for nearly a month. He never went into Aileron with the gang, he didn't dare risk a session on the grog, but he had a couple of beers at the end of the work day and it never bothered him, he wasn't tempted to wipe himself out. He wasn't sure what was keeping him on the straight and narrow the most. Was it the job? This was a good job; he liked this job. Or was it the fact that he didn't want to lose face in Laurence's eyes, knowing how the kid idolised him? Didn't matter either way: life was pretty good at the moment. And now on top of everything else, he was a bloody hero.

The rail corridor continued its relentless progression towards Alice, and barely a fortnight after the snake episode Matt was visited by another dream, a different dream altogether this time. This time he was neither in the Burmese jungle, nor was he in the Australian desert. This time he appeared to be on a train, a steam train, he could hear the clicketty-clack of its wheels on the track and the belching of steam from its funnel. And the train was travelling through countryside that could only be somewhere in Europe. He was passing by coppices and hedgerows, a white-washed farmhouse sitting prettily in a lush green meadow, then through the heart of a village, the train slowing down a little now, rows of quaint houses, a church with a steeple, people lining the streets, waving.

'*Bonjour, Australie,*' he heard them call: he was in France.

Then the voices of the men on the train calling back '*Bonjooa, bonjooa!*' – mangled French from raucous Australians. The men were in a cattle wagon, its door opened wide, some seated on the wooden floor legs dangling untidily over the side, others crowded behind eagerly taking in the view and waving to the villagers. They were young men all, and each wore the rank and file uniform of the AIF: tunic, breeches, bandolier, puttees and slouch hat. In wagonload after wagonload, relentlessly one after another, the boys were on their way to the front.

This dream differed markedly from Matt's previous dreams, for in this dream he was not an outsider viewing events from above and nor was he an unseen spectator moving among the men. In this dream he was one of them, one of these soldiers, and he was seated at the open doorway, his legs dangling over the side of the wagon as it passed through the village.

'*Bienvenue, Australie!*' Two pretty girls, arm in arm out on the footpath, were blowing fervent kisses to the passing troops. '*Bienvenue! Bienvenue!*' they called.

The soldier sitting next to Matt blew kisses back; he was a cheeky, freckle-faced young bloke, no more than nineteen. 'What a couple of crackers,' he said, nudging Matt in the ribs. 'Pity we're not stopping off here, eh, Withers?' He grinned. 'Give 'em a wave, cobber, go on, they're looking right at us.'

Matt returned his mate's grin and waved to the girls, who blew kisses back even more fervently. Then the train gathered speed, pulling out of the village and into the meadowlands, leaving the girls two small figures in the distance, still waving and still blowing kisses to the last of the wagons that passed them by.

When he awoke the next morning, Matt found he couldn't dismiss this dream with the ease he had the recurring dreams of several weeks back. It stayed with him throughout the day and, once again, although he wasn't sure why, he felt compelled to share it with Jess. He rang her late in the afternoon.

'I had another "visit",' he said wryly, 'at least I suppose that's what you'd call it.

'Oh.' Jess ignored the scepticism. 'Charlie came back, did he?'

'Nope. Not Charlie, someone entirely different.'

'Really? Who?'

'I'm not sure,' he admitted, 'in fact I'm pretty much in a state of confusion. Fancy a beer on Saturday? What are you doing late afternoon?'

'Hopefully hearing about your dream,' she said.

'Goodo. Where'll we meet?'

'Bojangles in Todd Street, you know it?'

'Who doesn't?'

They met at four-thirty for a beer at Bojangles, a colourful bar where the tables were beer barrels strewn with peanuts and where guests were encouraged to throw the shells on the floor. They took up a spot at the front overlooking the street, for the moment it was quiet enough, but come evening when the band arrived things would get noisy.

'So tell me,' she said when he'd returned from the bar with their drinks, 'who came to visit you?'

'A soldier from World War I,' he replied. 'I think he was me.'

'That's enigmatic.'

Jess sipped her beer and listened attentively while Matt told her every detail of the dream, which was still as clear in his mind as it had been three days earlier.

'I was on that train,' he said. 'I was one of those soldiers going off to the front and the bloke sitting next to me was a mate of mine. He called me by name, "Withers", he said. That's my nickname,' he added, feeling the need to explain. 'The men I work with call me Withers, always have, don't know why.' He gave a shrug. 'A bloke-type thing I suppose, men working together seem to adopt nicknames, at least Aussie men do.'

'Did you recognise this mate in the dream? Was he someone you know?'

'Nope. Never seen him before, wouldn't have a clue who he was, but in the dream I just knew that he was a really close mate.' Matt shook his head in hopeless surrender. 'I have no idea what to make of all this. I mean, seriously, what the hell's going on?'

'You've had another "visit",' Jess said, 'that's what the hell's going on.'

'Why did I know you'd say that?' They exchanged a smile and Matt took a hefty swig of his beer, which had so far remained untouched. 'Your turn, over to you,' he said, feeling once again strangely unburdened by the recounting of his dream.

'Do you have any relatives who died in World War I, Matt?' she asked.

'None that I know of.' He cracked open a few peanuts and chomped away while he waited for her to go on. 'So what do we do now?' he asked when she remained silent, and even as he asked he wondered why there *should* be anything to do.

'We go to my place,' she said.

She was already on her feet, so he made no enquiry, just knocked back the rest of his beer and they went outside to his car. Jess had walked to the tavern.

Back at the flat in Undoolya Road, she dumped her shoulder bag on the sofa and plonked herself down at the desk in the corner.

'My round,' she said, waving a distracted hand at the living room's kitchenette area as she focused on her computer, 'grab yourself a beer and one for me too.'

Matt obediently did as instructed. 'Do you want a glass?' he asked, lifting two cans from the refrigerator. She shook her head and he crossed to the desk, placing the opened beer can beside her.

'Make yourself at home,' her eyes didn't leave the computer screen, 'this shouldn't take long.'

He looked about the attractive open-plan sitting room. 'Nice,' he said, but she didn't answer, so he walked over to the windows and gazed out at the street. He was pleasantly distracted by the sight of a family in the front garden of the house opposite, a young couple sitting on the verandah steps watching their little boy play with a newly acquired puppy: charming.

He remained observing the scene for a full ten minutes before her announcement distracted him.

'Brian Francis Witherton.'

Her voice intruded upon his mindlessness and he turned from the window, from the boy and the puppy and the fond exchanges between parents to Jess, whose eyes were trained on the computer screen.

'Killed in action,' she said, 'France, 20 July 1916.'

He stared wordlessly back at her. What was she talking about?

'Records of service in the Australian Imperial Forces World War I,' she explained, glancing over to where he stood by the windows. 'Come and have a look for yourself.'

He took a chair from the four-seater dining table and joined her to stare at the page she'd called up from the Australian War Memorial site. There it was. *Private Brian Francis Witherton, 32nd Australian Infantry Battalion, killed in action, France, 20 July 1916, age at death 20.*

'It would appear you're not the only "Withers", Matt,' she said, watching as his eyes scanned the details listed on the screen. 'You said yourself Aussie workmates adopt nicknames. Well soldiers certainly would. This man in your dream wasn't you at all.'

He was about to interrupt, but she continued, urgent, insistent. 'I know, I know, you felt very strongly you were one of those soldiers, but that was simply a way of getting through to you, of making contact. At least I believe so.

The Withers in your dream wasn't you, Matt: he was family, he was your ancestor.'

She paused, thoughtful for a second or so, and Matt wondered what to say in response to such a statement, or rather he wondered what to say without causing offence, for she was clearly genuine in her belief.

'Who do you reckon he might be?' she asked. 'Your great grandfather perhaps, Charlie's dad?'

He shook his head. 'I wouldn't have a clue. My dad never knew his grandfather.' He wasn't answering her in all seriousness; How could he? Was he really expected to believe he'd been visited by an ancestor? But he found himself answering her nonetheless. 'Apart from his mother my dad didn't have any family.'

'They'd be the right age, Brian and Charlie,' she said. 'Brian could well have fathered a child at twenty. Perhaps his wife didn't know she was pregnant when he went off to war, just as Charlie's wife didn't.' The more Jess thought about it the more plausible the scenario seemed. 'Eminently possible I'd say, father and son, two generations of men killed in two world wars: not uncommon, wouldn't you agree?'

I have to put a stop to this, he thought, it's getting out of hand. She was sounding like a detective sleuthing a case; the whole thing was ridiculous.

'Yep,' he said, 'not an uncommon occurrence at all, and I agree that quite possibly this Brian Francis Witherton might be my great-grandfather or at least related in some way. It's an unusual name, so it's possible. But the whole thing is coincidence, Jess, nothing more than sheer coincidence.' Given the passion of her belief, and not wishing to be hurtful, he tried to sound reasonable rather than dismissive. 'I've been dreaming about railways because I'm working on the Ghan,' he said, his tone measured, but emphatic nonetheless. 'I dreamt about World War II and the Burma Railway because of my grandfather, yes, but I've read extensively about World War I and troop rail transport, so it's not altogether surprising I'd dream about that too. My subconscious mind is obsessed with railways, don't you see?' He smiled an apology, hoping she wasn't offended. 'Truly, it's that simple.'

Jess wasn't in the least offended. She was fully aware of his scepticism and also of his need to seek a rational answer, but she refused to argue either case, returning his apologetic smile with a disarmingly good-humoured grin.

'Fob me off as much as you like, but I won't give up. Charlie and Brian have put you in touch with me for a reason and I'm not going to let them down.'

'Fair enough,' he said with a laugh. 'So what's your plan of attack?' He'd go along with her simply because she delighted him.

She knew he was humouring her, but again she didn't care. Trying to convert a non-believer was a useless exercise that held no interest for her. Discovering the reason for the visitations, however, was of great interest. What was it Matt's ancestors were trying to communicate? Was it a warning of some kind? Could he or a member of his family be in danger?

'Tell me about your family, Matt,' she said, 'any siblings?'

'Nope,' he replied with a shrug, 'just my parents and me.'

But she wasn't to be fobbed off as easily as that. 'Uncles, aunts, cousins?' she queried with dogged determination.

Recognising her resolve, Matt surrendered himself to the grilling that followed and in answering her endless questions found himself talking as he'd never talked before. He told her about his parents and the loneliness of his boyhood and the influence of his Russian grandmother, surprising himself with his candour.

Jess was impressed to discover his mother was the artist Lilian Birch, whose outback paintings she so admired, but of greater interest to her was the relationship his parents shared.

'They appear completely at odds,' he said, 'you wouldn't believe the difference. Lilian's flamboyantly eccentric and demanding of attention while Dave's a loner who stays in the shadows; and yet they're soul mates, always have been. Their bond from the beginning was a mutual love of the outback, something they obviously passed on to me.'

'But it was your Russian grandmother who brought you up,' Jess said. 'Svetlana, right?'

'Oh yes, Babushka.' He smiled in fond recollection. 'Babushka was my world as a child, far more of a mother to me than Lilian ever was. But then Lilian wasn't born to be a mother,' he added without rancour. 'Dad and I both accepted the fact, but Svetlana didn't. There were constant rows between mother and daughter, formidable women.'

'What about the paternal side of your family?' Jess asked. 'You said your dad had no-one but his mother?'

'That's right, Peg. She was a war bride, married Charlie and had a couple of weeks with him, then off he went. Peg brought Dad up on her own; never married again. I didn't know her. She died in '64, well before I was born. She was only forty-seven years old, Dad told me, cancer.'

'And what of Peg's family? What do you know about them?'

'Nothing. There didn't appear to be any. She was adopted, apparently. Never knew her biological parents and didn't keep in touch with her adopted ones. A tragic life all round, when you think about it.'

'Yes, it is rather.' Jess frowned thoughtfully. 'Not much to go on is there?'

'In what way?'

'Your family tree. It's pretty sparse.'

He found her blatant disappointment vaguely amusing. 'What were you hoping for?'

'I don't know. A family secret, a skeleton in the closet perhaps, something your ancestors might want to make known to the current generation. Haven't you ever wondered about your family history?'

'Nope, haven't given it a thought. I don't think Dad has either. At least he's never seemed to. I remember Svetlana being angry that he was unable to provide a family tree: she'd get quite accusatory.' Matt grinned, recalling his grandmother's annoyance. '"Everyone needs a family history," she'd say, as if Dad had somehow mislaid his.'

'Everyone has a family history, Matt. It's just that some don't know theirs.' Jess felt on the verge of a breakthrough. 'Perhaps this is why your ancestors are making themselves known. Perhaps they feel the need to tell you of your past.'

'Perhaps they do,' he agreed obligingly and then he jumped to his feet. 'Hey, do you want some dinner? I'm starving.'

Jess looked at her watch. It was getting dark outside, she realised, the sitting room was becoming gloomy and she hadn't even noticed. She stood and turned on the overhead lights. 'Sure. I'll get us something here if you like.'

'No, no, we'll go out.' He'd seen the slightest hesitation and realised a cosy dinner at home might be crossing the line she seemed so determined to avoid and which he too wished to observe. He wondered again at the reasons for her fragility and wanted to tell her not to worry, that he had no intention of making any form of overture. Her friendship was of far greater value to him than a passing sexual dalliance. 'How about Sean's Bar?' he suggested. 'Do you like Indian food?

'Love it.'

Sean's Bar in Bath Street was within easy walking distance and the evening was mild, but at Matt's sugges-tion they drove. Again he was wary of putting Jess in an uncomfortable situation by leaving his car at her flat.

They shared a bottle of wine and a selection of dishes, discovering a shared passion for chilli and very much enjoying each other's company, and at the end of the evening they halved the bill the way mates did. Then, lingering over coffee, she surprised him.

'I'd like to meet your parents, Matt.'

During the meal she hadn't nagged him any further about his visitations; there hadn't seemed much point. She'd pushed him hard enough already and gained all she could. His parents were a different matter altogether, however, particularly his father, Dave. Perhaps Dave holds the key, she thought, or at least a piece of the puzzle that might offer a hint.

'I sometimes go down to Adelaide for a weekend,' she said casually, 'if I did, do you think they'd mind my calling in on them?'

Much as the suggestion surprised him, he grasped immediately her purpose. 'You mean do I think they'd mind if you pumped them for information,' he said drily.

'Yes, that's pretty much what I mean.'

'I'm quite sure if you told them their son had been visited by his ancestors they'd find the whole thing fascinating,' he said, 'in fact I know they would, particularly Lilian. But I don't think you'd get much joy out of them.'

'Why not?'

'They're atheists.'

'What's that got to do with anything?'

'Well, I've never asked them outright, but I very much doubt they believe in an afterlife.'

'Oh you'd be surprised,' Jess said airily, 'atheists often have strong spiritual leanings. So you'll check if they don't mind my calling in?'

'Of course I will. I'll ring them tomorrow.' He had to admire her tenacity.

They finished their coffee and said their farewells, Jess walking back towards the footbridge rugged up against the chill evening air and Matt driving off to the Heavitree Gap Hotel where he spent a night blissfully free of dreams.

*

He rang her the following day, late in the afternoon.

'Just been speaking to Lilian,' he said, 'I told her the whole story and she can't wait to meet you.'

'Fantastic, I'll go down to Adelaide next weekend.' Jess was thrilled. 'I'll book the hotel right away.'

'No hotel, you'll be staying at the house, Mum insists.'

'Oh no,' she said quite adamantly, 'I couldn't possibly do that.'

'Yes you could. I'm coming with you. I've owed them a visit for some time now and Mum's over the moon at the prospect. Let's make it the Saturday after next: I get a long weekend every second month and I'm due one then. I presume you can take the Monday off? You're pretty much your own boss, aren't you?'

She was being railroaded. 'Yes, but –'

'Great. We'll fly down together on the Saturday and come back on the Monday, more relaxing than just an overnight trip.'

'Um . . .' There was a pause while she wondered what to say. This put an altogether different perspective on things.

'Give us a break, Jess, you didn't honestly think I'd let you grill my parents without my being there,' he said jokingly, knowing full well the cause for her hesitation.

'No, I suppose not. I mean I suppose I didn't really think things through properly –'

'You didn't need to,' he interrupted briskly, 'there was never anything to think through. I've wised Mum up, she's under no misconception, she knows we're just mates. You'll be in the upstairs guest bedroom and I'll be in the flat out the back as I always am – we won't even be under the same roof at night!'

'Oh.' Another pause; Jess was now embarrassed at having been caught out. 'It's very kind of your mother to welcome a total stranger,' she said, feeling a bit silly.

'She's not welcoming a stranger; she's welcoming a friend.'

*

But upon their arrival two weeks later, Lilian ignored the strict instructions she'd received from her son over the phone and behaved outrageously, true to form.

'Oh my dear look at you, you're gorgeous,' she said as she met them at the front door, Dave by her side. She embraced Matt with gusto then Jess with equal gusto, enveloping them one by one in swathes of multi-coloured alpaca, then stood back to admire Jess with an artist's eye. 'You didn't tell me what a striking creature you were bringing home, Mattie –'

Dave interrupted, stepping forwards with outstretched hand. 'Hello, Jess, I'm Dave.' He shook her hand warmly, aware that the girl was confronted by Lilian's brazen appraisal. 'Don't take any notice of her. She just wants to paint you for the Archibald.'

'I do, I do,' Lilian said enthusiastically. 'I most definitely do! Just look at that face! Now come inside and close the door, for God's sake, it's bloody freezing out there.'

Adelaide was indeed undergoing a cold snap, the month of June ushering in winter with a vengeance.

They stepped inside to follow Lilian who like a ship under full sail led the way through to the downstairs main living room, where a log fire crackled cosily in the broad open fireplace.

Jess looked about as she went, at the sweeping central staircase, the high moulded ceilings, the large comfortable furniture and the artworks that abounded. The interior of the house was as impressive as its facade had promised, and Lilian somehow matched it to perfection. In fact to Jess, Lilian and the house seemed something of a pair, big and grand and a little overwhelming, but not pretentious – both just being what and who they were.

'Sit and get some hot coffee into yourself immediately,' Lilian ordered, throwing aside her alpaca shawl and lowering her considerable bulk into one of the armchairs pulled up in front of the fire. She'd put on quite an amount of weight over the past decade and was now a large woman, but she'd adjusted to her new size, which suited her and didn't in the least slow her down.

Everyone obediently sat as Lilian proceeded to pour mugs of hot milky coffee from the large silver pot on the table beside her. Matt had rung during the taxi ride from the airport and she'd prepared the coffee for their arrival. They'd eaten on the plane, he'd said, so no lunch was necessary.

'I loathe this cold weather and it must be particularly ghastly for you having just come from the Alice.' She didn't draw breath as she poured, handing the mugs one by one to Dave who obligingly passed them around. 'As soon as we've got you warmed up, Jess,' she said, 'I'll show you your room and you can settle yourself in. You're upstairs in my studio apartment.'

'It's very kind of you, Lilian, thank you so much.' Jess had no problem at all addressing Lilian by her first name as Matt had instructed she should. She'd asked him on the plane. 'Mrs Witherton, Miss Birch or Ms Birch,' she'd queried. The answer had been simple. 'Lilian,' he'd said, 'they're Lilian and Dave, never anything else. You'll see what I mean when you meet them.' She'd wondered how comfortable she'd feel, but Matt had been right, she had no qualms at all.

'Thank you too, Dave,' she said as he handed her a coffee.

'No worries.' Dave returned a smile.

'We're only too delighted you're here, dear,' Lilian continued. 'How else would we get to see our son? He rarely deigns to visit us these days.' She cast a mock glare at Matt, which although good-natured held a definite element of rebuke.

Matt just laughed. He was relieved Jess had accepted Lilian's initial onslaught; for a minute there at the front door he'd wanted to kill his mother. Good God, he'd warned her they were strictly friends and that Jess was fragile about relationships. Lilian's overt approval could have been shockingly misinterpreted. She just can't help herself, can she? he thought with his customary exasperation. Things could have been worse: at least she's not trying to pair us off.

Had Matt known what was going through his mother's mind twenty minutes later as she took Jess on a personal tour upstairs he might have had true cause for worry.

'You'll have this whole area of the house completely to yourself for the weekend, dear,' Lilian said as she ushered Jess into the huge airy studio with its separate bedroom and en suite. What a pity they're not a couple, she was thinking, I do hope the situation rectifies itself at some stage. During their chat over coffee Lilian had found herself as much impressed by the fierce intelligence she could sense in the girl as she had been by the striking racial mix of her appearance, which she did indeed long to paint. What a perfect choice for Matt, she thought, vastly preferable to poor, beautiful Angie. Lilian constantly lamented the fact that the ghost of Angie continued to haunt Matt to the point where he simply couldn't see any other woman as a potential partner. He's thirty-two, for God's sake, she thought: high time he found someone to share his life with.

'But Lilian,' Jess protested, looking about at the easel and the huge, scarred wooden table with its palettes and paints and pots of brushes; at the glorious works adorning the walls and the canvases leaning in haphazard clumps, 'this is your studio! I'm intruding, it's not right.'

'You're not intruding in the least, my dear. I won't be able to work this weekend anyway. I have an exhibition opening tomorrow with all the attendant bullshit, endless discussions on hanging and lighting and social chit-chat with gallery owners who are little better than used-car salesmen.' She halted abruptly. 'No,' she corrected herself, 'that's a terrible thing to say, I'm sure there are some very nice used-car salesmen. In any event, I shan't be working.' Even as the words flowed truthfully, Lilian wondered whether perhaps she should have lied. The downstairs spare bedroom served as a storage room these days and if she'd said she needed to work throughout the night Jess would have been forced to stay in the flat with Matt, which might have accelerated things. No, no, she chastised herself, Mattie would be furious. He'd know I was lying. I mustn't be pushy, I promised.

'The bed's very comfortable.' She threw open the door to the bedroom and ensuite. 'Just ignore all this mess,' she added, waving a hand that encompassed the studio in general.

But Jess didn't even glance at the bedroom. 'How could I possibly ignore all this?' she said, awestruck, her eyes wandering the studio walls from painting to painting. 'It'll be like staying in the most wonderful art gallery.'

'Well feel free to have a look around while you settle yourself in,' Lilian said, 'and then Mattie can show you the rest of the house.' She was already starting off down the stairs. 'There's a very nice park nearby if you want to take a walk in this wretched cold,' she said, calling a monologue over her shoulder as she went. 'Dave and I are off to the gallery shortly to check on the hanging. We'll talk during dinner – he's making one of his stews, so don't eat anything, they're frightfully filling, terribly messy and quite divine.' Her voice drifted back up the stairs long after she was out of sight.

Dave's stew that night was everything Lilian had promised. A massive mix of oxtail and vegetables swirling about in a rich, red wine gravy, it sat in a giant cauldron in the centre of the table, a large pot nearby to house the bones as they ate. Dave himself stood at the end of the table ladling the stew into huge bowls, which he passed around while Lilian tucked her napkin into the open neck of her shirt, Matt following suit.

'I warned you it's messy,' she said to Jess.

'Now I really know I'm home,' Matt grinned. 'Dad's stews are famous.'

Jess took the hint and tucked her napkin in at the throat.

They ate with spoons, the meat falling apart, and they sucked the marrow from the bones then threw them into the pot, and they dunked slices of crusty bread in the gravy and washed it all down with an excellent Shiraz. Jess felt as if she were in a time warp at some sort of medieval banquet, yet at the same time very much at home. She also felt hungry after the long, cold walk she and Matt had taken in the park.

'If we were standing on ceremony,' Lilian explained, 'we'd have plates and knives and forks and Dave would have served green beans on the side or something, wouldn't you, darling?' Dave returned a nod, aware no answer was necessary, and Lilian continued. 'You're getting the family treatment, Jess,' she explained, 'where he chucks every vegetable known to man in with whatever secret ingredients he uses. I've no idea what they are and I've never asked, but we like it this way.'

'So do I,' she said, 'it's delicious.'

They ate in relative silence until the initial pangs of hunger were satisfied and when they started to slow down they also started to talk, Lilian as always initiating the conversation.

'I must say I was fascinated by your interpretation of Matt's dreams,' she said, sitting back and taking a breather from the stew. She'd actually been far more fascinated by the idea that Matt was bringing a girl home to meet them, regardless of his protestations they were 'just mates'. It was surely a move in the right direction. She had, however, been genuinely interested in the girl's beliefs, and was now even more so having met her. Jess was clearly an intelligent young woman, and spiritualism was such an intriguing concept.

'The idea that he's been visited by the spirits of his ancestors is in itself enthralling,' she continued, 'but to then discover the death of Brian Witherton in World War I was nothing short of extraordinary. We both thought so, didn't we, Dave?'

Dave gave a dutiful nod, although he thought Lilian was being a little overly gushing, which of course was nothing new.

Jess interpreted Dave's nod as his customary way of dodging the issue and realised that, polite though he was, he didn't share his wife's enthusiasm. She couldn't help thinking how very often Lilian talked on her husband's behalf. Surely that must be irritating at times, yet it didn't appear to bother Dave in the least as he tucked into his stew.

'So you don't find it fanciful?' she queried. 'You don't think this is all mere coincidence?' She deliberately avoided Matt's eyes, but her tone inferred 'as your son does'.

'Not in the least. Dave and I are both atheists,' Lilian said, 'and it's probably because of our atheism that we have quite a strong spiritual affinity. I believe many atheists do.'

At that point Jess couldn't resist a triumphant I-told-you-so glance at Matt, who merely shrugged in return. He'd long since given up being surprised by his mother. One simply never knew in which direction Lilian's grasshopper mind might spring.

'At least *I* certainly do,' Lilian went on, 'and I know Dave does, to a certain degree anyway.' This time she didn't acknowledge her husband at all, but continued unabated and with passion: 'I think it's the outback that bred spirituality in us. Being in the desert where the light is so vibrant, feeling the land breathe – there's an energy surrounding one, a life one can't see but that one senses is there.' Her eyes met Dave's briefly before she turned back to Jess, adding with a hint of apology, 'But I'm preaching to the converted: you feel the same way, I'm sure.'

'Yes, I most certainly do.' In the brief exchange between husband and wife Jess had registered Dave's reaction, infinitesimal though it was. Well he's certainly content for Lilian to speak on his behalf when it comes to the outback, she thought. Jess had felt a strong, personal link with Dave's response. He feels the spirituality of the land as strongly as Lilian does, she thought, perhaps even more. Lilian may be voicing an artist's opinion, but she's expressing her husband's innate belief to perfection.

Matt helped himself to a second serve of stew while the others, finally sated, pushed their bowls aside.

'No clearing up,' Lilian announced, 'not yet. Ice cream a little later; time for talking now. Shall we attack the other bottle of wine, dear?'

Dave fetched the second bottle of Shiraz, which he'd opened and left on the sideboard to breathe.

'Matt said you wanted to pump us for information,' Lilian remarked, holding her glass out for a refill.

Jess cast an accusing look at Matt, who ignored her as he continued to hoe into his fresh bowl of stew.

'So fire away,' Lilian ordered.

'Right.' Jess took a deep breath and did so, directing her questions to Dave who had sat and was refilling their wine glasses. 'Matt says you knew nothing of your grandparents on either side of your family, Dave.'

'That's correct.' He answered with typical brevity. 'The Brian Francis Witherton you discovered might well be my paternal grandfather, but I really wouldn't know.'

Dave had found the discovery interesting, although the interpretations of his son's dreams were far too fanciful for his liking. He was of Matt's opinion.

'Matt's right,' he'd said abruptly when Lilian had told him of the phone call, 'pure coincidence. He's working on a railway so he has dreams about railways, pretty obvious to me.'

'Don't be so literal,' Lilian had scoffed, 'the whole thing's riveting and I for one can't wait to meet this girl.'

'Why? Because you think she might be the right one for Matt?' Dave had queried with a wry smile. 'I'd watch out if I were you: she's probably whacko.'

'You're narrow-minded, that's your problem,' Lilian had replied. 'Who knows what's out there in the ether? Who knows the receptive capabilities of the human brain? Who can *disprove* there's an afterlife?' she'd demanded triumphantly. '*There are more things in heaven and earth, Horatio . . .*'

Dave had opted out at that juncture. When she started quoting Shakespeare it was time to give up. But he'd happily agreed to indulge her whim and meet the girl. He'd answer whatever questions might be fired at him, although for the life of him he couldn't think what possible information he had to offer.

'I did a little more fact-finding, by the way,' Jess said. 'Brian was killed at the Battle of Fromelles.'

'Ah.' An interested nod; Dave waited for her to continue.

'I can't find any war pension record for a wife and child, though, so I doubt he was married when he enlisted.'

Lilian in true fashion was compelled to interrupt, 'which means if he's Charlie's father, as he might well be, the girl he left behind must have adopted his name when she gave birth to his baby despite not having married him.'

'It's a possibility,' Jess admitted; the thought had indeed occurred. She turned once again to Dave who was patiently waiting. 'And your maternal grandparents?' She felt a little intrusive asking intimate questions of a man who appeared so intensely private, but he was obviously expecting her to continue. 'Your mother was adopted, I believe.'

'Yes. Peg never knew her real parents and she never talked about the couple who'd adopted her.' There was a brief pause, Dave glancing at Lilian, perhaps expecting a signal, but none was forthcoming. He turned back to Jess, whose eyes remained trained upon him, and for some unfathomable reason he found himself telling a truth he'd shared with no-one but his wife.

'My mother ran away from home at sixteen,' he said, 'that much I know. It's my belief she was abused by her father throughout her childhood and that her mother was aware of it and turned a blind eye.'

Matt looked up, stew no longer of interest: this was news to him. Why was his father sharing this information with a virtual stranger, when he hadn't even told his son?

'Peg never told me that,' Dave went on matter-of-factly, 'but I'm quite sure I'm right. She detested her adoptive parents in equal measure, never referred to either by name. It was always "that nasty man" or "that nasty woman" or "those nasty people", pretending to shrug them off – rather childlike really. Then she'd change the subject as if it didn't matter. I've always believed those two were complicit in their contribution to a childhood that must have been hideous.'

He picked up his glass and sipped his wine, story over. Brief and unemotionally delivered as it had been, it had made a strong impact and silence reigned around the table, a silence into which Jess could read a great deal. She took a deep breath as something radical occurred. First and foremost, she was aware she had made a connection. How or why, she wasn't sure, but it was apparent that Dave had never mentioned these views to his son, and equally apparent that his wife knew everything. Why me, she wondered, why did he choose to tell me?

Lilian remained silent, but appeared glad Dave had spoken so openly, and Jess, emboldened by the connection she'd made and by what she saw as Lilian's approval, decided to push further.

'Have you had any unusual dreams yourself recently, Dave,' she asked, 'any images that seemed particularly vivid or strange?' He was clearly a non-believer and she hoped the question didn't offend him, but she sensed something receptive in Dave, something that perhaps he was unaware of himself.

'Nope, none whatsoever, sorry to disappoint.' The reply was not rude, but certainly brusque. Dave liked the young woman and didn't regret having been open with her for whatever strange reason had compelled him to do so, but he would not be drawn any further into this ridiculous realm of fantasy.

Lilian seemed the only one not to notice the awkward moment that followed.

'Why do you ask that, Jess?' she queried. 'Do you think it likely Dave might be visited by an ancestor, his grand-father Brian, perhaps?'

Matt looked sharply at his mother. For all her profess-ing to a fondness for things spiritual, was she being face-tious? If so it wasn't fair: Jess genuinely believed all this nonsense. But Lilian's interest appeared quite sincere.

'I don't know,' Jess replied, feeling self-conscious now, aware of the scepticism shared by father and son, but nonetheless determined not to back down. She would make no apology for her belief. 'I somehow doubt it. I think the contact is being specifically directed to Matt.'

Even Lilian could sense the awkwardness in the pause that followed. No-one seemed sure of what to say next, but the conversation was apparently over so she rose to her feet.

'Well, well, stranger things have been known to happen,' she declared. 'Are we ready for ice cream?'

They were, and the subject came up for no further dis-cussion, the unspoken agreement being there was no need. Jess herself certainly felt that everything she'd wanted to ask had been answered, and the evening continued along more mundane lines as they tucked into their ice cream and Lilian plied them both with questions about the Ghan.

Despite the momentary awkwardness of that night, Jess enjoyed every moment of a weekend she had originally thought might be daunting. On Sunday evening she and Matt went to the cocktail party and opening of Lilian's exhibition at the Hill Smith Gallery in Pirie Street.

After admiring the collection, which was a retrospective of Lilian's work and highly impressive, they stood with Dave watching as the gallery owners took to the podium and talked about art, congratulating themselves on their personal selection of Lilian Birch masterpieces and discussing the subtle change in her style over the years and what each phase represented.

Then Dave and Matt and Jess listened to two rather long speeches from dignitaries and finally they basked, all three, in Lilian's charisma as she enthralled a packed audience of admirers.

'She's in good form tonight,' Dave muttered. 'It's because you two are here. Usually at this stage of the proceedings she's so fed up with the "phoney bullshit" as she calls it, she just says "thanks for coming" and gets off.'

The following day as they said their farewells it was Lilian who broached the reason for Jess's visit.

'I hope we were of some help, my dear,' she said after warmly embracing her, 'at least I hope Dave was. I tend to be more an interference than anything, I always am; it's a terrible fault of mine.'

'You were both immensely helpful, Lilian,' Jess assured her.

'Really?' Lilian seemed both surprised and delighted. 'You feel you've learnt something then?' Her eagerness was engagingly ingenuous. 'You're on the verge of discovery perhaps?'

'Perhaps.'

Lilian did not push further, contenting herself instead with a raised eyebrow. 'How very exciting,' she said.

She did so hope this whole business would bring about a bonding between Mattie and Jess: they made such a splendid couple.

Dave had insisted upon driving them to the airport and Lilian stood on the front verandah waving goodbye, a colourful figure in her favourite alpaca.

Jess waved back through the car's open rear window and as Lilian dived inside the house out of the cold, she closed the window and sat back thoughtfully.

She studied Dave in the rear-vision mirror. As father and son talked, she noted the closeness between the two and how similar they were, in appearance and manner, private men, both. Matt, like his father, was a loner.

She would tell no-one, not even Matt, what she had discovered. How could she? She wasn't at all sure herself.

لسلام

1880

The women sit in the clearing between the two rocky outcrops. They have formed a circle and their fingers are tracing patterns in the dusty ground they have brushed clear before them. They are silent as they draw their pictures. The four have been chattering incessantly throughout the long days of their journey south and now, back in the flood-plain territory of their Arunta land, they are relating in the red sand the story of their travels and of recent events.

Letye's finger is strangely at odds with those of the other women, but neither her grandmother nor her mother-in-law nor her aunty notice, for although Letye's finger is white it draws the story as clearly as the black fingers of her family.

Nearby, young Kwala plays with Letye's baby. Letye and her husband Nyapi have called their little girl Antethe, the Arunta word for 'flower' because she was born in the spring when the desert blossoms were in full bloom. It had been Nangala, the matriarch, who had suggested the name. 'This is a good name for the child,' Nangala had said, 'for she is pale like her mother who was named after the white blossom of the bush orange tree.'

Kwala, fours year old and robust, is boisterous with little Antethe, who is barely twelve months of age. He plays with her as he does the dingo pups. When she rises shakily to her feet and totters a step or two he pushes her in the chest and laughs as she promptly falls on her backside. But Antethe does not mind in the least. She just sits there and gurgles with pleasure. Even when Kwala cuddles her roughly to him as he would a dingo pup, she continues to gurgle. Kwala and Antethe have become brother and sister. They love each other very much.

Atanum lolls beside the hillock of rock some distance away chewing on his bush tobacco — he always carries a wad behind his ear — and as he watches the children at play he feels content. He is a great-grandfather now, which is something of an achievement. He would rather Letye had given birth to a boy certainly, but his keen eyes detect the slightest swelling of her belly and he suspects she may once again be with child. He makes no enquiry, not even of his wife Nangala, for that is women's business, but he secretly knows he is right: he has an instinct for such things. He looks forward to the arrival of a great-grandson. Even a pale-skinned one like Antethe, he thinks, watching the bare bodies of the children entwined in play. A great-grandson would indeed be something to boast of.

Letye's fertility pleases Atanum. He had been deeply critical of the match between Nyapi and the white girl, but Nangala had insisted and he is now forced to agree that Nangala has been proved right. Letye is not only fertile, she is pleasant-natured and, a great deal stronger than she looks, she is a hard worker. Lazy, ill-tempered wives are of no use to a man, Atanum thinks. Besides, Nyapi loves her. It is good for a man to have a wife he loves.

Atanum lounges back comfortably against a flat rock that still holds the heat of the day. He enjoys the indulgence his age and seniority afford him. He is still fit but, without the speed and endurance of his younger days, the hunting of heavier game is left to his son Tjumuru and young Nyapi. Life is good, Atanum thinks contentedly, and looking about at his family he starts to sing.

The sound is pleasant to the others: it is a song they know well for Atanum often sings, either in the late afternoon while the meal is cooking as is now the case, or at night when they have eaten and are preparing to sleep.

The women look up from the pictures they are drawing in the sand. They smile at one another. Tjumura too acknowledges the song as he looks up from the emu he is cutting into sections for the cooking fire. The animal has already been plucked and gutted, the carcass singed in the fire and the fat removed. Now one by one Tjumura places the slabs of meat he has butchered directly onto the hot coals. Ankerre is a favourite food of all Arunta and the smell is appetising.

Nyapi does not look up from where he sits cross-legged on the ground, his focus remaining on the wooden bowl before him. The bowl contains the spinifex resin he has collected through much grinding and sifting and panning. In one hand he holds a flaming piece of bark over the resin while with the other he twirls a small stick, gathering up the gum as it melts. When the gum has formed a ball around the stick he will remove it from the heat and it will harden. Then he will carry the stick of gum tucked into his string waistband, portions of it to be melted when required for the making and repair of weapons and utensils. Gum is an all-important commodity of daily life.

But although remaining focused upon his task, Nyapi also acknowledges his grandfather's song, nodding in time to the rhythmic chant of Atanum's voice. This time of day before dusk sets in is a peaceful time, a time when the chores have been done; when the firewood has been collected and the sand cleared of vegetation and brushed smooth for sleeping; when, in the absence of surface water, a hole has been dug to one of the many underground sources known to them; when, dependent upon the weather, windbreaks or lean-tos have been erected; when, in preparation for the chill winter night, extra fires have been built to surround the family as they sleep, fires that will burn on until morning. There is often much work required in setting up camp.

Today, however, none of these duties have been necessary. They have built their cooking fire, certainly, and they have prepared their food, the meat now roasting on the coals and the pencil yams and bush potatoes baking in the hot soil, but no further labour has been required. There is a creek nearby which, at this time of year, invariably provides water and the women have gathered an ample supply; the spring weather is moderate and the night will not be unduly cold; the clearing nestled between the two hillocks of rock is sandy and comfortable, and the rocky outcrops themselves, one large and one smaller, form a natural windbreak. The family knows this place well for this is a favourite campsite and they are glad to be relaxing in such familiar territory after their trek north to meet with their Anmatyerre cousins.

As Atanum continues to sing and as the smell of roasting meat continues to waft ever more tantalisingly in the air, the women complete their pictures and break their silence, comparing drawings and admiring each other's work. Letye feeds Antethe, the child sucking hungrily at her breast while they examine the patterns and symbols each has drawn in the sand. Their drawings are all accounts of the same story, but told from different viewpoints.

The adventure they are reliving is the betrothal of Nyapi's younger sister, Tama. The family has returned from their journey to the land of the Anmatyerre, where twelve-year-old Tama has been delivered to her husband. His name is Luratjira and he is a fine young man sixteen years of age. Tama was promised to Luratjira at the age of eight when their respective families met at a ceremonial gathering of many clans.

For nearly two years now the women have been preparing Tama for this time when she must leave the family and embrace her new life with the family of her husband. The incisions in her flesh were made with infinite care, the lines and the placement of each cut needing to be precise in order to form the correct pattern. Following the cutting of the flesh, coal dust from the fire had been repeatedly rubbed into the wounds to irritate and prolong the healing process, resulting in prominent raised welts on Tama's shoulders and chest, scars that would remain with her for the rest of her life.

The preparation of young Tama had proved the final, and possibly the most intense, lesson in Letye's education. Letye had by then been with the family for well over two years and had recently married Nyapi. She was one of them now, an Arunta woman. But it had been through Emily's eyes that she had watched with horror the mutilation of the little girl who had become her sister. She had said nothing. She had not dared, but she had found the torture barbarous and she had wondered why Tama had not cried out at the pain inflicted upon her. But throughout the process, Tama had never once cried out. She had borne her pain with pride. And as the wounds had slowly healed to form fibrous patterns on her shoulders and between her budding breasts, Tama's pride had grown proportionately. Her scars were the badge of her womanhood and would be attractive to her husband.

It was then that the remnant of Emily remaining in Letye had recognised something beyond the comprehension of her previous self. Pain was tolerated with ease by these people who were now her family, she realised, for the pain borne and the symbols of that pain were a measure of status, gaining them respect in the eyes of others. The thought had not once occurred to Letye. In adapting to her new life, she had never questioned the scars her family members bore, male and female alike, nor had she pondered the missing front teeth of the men, an initiation into manhood: there had been far too many other lessons to be learnt. As the months had passed and as she had watched Tama caress her new scars with pride, Letye had realised that here was yet another lesson, and one of vast importance.

This is the picture Letye has drawn in the sand, a picture of Tama and the scars upon her upper body, and beside her a picture of her husband, Luratjira, and the scars upon his upper body also. The patterns of both are flawless, Letye has remembered them well, and in her drawing the scars symbolise perfectly the image of two young adults now bonded in marriage.

Beside her Tama's mother, Ngita, looks at the picture and smiles in recognition. Her own drawing

is simply a picture of Tama for she can think of
nothing else. She will miss her little girl who has now
become a woman, but she is happy for Tama: the
match is a good one. The other women, Nangala
and Macanti, have drawn far bigger pictures, the
meetings of the families and a map of the journey,
but Ngita likes Letye's drawing best.

Soon it is time to eat. Antethe is now fast
asleep and Letye beds her down in a cushion of
emu feathers nestled in a soft hollow of sand she
prepares while the women dig the vegetables out of
the hot soil. Tjumuru lifts a slab of meat from the fire
onto a flat stone and starts cutting it into chunks with
the sharp shard of quartz that is his favourite knife.
They will feast well tonight.

Tomorrow they will set off on their travels through
this familiar land of theirs to another favourite
campsite. But before they leave they will cover Letye
with mud from the creek, for they are not far from
the singing string. The white man's house that links
the singing string across the desert is barely a day's
walk from here and they do not wish her to be seen.

They are unaware that they are too late. Letye
has already been seen.

In the nearby scrubland barely fifty yards away,
the linesman crouches, watching the family as they
prepare to eat. He has encountered groups of
blacks before, but unless they are damaging the
telegraph line, which it is his job to protect and
maintain, he has no truck with them. It is a different
matter altogether if they are desecrating the line as
many of these heathens do, stealing the insulators
for the making of spearheads. If he catches them in
the act, he will most certainly shoot them, but this lot
appear a peaceable enough bunch.

He is about to creep away and return to his partner. He had only left their camp in order to relieve his bowels, but having done so, he'd been drawn by the aroma of roasting meat to investigate its source and had come upon the blacks as he'd expected he would. They are doing no harm, he decides. Then as he turns to go, he sees her.

He is astounded. A white woman! There is a white woman with the blacks! He gazes at her in amazement, her fair hair and pale skin clearly visible in the gathering dusk. She is a young woman, he guesses her to be no more than twenty, and she is naked. A naked white woman and black men? The thought disgusts him.

He turns from the sight and creeps stealthily back through the scrub to his fellow linesman and their camp. The woman must be rescued. They must make a plan.

PART THREE

PART THREE

CHAPTER NINE

'I been having lots of visits from Ken and Archie lately,' May said as they sat at the kitchen table, the pot of tea before them. 'Mum and Dad as well. And Rose of course,' she added with a smile, 'little Rosie's always with me. And the ancestors, they been around a fair bit too, I can feel 'em, you know?'

It appeared Aunty May was being constantly visited by dead people, her husband, her family and ancestors, but Jess wasn't quite sure who was visiting who. She had a feeling Aunty May might be conjuring up images from the past and ancestral spirits in her eagerness to join those who had gone before her. Not that she seemed in any way maudlin, just a little tired of life, which rather worried Jess.

'Have you been taking your medication?' she asked.

'Course I have. Take the pills every morning and every night, just like the doctor says, but they don't work anymore. I get these dizzy spells, see, and I'm tired all the time.'

Jess felt guilty that she hadn't visited Hermannsburg more regularly. She should have been keeping an eye on Aunty May.

'You need to go to the hospital,' she said, 'you need to see the doctor and get different prescriptions. We'll make an appointment and I'll take you into town.'

'Oh, done all that,' May replied breezily, 'seen the doctor, done tests at the hospital, got new pills from the chemist, I been into town any number of times these past few months. Millie takes me.' May drained her tea and as she replaced the mug on the table her smile couldn't have been prouder. 'Millie's the light of my life, Jess, and that's the truth. She's the light of everyone's life, she's changing this place for the better, she is. More kids going to school, more kids learning . . .'

Twenty-four-year-old Millie had returned to Hermannsburg and had been teaching at the school for quite some time now.

'. . . And that's all because of you.' May stabbed a forefinger at Jess in triumphant accusation. 'It all started that day you first come here. From then on Millie wanted to be just like you.'

May had been saying the same thing for years, in fact every single time Jess paid her a visit, but the compliment did not alleviate her niece's current sense of guilt.

'So what did the tests show? What did the doctor say?'

Again the response was breezy. 'Oh, they say it's the diabetes kickin' in, they reckon I'll have to swap to insulin injections. I don't like the idea of that, stickin' needles in myself,' May scowled, 'I don't like the idea of that at all.' She stood. 'Want another cuppa? I'll freshen up the pot.'

The question was rhetorical so Jess didn't bother replying, but watched while May topped the teapot up with hot water from the full kettle that sat simmering on the stove.

'These are good biccies.' Having returned the kettle to the stove and turned off the heat, May tipped another half dozen or so biscuits from the packet Jess had brought into the bowl on the table.

'I like these,' she said as she sat, 'good for dunkin'. Chocolate chips are my favourite.'

Jess had known they were, that's why she'd brought them – dumb choice, she now thought. 'You shouldn't have any more, Aunty May,' she said, 'they're full of sugar, no good for you.'

May gave a hoot of laughter. 'Bugger off, Jess,' she said, biting into her biscuit. 'Trouble is,' she continued as she munched away, 'I'm getting too old for this world. I'll be ready to leave soon.'

'Too old? That's rubbish,' Jess fired back. 'You're not even sixty!'

'Ken and Archie never made it to sixty,' May combated, referring to her husband and brother, 'crikey, Ken and Archie didn't get any further than fifty.'

'So? That doesn't mean to say *you* have to go prematurely.' Jess felt a touch of desperation, noting for the first time how drained May looked. Appearances could certainly be deceptive. Still a large woman, glossy-black face framed by a fine head of hair that was now silver-white, May remained an impressive figure, but closer inspection revealed shadows under her eyes and signs of fatigue. She looks tired, Jess thought, she looks tired and older than her years.

'You've got a long life ahead of you, Aunty May,' she insisted vehemently. 'Sixty's young these days.'

'Well now, that all depends, doesn't it?' May's eyes held a glint of rebellion. She always enjoyed a good argument. 'All those people who don't want to be old say "you're as young as you feel", don't they? Well I reckon it works both ways. You're as old as you feel too. And I feel old, bloody old. So what's wrong with wanting to go, eh? I reckon the tea's drawn now, don't you?'

Jess could do nothing but nod.

May poured them a fresh mug each, dunked the other half of her biscuit in her tea, rescuing it with perfect timing, and washing it down with a swig. Then as she leant back, the picture of contentment, she became suddenly aware of Jess's concern, which was patent.

'Crikey, don't worry about me, love,' she said, 'you mustn't worry about me whatever you do.' She was keen now to put her niece at ease – she'd only been talking for talking's sake. The last thing she'd intended was to worry the girl. 'I'm not going anywhere just yet,' she assured her, 'got enough to keep me around for a while. There's the grandkids, isn't there? All grown up now, some of them off the rails, I admit,' she added with a comic roll of her eyeballs, 'but some of them doin' real well. Like Millie, and there's young Jack too. He's down in Adelaide playin' with the Crows – you knew that, didn't you? Yeh, course you did. Everything he ever dreamt of, that boy. Footie'll keep him on the straight and narrow. That's a good thing to see that is, that makes me real happy.'

'Then why do you want to go?' Jess demanded. She wasn't buying May's sudden heartiness. 'If following your grandkid's careers makes you so happy then why do you want to go?'

May studied her niece shrewdly. This was what she loved most about Jess. The two of them always ended up having a real intelligent chat, sometimes even an argument. Jess called it a debate. May had missed that lately.

'I didn't say I *wanted* to go,' she replied with an air of smugness, 'I said what's *wrong* with wanting to go: that's got a different meaning altogether, that has.'

Jess remained combative. 'You said you'll be ready to leave soon. Those were your very words.'

'And I will be too, when my time's up.'

'And when will that be?'

'Not quite sure, can't tell right now, but I'll know when it comes.' May was happy to put the argument to rest at this stage. 'Life's got to be good, Jess, or what's the point livin' it?' Leaning forwards, she patted her niece's hand reassuringly. 'I just want to be prepared, that's all, love. Want to say hello to the family that's gone and to the ancestors, you know? Get 'em ready to put out the welcome mat, that's all, nothin' to worry about.'

The subject now exhausted, they talked about other things, Millie for the most part and the fact that she was seeing a nice young man who met with May's approval. 'Works for the council,' she said, 'I reckon a girl like Millie could do with someone a bit brainier myself, but he doesn't get rotten on the grog and that's all that matters in the long run.' Then they talked about the school and education in general, and an hour later, Jess took her leave, May walking with her to the front door of the cottage.

'You promise me you'll do everything the doctor says now,' Jess demanded.

'Course I will. Stickin' a few needles in here and there won't be the end of the world.' May shrugged. 'We'll see what happens. It'll work or it won't work, who knows?'

They hugged, holding each other close as they always did.

'That was good fun, Jess,' May said upon parting. 'You should visit me more often,' her wink was brazen, 'I won't want to go if you're around.'

Jess smiled. 'Are you blackmailing me?'

'Too right I am.'

'I'll visit once a fortnight from now on,' she promised then she set off towards the car, turning back to wave.

'Don't forget the biscuits,' May called after her.

As she drove the hundred and thirty kilometres back to Alice Springs, Jess wondered vaguely whether perhaps she'd been conned. She doubted it, but Aunty May was a wily old bird. She wouldn't put it past her.

The Ghan was taking shape, the four sections of its mighty rail corridor forging inexorably north and south from Katherine and Tennant Creek. These formerly sleepy outback towns, now industrial hubs, were thriving as workers flocked to the factories and labourers reported for work on the line. The law of supply and demand prevailing, local tradespeople and businesses had never had it so good. Everyone loved the Ghan.

Track was now being laid south of Katherine and in the sector running north from Tennant Creek, and this too was a thrilling sight to behold. The task was performed by colossal track-laying machines, behemoths the like of which had never been seen before even by the most sophisticated of locals. It was hoped the two lines would be linked by the end of the year, both central sectors being scheduled for completion well before the north and south lines that would eventually culminate in Darwin and Alice Springs respectively.

The creation of the rail corridor south from Tennant Creek was progressing as planned, the final leg from Ti Tree now well over halfway to Alice Springs. There were barely eighty kilometres to go, but the massive teams of workers and the flotilla of heavy machinery had reached the flood plains and progress was slower due to the necessary construction of bridges and culverts. The weather remained in their favour, however, and the corridor continued steadily to plough its way south.

Matt and his four-man team still worked roughly twenty kilometres ahead of the labour force, following the rough track left by the surveyors who had originally mapped the course, but there was less pressure now as behind them construction work slowed the overall process.

'Like being on holiday really, isn't it?' Pottsy remarked one afternoon as they lolled around taking an extra-long smoko. The weather was perfect, a clear day in late June, the temperature a pleasant twenty-seven degrees. They didn't even need to seek shelter from the sun during smoko the way they did in the baking, raw heat of summer. The nights were freezing admittedly, but this was a good time of year to be in the desert.

Gav and Baz and Mitch all grinned agreement, Gav and Baz lighting up a second cigarette apiece, but Pottsy's remark hadn't actually been made in jest. He'd directed the comment towards Withers, hoping for some reaction. He didn't get one. Sitting on a rock a few yards away, Withers continued to stare at nothing, his mug of tea untouched on the ground beside him. He'd poured it from his Thermos a good twenty minutes earlier and hadn't taken one sip. He was doing this sort of thing a lot lately and Pottsy was starting to get a bit worried: it wasn't like Withers to be so distracted. It wasn't like Withers to be so slack with the boys either. Not that the bloke was ever a slave-driver, but when there was less urgency required, as was now the case, it was Withers's form to keep his team working at the normal pace and then give the men a half day off, rewarding them for their efficiency. That was the sort of boss Withers was.

Pottsy waited until the boys had finished their smokes and then stood. He walked the several paces over to Withers and said casually, 'Want to get back to work, mate?' He didn't mean to be critical, but hell they weren't there to sit around all day.

Matt was jolted back to the present from wherever it was he'd been, and jumped to his feet, knocking over the mug of tea. 'Sorry, Pottsy,' he said, 'sorry, mate, I was off somewhere daydreaming, sorry about that.'

'No worries. You spilt your tea.'

'Didn't want it anyway.' Matt packed away his Thermos and mug. 'Righto, boys, back to work.'

The afternoon progressed smoothly enough until a couple of hours later when, towards the end of the work day, another episode occurred, which to Pottsy's mind was particularly worrying. He was overseeing the setting of the boundary pegs at the time, the distance from the centre line having been measured, Baz and Mitch setting the posts in place. Withers had instructed Gav to clear a thick clump of mulga and scrub up ahead that was directly in the path of the theodolite's next position where visibility would be required for the laser to make connection with the prism. Having left instructions for all, Withers had then disappeared with his map, presumably to scout the territory well in advance of their current position.

Pottsy, concentrating on the task at hand, had no idea there was anything amiss until he heard an almighty scream.

'Jesus Christ!' Two hundred metres away, Gav's voice rang out above the sound of the bulldozer and Pottsy and the boys turned just in time to see him hit the brakes, bringing the machine to an instant halt.

'Oh Jesus!' he yelled again, and slamming the gears into neutral he leapt out and belted around to the front, obviously to inspect whatever it was he'd run over.

Pottsy and the others raced to join him, presuming it was a kangaroo and wondering why he was so upset: these things did happen and Gav was hardly a wimp.

They arrived to discover it wasn't a kangaroo. It was Withers.

Gav had had no idea his boss was standing there in the clump of trees he'd been ordered to bulldoze. Why on earth would such a thought occur to him? When one of the trees in falling had caught Matt a glancing blow to the head, throwing him directly in the path of the machine, poor Gav had been horrified. His instincts had kicked in immediately, but he was nonetheless sure he'd run over the bloke.

By the time Pottsy and the boys reached them Gav was on his knees, an arm around Withers helping him to sit up. And Gav was freaking out.

'Jesus, mate, what were you doing?' he yelled. 'I nearly killed you! You were right in my path, I was on top of you for Christ's sake – I nearly ran over you! What the fuck were you doing there?'

Matt shook his head uncomprehendingly. 'I'm sorry, Gav,' he said, 'I'm sorry, really sorry.' What the hell had he been doing there? He had no idea.

Quickly assessing the situation, Pottsy realised that Gav was the one in need of attention. Gav was a twitchy mess bordering on hysteria.

'It's okay, mate,' he said, 'no harm done,' and bending down he helped heave Matt to his feet. 'You boys get Gav a cuppa,' he said to Baz and Mitch. 'You right, Withers?' he muttered. Matt nodded. 'There, see,' Pottsy gave Gav a reassuring thump on the shoulder, 'everything's jake. Go and have a smoke, mate.' Then he took Matt aside, not offering assistance, still playing it casual, but checking he was steady enough on his feet, which he was.

They sat in the sand beside the clump of felled mulga and Pottsy waited until the others were well out of earshot. 'Gav's got a point,' he said quietly. 'What the hell were you doing there?'

'I don't know,' Matt said, bewildered, 'I honestly don't know.' He tried his hardest to recall. 'I was walking further up the line to check out the map and do a bit of a recce – I remember that much. I must have cut through the thicket of trees I suppose, but instead of going on something stopped me.' He wondered how to describe the trance-like state he'd experienced, but it seemed impossible. 'I had some sort of mental blackout, Pottsy,' he said, 'I really can't explain it. I had no idea I was in Gav's path and I've no idea how long I was standing there. All I remember is being whacked over the head and finding myself on the ground with a bulldozer about to run over me.' He gave a tremulous smile, attempting to lighten the moment. 'Lucky it was Gav at the helm or I'd be so much squashed meat. You've got to give it to the bloke, his reflexes are bloody good.'

But Pottsy wasn't prepared to have the moment lightened. 'I reckon you should visit the doc, mate,' he said. 'I've noticed it for a while now. You've been a bit off the air lately, you know that?'

Matt nodded. Of course he knew he'd been 'a bit off the air' lately, and of course Pottsy would be the first to notice.

'You look tired too,' Pottsy added, 'bloody tired. Is everything all right?'

Matt was touched by the concern he could see in the sun-ravaged face of his friend. 'Yeah sure, Pottsy, everything's fine,' he assured him, 'really it is. I haven't been sleeping well lately,' he added in all honesty, 'that's the problem, just a case of fatigue, nothing more.'

Recognising conversation over, Pottsy smiled. 'Well go to the doc and get some sleeping pills, mate: we can't have you being run over by bulldozers.'

'You're looking tired,' she said.

It was several days later, a Saturday around lunchtime, and he'd met Jess at the Todd Tavern in Alice. They hadn't ordered lunch, neither was hungry, so they'd sat in the front bar at a table by the windows looking out over the street. They hadn't seen each other since their visit to Adelaide three weeks previously.

'As a matter of fact,' she said, studying him closely, 'you're not looking very well. Is everything all right?' She'd thought he sounded a little edgy over the phone. 'Want to meet up on Saturday?' he'd asked abruptly, and she'd sensed it wasn't just for a social chat, but she'd made no enquiry. 'Love to,' she'd said.

'Sure, everything's fine,' he replied sarcastically, 'just a few minor mishaps, falling asleep on the job, letting my team down, getting run over by a bulldozer, that sort of thing, nothing major.'

His response seemed somehow like a personal attack and she wondered why, but she let it go. 'What's happening, Matt? What's going on?'

'You tell me,' there was no disguising the hostility in his voice now, 'you're the one with all the answers.'

'I can't give you the answers if you don't tell me what's wrong,' she said coolly.

'All right,' he shrugged, 'I'm sorry.' It was an admission of guilt, but not an apology. His tone was still terse, his anger not actually directed at her at all, but rather himself. He was cross that he felt driven to tell her of his dilemma, even to seek her assistance, as if he believed all that mumbo jumbo of hers. He curbed his irritation as best he could. 'I've been having recurring dreams,' he said. 'Different dreams from the ones about the railway and the war. I was having them before we went to Adelaide, actually.'

'Why didn't you tell me?'

'I didn't think it was important. They seemed perfectly natural at the time.' He gave another shrug, trying to appear unconcerned, but not quite carrying it off. 'I'm working in the desert, so I dream about the desert, what could be more normal?'

'Tell me about them.'

'They were just images to start with, flood plains, granite outcrops, typical central desert landscape, but always seen from high above, an aerial view, harmless enough. At least that's the way they used to be,' he said, his manner once again becoming tense. 'They've changed lately.'

In describing the images, Matt had brought them alive and they were now stabbing into his brain with all their customary force, knife-like and alarming. 'I don't know how to explain it, they're still images of the desert, but they zoom in and out like a speeded-up movie,' he said, 'or they go around and around like I'm on a carousel. They've become distorted, crazy, they're driving me insane.'

Already he was beginning to feel dizzy. He always felt dizzy when the dreams awoke him at night. He quickly suppressed the images, the description was inadequate anyway, and it was surely better to stop before the headache set in.

'They're not dreams any more, Jess, they're more like nightmares, and they're having repercussions. They wake me every night, they revisit me during the day, and fatigue's taking over to the point where I have blackouts.'

'What do you do when the dreams wake you, Matt?'

'What the hell do you think?' Again the edge of irritation: the answer was surely obvious. 'Make myself a cup of tea, read a book, anything to fill in the time, I can't go back to sleep, that's for sure.'

She refused to let his manner affect her; he was clearly a troubled man. 'Tell me about the blackouts,' she said patiently.

Again Matt forced himself to calm down, aware he was behaving irrationally. 'I seem to go into some sort of trance,' he said, 'without any warning – it's inexplicable.' He went on to tell her about the bulldozer incident and Jess, although horrified to hear of such a narrow escape, made little further comment, waiting instead for him to continue.

'That sort of blackout's happened several times,' he explained. 'I don't know where I am or how long I'm out of it, but when I come back to the present from wherever it is I've been, I always have a headache. The dreams bring on headaches too.' He looked bewildered. 'I'm not used to headaches. I don't get them, never have, at least not until now.'

His tale concluded, he steeled himself for her analysis. 'I don't know what's going on, Jess,' he said, aware that whatever bizarre explanation she came up with was bound to irritate, and aware also that he had no option but to listen to whatever she had to say. 'I need your help,' he admitted. The same impulse that had urged him to tell her about his dream of the Burma railway those several months earlier, which now seemed a lifetime ago, was urging him to seek the answer from her.

Given his current mood Jess knew her reply would not meet with a favourable response, but in the firm belief she was right she decided to get straight to the point.

'They're deliberately making you sick in order to get your attention,' she said bluntly. 'You haven't been listening to them so they're taking drastic action.'

He found the use of 'they' and 'them' far more than irritating; he found it intensely annoying. 'I presume you're referring to *the ancestors*,' he sneered, 'good old Charlie and Brian, am I right?'

'Spot on,' she replied, undeterred by his sarcasm, which was exactly what she'd expected. 'Look, Matt,' she said reasonably, 'whether you choose to believe or not is immaterial at this stage. The truth of the matter is your dreams are becoming more persistent, more aggressive, and they're taking over your life to the point where they're making you ill. You have to start paying attention to what they may mean. I'm not being unrealistic. Any psychiatrist would tell you the same thing. Call it your subconscious if you prefer, call it what you like, but you're receiving messages from somewhere – you can't deny it.'

She was gratified to note the look of annoyance had gone to be replaced by an expression she found oddly defenceless, as if with nowhere else to turn he'd finally surrendered, and she realised that, despite his disbelief, he had decided to place his trust in her. Well he has little other choice really has he, she thought, but she couldn't help feeling touched nonetheless.

'I know you're determined to seek a logical explanation and I can understand why,' she continued, 'but try to accept the fact that some*thing* or some*one* might be trying to tell you something and that the situation itself is becoming more urgent. Perhaps time is running out. Perhaps they want to warn you of something that's about to happen – I have no idea. But be receptive,' she urged. 'Make yourself accessible. It's the only way you'll find out.'

He was silent for a moment. Then, 'What do I do?' he asked, 'tell me.'

She gazed out the window at the passers-by in Todd Street and those seated at the tavern's tables on the pavement, but she wasn't seeing the people at all. *What do we do?* She asked the question of herself and also of the ancestors hoping wishfully that they might perhaps make themselves known to her and offer up some mystical answer. They didn't. But then she hadn't really expected them to, after all Charlie and Brian weren't *her* ancestors.

With nothing forthcoming, she decided to adopt a practical approach in the hope he'd believe she knew what she was doing. It was essential she maintain his trust, even though she was forced to admit to herself she had no idea what the next step should be.

'Let's take a drive up to where you had your blackout the other day,' she said firmly, 'where you nearly got run over by the bulldozer.'

'And then?'

'And then we'll see what happens.'

They headed out of town in his Land Rover along the Stuart Highway, which was ever-busy these days with the constant transport of men and materials and machinery required for the construction of The Ghan. When they were far enough north they would take one of the many tracks that had been created to provide access to the rail corridor, which although roughly paralleling the main road was some distance to the east.

As Matt drove, Jess encouraged conversation in a deliberate ploy to distract him. The time for introspection lay ahead, for now it was important he should relax.

'How are Lilian and Dave?' she asked. 'Have you spoken to them recently?'

'I most certainly have,' he replied, only too happy to be distracted and discuss something 'normal'. 'Before we left Adelaide Lilian made me promise faithfully I'd ring every week from now on. She said our visit had served as a *shocking* reminder of how *shamefully* I'd neglected her and Dave for the past six months.'

Jess laughed. Without actually mimicking his mother, the over-emphasis had been spot on. 'Yes, I can just hear Lilian saying that.'

'She puts Dad on the phone and we chat for five minutes – of course Dave doesn't care whether I ring or not – and then I cop Lilian for another half hour at least, usually longer.'

'They're a great couple, your parents,' she said, 'I liked them a lot.'

'They liked you too. You made a huge impression, particularly with Lilian – she's always asking after you.' A little too much, Matt thought. He strongly suspected his mother was bent on matchmaking, although in Lilian's defence she did appear interested in Jess's beliefs, to the point where at times she even sounded like a convert.

'Such an interesting young woman,' he recalled his mother saying the first time he'd made his obligatory call, 'such a mixture of the practical and the spiritual, and *frightfully* intelligent. I find that *so* attractive, don't you?'

'Yes, yes, Mum.' He'd been instantly dismissive. It was clear she wanted to pair them up as he'd suspected she might, and he wasn't having any of it.

But Lilian would not be dismissed. 'No, no, dear,' she'd insisted, 'I'm serious. A girl like Jess renders the concept of spiritualism eminently believable. At least she does to me. I'm most fascinated to learn of the outcome of her investigations. Has she told you what she gleaned during her Adelaide visit? I'm dying to know. I didn't push when she hinted at the fact,' Lilian's rich laugh had echoed down the line, 'kept my big mouth shut for once. Rather admirable on my part I thought, but I can't wait to hear exactly what it *was* that she gleaned during her time with us. Has she said anything to you yet?'

'I wasn't aware she'd *gleaned* anything at all in Adelaide,' Matt had replied. Only my mother would use that word with such abandon, he thought.

'Oh yes, she definitely learnt something. In fact she hinted she might be "on the verge of discovery"!' Even while lending the phrase dramatic emphasis, Lilian had forgotten that the words were actually her own and that Jess had said no such thing. 'I found that tremendously exciting, I must say.'

Accustomed as he was to his mother's flair for the theatrical, Matt hadn't paid much attention to the conversation. And during the two further obligatory phone calls he'd made over the ensuing fortnight when Lilian had continued to plague him about Jess and her investigations and whatever it was she had learnt in Adelaide, he'd paid even less attention. 'I haven't seen Jess, Mum,' he'd said, much to Lilian's disappointment. 'Oh what a pity,' she'd replied, and then chatted away animatedly about any number of things that could quite possibly have been fascinating, but he'd clocked off altogether. He was tired by then, the dreams were getting to him and he didn't have the energy to take an interest in anything his mother had to say, or anyone else for that matter.

Now as he drove and as the two of them talked of her, Matt recalled his initial phone conversation with Lilian and his curiosity was distinctly aroused.

'Mum told me you'd discovered something in Adelaide,' he said.

'Did she?' Jess responded blandly, giving away nothing.

'Well, "gleaned" was the word she used, actually, which I found just a touch mysterious. Then she said you felt you were "on the verge of discovery".'

'Hardly. They were Lilian's words, every one of them. Including "gleaned",' Jess added with a smile.

'Yes, I thought the whole thing sounded rather like her, but she was very insistent.' Matt's eyes left the road for a moment to study her keenly. Melodramatic his mother might be, but Lilian never lied. 'Did you really feel that you'd learned something?'

'Oh probably not,' Jess said with a shrug. Now is certainly not the time to tell him, she thought. 'Just a gut feeling, a sort of hunch: I'm probably completely wrong.'

He wasn't prepared to buy that. 'Gut feelings and hunches,' he said, eyes once more on the road. 'Aren't they more or less what we're following right now?'

There was a brief pause then, 'Yes,' she admitted, 'yes they are. I'm sorry. I didn't mean to fob you off.'

'Oh yes you did.' Another glance and in his eyes was accusation, but his tone was not unkind. 'You most certainly did.'

'I'll tell you when I know, Matt,' she said. 'I'll tell you when I feel really sure that I'm right. I promise.'

'Fair enough,' he agreed.

They continued to chat about inconsequential things, just two good friends out for a drive, while Matt kept a sharp lookout for the track that would lead off to the right.

'That's where we turn,' he said eventually, pointing up ahead to a bush track that was all but invisible to Jess.

They turned off the main road and followed the track for about twenty kilometres. They were quiet now, free of the traffic and the busyness of the highway, both enjoying the tranquillity and surrounding scenery.

Beautiful country, Jess thought, as she always did. Without the dramatic grandeur of the towering rock edifices and gorges and rock pools that attracted the tourists, some might consider it repetitive, some perhaps even boring, but she loved the flood plains. The endless stretch of red earth, the mulgas and acacias and elegant coolabahs, the healthy growth of grasses and vegetation that sprang from underground water sources, here was yet another face of the ever-changing desert.

They reached a T-junction with another rough bush track and Matt took a further right turn.

'We're on the original surveyors' track now,' he said, 'the one my team's been following as we chart the course. 'You can see our pegs over there marking the path of the rail corridor.'

She looked where he was pointing and could see the centreline pegs and the boundary posts defining the allowances for firebreaks and service roads. The course was clearly delineated for the contractors who would mark out the final rail construction path that the teams of workers and heavy earth-moving equipment would follow.

'We need to head back south a few Ks,' he explained, 'that'll get us to where we were working on the day of the bulldozer incident.'

They drove along the track beside the marked-out route of the rail corridor and five minutes or so later Matt pulled the vehicle up.

'Here we are.' He indicated the spot. 'It happened over there.'

Jess looked towards the clump of felled mulga. 'Right,' she said, 'that's where we start,' and they climbed from the vehicle.

'What do I do?' he asked when they'd crossed to the fallen timber and he stood near the spot where he'd had his blackout.

Jess pondered the matter momentarily, not sure of the right answer. She recalled her first spiritual encounter that day at Emily Gap, when she had felt the ancestors of Mparntwe welcome her. The experience had changed her life. Since then the contacts she'd had with the spirit world, brief as they'd been, had occurred automatically, she'd never had to analyse how or why she was receptive. What instruction could she possibly offer a confirmed non-believer, and a white man at that? How did one teach a person like Matt to open his heart and his mind to another plane of existence?

'I don't suppose you've ever given meditation a go?' she asked hopefully. The response was nothing more than the whimsical raise of an eyebrow. 'No, I thought not,' she said. 'Well, why don't you close your eyes and breathe deeply ...' she suggested in a suitably assertive manner 'and you might want to start by slowly counting –'

'I know what meditation is, Jess.'

'Oh. Right.' She was relieved to note that her school-teacher antics had amused more than anything, and he certainly seemed relaxed, which was a very good sign.

'I'm quite prepared to make myself accessible, as you put it,' he went on, 'but shouldn't I focus upon something, and if so, what? Seriously, I mean it. Charlie? Brian? I don't even know what Brian looks like.'

She wondered if he was being facetious then realised that he was in deadly earnest. Good question too, she thought, but the answer's much simpler. 'Focus upon the images in your dreams, Matt,' she said. 'You've been sent pictures of the land for a reason. Think of the dreams and give yourself up to them.'

He nodded obediently, although he didn't relish the dizziness and the headache that were likely to result. Best to get it over and done with, he thought, but he determined nonetheless to give it his best shot. Without another word he turned from her, stood very still and closed his eyes.

'I'll go and wait in the car,' she said, feeling suddenly superfluous. 'I'll leave you to it.'

She walked away and Matt relaxed, the rays of the mild mid-afternoon sun pleasant on his face. Then, after taking several deep breaths, he willed the images he'd been so assiduously avoiding back into his mind.

From thirty metres away Jess watched through the car's open passenger window. He was utterly motionless, a lone figure in the desert, just Matt surrounded by the wilderness. What was happening? she wondered. Were they making themselves known to him, his ancestors? Was he seeing them, Charlie and Brian, was he hearing their voices, was he feeling their touch? She longed to know.

She didn't take her eyes from him for a full half hour, during which time there remained no movement at all, a passing breeze ruffling the sleeve of his khaki shirt, nothing more.

Then even as she remained watching, he turned to her. Or rather he turned to the car. And then he was striding purposefully towards the vehicle, opening the door, climbing in, turning on the ignition.

She didn't say a word as they drove off, although she ached for answers. Instead she waited for him to offer information, which he did, to a certain extent anyway.

'We need to head further south along the old surveyor's track,' he said.

'Right you are.' She tried not to scrutinise him too obviously, but in her peripheral vision she searched for changes. Had he had a life-changing experience? It didn't seem so. He appeared purposeful, certainly, but apart from that he was absolutely normal.

'Just on the border of the flood-plain territory,' he said. 'Two granite outcrops: I'll know them when I see them.'

Jess's mind was teeming with questions. How will you know them? Who told you? What happened back there? She longed for the answers, but didn't dare enquire. There appeared nothing at all mysterious in his manner, he was simply following instructions. But whose instructions was he following?

Had she asked, she would have been disappointed in the answer. Matt had experienced no epiphany, no life-changing moment. In calling up the images of his dreams and focusing upon them, they had simply become clarified. A course had been set out before him as clearly as any surveyor's map and he was following it without hesitation. Perhaps later he might question who or what was guiding him, but for now he was simply noting each of the passing landmarks that had been presented to him, in the knowledge they were getting closer to their destination with every passing minute.

He described the site to her, vivid as it was in his mind's eye. 'The rocky hillocks are about ten metres apart,' he said, 'surrounded by spinifex grasses and a few trees with a natural clearing in the middle. There's a creek about fifty metres out. One of the outcrops is a lot bigger than the other and has a sign carved on a rock about halfway up. I can't see exactly what the sign is, but we'll find out when we get there.'

'Great.' Jess's reply was suitably laid-back, but she was astounded. He can *see* the rocks, he can *see* the sign, he can *see* the creek, but he's not questioning how or why, she thought. He still doesn't believe the ancestors are leading him. How fascinating. 'That's really great, Matt,' she said and she sat back and enjoyed the ride.

They'd been travelling a good half hour or so when up ahead on their right, two rock formations came into view.

'There they are,' he announced, according to his reckoning they were by now roughly thirty kilometres from Alice Springs. 'Yep, that's the place all right,' he said as they drew nearer, and again Jess was amazed by the normalcy of his manner. They might have been arriving at a favourite picnic spot.

Upon reaching the site he brought the Land Rover to a halt and they climbed out in order to walk the twenty metres or so from the track to the rocky hillocks.

The place is exactly as he described it, Jess thought, two granite outcrops about ten metres apart, one a lot larger than the other, a natural clearing in the middle, how extraordinary. She found the larger of the hillocks impressive, rising out of the surrounding flat terrain, the late afternoon sun lighting up its fiery redness, and she searched for any evidence of the sign he'd mentioned. But she couldn't see anything: perhaps it was on the far side.

As they reached the rocks and walked into the centre of the clearing, Jess's eyes continued to rake the larger outcrop seeking the sign and suddenly there it was. From this particular angle she could just make it out. Halfway up the hillock and indistinct in the glare of the sun, it would have been all but invisible had she not been searching. She wondered what it could be. Early Aboriginal artwork perhaps, as yet undiscovered? They were in a remote spot; it was quite possible no-one knew of its existence. The prospect was exciting.

'I can see it, Matt,' she said, her voice hushed, not wishing to disturb the silence. 'The sign, it's there. I can't make out what it is though,' she said, squinting up at the rock face.

She received no reply. Beside her, Matt appeared to be in a state of semi-consciousness. He remained deathly still, his eyes open, but trance-like: he was in another place altogether, hearing and seeing nothing, or so it seemed.

Jess found the sight unnerving, but, realising he was having one of the blackouts he'd talked of, she knew she must not disturb him. Even now the ancestors may be making themselves known; under no circumstances must she intrude.

She backed away quietly, feeling like an interloper in a moment of such intimacy, but even as she withdrew, she sensed some strange connection of her own. What was it? She felt no spiritual presence – but rather a kind of *restlessness* that emanated from the land itself. She was uneasy in this place.

She decided to climb the larger outcrop and examine the sign, leaving Matt in his trance-like state, buying time, putting distance between them. When she returned he would hopefully have regained consciousness and they could discuss what it was he had learnt from the ancestors.

The hillock was not difficult to climb, but she moved very slowly, choosing each hand- and foothold with infinite care, wary of dislodging any loose rock that in falling would disrupt the silence.

Travelling at the rate she was, it took her some time to reach the sign and when she did it proved strangely disappointing. Carved roughly into the flat surface of one of the granite rocks, it was weathered and had clearly been there for some time, but apart from its age little else appeared of significance. It was not the ancient Aboriginal artwork she'd hoped for, but of course she should have known that, she told herself. In recounting his vision of the site Matt had said the sign was carved into the rock. The artwork of the central desert Aborigine was never carved, but painted in kaolin or ochre. The iconography was not familiar to her either, and if it had been Indigenous she would most certainly have recognised it. So what did the sign mean? Who had put it there? Jess wondered.

At first glance the roughly hewn pattern might have been a bird, but upon closer examination perhaps it was a caterpillar, how could one tell? The simplistic squiggles were impossible to decipher. What on earth could it mean? It signified nothing to her. But then perhaps it was not intended to signify. Perhaps it was simply a form of graffiti, old indeed, but graffiti nonetheless. It may have been left by men working on the Overland Telegraph Line a hundred and thirty years back. If so, how interesting, she thought. Some things never change. Men always need to leave their mark.

She turned and was about to slowly make her way back down the hillock when below in the clearing she saw Matt drop to his knees. He started to rock back and forth and she could hear his voice. He was calling out, one word, over and over, and she couldn't believe what she was hearing.

Abandoning care, she scrambled down the rocky outcrop, bringing with her a shower of stones, slithering on her backside, scraping her elbows raw as she went.

Upon reaching the clearing she ran to him. His face was bathed in sweat, his whole body shaking, his eyes staring unseeingly at the ground, and as he rocked back and forth he continued to call out the one word, again and again.

'*Arrtyaneme! Arrtyaneme! Arrtyaneme!*'

She crouched beside him. He was speaking Arunta. 'Run!' he was calling out. 'Run! Run!'

لسلام

1880

The linesmen have made their plan. There is no turning back. The mere thought that a white woman is being defiled by black heathens is abhorrent to them, as it would be to any decent man of Christian faith, they agree. It is their bounden duty to rescue the unfortunate creature even at their own peril and they will not be deterred. But the motive that drives them is not altogether altruistic for they firmly believe their noble action will reap a sizeable reward.

Upon returning to the campsite Wilt had recounted what he'd seen to his partner.

'A young white woman, Col,' he'd said, 'buck naked like the black savages themselves. They clearly have their way with her. I tell you here and now I was fair sickened by the sight.'

Colm Doherty, a tough, savvy Irishman, had been equally appalled, but in his customary manner also quick to recognise an advantage in the discovery.

'Do you think it's at all likely it could be the McQuillan girl?' he'd asked.

The thought had not occurred to Wilton Baker. He too was tough, a Yorkshire man who, like Col, had been working the line for five years, but Wilt did not possess Col's opportunistic eye.

'It's possible,' he replied after a moment's consideration. 'She'd be of an age that would fit, around twenty by my reckoning, and they say the McQuillan girl was sixteen when she disappeared.'

Both men had read all about Emily McQuillan. Everyone had. The story had been headline news throughout the whole of South Australia. James McQuillan, one of the state's wealthiest men, found dead from a snakebite barely two miles west of his cattle station in the remote lands far north of Adelaide. He'd been out riding with his young daughter. Emily's horse had returned to the homestead, but there'd been no sign of the girl herself. Nor had her body been discovered, despite the efforts of costly and extensive search parties over the ensuing months. Huge reward offers had appeared in the newspaper; posters and leaflets had been distributed throughout remote areas, all seeking information and offering rewards, but no-one had come forward. Young Emily McQuillan had simply disappeared.

'But do you really believe,' Wilt said, 'that the savages would have kept her these past four years? Wouldn't you think they'd have killed her after having their way with her?'

'Nope,' Col replied, 'she'd be a novelty to them, they'd have fun passing her around – nothing's sacred to those black bastards. I swear to you, Wilt, it's our duty to save that girl from a life of unspeakable shame and degradation.'

Wilt nodded. He couldn't possibly disagree with that.

'And even if it turns out not to be the McQuillan girl,' Col went on, 'there'll be a family out there only too happy to reward us for the return of their daughter. The McQuillan purse would be preferable, I grant you, but either way I'll warrant there's money for us in this.'

Again Wilt nodded. Col was making infinite sense. The two had only recently partnered up, as linesmen they normally worked alone, but Wilt had quickly come to realise it was wise to listen to Col. Col was smart. So as they'd loaded their weapons and set about making their plan he'd paid close heed to all Col had to say.

'We shoot the men first. Three of them, you said, am I right?'

'Yes, I counted three, an older one, grey-haired and two younger ones.'

'Three, good,' Col says, 'that won't be difficult, and when we've done with them the women will be easy. You didn't count the women?'

'No, but there were two, maybe three.' While systematically feeding the bullets into the magazine of his Winchester repeating rifle, Wilt casts a querying glance at his partner. 'We don't need to shoot the women, do we?'

'Ah well now, you never know,' Col appears dubious. 'If they get hysterical and out of control they can turn like rabid dogs; let's not forget these are savages we're dealing with. We'll just have to see what happens.'

There is a gleam of anticipation in Col's eyes as he loads his twin Colt revolvers. They are .45 calibre 'Peacemakers' recently purchased from a gunsmith in Adelaide. Formerly the property of a wealthy American mining engineer who'd settled in Australia during the gold strikes, the revolvers are Col's pride and joy. A 'man's man', guns are his passion: he loves nothing more than the hunt. And on this cloudless evening with the moon near-full, conditions are perfect. Col is very much looking forward to the night's sport.

The family has feasted well. Curled up next to his mother, little Kwala, his belly full, is already dozing off. Even the two pet dingoes that assist the men with their hunting are replete, the desultory gnawing of bones being for pleasure rather than hunger.

Nangala is seated beside the flat stone that has served as a cutting table. One by one and with great care, she is wrapping the several spare slabs of raw meat in emu feathers. They will be kept for the following day. She and her grandson and his wife work as a team. When Nangala has completed a parcel she passes it up to Letye who in turn passes it on to Nyapi who is standing some way from them beside an acacia tree. Nyapi then ties the parcel into a fork of the tree's limbs, keeping it safely out of reach from marauders while Letye returns to await the next parcel.

Ngita is digging out from the hot soil the several yams and bush potatoes that were not eaten, these too will be kept for the following day, while nearby Atanum and Tjumuru lounge lazily in the sand by the cooking fire, Atanum chewing his bush tobacco. Soon he will sing.

The family is unaware of the danger that lurks barely twenty yards from them. Even the dingoes have sensed nothing, for the linesmen, experienced hunters both, have made their approach from downwind.

Then the double click of the Winchester being cocked cuts through the silence, startlingly loud.

It is a sound foreign to the family and all eyes turn in the direction from whence it came, a thicket of ti tree bushes at the edge of the clearing.

A moment frozen in time as the family waits, not alarmed, but rather puzzled, watching for something to materialise and make itself known to them. And then something does. Stepping from the thicket are two white men with weapons raised.

The realisation hits in that second that here is cause for alarm indeed, and the same collective thought flashes through the minds of the three Arunta men. 'Run,' they want to scream to their women, 'Run! Run!' They are willing to fight, but they know their spears are no match for the weapons of the white men. There is not time enough to issue the warning, however, not time enough for any reaction at all as gunfire shatters the night.

Atanum and Tjumuru are the first. Easy marks in the light of the cooking fire, they slump back without a sound, victims of Col's twin Peacemakers. For good measure, he shoots the woman beside them too. Ngita does not even have time to cry out.

But the other women do. In the seconds that follow, Nangala's screams rend the air, as do those of Macanti as she seizes her now wailing child and holds him close to her, shielding Kwala with her body even as she waits for death.

Wilt is frantically searching the group for the other man. There had been three: where is the third? He has no desire to kill the women, but the men? They must kill all three in order to rescue the white girl.

Less evident where he stands by the acacia tree, Nyapi has had these precious seconds to prepare. He races for his spear, gathers it up and starts charging the white men. He will die fighting.

In those same precious seconds, Letye too has assessed the situation. White men are killing her family, white men whose language she speaks, men with whom she must surely be able to communicate.

'No!' she screams, 'No! Stop!' She has not spoken English for four years. If she had ever thought upon the matter, which she has not, she would have presumed she had forgotten altogether the language of her former life.

'Stop!' she screams. Nyapi continues his charge, the white man's rifle is at the ready, only ten yards separate them, and she hurls herself forward, directly into the path of her husband, arms outstretched in a desperate appeal. 'You must . . .!'

The .44 calibre bullet from Wilt's powerful Winchester slams into her chest, killing her instantly. But it does not stop there. The bullet passes right through Letye and into her husband, felling him. Nyapi does not die in that moment, but mortally wounded and incapable of further action, he writhes in silent agony.

Wilt is horrified by what he has done. The white girl's body lies in the dust at his feet, a gaping hole in her chest. He stares down at her in a state of stupefaction, oblivious to the mayhem that surrounds him. How has this happened?

Col has continued on his killing spree, unaware of the awful mistake that has occurred. He had known the last of the men, the young one who had taken up his spear, was well in Wilt's sights, so he'd advanced, concentrating instead upon the women. First he shoots the old one who, having risen to her feet, is screaming, then he shoots the other one, hunched over by the fire. He hadn't realised she was shielding a child, but when the boy is revealed, he shoots him too: best to make a clean sweep. Then, with the pet dingoes going berserk he shoots them as well, all in the name of sport, dingoes, blacks, same thing really. Col is having a fine night.

Within barely a minute it is over. Col wanders

among the fallen discharging an odd bullet here and there to ensure no life exists then turns back to Wilt, triumphant.

But Wilt is still staring at the body on the ground . . . the white body on the ground.

'Oh sweet Jesus!' Col exclaims. 'What have you done?'

Crossing to join his partner, Col notes that the young savage who'd been on the attack is still alive. A gut shot, he realises, and puts a bullet through the man's brain. He never leaves animals to suffer.

'What have you done, man?' he demands. 'In God's name are you mad?'

Wilt is shaken from his stupor. 'I didn't even see her. She came out of nowhere. I had him all lined up,' he gestures at the young black, 'and she threw herself in front of him. There was nothing I could do. I didn't mean to kill her. Oh dear God in heaven, I didn't mean to kill her!'

Col is annoyed that their chance for a reward has been thwarted, but he realises there is no point in taking his frustration out on Wilt. Wilt is badly unnerved, he can see that, and with just cause. He must put the man at ease and they must make plans.

'Ah well, what's done is done,' he says, clapping his partner on the shoulder. 'No fault of yours – an accident is all. Don't be too harsh upon yourself. We shall have to bury her though,' he adds, looking down at the body, 'we can't have her found, that's for sure.'

'No, no of course we can't.' Col always knows best, Wilt thinks. He will do whatever Col says. 'We shall bury her, that's it, and no-one will ever find her. They won't, will they?' he asks fearfully.'

'No-one will ever find her,' Col assures him. 'You'll be safe, I promise.'

They return briefly to their own campsite where the horses are tethered and fetch tools that are part of their travel equipment at all times.

Between them, with pick and shovel, it does not take long to dig a grave of suitable depth. But as they labour a thought occurs to Wilt.

'Without any just reason now for killing the blacks,' he says, 'what will we do with their bodies? Should we bury them too?'

'Must one have a just reason for killing black heathens?' Col replies. 'But yes, you may be right. Questions could be asked, there might be repercussions.'

'So we bury them too?'

Col leans on his pick, taking a breather and giving the matter a moment's consideration. 'No need,' he decides, 'let them be found. We'll be well clear by then and folks are bound to associate the killings with Barrow Creek. Police are still wreaking revenge where they can, and good riddance I say.'

The argument makes sense to Wilt. The killing of two white men at the Barrow Creek Police Station several years previously by a group of Kaytetye had led to endless reprisals. Some said the Kaytetye had attacked in retaliation for the white men's treatment of their women, others said it was a rebellion against the denial of access to their water source, but either way retribution had been swift and brutal. Blacks from all surrounding areas, men, women and children, had paid the ultimate price.

Wilt stops shovelling dirt from the now nearly completed grave and looks at the black bodies strewn on the ground, seven in all. Who would ever consider this the work of two innocent linesmen? No, this would be seen as further revenge killing by members of the mounted police and no questions would be asked. Col's decision, as always, is the right one, Wilt thinks.

Several minutes later Col calls a halt. 'That's deep enough,' he says throwing aside his pick and crossing to the girl's body. 'You take her legs.'

He grasps the white girl's wrists, Wilt takes a hold of the ankles and together they carry her to the grave.

Wilt averts his eyes from the girl's nakedness. Her pubic covering hangs to one side and her private parts are exposed, which he finds shockingly indecent. When he visits the whores in the brothels he never looks at their private parts: the business of coupling is always conducted in the dark. And this young woman is not at all like the whores he has come to know. Even in death this appears to be a young woman of breeding. Guilt overwhelms him.

Wilt is plagued by something far greater than the fear of discovery and the possible threat of a manslaughter or even a murder charge. He fears the wrath of God will be visited upon him for the death of this girl. Fervently he prays that the Lord will recognise it was an accident.

They place her gently in the grave, Col too respectful. He has no compunction about burying the evidence of this terrible accident — what alternative is there? But he is thankful he is not the responsible party. To kill a white woman is to invite divine retribution.

They labour for a further ten minutes, filling in the grave, stamping down the earth, covering it with rocks and vegetation, rendering it invisible. Then when the task is completed Wilt stands silently for a moment, head bowed. Col isn't sure whether he is paying his respects to the dead girl or offering up a prayer for forgiveness, but either way he remains silent himself, not envying the threat of eternal damnation that must plague his partner's conscience.

It is in this mutually observed silence that they hear the strange muffled whimpering sound. At first Col thinks it is one of the dingoes that must have survived, although he was quite sure he had finished them off neatly.

A quick examination proves him right. There is no life left in any of the bodies, animal or heathen.

And then they discover the baby. Nestled in a soft hollow of sand and swaddled in emu feathers is a little girl around one year old. And she is white.

Both men find the sight confronting, even Col. If the baby had been black he would have shot it without giving the matter a second thought, but a white child? He watches as Wilt picks her up, swaddling and all, from her sandy nest.

'There's black blood in it, Wilt,' he says, trying to convince not only his partner, but also himself of the action they must take. 'There has to be. This is a product of the heathens raping the white girl. We have to kill this baby. We have to kill it and bury it along with the mother. There must be no evidence.'

But this time Col's decision is not the right one for Wilt. 'I have enough to answer for,' he says in a manner that brooks neither argument, nor discussion. 'I'll pray God understands that the girl was an accident, but I'll not suffer hell's fires for the child.'

'What do you plan to do?' Col is apprehensive and prepared to disassociate himself from Wilt here and now. He wants no part in any action that might lead to questions about the white girl.

But Wilt is asking nothing of Col. 'We're less than twenty miles from the telegraph station at Stuart. I'll take her there now and leave her on the verandah by the front door, where she'll be safe.

The telegraphist rises at dawn, as we both know: he'll discover her first thing.'

Col nods. He does indeed know the operator at the Central Mount Stuart repeater station. They were there only recently before embarking on their long trek north. There is no possibility the man will associate the mysterious child on his doorstep with them.

He agrees to the plan and they return to their campsite, Wilt carrying the child, Col the pick and shovel, and once there they make immediate preparations for their departure. Each will travel throughout the night. Col is keen to put distance between himself and the massacre.

'You follow the line north towards Barrow Creek,' Wilt instructs; it is now he who is giving the orders. 'Keep working normal like always and I'll catch up with you somewhere further along the track.'

They mount their horses, Wilt's left arm clutching the child close to his chest, a little hand reaching out from the swaddling to clasp the collar of his shirt.

'Might take me a couple of days,' he says. 'I'll cut across country and steer well clear of these parts on my way back from Stuart.' You can be sure of that, he thinks as he sets his horse off at an easy pace. These parts are destined to haunt him for many a year.

Col watches for a moment. He rather regrets having accepted this partnership of theirs. Company during the long and lonely months in the wild is a fine thing, but the life of a solitary linesman is far less complicated.

He turns north and the two men go their separate ways.

CHAPTER TEN

'*Arrtyaneme! Arrtyaneme!*' Matt continued to cry out the word over and over, rocking on his knees, staring blindly ahead. '*Arrtyaneme! Arrtyaneme!*'

With a strength she hadn't known she possessed, Jess hauled him to his feet, aware she must get him away from this place.

Shaken from his trance-like state, he allowed himself to be roughly dragged from the clearing, his cries fading to mumbles then finally dying away altogether.

By the time they'd reached the car he'd regained his senses, but she could see he was disoriented. She opened the passenger door. 'Get in, Matt. I'll drive.'

He did as he was told like an obedient child and she climbed into the driver's seat. Turning on the ignition, she made a U-turn and started heading back towards the track that would lead them to the main highway.

She kept an eye on him as she drove. He was shaken, certainly, and still a little dazed, but he appeared more confused than anything. She waited for him to speak.

Finally he did. 'What happened back there?'

'You tell me,' she said. But he made no reply, merely staring through the windscreen at the track ahead. 'What did you see, Matt?' she insisted. 'Tell me what it was that you saw.'

'Nothing. I saw absolutely nothing.' He turned to her, mystified. 'But I know something happened back there.

I think I had one of my blackouts, I can't be sure, but I started convulsing: I remember that much. It was like an electric shock. My whole body was shaking, I couldn't stand up. That's all I remember.'

'You don't recall yelling out?'

'No. Did I?'

'Yes, you were yelling "Run! Run!" You kept yelling it out over and over.'

'Did I really?'

'Yes you did.' Jess slowed the vehicle to a halt and turned off the ignition. He had recovered now – it was time to talk. 'But Matt,' she said, 'you were yelling it out in blackfella language.'

'What?' He stared blankly back at her.

'"*Arrtyaneme! Arrtyaneme!*" That's what you were saying. You were speaking Arunta.'

His expression was one of disbelief. 'How could I have done that? I can't even say hello in Arunta. I don't speak a word of the local lingo.'

'No. But your ancestors do. Or rather they did. And they were speaking through you. That's what happened back there.'

'What are you trying to tell me?' He was thoroughly baffled by now.

'I'm trying to tell you your ancestors are black.'

The reply was so unexpected that after the second or so it took him to register what she'd said Matt gave a bark of laughter, which in his current jangled state sounded vaguely hysterical. 'What? Good old Charlie and Brian were black? Is that what you're saying?'

'That's what I'm saying, yes.' She'd expected nothing less than derision and was prepared for combat. 'The mob getting in touch with you back there were Charlie's and Brian's ancestors. At least that's my firm belief.'

'Oh come off it, Jess,' he scoffed, the idea was preposterous, 'I've seen a picture of Grandpa Charlie and he sure as hell wasn't black, and I can tell you here and now the bloke in my dream on his way to the Somme, the Withers bloke you're so convinced is Great-Grandpa Brian, *he* sure as hell wasn't black either.'

'Of course,' she said, patiently riding his scorn, 'they didn't *look* black. They may not even have *known* they were black. A lot of people don't.'

His disdain was so obvious that Jess, determined to break through the barrier, allowed the anthropologist in her to take over.

'Did you know that in the 1930s "biological absorption" was considered the key to "saving" the Aboriginal race? Children who were taken from their families and made wards of the state could be "bred out" within three generations, four at the most, for their own good of course. The authorities had discovered that, unlike many other native populations, there are no "throwbacks" with the Australian Aborigine. Each crossbred generation becomes whiter, which to the protectors at the time seemed the ideal solution, even though the people under their protectorate had no desire at all to be "absorbed". In fact Auber Octavius Neville, the Chief Protector of Aborigines in Western Australia so strongly advocated the practice he was recorded as saying, "the sore spot requires the application of the surgeon's knife for the good of the patient and probably against the patient's will." That's my favourite quote of Neville's,' she added wryly, 'and he came out with some beauties, believe me.'

'Right, I get the message.' Matt decided to bring the subject a little closer to home. 'And you believe somewhere in the distant past a black ancestor of mine was a victim of this practice.'

'Yes I do. Several generations after their forebears have been farmed out to white people there are many who have no idea of the blackfella blood in them. Your father certainly hasn't.'

She'd dropped the bombshell deliberately in order to cut through the argument she could see looming and the ruse worked to perfection. Matt was rendered speechless.

'That's what I "gleaned", to quote Lilian,' she said gently, with a smile that she hoped might in some way mollify. 'When I was in Adelaide I sensed a connection with your father, a feeling of blackfella blood – I can't explain why or how, but it was there. At first I thought my imagination was working overtime and that it couldn't be possible, but I'm sure now I'm right. Dave's ancestors, about whom he knows nothing, were black, I'm convinced of it, and they came from around here. Those same ancestors are reaching out to you now, Matt. You felt it back there in that clearing, you know you did,' she urged. 'They guided you to that place, they communicated with you. Surely some instinct must be telling you I'm right.'

Matt said nothing. Was she right? Was she wrong? He didn't know what to believe. But he did know that he had experienced something back there, something of immense power.

'I felt it too, Matt,' she said, aware of his turmoil. 'Not a connection with the ancestors as you did, but with the land itself. Something happened in that place, something of great significance.' Then the thought hit Jess with such force that she wondered why it hadn't occurred to her sooner. 'Those rocky outcrops and that clearing,' she said, 'they're by the old surveyors' track. They'll be right in the path of the rail corridor, won't they?'

'Yes, I'd say so,' he agreed. 'I'd need to check out my maps and the original route, but yes I'd say they'd be slap-bang in the middle.'

'Of course,' she said, 'that's it!' All the pieces of the puzzle suddenly seemed to fit, and the words poured out of her. 'That's why the ancestors made their initial contact through Charlie and Brian,' she said, 'they didn't want you to feel alienated. It's why they led you to that place today. It's what they've been trying to tell you all along, but you wouldn't listen. It's why the dreams have been becoming more urgent, because time is running out!'

'What?' he said in the brief pause that followed. 'What were they telling me, for God's sake?' Her urgency was so contagious he forgot for a moment that he didn't believe any of this.

'They were telling you that place is a sacred site. They were telling you it must not be desecrated.'

'So?' A moment's further confusion. 'What am I supposed to do?'

'You're supposed to alter the course of the Ghan.'

'Oh.' She has to be joking, he thought. She has to be fucking well joking. But one glance at her told him she wasn't. He leant back and stared through the windscreen at the surrounding landscape, vaguely aware that the sun would soon be starting to set and that with the scattered cloud cover about it was bound to be beautiful. 'Oh, is that all?' he replied. What else could he say?

The blatant irony of his reaction appeared to have escaped her. 'So how do we go about this?' she asked, eagerly. 'What do we do? Where do we start?'

'We start by heading back to Alice.' Climbing from the passenger side, he circled the car and opened the driver's door. 'Shuffle over,' he said, 'I'd like to hit the highway before dark.'

She shuffled over and remained silent as they drove on down the track, sensing it wouldn't be wise to push him any further, not at this stage. She'd been pretty full-on, she told herself, and in any event he was preoccupied. Having grabbed a map from the back seat he'd placed it between them and was tracing directions with his finger while checking the vehicle's compass and odometer. She presumed he was establishing the specific position of the site, and decided it best not to disturb him.

The sunset was in full flood by the time they reached the highway, a glorious sunset as desert sunsets invariably were.

'Magnificent, isn't it?' Jess said, looking out at the fiery panoply of colour that panned the sky. 'I'm lost in awe every time. I never tire of the sight.'

He didn't appear to hear her. No longer following the map and the instruments he seemed deep in thought, but she couldn't be sure. Perhaps he'd just switched off altogether. Then out of nowhere . . .

'Did you see the sign?'

'What?' The question took her by surprise.

'The sign,' he reminded her. 'There was supposed to be a sign halfway up the larger outcrop of rock. Did you see it?'

'Yes.'

'And did it offer any further clues that might help us, any evidence of an Aboriginal sacred site?'

Us, she thought, he just said *us*. 'Unfortunately no,' she replied. 'It was old, certainly, but to my mind probably just graffiti left by workers on the Overland Telegraph Line. There was no Aboriginal significance to it: that much I know.'

'I see.'

He lapsed into silence once again and she wondered whether he was forming a plan of action or deciding to dismiss the whole thing.

'I'm afraid this is one of those situations that requires a leap of faith, Matt,' she said, to which he returned an odd smile that seemed to say '*Oh really?*' – leaving her none the wiser.

She was still none the wiser when he dropped her off at the flat in Undoolya Road.

'Where to from here?' she was forced to enquire, unable to see his face properly in the dark and still trying to assess his reaction.

'Sunday tomorrow: can you come out to the donga camp? It's not far, less than halfway to Ti Tree now. They've moved the workforce a hundred Ks further south.'

'Of course.' She presumed she was to drive herself there, but it turned out he had other plans.

'Right. I'll pick you up around nine thirty – we'll talk on the way,' and leaving her standing in the street hugging herself against the freezing cold night, he drove off to the Heavitree Gap Hotel.

A man of few words, she thought, but they were a few words that sounded distinctly promising.

The following morning during the drive north, Jess was not disappointed. Matt had made a study that night of the surveying maps that were always kept in the back of his Land Rover.

'You were spot on,' he said, 'the site's directly in the path of the Ghan.'

'Right.' She was hardly surprised by the news, but very much encouraged by the fact that he'd given the matter serious thought.

'But although it's on Arunta land, there's been no claim of a sacred site to be avoided in that area. Why?'

'Because it's not a site that relates to the Dreaming,' she replied, 'nor is it a site that's reserved for ceremonial occasions or for secret men's or women's business. Something happened there that even the locals don't know about, Matt. That's what your ancestors are telling you. This is something that personally relates to them –'

He interrupted, not rudely, but briskly, getting down to business. He'd expected her reply to be along such lines. 'So we can't make our approach through the Central Lands Council or other official channels,' he said. Then he continued without pause, reasoning as much to himself as to her, 'Not that there'd be time for all the palaver and bureaucratic bullshit they'd come up with anyway. The heavy earthworks crews are roughly forty Ks from the site; it's only a matter of weeks before they get there. We have to do this in secret and we have to move quickly.'

We, she thought, he said *we*. Jess felt a wave of relief, mingled with exhilaration. We're a team, she told herself. There's been a breakthrough. Whether or not he believes, he's committed to preserving the site. Something in him recognises its importance.

She kept her feelings well in check, however, and her voice as steady and business-like as his. 'So what do we do, Matt?'

'We lie,' he said. 'We lie to everyone except Pottsy. We can't do anything without him. Pottsy's my assistant,' he explained, 'and a good friend: we can trust him.'

She nodded, remembering the wiry, ginger-haired man she'd been introduced to the day she met Matt.

'But we'll have to spin a bit of a lie even to Pottsy,' Matt went on, 'the poor bastard can hardly be expected to believe any of this . . .' He couldn't bring himself to say 'nonsense' or 'bullshit' – he'd been too affected by recent events – so he simply left it at that. 'No talk about visits from my ancestors, Jess, okay?'

'Okay,' she said. 'So which particular lie are we spinning? You'd better fill me in.'

They had everything well worked out by the time they reached the donga camp.

As Matt had said, the camp had been shifted further south and was now more or less equidistant between Alice Springs and Ti Tree. The workforce had been re-located, as each workforce was approximately every three months during the progression of the rail corridor, new labour contracted, seasoned labour staying on, the work never ceasing.

Jess couldn't help but marvel at the speed and effi-ciency with which a virtual township housing around two hundred men had been transported literally overnight. Some of the donga camps' core units like kitchens and ablution blocks were kept in situ along the route, awaiting the arrival of those workers involved with the next phase of construction, but as far fewer men were needed for the track-laying operation the majority of transportable accommodation units were simply picked up and moved on to where a new kitchen and ablution block had been erected and life continued as normal. Jess, like most, found the process quite extraordinary.

Upon arrival, they sought out Pottsy who, as Matt had expected, was lounging in the canteen over a mid-morning cup of tea, engrossed in the latest crime novel he'd acquired. The canteen was relatively deserted, most of the workers, those not on the Sunday shift, having headed for the tavern at Aileron or into Alice Springs for a few beers before a pub lunch. Pottsy would probably join them later, but he always enjoyed a quiet read on his own. He was an avid reader, particularly of the crime/thriller genre, and regularly swapped copies with the several like-minded men in camp who, as opposed to the majority, preferred novels over the free-to-air television that was provided for the workers.

He looked up as Matt gave him a nudge. 'Oh, g'day, Withers,' he said, 'thought you'd gone into Alice for the weekend.'

'I did, came back a bit earlier than usual that's all. Do you remember Jess Manning? She's a negotiator. You two met a few months ago. Jess, this is Craig Potts, otherwise known as Pottsy.'

'Course I remember,' Pottsy said rising to his feet and shaking hands with the young Aboriginal woman who stood beside Withers. 'G'day, Jess.' How could he forget? She was quite a looker.

'G'day, Pottsy.'

'We've got something we want to run by you, mate,' Matt said, 'something that needs to stay strictly hush-hush. Mind if we have a chat?'

Pottsy earmarked the page in his book, tossed it aside and gestured at the seats. 'Pull up a pew, I'm all yours,' he said and the three of them sat.

'Jess in her role as negotiator's been thrown a curve ball,' Matt said, 'and we're trying to figure out how to handle it.'

The remark was instant shorthand to Pottsy who, like Matt, was accustomed to fielding all forms of bureaucratic interference from those they both considered incompetent.

'Some boundary claim that's been overlooked, I take it,' he said to Jess, aware of the disputes between local Indigenous groups and government regarding boundary lines and land ownership. 'I thought all that had been sorted out years ago.'

'It was.' The reply came from Matt. 'But this is something not altogether dissimilar in the way that it *is* a claim of a sort. Anyone want a cup of tea?' He stood, a signal to Jess, who nodded. It was their plan she should have a little one-on-one time with Pottsy.

'Thanks,' she said.

'Yeah, I'm up for another one.' Pottsy gave a nod.

'Right, won't be a tick.' Matt started to walk off to the self-service counter then turned back as if in afterthought. 'Tell Pottsy about the ancestors, Jess,' he said and left them to it.

Jess proceeded with the story she and Matt had concocted, which was very close to the truth. They were lying really only by omission they'd agreed, the one element excluded being Matt's personal involvement.

'I've been contacted by an Arunta mob, Pottsy,' she said, 'a large extended family, all of whom are very agitated about a sacred site of their ancestors being desecrated. They believe it lies directly in the path of the Ghan. Matt checked the location out for me yesterday and the family's fears are justified: the rail corridor will run right through it.'

'But all sacred sites were agreed upon ages ago,' Pottsy was clearly puzzled, 'they've been mapped and avoided accordingly.'

'Yes, they have,' she said, 'all those with historical and ceremonial significance known and shared by the local people, but this is a slightly different case. This site is personal. It is sacred only to this particular Arunta family and has been for several generations, which is why its location didn't come up for discussion in official meetings with Indigenous landowners. Until recently the family had no idea that the site lay directly in the path of the railway.'

'How come they know now?'

'The spirit world has made contact. The ancestors have told the family their sacred ground is about to be desecrated, and the family is desperate.' Jess was aware the average white person would find the story implausible and that she was leaving herself open to ridicule, but Matt had instructed her not to hold back.

'Be direct with Pottsy,' he'd said. 'He has a great deal of respect for Aboriginal beliefs. You'll find far more empathy in him than you did in me. In fact,' he'd added only half-jokingly, 'if you'd asked me to come up with a white bloke who had blackfella blood in him, I would have picked Pottsy myself.'

'The ancestors have become increasingly anxious,' she continued. 'They say time is running out, so the family has turned to me for help.' Having stated her case Jess came to a halt, wondering whether Matt would prove right or whether she was about to be ridiculed.

Matt proved right. Pottsy did not ridicule nor did he even question the notion of contact from the spirit world. But he was gobsmacked nonetheless.

'You mean they want us to change the route of the rail corridor,' he said incredulously.

'Yes. If it's at all possible that's what they want and that's what I'm asking on their behalf.'

'Pretty big ask,' he replied in wry understatement. 'What's Withers got to say about it all?'

Pottsy was unaware that Matt had returned and was now standing directly behind him.

'Withers reckons we should give it a go.' Matt placed the three mugs of tea on the table and sat. 'White and two sugars,' he passed Pottsy his, 'white and none,' and passed Jess hers. 'What do you say, Pottsy? The site's not near any boundary line; there'd be no grounds for dispute.'

There was an element of suspicion in the flinty blue eyes that flickered from Matt to Jess and back again. Pottsy was wondering if the two were having an affair. They were very familiar with each other and Withers had been going into town a lot lately. Is this why he's behaving so out of character? Pottsy wondered. Withers would normally be the first person to label the whole thing a load of superstitious nonsense: is he doing the girl a personal favour?

Every single thought flashing through Pottsy's mind was readable to Matt. 'Uh uh,' he said shaking his head, 'we're just friends, mate – very good friends I admit,' he added, his smile including Jess, 'but that isn't why I believe we should do this. I believe we should do this because it's right. Exactly why it's right I don't know,' he added with a shrug. 'I guess only the ancestors can answer that. I'm afraid this is one of those situations that requires a leap of faith, Pottsy.'

Matt and Jess shared a smile of recognition, which led Pottsy to suppose it was Jess's influence that had wrought the change in Withers. During the long years of their friendship Withers had always been the cynical one.

'Oh well,' he said, 'it's their faith, isn't it? Their faith and their land. Seems only right to me. I'm willing to give it a go.' He took a swig of his tea. 'So where's the site?'

'About a half hour's drive from where our team's currently working. I've marked the location on the map, it's around thirty Ks north of Alice.'

'We'd better take a look at it then, eh?'

They downed their tea and set off in Matt's Land Rover, Jess in the front passenger seat and Pottsy in the back.

'Are you happy to have a late bite of lunch in Alice after we've shown you the place?' Matt asked Pottsy. 'I'll need to take Jess back to town.'

'Sure,' Pottsy agreed amiably, 'good idea.'

They chatted comfortably during the drive, keeping the conversation general, the tacit agreement being there was no point in planning a course of action until they'd seen the site. But as the rock formations came into view, Jess could sense Matt's trepidation. She found it understandable for she was thinking very much along the same lines. Would he have another blackout? Would he start yelling in Arunta? If so it would be a difficult situation to explain to Pottsy.

Matt wasn't thinking of Pottsy at all. As the rocky outcrops loomed closer and closer, Pottsy's reaction was the last thing on his mind. The prospect of undergoing a repeat experience brought with it a mounting wave of anxiety. The events of the previous day had had a profoundly unnerving effect on Matt Witherton.

He pulled the vehicle up, the three of them climbed out, and as they walked the twenty metres or so to the site Jess took over, striding on ahead.

'The site encompasses these two granite outcrops, Pottsy,' she called back over her shoulder and upon reaching the rocks she marched into the centre of the clearing. Once there, she turned to face them arms outstretched, an authoritative figure in the desert surrounds, and the men came to an automatic halt. 'The family is very specific about its dimensions,' she said, 'these two rocky hillocks and this clearing where I'm standing. This is the site that is sacred to their ancestors.'

Her eyes met Matt's and he returned a nod of gratitude. He couldn't possibly stand in the clearing. Even where he was on the periphery the place gave him a sense of unrest, a sense that anything could happen at any moment.

Nothing untoward did happen, however. They took the maps from the car, referencing the position of the site, then Pottsy roughly paced out its measurements, jotting down notes in a work pad while Matt disappeared to explore the surrounding area where the route would be redirected.

A half hour later he rejoined Pottsy, who was by now studying the map laid out on the Land Rover's bonnet and jotting down further notes, Jess standing quietly to one side, careful not to disturb him.

'There's a watercourse with a rocky embankment nearby,' Matt announced. 'It could prove a problem in flood.'

'Oh yeah?' Pottsy's reply held an element of 'so what?' as he looked up from the map. He didn't quite get Matt's drift.

'So that's our story should there be any questions asked,' Matt went on to explain. 'We made a deviation to the route in order to avoid a possible floodwater problem. Hell,' he added when Pottsy was slow to respond, 'we can hardly say we altered the path of the Ghan because some anxious ancestors got in touch with their family, can we?'

'Ah,' Pottsy's grin was laconic, 'yeah, point taken. I don't reckon we'll cop too many questions though,' he added carelessly, 'this is the Northern Territory, mate – nobody's doing things strictly by the book. Hell, half the time they're making it up as they go along.'

Matt rather envied his friend's cavalier attitude, but he wasn't so complacent. 'This might be the Territory, Pottsy,' he cautioned, 'but progress checks are made and construction reports sent through nonetheless. We want to hope like hell that any questions asked don't come from down south.'

The two discussed the matter further during the drive into Alice, Matt's principal concern being not so much the redirection of the route itself, but how well they could keep it a secret.

Jess, having insisted upon taking the back seat, remained very quiet while drinking in their every word.

'We'll have to run it by Fritz,' Matt said. 'I'll tell him you and I have done an advance recce and that we're in agreement the watercourse could prove a bit of a problem.'

Peter 'Fritz' Jermyn was the Senior Surveyor, who worked hand in glove with the teams of engineers and designers employed on the construction of the southern rail corridor section. A fifth-generation Australian who hailed from Brisbane and specialised in outback projects, he'd never been to Germany, his one experience of overseas travel having been a week's trip to Fiji, but as surnames were always fair game he'd been stuck with the label 'Fritz' for the whole of his working life.

'Fritz won't give a shit.' Pottsy's attitude again was distinctly laissez-faire. 'He'll just say "That's your department, up to you, mate." You can bet on it – the bloke's doing a juggling act as it is.'

Matt tended to agree, Fritz was certainly laid-back, and certainly busy serving many masters, but again he couldn't help wishing he had Pottsy's supreme confidence.

'And what about the boys?' he asked. 'What do I tell the boys?'

'What do you tell the *boys*?' Pottsy's sandy eyebrows shot up comically as if dumbfounded by the question. 'You don't need to tell the boys a bloody thing, mate! Even if they guessed what was going on, and they very well might, Baz and Mitch'd never question a decision of yours, and Gav wouldn't understand even if you tried.'

Matt grinned. He knew exactly what Pottsy was doing. Pottsy was going out of his way to put him at ease, knowing only too well that, as leader, Matt was bound to question every element of the undertaking. He shared a smile with Jess in the rear-vision mirror.

'A good man to have on our side,' he said, to which she returned a vigorous nod.

'Actually, Jess,' Pottsy swivelled about to face her, 'your Arunta mob got in touch with us in the nick of time. We'll be surveying and defining that area in just a couple of days: if they'd left it any longer they would have dipped out altogether, we wouldn't have been able to go back and change things. Isn't that so, Withers?' he queried, turning to Matt.

'Yep,' Matt agreed. 'They were running out of time all right.'

'Just as well the ancestors made contact then, isn't it?' Jess said. 'No wonder they were getting anxious.' She directed her comment to Pottsy, deliberately avoiding the rear-vision mirror now.

As they drove through Heavitree Gap, the men discussed venue options for a late lunch. The Tavern, Bojangles, the café in the Mall . . .? Somewhere they could spread out their maps and discuss the route redirection . . .

'My place,' Jess interrupted. 'It'll be quieter and you'll have more space. Besides, I've got beers in the fridge and I make a bloody good steak sandwich.'

'You're on,' Matt said.

Back at the flat, they cleared the dining table, Matt and Pottsy laying out their maps and sitting to make notes over a beer while Jess defrosted the steaks in the microwave and fried up some onions.

She was impressed as she listened to the men, although she found their muttered calculations something of a mystery. After agreeing the route redirection should be at least fifty metres sideways to the east to allow space for access tracks, they went off at a tangent that lost her altogether.

She heard from Matt '. . . total length of deviation I'd say around fifteen hundred metres, wouldn't you?' and from Pottsy, 'Yep, first curve seven-fifty before the site, final curve to finish seven-fifty after. That should about do it, I reckon.'

There seemed to be quite a bit of chat about curves, all of which was a little confusing. 'Does everyone want tomato sauce?' she asked as the toaster popped up a third round.

'Yep,' Matt answered, 'and hot mustard if you've got it.'

She waved a jar of Hot English triumphantly in the air.

'Same for me,' Pottsy said and within seconds the table was cleared, the smell of fried onions reminding the men they were ravenous.

'Would somebody like to explain what all that was about?' Jess sat, placing three dinner plates on the table, each sporting a huge toasted sandwich untidily bulging steak and onions from its sides.

'All what?' Matt asked, unceremoniously wolfing into his.

'All that business about curves,' she said, just as hungry, picking up her own sandwich and applying herself to it with gusto.

Matt gave Pottsy a nod that said 'over to you' and Pottsy, through mouthfuls of steak sandwich, offered a detailed account of the transition and circular curves essential in the design of railway tracks. When he'd finished she still appeared a little baffled, so he added by way of explanation, 'The straight centreline transitions into a circular curve with a radius of sixteen hundred metres, which is needed to allow proper curves, you see, and after that it transitions back to the next straight.'

Jess cast a mystified look at Matt, but nothing was forthcoming: he was too busy concentrating on his sandwich.

'Some well-designed roads follow the same principle, although it's not necessary,' Pottsy continued, 'because a motorcar's front wheels change direction progressively. Are you with me?' She wasn't really, which didn't matter as he went on regardless. 'Transitions are absolutely vital in rail design, however, because a train's wheels are fixed and it's the tracks that need to change direction progressively.' Another huge bite of sandwich, 'Of course we're only making rough notes at the moment,' he said, chewing away vigorously, 'the changes will be made using the theodolite and prism.'

'I see.' Jess was left wondering why she'd bothered to ask, but fascinated nonetheless. 'I'd love to come and watch,' she said, loath to be on the outer at this stage of the proceedings. 'Can I, Matt?' she pleaded.

'Nope.' The answer was brisk and unequivocal. 'Sorry, no way. We don't want anything that arouses attention and your presence would be definite cause for comment. You'll have to stay well away for a while, Jess, but I'll keep you posted.'

'Sure. I understand.' Disappointed though she was, Jess felt a thrill of anticipation. It appeared the unimaginable was about to happen. They were about to alter the course of the Ghan.

The reaction from Fritz turned out very much as Pottsy had predicted. In fact Fritz's opening comment was virtually Pottsy's prediction verbatim.

'No worries, mate, go for it,' the gangly Queenslander said when Matt approached him, 'the advance survey's your area, you're the expert. And if some local bureaucratic prick wants to stick his nose in and hold up proceedings,' he added, 'you'll have my backing.' Fritz detested the bureaucrats in much the same way Matt and Pottsy did. But he made a further comment that touched upon the area of most concern to Matt.

'Course it's those pricks from down south I can't help you with,' he said, 'those pricks who arrive on site to run a spot check or those pricks who study reports trying to catch us out when they can't run a fucking country dance themselves.' He gave a laconic shrug that said it all. 'Can't help you with them, I'm afraid, Withers. Ball's in your court there.' And Matt was left with his major concern still looming large on the horizon.

Jess kept well out of the way as instructed. Much as she longed for a progress report she didn't contact Matt, but concentrated on her own work, boring phone calls, emails and paperwork at the Central Lands Council offices for the most part, work she'd been avoiding for some time. These days she seemed to negotiate as much with government departments as she did with local communities, the Central Lands Council being a sea of bureaucracy. Even serving in the diplomatic position she did, Jess, like the surveyors, found the bureaucratic process intensely frustrating.

Then ten days later Matt rang. It was a Thursday.

'We've completed the route redirection,' he said. 'Everything's in place. Now we sit back and wait for the contractors to set out the final rail design and then the construction teams arrive and get on with the job.'

'And when will that be?'

'Oh several weeks yet; nothing'll happen until then. What are you up to this weekend? How about lunch at the Tavern Saturday?'

'Great. See you around one o'clock.'

But she rang him back just the following day and cancelled lunch. 'I have to go to Hermannsburg,' she said. She didn't say why and he presumed it was business, but it wasn't business at all. She'd received the phone call that very morning.

'Aunty May asked me to ring you, Jess,' Millie's voice down the line. 'She says she's going to die tomorrow and she wants to watch the sunset with the family around her. She wants you there particularly.'

'I'll be there. What time should I turn up?'

'Late afternoon – she wants to have a cuppa with you. I'll let her have a good long sleep after lunch. The medication makes her tired and I don't want her too worn out to enjoy the sunset with us. She's really looking forward to that.'

'I'll be there at four o'clock.'

'She said don't forget the biscuits.'

'I won't.'

They could still hear the smiles in each other's voices as Jess hung up the phone.

May's health had plummeted dramatically over the past several weeks. Tests had revealed pancreatic cancer, a diagnosis which May herself had taken very much in her stride.

'The doctors are talkin' surgery and chemotherapy and things,' she'd told Jess, 'but nah,' she'd scoffed. 'I don' want any of that stuff. Time's up. I'll say my goodbyes and be off soon.'

Millie's call had not been unexpected.

'G'day love, come on in.'

Millie ushered Jess into the little back bedroom where May sat bolstered up by pillows receiving her guests like royalty.

'Good to see you.' May held her spindly arms out wide and Jess walked into the hug, bending to embrace the frail body. She'd been shocked by her aunt's weight loss during her last visit, and now only a fortnight later the once burly frame seemed to have withered away to nothing.

'G'day, Aunty May.'

'I'll bring in the tea; it's all ready,' Millie said and disappeared.

'My angel she is,' May gazed lovingly after her grand-daughter, 'my own personal angel and a tower of strength, that girl. She's the one'll lead this family when I'm gone. Take a seat, Jess.'

Jess sat in the only chair, a rickety hardback that was pulled up beside the bed to accommodate the visitors who'd arrived to pay homage, one by one, throughout the morning. Millie had intermittently ushered family members in for brief meetings, monitoring the time in order not to overtax her grandmother. She'd been given strict instructions, however, regarding Jess. 'Leave Jess till last,' she'd been told, 'after I've had my nap when I'm good and fresh. I want a cuppa and a chat with Jess.'

'Glad I got myself prepared,' May said with a smile bordering on smug, 'they're all lined up in the spirit world ready and waiting to give me the big welcome – pretty good, eh?'

'Yes, pretty good, Aunty May.'

May's smile faded as she reverted to Western Arunta, she was in deadly earnest now. *'You know the best thing you ever did, girl?'* The question was obviously rhetorical so Jess waited for the answer. *'The best thing you ever did was to come home and find your family. Family is who you are, Jess. We're who you are and we're where you come from, the good and the bad of us, you need to know that.'*

Jess nodded, again aware no answer was required, and again waiting for her aunt to continue, but the door opened and there was Millie with the tray, perched upon it two mugs of tea and a plate of biscuits.

May's withered face cracked into a grin as Millie placed the tray on the bedside table. 'Ah good girl, Jess, you remembered the biccies. Chocolate chip too,' she said, then with a nod to her granddaughter: 'Thanks, Millie love.'

Without uttering a word Millie crossed back to the door.

'Aren't you joining us?' Jess asked.

'No, thanks.' Millie turned and gave the slightest shake of her head. She'd blossomed into an attractive young woman fulfilling the prettiness of her childhood, but it was her assurance that most impressed. There was an air of quiet command about Millie. 'No, I'll leave you two to it.' Her look told Jess everything that needed to be said. *'Aunty May is making her personal goodbye speech to you, Jess,'* is what Millie's look said.

She left, closing the door quietly behind her. Aunty May had been making a personal goodbye speech to every single member of the family, as was befitting her position as elder. Millie knew that such moments were precious and demanding of respect.

Determined to make the most of what little strength she had left, May ignored the tea and biscuits and continued directly from where she'd left off.

'*You told me a long time back you'd studied our people at university,*' she said, '*our history and our culture and languages, that's what you said. Well that's good,*' May nodded approvingly, '*education and learning's good. You probably know more about our people than we do ourselves,*' she added in all seriousness, albeit with a smile. '*But there's something you can't learn from books, Jess, something that comes from here,*' bony fist tapped emphatically on bony chest, '*from right here, deep inside. Family gives you that. Family's real important. You know what I'm saying?*'

'*Yes, Aunty May, I know what you're saying and I agree. You're right. The best thing I ever did was to come home and find my family. I'm a much stronger person for having done so.*' It's true, Jess thought, it's most certainly true.

'Righto,' May reverted to English, 'time for tea and biccies, that's tired me out that has.' Jess passed her aunt a mug of tea and May took one of the biscuits from the plate she was offered. 'Your turn now,' she said. 'Tell me all about what's going on in your life and don't worry if I doze off. Just wake me in time for the sunset.'

Jess talked about things in general. May was particularly interested to hear about the progression of the rail corridor, which was now not far from Alice Springs. 'They'll be laying track early next year,' Jess said, 'or at least so I'm told.'

But before long May's eyelids were drooping, the mug still three quarters full resting in her lap, the biscuit, which had received one brief dunk and one small nibble only, clasped in her other hand. Her appetite was so diminished she couldn't eat biscuits anyway. The request for them had been merely an act of bravado, but she'd so enjoyed seeing them on the plate.

Jess gently took the mug and the biscuit from her aunt's hands and sat watching as May dozed off.

Less than ten minutes later the door quietly opened and Millie put her head around it to take in the scene.

'Didn't mean to interrupt,' she said apologetically, 'but I was pretty sure she'd be asleep by now: she doesn't last long these days. Come out and join us, Jess. Evie and the girls have made chicken sandwiches. We're going to have our tea early while we wait for the sunset.' When Jess cast an uncertain glance at her aunt, Millie added, 'She won't want to eat anything and she'll sleep until we wake her.'

Jess joined the others crowded into the front room, fifteen in all, sitting cross-legged on the bare floor or squatting on sleeping bags, sipping from mugs of tea and chattering among themselves as platters of sandwiches were handed around. There was May's son and nephew with their spouses and children, grown now, including young Jack, who'd flown up from Adelaide that morning. There was May's daughter, Eve, and her husband and their three children, also grown, who'd driven throughout the night and day from Katherine over a thousand kilometres to the north. The clan had gathered in force to say their goodbyes.

The tone was respectful. There was no alcohol present, even the heaviest drinkers among them abstaining that day. The family's general mood, however, was not one of gloom, but rather of sharing. There were smiles and spatters of laughter as, in their own language, two generations exchanged stories of misdemeanours that had incurred the wrath of Aunty May. 'Do you remember when . . .' led from one tale to another, and Jess, sitting there watching and listening and laughing along with them, felt very much a part of it all.

Shortly before sunset, Jack and his cousin Bobby lifted May's special armchair out into the street, positioning it perfectly where she'd have the best view. Then five minutes later Millie and Eve fetched May herself, rugged up against the cold in her favourite cardigan. They supported her between them, May determined to walk.

Once she was seated upon her throne, the family gathered around her, some squatting in the dust and others standing, but all silently watching as the rays of the setting sun slowly painted the sky.

Jess found herself casting furtive glances at May. The look of rapture on her aunt's face was hypnotic. But after a little while she concentrated upon the sky as the others were doing, it seemed disrespectful to intrude upon May's connection with the universe.

At the very peak of the sunset's beauty someone finally spoke and the voice was May's, clearly and loudly addressing the family as a whole.

'I'll be part of that,' she said, her gaze still focused upon the sky, 'I'll be a part of that every single day.'

The announcement was extraordinarily effective, as had been May's intention. Everyone present knew they would never again look at a sunset without being in the presence of Aunty May.

They went back inside half an hour later while the sky was still gently aglow; it was cold and May was ready to go to sleep.

Eve and Millie put her to bed, but when they returned to the front room, Millie whispered in Jess's ear. 'She wants to see you, Jess. Pop in and say goodbye.'

Jess approached the bed quietly, May appeared asleep and she didn't want to disturb her. But the black eyes sprang open, still startling in their intensity.

'I'll say hello to your mum for you, Jess,' she said. 'I'm lookin' forward most of all to seein' Rose. You go on home now, love. No need to hang around. I'm glad you came.'

Jess wasn't sure what to say. 'Goodbye, Aunty May.' What else was there?

'Goodbye, love.'

She crossed to the door, but the voice, although a little weaker, still reached her clearly as she opened it.

'You belong real well in two worlds, Jess, and that's something to be proud of. Not many do. I'm right proud of you myself, I must say, and I know Rose is too.'

'Thanks, Aunty May.'

'Go on home now, there's a good girl.'

May closed her eyes and Jess quietly stole away.

But she didn't go home. She stayed with the family, talking and drinking more cups of tea and eating biscuits and potato crisps from the packets the younger ones had bought from the grocery shop earlier that day. Then she curled up in a spare sleeping bag in the corner of the little bedroom shared by the unmarried girls of the clan. The only single female member not present was Millie. Millie was keeping a vigil by May's bedside.

Sleep evaded Jess that night, not through physical discomfort, she was a good sleeper under any conditions as a rule, but because her mind was running riot.

It was well after two in the morning when she crept through the cottage, the sleeping bag blanketed around her shoulders, past her aunt's bedroom door and outside to sit on the porch step looking at the moonlit backyard, May's words about the importance of family still echoing in her mind.

She thought of her mother, of how Rose had had no family and how that loss of identity and belonging had destroyed her. And she thought of herself. What of her own life? What might have happened had she stayed in Sydney in the artificial bubble of Roger's world? She, too, would have been destroyed. But most of all her thoughts were of Matt. Matt and his father Dave were uppermost in Jess's mind as May's words echoed like a mantra.

'Family is who you are, Jess. We're who you are and we're where you come from, the good and the bad of us, you need to know that.'

Surely Matt and his father need to know that, she thought. There's too much mystery surrounding their past. Surely they need to discover the truth, to find out who they really are.

She wasn't sure how long she'd been sitting there. Huddled up in the sleeping bag she must have dozed off, for the first hint of dawn was in the sky when Millie stepped outside.

'She's gone.' Millie sat beside her on the porch step. 'Slipped away in her sleep, didn't wake up.'

Jess took the girl's hand. Even in the half-light she could see the glisten of tears. 'Aunty May willed herself to go, Millie, just as she said she would.'

Millie nodded, not trusting herself to speak, and Jess draped the sleeping bag about her shoulders to ward off the cold, gently pulling her close and cuddling her as she might a child. For all Millie's strength it was only natural she would be bereft. Her grandmother had been the one solid thing in her world, the person who had been an anchor throughout her entire life.

Millie allowed herself to be cuddled, even giving in to a brief silent weep. Then she gathered herself and pulled away.

'Thanks, Jess,' she said, 'I needed a bit of that.'

'You're the new leader now, Millie. You'll take up the baton and lead the next generation.'

'I know.' Millie smiled. 'That was Aunty May's goodbye speech to me.'

They sat quietly together watching the sun's first rays appear over the horizon. Then Millie stood. 'I'll let them know now,' she said.

They embraced each other and Jess left the family to grieve, driving back to Alice Springs through a glorious sunrise.

CHAPTER ELEVEN

Aunty May's burial was an eclectic affair involving various funerary practices, as was often the case with highly respected elders. Word was relayed and many travelled from other communities to join the family and those at Hermannsburg for a traditional send-off. There was the chant of mourning songs and the performances of ritual dances, with the male members of the family painted white, the clicking of many sticks and the haunting dirge of the didgeridoo. There was the smoking ceremony, selected native plants ignited to smoulder and waft among the guests, cleansing the air and helping the spirit on its way to join the Ancestral Beings. And after all due ceremony had been observed May was given a Christian burial in the Hermannsburg Cemetery, the service conducted by the Aboriginal pastor of the Bethlehem Lutheran Church, a man with whom she had been well acquainted. For practical purposes May had always paid great respect to the church, believing her position in the community dictated she should, but even the pastor knew she had never converted, that her beliefs were purely blackfella.

'It was a great send-off, Dad,' Jess said to her father over the phone after a full account of the proceedings. 'I wish you'd been here,' she added regretfully.

'I wish I had too.' Toby's voice held a distinctly critical edge. 'You should have told me. I would have dropped everything and come up, you know I would've.'

'Yes,' Jess felt duly chastised, 'and I know Aunty May would have loved you being there too; she often talked of her "white brother". But everything happened so quickly, Dad. She just decided to die and that was that.'

Toby wished he hadn't sounded critical. He could hear the faintest echo of something wistful in his daughter's voice. What was it? An ache, a need? Something was wrong. 'I can cancel my recording sessions and come up now if you like,' he said, playing it cool, not sounding alarmist; the call was Jess's after all, but God how he'd love to see her. He missed his daughter and thought of her constantly, but he would never intrude. His pride in her achievements and the success of her life outweighed his personal need for her company.

'No.' Jess's decision was instant. 'Don't come to Alice; I'll come to you.' Her father had read her correctly. Jess ached to pour everything out, to share all the secrets of the past several months, and the only person she could pour it all out to was Toby. There was no-one else in whom she could place her complete trust. 'I'll arrange a few days off in a week or so and fly down to Sydney – okay with you?'

'Sure, why not?' The response came back in Toby's typically laid-back Irish style, but he was having trouble disguising his elation.

'I'll give you a ring when I've made my plans.'

'Right you are then.' After hanging up the receiver Toby let out an almighty whoop of joy, startling Ringo, the five-year-old Cairns terrier/blue-heeler/cocker spaniel/ 'whatever-else' cross he'd recently rescued from the pound. Jess hadn't met Ringo yet, but the dog was just the sort of scruffy, mongrel-mix she adored and Toby couldn't wait to introduce them.

Jess's plans were slightly delayed, however, by a further unexpected decision that seemed to pop up out of nowhere.

It was just several days later, the following Saturday, when she'd agreed to meet Matt for lunch at the Tavern.

'Only a couple of weeks to go,' he said, digging into his steak. 'It'll be coming up to nail-biting time shortly.'

'What will?' She'd been thinking of something else.

'The contractors arriving at the detour . . .?' His reminder was heavily laced with irony – how could she possibly have forgotten? But he could tell she was distracted, she hadn't even started to tackle her steak. He wondered what was on her mind, but decided not to ask. She'd get around to it in time. Jess always spoke her mind and he was happy to wait.

He didn't need to wait long. Jess took just one mouthful of her Scotch fillet, chewed thoughtfully for a while, then after swallowing seemed to forget her meal altogether as she launched into the topic that had remained uppermost in her mind since Aunty May's death.

'Don't you ever think about your family's history, Matt?' she asked. 'Don't you ever wonder where you come from?'

Ah, so that's it, he thought. 'You asked me virtually the same question months ago,' he replied with a smile, 'and I said no. I take it now you're convinced that my ancestors are black, you're presuming I've had a change of mind, is that right?'

She ignored the fact that she was being sent up. 'Yes probably. Don't you want to know? Don't you want to find out the truth?'

Matt wondered if he'd been insensitive. He supposed he had: this was obviously not something he should joke about. It was also not something to which he'd given a great deal of thought, surprisingly enough. He'd been concentrating so hard on the practicalities of re-directing the route of the rail corridor he'd ceased questioning why they were doing it. But even as he stopped attacking his T-bone and prepared his answer, Jess barrelled on.

'Wouldn't Dave want to know the truth?' she insisted. 'Don't you think he'd want to find out?'

'I have no idea,' Matt answered in all honesty. 'For some unknown reason Dad's never professed an interest in his family's background.'

'But now we know what we know don't you think that would alter the case?'

Now we know what we know, he thought. *But what do we know, Jess? Truly, what do we know?* He remained silent.

She could hear the doubts rattling around in his mind. 'Have you had any more dreams,' she demanded, 'any more blackouts, headaches, sleeplessness?'

'No.'

'So doesn't that tell you anything? Doesn't it prove we're on the right track?'

On what track? What does it prove? Still he remained silent.

'We're doing what your ancestors want of us, Matt,' she urged, 'so they have no need to torment you further. I don't pretend to know *why* they want this of us, but it proves they've successfully made contact and it proves who they are.'

Proves who they are? But who are they? This conversation seems to be going on between you and my brain, Jess.

'Don't you want to find out more about them? Isn't it your duty to trace your background?' Jess knew she was nagging, but she couldn't seem to stop. 'Wouldn't your father want to know about his family?'

Matt's brain stopped conversing at that juncture and the words just popped out. 'You reckon we should tell Dad, do you?'

She hadn't been heading in that specific direction and the 'we' came as a complete surprise, but yes, she thought, yes, Dave should be told. 'Well, I certainly think you should tell him,' she replied firmly.

'He wouldn't believe me without you, Jess.' Matt looked her squarely in the eye. 'Dad honestly would not believe me without you: we'd have to tell him together.'

'I take it I'm being dared,' she said, meeting his gaze with equal intensity. Telling a white man he was black was certainly something of a dare.

'Yes. You're being dared.'

'When would you suggest?'

'Next Saturday – I have a long weekend due. We'll fly down to Adelaide for a few days, what do you say?'

'All right.' She accepted the challenge without further thought. 'But just Saturday for me,' she said. 'I'll go on to Sydney the next day. I've planned to visit my father.'

'Just Saturday it is then.' He shrugged reluctantly, not bothering to disguise his disappointment; he would have enjoyed a long weekend with her in Adelaide. 'Now are we going to eat these steaks before they congeal?'

'We most certainly are.' She picked up her knife and fork and attacked her Scotch fillet with zeal.

He watched, loving as he always did the way she ate with the appetite of a navvy.

'Jess darling, how *wonderful* to see you!'

Lilian's welcome was as effusive as ever, her embrace all-engulfing, and this time Jess found herself smothered, or rather entwined, in voluminous lengths of red and orange silk. The early spring weather being mild, a selection of lightweight scarves had replaced the alpaca.

'And Mattie darling, you look so *well*!' Matt's turn to be engulfed, after which Lilian disengaged herself and stepped back to admire the pair of them. 'You *both* look so well, you really do!' God they're a handsome couple, she thought. 'Come in, come in, Dave's making the coffee.'

Once again Matt had refused his father's offer to pick them up at the airport, insisting they'd catch a cab. 'Too much hassle parking and all that, Dad, much easier to get a cab.'

They followed Lilian, who led the way like a glorious sunset through to the main living room, talking all the while.

'So sorry to hear you're only staying with us the one night, Jess,' she called back over her shoulder, 'we could have arranged a day's visit to the wineries all four of us. I'd have adored that.'

'Hello, Jess. Good to see you.' Dave was placing a tray of sandwiches on the coffee table as they entered. He gave Jess an avuncular peck on the cheek, which rather surprised her, but he was merely obeying instruction.

'Make her feel especially welcome, dear,' Lilian had begged, 'treat her as if she's one of the family; do please, please for my sake.'

Having obliged his wife, Dave embraced his son. 'I know you said you'd be eating on the plane, but I made sandwiches anyway.'

'You shouldn't have, Dad.'

'Yes I should, it's lunchtime, they're leg ham fresh off the bone, and I'm hungry.'

'Fair enough.'

Father and son shared a grin, everyone sat, and when the sandwiches were passed around they proved so delicious Matt and Jess ate their share anyway.

'We're all hot mustard fans, I'm glad to see,' Dave said, 'I thought I might have whacked on a bit much for you, Jess.'

'No way,' Matt answered, 'she's a Hot English freak from way back,' to which Jess, chewing vigorously, nodded agreement.

Lilian beamed happily from one to the other, enjoying the pair's familiarity, but studying them with serious intent. Did she detect something a little different, she wondered, something a little more than 'good mates'?

Yes surely she did. Something's happened between them, she thought. I wonder if they've become lovers. Oh I do hope so. How wonderful.

As the small talk continued and the sandwiches dwindled and second cups of coffee were downed, she decided to test the waters.

'Oh my goodness, we've thrust lunch upon you and talked for an hour and you haven't even unpacked,' she said. 'You've probably been dying to freshen up, Jess.' She turned to her son in seeming innocence. 'The studio or the flat, Mattie darling?' she asked. Then upon receiving a dagger-like look she continued without drawing breath, 'Yes, the studio of course, same as last time.' What a pity, she thought.

'So long as I'm not intruding upon your work, Lilian,' Jess said. 'I'm more than happy to bunk down on a sofa: I'm a very good sleeper, I promise you.'

'You're not intruding in the least, dear, and I will not have you "bunk down". Come along,' she stood, 'we'll go upstairs together.'

'I know the way, really, no need to bother.'

'Allow me, please, I like to play hostess.' She didn't. She never played hostess, much preferring people look after themselves, but she wanted to get away from the hostility emanating from her son. 'We'll leave the boys together for a while. I have some new pieces you might be interested in. I've been painting up a storm recently – cityscape themes, something a bit different.'

'How wonderful.' Jess jumped eagerly to her feet. What a privilege, she thought. 'I'd love to see them,' she said, picking up her small case. She was travelling light, with only cabin luggage.

As she followed Lilian up the stairs, Jess wondered whether, in her absence, Matt would tell his father of the latest developments, or rather she wondered how much he might tell his father. He certainly wouldn't mention her belief in their family's black ancestry, she knew that much, but he'd also warned her he didn't want to tell his father about the re-routing of the rail corridor.

'I don't think it's necessary, Jess,' he'd said. 'Dad's been the leading surveyor on projects like this all his life and he might not approve. It's a pretty unconventional step we're taking, unprofessional even, and he's a bit of a stickler when it comes to work.'

Jess found the excuse rather lame. What, she thought, Dave won't approve of your altering the route or he won't approve that, in doing so, you must deep down believe in the necessity to do so? She strongly suspected the latter. You don't want to be caught out in case he scoffs at you, Matt. But she pretended to accept his explanation.

'So what *will* you tell him?' she asked.

He knew she was questioning the reason for his evasion and he could understand why she might, but it was not his father's scorn he was avoiding at all. He simply did not want to tell anyone of his intention to alter the route of the Ghan. He didn't want to hear himself say the words out loud, even to his own father. If all went according to plan, he would tell Dave one day, certainly, but now with everything hanging in the balance any mention of the subject seemed to be tempting fate.

'I intend to tell Dad everything that's necessary, Jess,' he said firmly. 'I'll tell him about my recurring dreams and my blackouts, and how I was directed to what you believe to be a sacred site. I'll tell him what happened to me at the site too. I'll be straight with him, I can promise you. The effect that place had on me was profound, as you well know. I'm willing to tell Dad all of that and you can take things from there. What do you say?'

'Sounds like a plan,' she'd replied.

'Well here we are, dear,' Lilian said as they arrived at the top of the stairs, 'I'll leave you to wander around and settle in while the boys have their chat.' Having successfully escaped her son's hostility, Lilian was now eager to escape playing hostess. She really couldn't be bothered chatting about her paintings, even to someone as gorgeous as Jess. Talking about art was always so boring. You either liked what you saw or you didn't: people should leave it at that. She would retire to her office downstairs and catch up on her emails, she decided. 'We'll re-group in an hour or so, shall we?' she said. Mattie would have forgiven her by then.

'Lovely, one hour it is then. Thank you, Lilian.'

But the question had been rhetorical. Lilian had already done an about-turn and was off down the stairs, scarves wafting ethereally in her wake.

Jess dumped her case on the floor. She wouldn't bother to unpack, not yet. She was much more interested in examining the several new paintings, which, far from being properly mounted, were strewn about haphazardly as usual. They differed in subject matter from the outback topics normally favoured by Lilian, but each was in typical Lilian Birch style, bold and provocative. Here the bright red door of an attractive sandstone terrace house, the redness reflecting the heat of the mid-afternoon summer sun, the door temptingly ajar, beckoning one inside; here a park bench and a wintry dawn, a woman seated, viewed from behind, staring out over the river, straight-backed, body language depicting her deep in thought, but is she happy or sad? One longs to see her face. Here a modern office block at dusk, other city buildings and the central square's autumnal trees reflected in its shining surfaces, but no people rushing about after work, just one lone figure standing by the main doors. Is it Sunday, and if so what is he doing there?

Jess was entranced. Each painting seemed to raise a question that teased, and the lighting in each denoted not only the season but the specific time of day, making a further comment. Lilian's mastery enthralled as always, but even while admiring the pieces, Jess couldn't help her mind now and then wandering to father and son. Just how much was Matt telling Dave?

Quite a bit as it turned out.

She joined them in the sitting room an hour later, having finally unpacked her case and freshened up as Lilian had suggested. She'd deliberately whiled away the time to allow for the full hour, but Lilian was there well in advance, pouring herself a glass of red wine from the bottle on the cabinet as the men tucked into their second beers.

'Jess darling, I was just about to come and get you,' Lilian said with a touch of impatience the moment she appeared, 'what on earth took you so long?'

Jess ignored the look from Matt, a mixture of exasperation and sympathy. 'Sorry,' she said, 'didn't mean to keep you waiting.'

'The boys have been telling me about the latest *fascinating* things that have been going on and Mattie now says the rest is over to you.'

'Oh.' Jess was instantly daunted, but saved the necessity of further comment as Lilian continued.

'They've already downed a beer, but as I don't drink the stuff I'm hoping mid-afternoon isn't too early for you to join me in a wine.' She held the bottle aloft. 'It's a Barossa Shiraz, and a very nice full-bodied one I promise you. Or would you rather a beer?'

'I don't think it's too early at all, Lilian. I'd love to join you in a wine, thank you.'

'Oh goody.' Lilian beamed. 'I've never understood the lust for beer myself, wonderful I'm sure after a strenuous game of tennis, but I don't play tennis.' She took another glass from the cabinet and poured Jess's wine. 'Cheers,' she said as she handed it to her.

'Cheers,' Jess responded and they clinked glasses and sat.

The wine was certainly full-bodied, Jess thought as she took a sip. She put the glass down warily, waiting for whatever cue was coming her way. She'd need her wits about her to tackle what lay ahead. How was she to approach things? she wondered. Perhaps she could open with the spiel she'd given Matt about the 1930s 'biological absorption' scheme and how many apparently white Australians didn't know of their black ancestry.

'I've been hearing all about Mattie's recurring dreams and blackouts,' Lilian said, 'most unpleasant. And then about the visions he had that directed him to a site you believe is sacred, Jess, how extraordinary.'

Dave took over at that point. 'Yes, it's quite remarkable that the images Matt had in his mind proved so precise – the larger and smaller rock outcrops, the clearing, the sign . . . You must have found that amazing, Jess.'

'Yes,' she said, 'I did.'

'And he says he can't remember what happened at the site,' Dave went on, 'but that you told him afterwards he was yelling out in a local language.'

'That's right. He was yelling "run" in Arunta, over and over.'

'Remarkable,' Dave shook his head, 'quite remarkable.'

'And that's as much as the boys have told me,' Lilian could contain herself no longer, 'and now Mattie won't tell either of us anything more. He says the rest is over to you.'

There was an air of expectancy. Jess took a deep breath.

'Well, as Matt has mentioned, I believe the site is sacred.' She started out cautiously. 'I believe the dreams he was having right from the start, the dreams about railways evoked by his grandfather Charlie and possibly his great-grandfather Brian, were leading him towards the discovery of this site . . .' She paused; Where to from here?

'Yes, yes,' Lilian urged, 'go on, go on.'

'I don't know why the site is sacred,' Jess said, still buying time. 'It's not officially recognised as such. Perhaps something happened there a long time ago, something that was of personal significance to a local family; in any case Matt was certainly led there for a purpose . . .'

How unlike Jess to flounder, Matt thought, she needs help. He decided to cut to the chase.

'Jess reckons it was our ancestors who led me there, Dad,' he said, 'she reckons we've got blackfella blood in us.'

Complete silence followed, Dave and Lilian staring dumbfounded, Matt now the expectant one awaiting a reaction and Jess, although surprised by the bluntness of his statement, grateful to have been saved further delay tactics. Who would be the first to speak?

It was Lilian's bewilderment that finally won out. 'What ancestors?' she asked. 'Charlie and Brian?'

'Well, the ancestors of Charlie and Brian, yes,' Jess said.

'But Charlie and Brian were white.'

Now's the right time, Jess thought, and she launched into her discourse on the government's 'biological absorption' scheme, which Lilian in particular appeared to find spellbinding.

'Several generations on,' she concluded, 'when children have been adopted out with no knowledge of their background, there are many left totally unaware of their black ancestry.'

'So there you go, Dad,' Matt remarked, 'it seems we come from central desert blackfella stock.'

'How thrilling,' Lilian said.

Jess looked from mother to son, wondering if either or perhaps both were being flippant, but it appeared not. She looked then to Dave for his reaction. Was the man shocked, offended or merely in a state of disbelief? He appeared none of these – perhaps he was simply as spellbound as his wife. But he was silent. Was he waiting for her to go on, and if so what more was she expected to say?

'Matt tells me you've never professed an interest in your family's background, Dave,' she said. 'Forgive my impertinence, but haven't you ever wanted to trace where you come from?'

'No, strangely enough.' The reply was simple, but Jess could tell she hadn't offended.

'Why not?'

'My mother,' Dave said. 'I can only suppose I was being protective, but Peg wanted no part of her past. She'd talk about Charlie and the great love they'd shared, brief as it had been, but she never spoke of her family. I was her world and she was mine and it didn't seem right to invite the past in. Or rather, it never occurred to me to do so.'

'And it still doesn't?'

'Oh yes it does. *Now* it does.' Dave glanced at Lilian and they shared a moment of complicity. 'I already have, or rather *we* have.'

Jess's turn to be mystified. 'In what way?'

'At Lilian's insistence I traced the background of Brian Francis Witherton. The records show his father was Thomas James Witherton, born 1872, died 1935. His mother was Anne Featherstone, born approximately 1878 or '79, died 1947.'

'Approximately?' Jess queried.

'Yes. It seems she was adopted by the Featherstone family from an orphanage in Adelaide when she was around three years old. No-one knew who she was or where she came from or her exact date of birth.'

Once again a telling silence, Lilian's the most telling of all, and it was naturally Lilian who chose to break the moment.

'Things seem to fit rather neatly, don't you think?'

Much general discussion followed after that. It was obvious to Jess that Dave had difficulty believing his son had been visited by the spirits of their family's ancestors, but then so did his son. Even Matt, profoundly affected as he'd been by his experience at the site, found the spiritual connection hard to swallow. But both men were in agreement that something inexplicable had taken place, and both were surprisingly accepting of the possibility, even probability, of their black ancestry. As for Lilian, well Lilian wholeheartedly embraced the notion.

'It explains so *much*, Dave,' she said with her customary zeal, 'you've always been drawn to the central desert, always so at home there. It explains above all your bond with the land – you'd have to agree with that, surely.'

I'd certainly agree with that, Jess thought, watching the family in discussion and exchanging a smile with Matt. Telling a white man he was black hadn't been that difficult after all.

She said as much to Matt the following morning when he dropped her off at the airport.

'Things went pretty well really, didn't they,' she said, standing by while he lifted her case from the boot and raised its handle for her.

Bit of an understatement, Matt thought. 'Bloody oath they did. Things went exceptionally well, I'd say.'

She grasped the case's handle and gave one of those irrepressible grins that always won him. 'See you in Alice,' she said and walked off.

'See you in Alice,' he called after her.

'He has a perfect ear,' Toby said, 'just listen to this.'

It was later that same day and they were seated in the studio, Toby at the synthesiser and Jess on the sofa, Ringo, tail wagging in eager anticipation, standing between them with his gaze fixed on Toby.

As Toby had predicted Jess had fallen in love with the scruffy mongrel he'd adopted from the pound. Medium sized and sturdily built with wiry terrier-hair, mothy-grey colouring and donkey-like ears, the dog was adorably ugly. But Ringo had skills Toby was eager to show off.

'Sit,' Toby commanded and the animal obediently plonked itself on its hefty backside and froze, bushy-browed eyes gazing up expectantly; Ringo loved this game.

Toby hit a note on the keyboard and the dog threw back its head and let out a brief howl. 'See, what did I tell you? A perfect A,' Toby boasted. Then he hit an E and then a G and both times the dog changed pitch, not altogether on the note but impressive nonetheless. 'He can sing a whole C scale: you just listen to this.'

Toby proceeded to play the scale and the dog gave voice, howling along raucously, moving up with each new note, although rarely on key.

'Well perhaps I exaggerate, not altogether perfect,' Toby said as Jess applauded, 'but three out of eight's not bad – better than some singers I've known.' He dropped his voice and whispered conspiratorially, 'But you want to know the real secret?'

'What's that, Dad?'

'The dog's actually a drummer. Watch this.'

He hit the synthesiser's percussion key and slid the volume up loud; as the drums belted out the dog went wild, chasing itself in circles and racing around the room in a frenzy of tail-wagging, ear-flapping excitement. Ringo was mad about the drums.

Jess roared with laughter at the sight. They both did: the dog's joy was lunatic. Then as Toby lowered the volume Ringo's antics became less and less frantic until finally when silence once more reigned he was thoroughly placid.

'The louder it is the more he likes it,' Toby said, 'a true drummer.'

'A true muso's dog, Dad,' Jess replied, still fighting to contain her laughter. 'He's picked it up from you.'

'No he hasn't, that's just it,' Toby insisted. 'He was like this when I got him. Ringo's a natural. Isn't that the most wonderful thing?'

Toby and Jess were revelling in each other's company. They'd agreed that over the past six months they'd both been so busy with their work they hadn't realised how much they'd missed each other. At least that's what they'd both said. He'd never tell her to her face but Toby always missed Jess.

They went to a gig of his early that evening, a jazz gig at The Union pub in Balmain.

'Just a fun gig I do from time to time, Jess,' he'd said, 'playing guitar with Georgie and his band. I can easily get out of it, Georgie won't mind, he's got guitarists queuing up to play with him, but I thought you might like a touch of the old days.'

'I can think of nothing I'd like more,' she said.

She watched them, her father grooving with George Washingmachine and the others, everyone taking their lead from George. Paris jazz at its finest; she might have been listening to Stéphane Grappelli – George was a master on the violin. And her dad was holding his own every step of the way, the crowd showing its appreciation, the pub packed as it always was when George and his band were playing.

Looking on with daughterly pride, Jess recalled Roger's demeaning remark all those years ago: 'He's not exactly a *musician*, darling. Your father's a sound engineer. It's not quite the same thing.' How wrong, she thought, how wrong and how very ill informed of Roger. Toby Manning had always been a fine musician, which was precisely why he was one of the best sound engineers in the country. Music flowed through his veins. That's what he used to say about Mum, Jess thought fondly. 'Your mother's the true musician in the family, Jess,' he'd say, 'music flows through her veins and that's a fact.'

The evening brought back many a childhood memory for Jess of the pub gigs she'd go to with Rose, and the jam sessions in the studio at the end of a recording day when she and her mother would sit up the back watching Toby groove with the musos.

'You were right, Dad,' she said several hours later as they wended their way home through the night-lit,

Sunday-busy streets of Balmain, where people were leaving restaurants and pubs and bars, 'that was definitely a touch of the old days.'

'Thought it might be.' Toby grinned, pleased. 'So what's on the agenda for tomorrow?' He'd taken Monday off, she wasn't flying out until Tuesday afternoon and they'd have the whole day to themselves. 'Your choice.'

'Ferry to Manly?' she asked, and he laughed. Another touch of the old days; he'd known she'd say that.

The Manly Ferry had been a regular outing for Toby and Rose and little Jess, and now as father and daughter stood by the starboard railings watching the sails of the Sydney Opera House glide by they shared a poignant moment, each knowing the other was thinking of her, each hearing her voice.

'Just look at that, love,' Jess could hear Rose say. 'If you concentrate on the sails and the sky you'd swear it's a ship going past and that we're just standing still.' Rose had always found the Opera House a source of great wonder.

The voice in Toby's mind was the voice that lived with him constantly. Rose was singing as they passed the Opera House and, as always, she was singing just for him. The music that had flowed through Rose remained forever in Toby's blood. He was never without her. And now with Jess beside him, Rose's voice was stronger than ever.

When they alighted from the ferry they walked away from the harbour through The Corso, the pedestrian mall that led to the ocean side of the peninsular, where they bought fish and chips, all part of a bygone routine. They didn't even discuss other options.

The weather was pleasant, the day clear, an early spring nip in the air and a breeze with a bite coming off the water, but they were in sweaters, they were prepared.

They sat on the beach eating their fish and chips and looking out over the ocean and Toby waited for her to tell him about whatever it was he'd sensed on the phone. He could sense it still – he had from the moment she'd arrived – she needed to talk, but in her own time. Well now seems as good a time as any, he thought, and he waited.

They finished their fish and chips. He found a bin for the refuse and returned to sit once again beside her, but still no word as she continued to stare out to sea.

'Would you like a coffee?' he asked. 'Shall we find a cosy caff? It's a bit breezy don't you think?'

'No thanks, Dad. I'd rather stay here if you don't mind.'

'Course I don't mind. Right you are then, no coffee, didn't want any anyway.' He left it barely a minute before taking matters into his own hands. 'Come on, Jess, what is it? Spit it out, there's a good girl.'

And she did. She'd been on the verge of doing so anyway and now there was no holding her back. She told him absolutely everything: about Matt and his dreams; about the site and the rail corridor; and she even told him about the redirection of the route, swearing him to secrecy as she did so.

'You're the only one outside the inner circle who knows, Dad,' she said, refusing to feel guilty – she'd sworn no oath to Matt and she would trust Toby with her life.

'Not a word,' he promised, 'cross my heart.'

Then she made her true confession. She was distracted, she said. 'It all started out as a favour to a friend,' she admitted. 'Matt's dreams were distressing him and I was a sounding board, someone he could talk to. Then I started coming up with answers. They were answers that admittedly he didn't believe for the most part and probably still doesn't, particularly with regard to the ancestors, but I'm consumed by the desire to find out more. It's become an obsession,' she said. 'I know that the site is sacred; I can feel it. And I know we were meant to save it from desecration. But what happened there? Why are Matt's ancestors guarding the place?'

The questions being rhetorical and unanswerable anyway, Toby just sat in silence, letting her get things off her chest.

'I play it as low-key as I can with Matt,' she said. 'As far as he's concerned I'm just an Aboriginal woman who believes in the spirit world, but I've become so personally involved! I'm obsessed with finding out the truth.' She smiled ruefully and gave a helpless shrug. 'Which is silly really, isn't it? Unless the ancestors pay me a personal visit and fill me in, I'll never know, so what's the point in agonising?'

'No point at all, I'd say. But it's a bloody fascinating story, I'll give you that much.'

'Yes, it is, isn't it?' She hugged him gratefully. 'Thanks for listening, Dad.'

'My pleasure. Any time.' Toby couldn't have been happier. He had indeed found the story fascinating – who wouldn't? But there was something else he had read in his daughter's confession. Jess loved this man she called a good friend. She didn't know it yet, but hopefully she would in time. And even if nothing were to come of the relationship, Toby was still happy. It seemed the damage Roger Macready had wrought upon his daughter, damage which Toby had worried might be irreparable, was now a thing of the past. Jess was no longer closing men out of her life.

He insisted upon driving her to the airport the following day. 'I'm not cancelling any work, I promise you,' he said, 'I've got a night recording session and that's it.' He was lying – he *had* cancelled an afternoon session.

They talked about Christmas on the way. They'd agreed she should come home to Sydney for the break. They'd missed each other altogether far too much. They must not leave it so long between visits.

'I'll arrange another gig and we'll do another ferry trip,' Toby promised.

Then as they pulled up at the quick drop-off area outside the terminal and she piled from the car, cabin luggage in hand, Toby made the casual suggestion.

'Why don't you bring your friend Matt with you?' he said. 'I'd like to meet him. He sounds like an interesting bloke.'

'Oh no, Dad,' Jess replied, oblivious to any ulterior motive in the invitation, 'Matt'll be on a promise to his parents at Christmas.'

'Right you are.' What a pity, Toby thought.

CHAPTER TWELVE

'It's about to happen.' Matt rang her the week after she'd returned from her brief Sydney trip. 'Fritz told me the contractors are nearing the redirected section of the route. They'll soon start pegging out the final construction path. Now we just sit tight and keep our fingers crossed.'

'When will we know?'

'If nothing happens within the next week we should be safe. I'll give you a call. In the meantime we play the waiting game.'

Matt sounded his customary unruffled self, but in truth he was feeling tense. No longer plagued by recurring dreams and sleepless nights, no longer visited by inexplicable blackouts and headaches, the force that had been driving him seemed itself to have become no more than a dream. He was beginning to question why he'd undertaken the drastic action he had. If it was discovered that, without any form of authority, he'd secretly altered the course of the Ghan, his credibility and indeed his very career could be ruined.

Two days later his worst fears were realised.

'Hey, Boss!' It was Gav, leaping from the four-wheel drive after bringing it to a screeching halt in a cloud of red dust.

Matt was several kilometres to the south of his team, having left the others working while he conducted an advance recce, as was his habit. He'd been watching the vehicle tear across the desert at top speed, wondering why the bloke was in such a hurry.

'What's up, Gav?' he asked as the burly worker arrived at his side.

'Some smartarse bastard from the city's arrived. I reckon he's out to cause trouble.'

'Oh?' Despite an instinctive stab of alarm, Matt told himself there was probably no real cause for concern. Gav had no idea about the route deviation, and in his eyes every 'smartarse bastard from the city' was out to cause trouble. The official reason for the visit might well be something mundane, another time-wasting bureaucratic exercise. 'What sort of trouble?' he asked.

'I dunno.' Gav shrugged. 'He was talking to Pottsy when I left, but it's you he wants to see. Pottsy tried to radio you but you weren't in your car.'

'Rightio.' Matt crossed to his Land Rover some distance away. 'Thanks, Gav,' he called back.

The two men climbed into their respective vehicles and took off together, travelling the several kilometres back to their current work site.

But when they arrived the official from the city was nowhere to be seen. The AdRail vehicle he'd driven from Alice Springs was there – one of the shiny Toyota Land-Cruisers kept in mint condition for visiting dignitaries or inspectors from down south – but no sign of the official himself. No sign of Pottsy either.

'What's happening, boys?' Matt continued to play it cool as he questioned Baz and Mitch, although he was starting to feel uneasy. 'Who's this bloke that's arrived?'

'Introduced himself as Lewis Bisley.' Mitch exchanged a glance with Baz. 'He's an engineer up from Adelaide.'

Matt knew the name, on paper anyway; he hadn't met the man in the flesh. Alarm bells were starting to sound. 'And where is he now?'

'Pottsy took him about ten Ks back down the line.' Mitch once again was the spokesman. 'Said he was going to show him a watercourse.'

A further exchange of glances between Mitch and Baz did not go unnoticed by Gav standing nearby. But Gav had noticed many such glances over recent weeks. He'd even heard the odd mutter between the two young assistants some time back. 'Withers knows what he's doing,' he'd heard Baz say, 'don't know why he's doing it, mind you.'

Then agreement from Mitch: 'I don't know either,' he'd said, 'I just hope it doesn't come back to bite him.' When the two had noticed him watching from the sidelines, they'd instantly shut up, but Gav wasn't stupid. Something's going on, he'd thought, something that could get the Boss into trouble.

About ten Ks back down the line. The words echoed ominously in Matt's brain. The route deviation was ten kilometres back down the line. And he'd told Pottsy they could use the adjacent watercourse as a possible reason for the change should questions be raised. Questions obviously *had* been raised. I'm in trouble, he thought.

'Right,' he said briskly, 'I'd better get on down there and meet the bloke, hadn't I? Radio ahead to Pottsy,' he instructed the boys, 'and tell him I'm on my way.'

He climbed into the Land Rover and drove off, his mind racing. It was Lewis Bisley's name and signature that appeared on the final design drawings that were based upon his own mathematical data and route measurements. The drawings were then provided to the contractors for use in their pegging and layout and rail construction. It was from this quarter that he'd anticipated possible trouble, not Bisley. He'd presumed Bisley was just a bureaucrat ticking boxes, but obviously he wasn't. The man was out for answers.

As he drove, Matt was so deeply in thought that he was unaware of the four-wheel drive following closely behind.

Gav had jumped into his vehicle and taken off after Withers. He wasn't sure what he was going to do, but if the Boss was in trouble he'd be there to help. As a member of the team, Gav was eager to play his part.

Matt passed the site to his left, the hillocks clearly visible, and it was only a minute or so later that he saw the two men up ahead waiting for him. Pottsy was lounging against his dusty four-wheel drive, rust-coloured hair and vehicle melding in with the surrounding desert, while the engineer, a well-built, rather stylish man in his early forties with a folder in his hand, was standing somewhat to attention, wearing a suit and looking distinctly out of place.

'Lewis Bisley I take it,' Matt said as he alighted from the Land Rover. 'G'day.' He strode forward, offering his hand.

'Mr Witherton.' They shook.

'G'day, Gav.' Pottsy was peering over Matt's shoulder and Matt turned, surprised to see Gav, who'd climbed from his vehicle and was standing respectfully several paces away.

'This is a member of my team,' he said to Bisley, 'my machine operator, Gavin Johnstone.'

The introduction invited a handshake, but Bisley made no offer, giving a curt nod instead, and Gav stood his ground, glaring at the slick city bastard. What sort of dumb cunt wears a suit in the desert, he thought. A suit and a fucking tie, for Christ's sake.

'What can I do for you, Lewis?' Matt started out on a first-name basis, keeping his tone friendly and accommodating, although his reaction was rather along Gav's lines. This is one stitched-up prick who wants to pull rank, he thought.

'I'll get straight to the point,' Bisley said, 'nothing to be gained by beating about the bush, is there?' A rhetorical question to which Matt made no response – pompous to boot, he thought. 'Besides, in your *absence*,' the engineer continued, his emphasis managing to lend an accusatory edge, 'I've discussed the matter in some detail with Mr Potts here.'

'Oh yes? And what matter would that be?'

Bisley waved the folder in an authoritative manner. 'I have a copy of the final design drawings, together with a map of the originally proposed route, and there appears to be a distinct discrepancy.'

'Is that so?' Matt glanced at Pottsy, who proffered a helpless shrug that said *I did what I could, mate*, then returned his attention to Bisley, waiting for the man to go on.

'Yes, that is most certainly so,' the engineer replied archly. 'Mr Potts has shown me a watercourse that you apparently believe could pose a threat during flood, but this has not appeared in any report my office has received.'

'There are often things that don't appear in reports, Mr Bisley,' Matt said, trying not to sound arch himself. 'You must understand this is difficult, uncharted terrain. If we had to await approval from down south for every slight allowance that needs to be made given the conditions the wilderness throws at us, the Ghan would never see the light of day.' He was starting to sound pompous himself, he realised, but he was desperately trying to buy time. What should he do? What was there he *could* do?

'This is hardly a "slight allowance", Mr Witherton.' Bisley's tone was more than arch, now – he was positively scathing. Did the surveyor take him for a fool? 'I have seen the watercourse, it would pose no threat in flood, and yet you have taken it upon yourself to alter the final route measurements without the authority to do so. I must warn you, I am here in an official capacity, and I can tell you right now –'

Gav to the rescue . . . 'If you're here in an official capacity, mate, I've got a complaint to make.' He strode over, coming nose to nose with the man, burly and belligerent.

Bisley flinched involuntarily, but to give him his due he did not back away. Lewis Bisley was not one to be intimidated by a common thug. 'And what complaint would that be?' he asked icily. He would have preferred to turn his back on the man, but it wouldn't look good if he ignored a worker's genuine grievance.

Gav could have decked the bloke. What gave the bastard the right to piss on him? This was just the sort of prick he'd like to take apart, but that wouldn't do the Boss any good.

'A legitimate complaint, that's what,' he said, 'faulty machinery. You tell that to your cronies down south. Faulty machinery can kill a bloke, you know. There'll be some hefty lawsuits when that happens, won't there? I've got a bulldozer that's a fucking death trap. You wanna come and look at it and make a report? You better, 'cos otherwise I'll say you refused.' Gav stabbed a beefy forefinger at the engineer's chest, stopping just short of bodily contact – there was nothing to be gained by an assault charge. 'And that won't go down too well, will it. The bosses refusing to listen to complaints from the workers? That sort of thing can cause strife with the union –'

'Okay, Gav, one thing at a time,' Matt said, interrupting the tirade. 'I'm sure Mr Bisley will file a complaint report on your behalf after we've addressed this current situation. Isn't that right, Mr Bisley?'

The engineer gave another curt nod, turned dismissively from Gav and was about to continue where he'd left off, but Matt got in first.

'In the meantime,' he continued 'why don't we take a walk, just you and me? We can follow your map of the originally proposed route, and you can see for yourself the deviation allowed for the watercourse. Which,' he added as if it was a matter of great significance, 'actually reappears up ahead as many of these creek beds do.'

'If you wish.' Bisley obviously saw no point in the exercise but, keen to get away from the oaf confronting him, he waited with tellingly frigid patience while Matt fetched a compass from the Land Rover.

Pottsy watched the two set off. He was mystified. What was Withers up to? The watercourse didn't reappear up ahead at all. The creek bed and rocky embankment he'd shown the engineer was the only evidence that could have held any possible validity for the route deviation. Withers doesn't stand a chance, he thought.

While Pottsy was watching them walk away, Gav was climbing into his four-wheel drive, bent on getting back to the worksite where he could tinker with his faultless bulldozer.

They didn't talk as they walked, the engineer purse-lipped, compass in hand, following the coordinates on the map while Matt silently offered something up into the ether that seemed suspiciously like a prayer. He was grateful to Gav – the interruption had bought him time to think. His thoughts had produced no concrete answers, admittedly, apart from the obvious fact that any further discussion with Bisley was useless, but he had come to a decision nonetheless. A desperate decision requiring a leap of faith that he very much doubted was in him.

If you're there, he thought – Charlie, Brian, any of the rest of your mob – I need help. It's up to you now. I can't save your site on my own. Everything's over to you. Where do we go to from here? Tell me what to do.

Even as he sent up his thoughts, a part of him questioned his foolishness. What the hell am I doing, he wondered, what sort of ridiculous nonsense is this? But as they approached the rocky hillocks, he found himself seeking contact with ever-increasing urgency. I must think the way Jess thinks, he told himself. I must think of the spirit world, of the ancestors. Save yourselves, he urged as if he actually believed they were there and could hear his plea. This man will destroy your site. Save yourselves! Save your sacred site! Tell me what to do!

But nothing was happening. He felt no contact at all. No images appeared, sending messages and instructions as they had before. There was no dizziness, no headache, no threat of an impending blackout.

As they stepped into the clearing, Matt didn't know what to expect, although he was tense and certainly wary given his previous experience. But walking between the rocks and into the clearing's centre, he continued to feel absolutely nothing.

Lewis Bisley, however, did. For the past ten minutes, as he'd slowly traced every step of the route, Lewis Bisley had begun feeling increasingly ill. At first it was biliousness and, remembering the breakfast he'd had on the plane up from Adelaide, he'd wondered whether he'd contracted food poisoning. Then he'd felt hot and clammy beneath the light suit jacket, then just as suddenly he was chilled to the marrow, shivering even. Surely he was coming down with some sort of flu virus.

Now as they walked into the centre of the clearing the real nightmare began. All of a sudden he was under attack. Things were crawling over him – torturous, unseen things – poking, prodding, jabbing. He dropped the compass and folder, papers spilling out onto the sand. He raked his face with his fingers, frantically trying to rid himself of the creatures that were attempting to crawl inside his nose and his ears and his eyes, intent upon invading his body in order to attack from within. What was happening to him? Where had these repulsive assailants come from? What hideous force had set upon him? Lewis Bisley had never known such terror.

'Are you all right, mate?'

Lewis didn't hear Matt's concerned query. He fell to his hands and knees, gagging. He couldn't breathe. Some invisible power was strangling him.

Matt dropped down beside the man. 'What's happening, Bisley? Are you all right? Can you walk?'

Lewis heard this time, but couldn't reply. He shook his head. Of course he couldn't walk, he couldn't even talk. He was dry-retching now, dry-retching and suffocating, tearing at his tie and his shirt collar. He wanted to scream 'get me out of here', but no words would come, just ghastly choking sounds. He'd be dead any minute,

The man's having some sort of fit, Matt thought, perhaps he's epileptic or suffering a severe asthma attack. But just in case the seizure had something to do with the site, he grabbed Bisley under the armpits and dragged him out of the clearing.

Once well removed from the site, Lewis Bisley seemed to recover. He sat hunched on the ground, his grateful lungs heaving in gobs of air. Squatting beside him, Matt was relieved the man's condition had improved. Things had seemed a bit scary back there, he thought. Then suddenly Bisley was once again on all fours, this time puking into the dirt.

Lewis looked down at the mess spewing from his mouth and pooling on the ground before him. This was not the breakfast he'd had on the plane. This black muck was not normal. This was evidence of his body's invasion. Something horrendous had happened. He retched violently another two times, then finally it was over and he flopped back in the dust, exhausted.

Matt wasn't sure what to say. 'I'll collect the file and the compass, shall I?' he offered lamely, gesturing at the papers that lay scattered about the clearing. Not unsurprisingly, he received no answer.

He walked back into the centre of the clearing and, when he'd gathered the material together, he looked about the site, trying to feel an unearthly presence. Was that your doing? he asked, seeking a response. If so it was pretty brutal. No criticism intended, but you were a bit tough on him, don't you reckon? He felt no unearthly presence and he received no response.

Bisley had hauled himself to his feet by the time Matt returned. He was kicking dust over the black vomit and adjusting his tie and shirt in an effort to restore his dignity, but Matt could see he was a nervous wreck.

'I don't suppose you want to take a look at the watercourse over there,' he suggested, pointing to the other side of the site where there was no watercourse at all. It was not his intention to torture the man further, he simply had to be sure there was an understanding in place.

Bisley shook his head and, taking the folder Matt held out to him, set off in the direction from which they'd come.

Matt kept pace beside him. They did not walk fast. Bisley was still in a dazed state, shaken to the core. Matt felt sorry for the man.

'Actually, Lewis,' he said, 'I must tell you in all honesty that there have been other strange happenings back at that place. I've had a weird experience there myself, something totally inexplicable.'

Bisley halted, and for the first time since the incident he looked Matt straight in the eyes, a look that Matt found extraordinarily vulnerable.

'Some things are very difficult to put on paper,' Matt continued with care, 'virtually impossible to describe in a report. I thought, given the strangeness of that site . . .' he paused, then added firmly in order that there should be no misunderstanding, 'together with the watercourse, naturally, which was of some concern, that a slight deviation to the route was warranted.'

Lewis did not trust himself to speak. He wasn't even sure if he was capable of speech. His throat hurt and his head ached. But the nod he gave Matt clearly stated that they had an agreement.

They walked on together in silence, and when they reached the vehicles where Pottsy remained patiently waiting, the three men shook hands all round.

Pottsy was taken aback by the engineer's dishevelled appearance and change in his demeanour. What had happened to the bloke's arrogance? But he made no comment, and Lewis, now in the company of the Assistant Surveyor, felt obliged to offer some verbal comment.

'All appears to be in order,' he said with Herculean effort, his voice rasping.

Then he climbed into his AdRail Land Cruiser and set off back to Alice Springs. No mention was made of Gav's bulldozer.

Pottsy openly gawked at Matt.

'You won't believe it,' Matt said, looking at the Toyota receding into the distance. 'You won't believe what happened out there, Pottsy. I sure as hell can't.'

'Hey Withers, fancy a beer?'

It was several days later when Fritz dropped by his donga, a couple of cans of 4X in hand. Matt had just come back from the ablutions block having showered at the end of a long work day, but Fritz hadn't freshened up at all. Upon his return from working with the teams involved on the rail corridor's construction Fritz had gone straight to the canteen and when Matt wasn't there he'd grabbed a couple of beers and sought him out.

'Sure, thanks Fritz.'

Matt took the can he was offered and the two of them sat side by side on the donga's low front step, the lanky Queenslander spider-like, all knees and elbows. There appeared no-one else about, the doors of the other dongas closed, the majority of workers having headed directly for the canteen, but Fritz kept his voice low just in case.

'You're in the clear, mate,' he said. 'The corridor's followed your centreline to a tee and no-one's said a bloody word. If any of the head honchos thought the route varied a little from the originally mapped path they never uttered a boo, at least they didn't to me, and I'd be the one they would have headed for if they'd wanted to raise queries. The contractors just went right ahead setting out their pegs for earthworks and rail construction based on your final route measurements and now the corridor's gone through. End of story.'

'What about the progress reports?' Matt asked.

'Everything reported as normal, nothing untoward that the buggers down south could question, and no smart-arse inspector turned up to run a spot check in order to big-note himself.' Fritz clearly hadn't heard about Lewis Bisley's visit and Matt decided not to tell him; it wasn't really necessary.

The two clinked beer cans and drank a wordless toast.

'Bloody lucky,' Matt said.

'Yep,' Fritz agreed, 'bloody lucky all right, but there's a reason, at least in my opinion there is.'

'Oh, and what's that?'

'I think the closer we get to Alice the less questions are being asked all round. We're ahead of schedule and the field bosses can see the end in sight, so they're not going to let up the pace now.' He took another swig of his beer and added with a grin, 'There's a bonus for coming in ahead of schedule you know.'

Matt returned the grin, inwardly breathing a sigh of relief. It appeared the waiting game was at long last over.

He shared the news with Pottsy and quite a few more beers went down that night – in fact the two got rather drunk, something they never did mid-week. But then covertly changing the route of a mighty railway like the Ghan was hardly a run-of-the-mill achievement, was it?

'What a coup, eh, Withers?' Pottsy said as they toasted themselves yet again with their fourth 4X. 'What a down-right, bloody coup.'

They were celebrating their cleverness in achieving a feat so audacious – they both knew that. In their excite-ment neither of them was dwelling upon the reason for their audacity. Certainly Pottsy had initiated the toasts with a big thank you to the ancestral spirits for scaring off Lewis Bisley, a fact that he'd found plausible from the outset. Indeed it rather surprised him that Withers still appeared resistant, persuading himself that Bisley may actually have had some form of seizure. Typical Withers, Pottsy thought fondly, everything had to have a logical explanation. But no matter. Right now they were concentrating on the self-congratulatory aspect of the exercise.

The following Saturday in Alice, however, when he celebrated with Jess, Matt was reminded of their true purpose.

'We did it, Jess,' he said as they sat in the Tavern at the window table that seemed to have become theirs, 'we actually did it,' and he raised his glass.

'You did it, Matt,' she said after they'd clinked and drank, 'you and the ancestors.'

When he'd told her of the episode with the visiting engineer from Adelaide, Jess had of course been adamant in her belief. 'The man didn't have a fit at all,' she'd stated categorically. 'Whether or not you were aware of it, you made contact with the ancestors. You asked for their help and they came to your aid, simple as that.'

'Whatever sacred purpose the site serves it will never be desecrated,' she now said, raising her glass and saluting him again, her smile jubilant. 'You've preserved it for all time and the ancestors will thank you forever.'

Jess's elation should have meant the world to Matt, but instead it had a surprisingly sobering effect, reminding him as it did of the past months, during which the two of them had explored realms he had never known existed, realms he still didn't altogether believe in, but which he felt in some way he'd been given license to enter.

Where do we go to from here? He thought his own sense of elation skidding to a halt. Where do we go to from here? He felt becalmed, a ship on a windless sea, sails luffing uselessly. What were they to do now? Where was the force that had been driving them?

His instant deflation was readable and at first Jess wondered why he'd become so withdrawn. Then she realised that he'd simply been celebrating the success of the undertaking, not the reason for it. Her reminder had brought him down, she thought, why? Surely he can't doubt our purpose! Surely he can't be questioning the very motive behind the action he's taken. He mustn't do that. He mustn't!

'Don't doubt the goal we set ourselves, Matt,' she urged. 'Please, whatever you do, don't underestimate the importance of preserving the site. Whether or not you believe in its spiritual significance, it must remain untouched. I know this.' Her eyes implored him. 'Don't ask me how because I wouldn't be able to tell you, but trust me, I do know this.'

'I know that you know, Jess,' he said reassuringly – she appeared worried, 'and furthermore I accept the fact that you're right.' Then he added with an air of self-mockery, 'I have no idea why I accept the fact that you're right, but somehow I do. And unquestioningly, what's more.'

She smiled. 'A leap of faith?'

'Yes,' he smiled back, 'we'll put it down to a leap of faith.' He took a swig of his beer. 'So what do we do now?'

Despite his reassurance Jess sensed an empty feeling remained and she had to admit she felt rather the same way.

'I think we should return to the site,' she said, and in the instant she said it she knew she was right. He needs to reconnect with the ancestors, she thought, he's bound to experience some form of reaction at the site, something that will make him aware of its significance.

Several moments passed before Matt replied. 'I'd rather not, Jess, at least not until the rail corridor's completed right through to Alice; then we'll know for certain there can be no turning back.' He wasn't sure of the reason for his delay tactics. There would be no turning back now, not according to Fritz and not according to his own knowledge of procedure. Everything had gone according to plan and the route of the Ghan was locked in. But Matt didn't want to return to the site. Something told him he mustn't, that he was not ready yet, that he would not be ready until the corridor was completed.

'And when will that be?' Jess asked.

'Early in the New Year,' he replied, 'when they do the rock blasting just north of town. We'll visit the site after that. Okay by you?'

'Sure,' she replied. A long time to wait, she thought, but the decision had to be Matt's. 'Okay by me.'

They sat silently, sipping their beers, comfortable in each other's company as they always were, but the mood remained slightly lost: both felt rudderless, purposeless, wondering, 'What next?'

'What are you doing at Christmas?' she asked. It was still only October and Christmas seemed so far away, but there didn't appear much else to talk about.

'I promised Lilian I'd spend it in Adelaide,' he said. 'She's invited you too, by the way.'

'How kind of her.' The reply had been just as Jess had expected. 'Do give her my thanks, but I've promised Dad I'll go to Sydney.'

'Yes I thought that'd be the case.' Matt downed the remains of his beer. 'My round,' he said and left for the bar.

Fritz proved right. Over the ensuing weeks the southern leg of the rail corridor from Tennant Creek to Alice Springs continued to progress ahead of schedule – and it wasn't the only section of the Ghan to do so. On 10 December the longest bridge on the entire project, the Elizabeth River Bridge south of Darwin, was completed three months ahead of its due date, and on 13 December the final Thermit weld linking the two sections of the line between Katherine and Tennant Creek was ignited, the molten metal forging the two tracks into one.

It was becoming evident to all concerned that the whole of the Northern Ghan from Alice to Darwin was destined for completion well ahead of schedule, a fact that delighted not only the government, the consortium and the contractors, but the Territorians themselves, who could now see their long-awaited dream approaching fulfilment.

Jess's Christmas break in Sydney ended on a raucous note. The first two days had been quiet enough. Christmas Eve was pleasant father–daughter time, the customary ferry trip to Manly and the night spent curled up on the sofa, Ringo between them, watching soppy, romantic films on television, the sort they both agreed that Rose had always loved. Christmas Day too was pleasurably quiet while also highly indulgent, Toby having booked a table for two at a very expensive restaurant overlooking the harbour.

'Who wants to cook?' he'd said and they'd lingered over a long lunch starting with Sydney rock oysters and seguing on to a number of small courses, ignoring the 'Classic Christmas Fare' favoured by most of the patrons. No doubt annoying the restaurateur and chef, both of whom had considered limiting the menu to a set lunch, but had thought better of it given the restaurant's international reputation.

Dawdling over their respective crêpes Suzette and crème caramel, swapping tastes, savouring every mouthful, while the majority of other diners waded through the traditional plum pudding and brandy sauce, albeit flambéed in haute cuisine style, Toby and Jess felt the day was theirs and theirs alone.

Boxing Day, however, was a vastly different affair. Toby had accepted an offer to fill in for a regular member of The Hotdogs, a jazz band that was booked to play a gig at the Coogee Bay Hotel during the late afternoon and into the evening. He'd been only too happy to take up the offer, given the youthful attendance the pub's gigs attracted.

'Should be fun, Jess,' he promised. 'Buddy Boyce and the Hotdogs are a really hot trad jazz band – hell, Buddy's one of the best clarinettists in the country, and the Coogee Bay Beer Garden always draws a great crowd. A young crowd,' he added meaningfully, 'and the kids all love to dance. You'll be able to throw yourself around the dance floor for a change.'

'I'll be more than happy to sit and listen to the band, Dad,' Jess replied.

'Rubbish,' he insisted, 'you have to dance, girl – it's only right and proper you should. Time you mingled with those your own age instead of spending every waking hour with your poor, tired old da.'

Jess gave a snort of laughter, knowing he was sending himself up. Poor, tired old da indeed, she thought. Despite the grey in his ponytail Toby remained, although a little dated, ageless in spirit. She felt distinctly the older of the two these days. And *kids*? He seemed to forget she was a divorcee and thirty-one; she hardly needed to groove the night away with twenty-year-olds.

'We'll see,' she said in order to humour him.

'Want to dance?'

'Sure.'

Jess had barely been off the dance floor for the past hour. Not that it was really a dance floor at all, more just a space near the band at the end of the vast pot-plant-strewn, palm-surrounded beer garden, where early arrivals had garnered tables and others were crammed about the perimeter, drinking and talking and intermittently dancing. The Boxing Day Jazz Concert at the Coogee Bay Hotel was the hot gig everyone had known it would be.

From up on the rostrum with the eight-piece band, Toby watched his daughter, happy to see that she was enjoying herself just as he'd planned she should.

They'd arrived half an hour earlier than the band's scheduled four o'clock start; the heat of the afternoon had been alleviated by the breeze that swept in off the ocean. The Coogee Bay Hotel, which stood in pride of place overlooking the sea, was grandly evocative, an architectural reminder of a bygone age when it had served as a nineteenth-century beachside resort. These days it served many purposes, not the least being a venue for music events that attracted the young, which was precisely why Toby had accepted the gig.

Upon his suggestion she'd sat at a table near the dance area, and sipped at a beer while he and the boys set up. He'd known she wouldn't be on her own for long; you didn't get a table to yourself at a gig like this. Sure enough barely twenty minutes later half a dozen young things, four boys, two girls, had bagged the table with her, introductions had been made and Jess had become part of the gang. That was the way things worked.

Toby may not have been surprised at the way things had panned out, but Jess certainly was. She'd lost touch with the camaraderie that attended youthful gatherings such as this. She'd felt a little intruded on when the gang had settled at the table, pleasant though they'd been in introducing themselves, and as the concert had got under way and the beer garden had started to fill she'd downed the last of her beer, thinking she should leave and join those standing around the periphery. But as she'd made to go her new friends wouldn't have a bar of it.

'No, no love, stay,' Jason had insisted, 'you've scored us a prime spot, we owe you one. Next round's on me.' Jason was in his early twenties, a personable young man who wore a bright red bandana around his skull in true pirate fashion. The obvious leader of the group, most of whom she was later to discover were backpackers, he was colour-ful and good-looking, but it was the Irish accent that won her – something reminiscent of a young Toby Manning, Jess supposed.

The 'next round' that Jason, or Jase as his mates called him, brought back to the table was a repeat of the previous round, and the apparent tipple of everyone's choice. They were drinking directly from their bottles and Jess accepted hers graciously guessing it to be some sort of vodka and orange mix that was currently the trend. It was nice enough, so she shouted another round of the same when it came to her turn, making a conscious decision to abandon beer for the rest of the evening. It was obviously easier to just go with the flow.

Jase and his mates being two girls short, Jess saw quite a bit of action on the dance floor; and as the evening wore on, not only was she asked by those at her table, but by others in the beer garden whose attention had been drawn to the attractive Aboriginal girl who really knew how to move.

From up on the rostrum, Toby watched his daughter in the throng of writhing youth. Her grace was mesmeric: she moved like she walked, relishing the rhythm of her body. And she's so at one with the music, he thought, just like her mother. Look at her, Rosie, just look at her, he thought. No wonder they all want to dance with our girl, Doesn't she make you feel proud, Rosie love?

But even as Toby delighted in his daughter's enjoyment, he remained wary, keeping an eagle eye out for those who might overstep the mark. They were young men after all and young men always wanted something more than the dance.

Toby was aware that any concern on his part was quite unnecessary and that Jess was more than capable of looking after herself, but hell, he couldn't help it, could he? Worry was what a father did, wasn't it?

Jess was indeed fending off the odd grope, but with minimal difficulty, finding the advances boyishly gauche for the most part. She'd quickly registered those who viewed dancing as either a form of foreplay or an opportunity for a chat-up and when they returned for a second bout she feigned fatigue and said no. But she was enjoying herself immensely. She hadn't danced for years. She'd forgotten how much she enjoyed dancing – it was even fun with those a decade her junior.

'Hello, Jess.'

The voice, raised above the sound of the band, was one she recognised instantly and, looking up from where she sat, she saw the face she'd been forcing from her mind for the past several years. The moment their eyes met she could tell that he was laying claim to her. Why? she wondered. We're divorced.

'Hello, Roger,' she said.

'Would you care to dance? There's really not much point trying to talk above the noise, is there?' It was clear he would have vastly preferred to talk.

'Good jazz is not "noise",' she said pleasantly but pointedly, 'and that's Dad on rhythm guitar.'

'Oops, so it is.' He gave a wry grimace. He hadn't noticed Toby. He hadn't paid any attention at all to the band, his eyes had been solely upon her. 'I sincerely beg your pardon, Jess, really I do.'

'No apology necessary. I'm a bit danced out anyway.' She steeled herself. This moment was destined to have occurred some time or other – she might as well confront it now. 'Would you prefer to go for a walk?'

'I'd love to.'

She excused herself from the table saying she was off for a walk, leaving Jason distinctly disappointed. He liked older birds and this one was sexy as all get out.

'Shall I save your seat?' he enquired, wistfully hopeful.

'Yes, that'd be great, thanks, Jase.'

Jase gave a broad grin and plonked his jacket on her chair. He watched as the two walked off. Looks like they're just mates, he thought thankfully, and the bloke's far too old for her anyway.

At the beer garden's grand, stone-arched exit that led out onto Arden Street, Jess turned back and caught her father's eye. She presumed he was keeping an eye on her as she'd known he had been throughout the concert, a fact that greatly amused her, and of course she was right. She pointed to the street and gave a wave intimating she wouldn't be gone long.

Toby returned a nod. The band was due to take a meal break soon and he'd presumed he and Jess might have a hamburger together, but it was clear now they wouldn't.

Toby was worried. He hadn't noticed Roger in the crowd. Good grief, what was the man doing here? Roger Macready would detest trad jazz. He gazed after the two of them as they walked beneath the stone arch, Roger offering his arm in that proprietorial way of his, Jess automatically accepting it. The bastard's no doubt hoping a romantic stroll by the sea might rekindle the flame, Toby thought. He desperately hoped that it wouldn't.

They crossed the broad boulevard of Arden Street, with its stately Norfolk Island pines, Jess thinking distractedly how ubiquitous the trees were. It seemed the main ocean-front street of every major seaside suburb in every state in the country was lined with Norfolk Island pines.

'You always know where the sea is, don't you?' she said.

The non sequitur received a raised eyebrow from Roger.

'The pines,' she said with a wave of her hand.

'Yes indeed.' He smiled agreeably to put her at ease, her small talk was clear evidence she was nervous. 'When in doubt head for the far-distant pine trees and you're bound to hit the coast.'

They walked through Goldstein Reserve and sat on the broad arc of steps that dominated the seafront, leading down to the beach in an impressive series of terraces. The sunlight was prettily fading to dusk and the water relatively calm although several diehard surfers still bobbed about on their boards, waiting for those last waves before dark.

'Gorgeous, isn't it?' Jess said as she looked out over the sweep of Coogee Bay. 'I've missed the ocean, I must say.'

Roger's hesitation was minimal and Jess, focused upon the view, wouldn't have noticed it, but he was actually caught out. He hadn't expected she would be the one to lead the conversation and in such a direct manner. He'd anticipated a little more small talk. She doesn't appear nervous after all, he thought.

'So how are you enjoying Alice Springs and the Ghan?' he asked.

'I love it.' She turned from the view to face him. 'I love Alice and the Ghan and the Territory and the people, I love everything about my life up there.'

'Excellent.' He nodded approvingly as if she was a student who'd answered a tricky question correctly. 'And the flat? You're happy with the flat? Nice and central Undoolya Road, a short walk into town, most convenient I would think.'

How quickly he'd managed to take control, she thought, the manipulative Roger of old. The ease with which she'd opened the conversation had surprised herself as much as him, but she was now supposed to display gratitude, she realised, to admit that she was beholden to him, which of course she was.

'Yes, I'm very happy with the flat,' she said. 'I love the flat just as I love everything else in Alice. And I'm grateful of course,' she added a little tightly. 'It was very generous of you, Roger.'

'It was the very least I could do for you, Jess. Good God, what else was I *capable* of doing under the circumstances? I can't tell you how worried I was when you just disappeared, leaving instructions I was to communicate only through your lawyer. Of course I had to make sure you were well looked after, my darling, that was my duty above all else . . .'

Jess watched him, detached, studying each step and each nuance that appeared somehow rehearsed. First the expansive benefactor, then the victim, a perfect mix of distress and accusation, and finally the paternalist she'd so often seen, treating her as if she were a child incapable of looking after herself. She felt as if she was watching a performance.

She was. Roger's current performance was not dissimilar to the one he'd offered up to his colleagues when she'd left him.

'I've looked after her, of course,' he'd said, 'set her up in a nice little flat in Alice Springs, lined her up a job as negotiator with the Central Lands Council . . .' Through his contacts he'd had no trouble finding out where she'd gone and the job she'd accepted. 'I'm devastated our marriage didn't work out,' he'd lamented, 'and I'll always love Jess, but things are probably better for her this way. She has family at Hermannsburg and she'll be near her people. The truth is she's rather naive and a little lost in the city,' he'd confided, adding with his superior knowledge of all matters Indigenous, 'as of course is so sadly often the case.'

Roger had most certainly been devastated when Jess had left him. Her desertion was so unexpected that he'd been in a state of shock and disbelief. How could she have done such a thing? He was everything to her – lover, husband, mentor – and without him she was nothing. At first he'd persuaded himself it was just a rebellious gesture and that any day she'd come back, begging the forgiveness that of course he would grant her. But she hadn't come back, and he'd been forced to face the fact that she never would. The lies he'd concocted in order to cover his humiliation had very quickly become the truth to Roger. Unfortunately for him, those of his academic colleagues who'd known and worked with Jess didn't believe one word he said, which only served to make his humiliation all the more profound.

These days he tried to avoid anyone who'd known his wife, although it was difficult, she'd made a strong impression upon many.

'Anyway, Jess, I'm delighted to hear you're happy.' Aware that his speech wasn't making its intended impact, Roger brought it to a halt. He paused for a moment, somewhat at a loss. 'I think of you often,' he said in all honesty, 'and I wish you well.'

'As I do you, Roger,' she replied, which was not in the least honest. She'd been trying so hard to forget him that she hadn't wished him well at all. And then the realisation hit Jess that for some time now she'd given him no thought whatsoever. I've been free of him without even knowing it, she thought and wondered why. When had this happened?

Time to change the subject, she decided. 'So what are you doing at a trad jazz concert?' she asked. 'Jazz of any kind was never your scene, or has your taste changed?'

'Hardly,' he said, relieved that they were now on the safe ground of small talk. He found her confidence most disconcerting. 'But some important corporates I'm currently working with are keen enthusiasts so . . .' His shrug said it all.

'Of course. The bread and butter . . .'

'Exactly.'

They smiled and for one brief moment something passed between them, something that might have been fondness until Jess remembered how deeply thankful she was to no longer be a part of Roger's shallow, shallow world.

'Let's go back to the pub, shall we?' she suggested.

'Yes,' he agreed, aware there was nothing more to be said.

They stood and once again he offered his arm, but this time she didn't take it, pretending not to notice. Her previous response, she now realised, had been simply automatic, nothing more than habit.

She's changed, he thought, matching her pace as they strode across the road, she's certainly changed. But Roger failed to recognise that this was the Jess he'd first met, the Jess who had existed before he'd set about casting her in the mould that suited him.

The band members were having their meal break, seated at a table downing hamburgers, and Toby's eyes had been focused on the stone-arched gateway awaiting Jess's return. The moment the two of them appeared he felt like rejoicing. Thank Christ for that, he thought. The walk by the sea hasn't rekindled the flame. In fact, I'd say it's bloody well doused it once and for all, and a damn fine thing too.

'Hello, Roger,' he said, rising and offering his hand as the pair approached, 'long time, no see.'

'Hello, Toby. Yes, a long time indeed.' Roger's smile as they shook was polite. 'I've been enjoying the music.'

Liar, Toby thought happily. 'Yeah, they're a damn fine band all right.' Then to Jess, 'Do you want to join us for a hamburger, love?'

'No thanks, Dad. I'm not hungry.'

'Right you are then, I'll see you after the gig.' With a nod to Roger, Toby returned to his seat, his hamburger and his muso mates, who had remained huddled in deep conversation.

Roger felt obliged to make the offer, although he was sure she'd refuse.

'Would you like to join us at our table?' he asked, gesturing to the far end of the beer garden where several smartly dressed middle-aged men were gathered.

'Thanks, but no thanks.' She glanced at the table nearby where Jason was openly staring at them, willing her to come back to him. 'I'll stick with the young gang that's adopted me.'

They parted company and Jess returned to the seat that Jase had been zealously guarding. His welcome was effusive. The 'old mate' was obviously no competition at all.

The evening progressed much as it had started out, with constant rounds of vodka mixes interspersed with dancing.

Roger could barely take his eyes off Jess. He wondered how she could possibly enjoy the company of those young people. But watching her as she watched the band and watching her as she moved around the dance floor the way she did, he realised it was the music itself that was turning her on.

An hour later he decided to leave. Bugger his corporate colleagues and their love of trad jazz. He couldn't stand the music and he couldn't stand watching Jess, remembering the silken touch of her and the way she was in bed. But for appearance's sake he'd have to make his farewells. He couldn't just slink off into the night. It would be tantamount to admitting defeat.

He waited until she was seated back at her table regaining her breath between dances.

'I really enjoyed catching up with you again, Jess,' he said as if to an old friend, 'You look after yourself now.'

'You too, Roger.' She tried to feel sorry for him, she could tell he was lonely, but she was having trouble dredging up sympathy. 'And give my best to any of the old gang you think might remember me.'

'Oh they all remember you, Jess, you can bet on that,' he said with a smile that actually appeared genuine. 'You're difficult to forget.' Then he walked away.

She didn't watch him go. Someone was already claiming the next dance.

The band's performance was finally coming to an end and Jason was demanding she dance the last bracket with him.

They stayed on the dance floor until the music ceased and then returned to the table to finish off the round of vodka mixes that sat there.

Jess glanced over to where the band members were bumping out their gear so the night's DJ could set up. The beer garden was destined to rock on for quite some time. Realising Toby would be another ten minutes or so, she sipped her drink slowly; the vodka mixes were not as innocuous as they tasted and she was feeling the effects.

'My round,' one of the young backpackers, a British student named Col, announced as he rose from the table. Col, just turned nineteen, was taking a gap year from his studies before returning home to embark upon his university course.

'Not for me, thanks, Col,' Jess said, 'I'll be going soon. I was only here for the live music.'

'Right you are then.' Col set off to fight his way through to the bar.

Jason was delighted. How opportune. Things were looking extremely promising. He and Jess could leave the gang there and go back to the house, where they'd have the whole place to themselves.

'I'm with you there, Jess,' he said in hearty agreement. 'DJs aren't my bag either – it's not the same thing at all. Give me a live band any time.'

'Particularly a live *jazz* band,' she said. 'They were terrific, the Hotdogs, weren't they?'

'Bloody fantastic, I'm just crazy about jazz.' He polished off his vodka mix and homed in without further ado. 'No point staying really, is there? Let's go back to my place for a nightcap,' he said. 'I'm in Bondi right near the beach.' He always managed to sound as if he owned the place although he actually shared the lease on the rundown house in Bondi with plenty of others, his enterprising landlord only too aware of the money to be made from the quick turnover in backpacker trade. 'We could play some jazz,' he said, dazzling her with one of his killer grins. 'I've got a great CD collection.' He didn't have a great CD collection at all, and certainly no jazz, but they both knew he wasn't really talking about music.

'No thanks, Jase. I've got a date for tonight.' She smiled amiably, polished off her drink and stood. 'See you, guys,' she said to the table in general.

'See you, Jess,' the others called as she walked off.

The abruptness of her departure took Jason by surprise.
He watched her cross to the band then surprise turned to
amazement as he saw her embrace the old bloke who'd
been on rhythm guitar. No way! The bloke looked so
retro he might have just stepped out of the sixties. He's
the oldest member of the whole bloody band, Jason
thought, old enough to be everyone else's father, for
Christ's sake!

He stared after the two of them as they walked off
together, arm in arm, chatting animatedly, eyes for no-one
but each other. Oh well, he thought with the slightest
shudder of revulsion, no accounting for taste.

Jess awoke the following morning feeling decidedly seedy:
she hadn't realised the vodka mixes would have such a kick.

'You're not used to hangovers, I see,' Toby said when
over coffee in the kitchen she admitted to being a little the
worse for wear.

'Not this sort. We don't seem to drink anything but beer
in Alice.'

'A big greasy breakfast, that's what you need. We'll
have another cup of coffee then we'll go for a walk.'

An hour or so later he took her to a cafe in Darling
Street that did all-day breakfasts. By now it was time more
for brunch really and Toby was very much a brunch man
himself. He couldn't be bothered preparing meals, and going
out for a feed at eleven took care of breakfast and lunch
simultaneously, leaving more studio time.

'This is my favourite caff,' he said as they sat at an
outdoor table watching the passers-by, 'all-day brekkie
with none of the fancy yoghurt and muesli stuff that's the
rage these days. They do the real thing here.'

After a pile of bacon, eggs, mushrooms and hash browns
Jess had to admit that she felt distinctly better.

It was a beautiful midsummer's day, hot but not stiflingly so, and they walked along Balmain's main road,

ducking here and there into side streets, all the while discovering new restaurants, bars and cafés, exploring the odd secondhand book shop and antique store.

The exploration was as novel to Toby as it was to Jess. He knew well the Balmain pubs that employed live bands and where the musos hung out, just as he knew every such pub throughout the whole of Sydney, his nightlife and weekends were extremely active socially. During the day, however, he tended to stick to the caff and his studio.

It was lunchtime when they returned home and Jess disappeared to her room to gather her things preparatory to leaving. Upon her reappearance she steadfastly refused to allow her father to drive her to the airport, and when Toby tried to insist, she informed him that she'd already rung a taxi on her mobile.

'It'll be here in five minutes,' she said.

'But I took the whole day off.'

'I know you did and you shouldn't have,' she said firmly, then gave him a grateful hug. 'Thanks for our morning together, Dad, I loved it, but I can't let you waste an entire afternoon just to take me to the airport. I felt terribly guilty when you did that last time.'

'Too late,' he announced with an air of triumph, 'I've already cancelled a recording session.'

'Then you can use the afternoon to get on with your mixing, can't you?' she replied. The laborious job of sound-mixing, which Toby loved, consumed most of his studio time, as Jess well knew.

He was about to protest further when the toot of a car horn sounded outside.

'Taxi's here,' she said, bringing the argument to a close.

Out in the street they put her case in the boot and hugged each other.

'It's your turn next time,' Jess said. 'Why don't you take a few days' holiday and come to Alice? You work so hard you deserve a break and you know you love the desert.'

Toby gave the matter barely a second's thought. 'How about Easter?' he suggested. 'No-one records stuff over the Easter weekend.'

'Easter it is,' she said.

They hugged once again and she climbed into the car's rear seat, waving as the taxi pulled away from the curb.

'Is it the domestic or international terminal you wish?' the driver asked, although he'd already presumed from the cabin luggage she'd stowed in the boot that she was travelling domestic.

'Domestic thanks. Qantas.' Jess leant back in the seat and closed her eyes. The beneficial effects of the big breakfast brunch and the walk around Balmain were starting to wear off and the ramifications of last night threatened to resurface.

'It is a very fine day for travel,' the driver said. 'What is your destination, may I ask? Do you fly interstate?' He was a swarthy-skinned man of around forty-five whom, by appearance and from the colourful lilt of his voice, she took to be Pakistani.

'Yes, the Northern Territory,' she replied, keeping her eyes closed in the hope he'd register she didn't want to chat, 'Alice Springs.'

'Ah, the very *heart* of the country, the *Red Centre* as it is called . . .' his clear enunciation and emphasis lent added romance to the term 'I have never been there myself, but they say the area is very beautiful. Is the earth truly as red as the pictures depict?'

Heaving a sigh, Jess opened her eyes; the man clearly had not taken the hint and he was so polite she couldn't bring herself to be rude. 'Yes,' she said, 'the earth is very red.'

'Ah,' he nodded, pleased to hear it, 'and you live there in Alice Springs or you go there to visit?'

She looked into the rear-vision mirror at the intelligent brown eyes so alive with interest, and painted on a smile. 'I live there,' she said.

The man returned the smile, delighted they were now engaged in conversation; Tahir always loved to chat to his passengers.

'I believe it would be very, very hot there now at this time of year,' he said.

But Jess's smile had disappeared. She'd seen the sign that dangled from the mirror. A rectangular object no more than six or seven centimetres wide, it appeared to be some sort of good-luck charm, a silver symbol dangling on a silver chain. The pattern was quite clear, but the meaning obscure, a series of swirls and loops that she took to be some form of ancient calligraphy. In a more roughly hewn form they might appear like a bird, or even a caterpillar, impossible to distinguish, but of one thing she was sure. The sign was the same as that on the rock at the sacred site.

Tahir waited for a response from the attractive young woman whom he guessed to be of Aboriginal blood, but none was forthcoming. He would like to have asked if her people came from Alice Springs, he would be most interested to know, but that might perhaps be a little intrusive, he decided, particularly as she seemed distracted. He was about to comment upon the Sydney weather instead, but –

'What is that sign?' she asked. 'What does it mean?'

Ah, so the symbol is the source of her distraction, Tahir thought. The fact pleased him greatly. A number of his passengers had made enquiries and he was always happy to tell them of the symbol's meaning and the reason he displayed it in his taxi.

'It is an Arabic word,' he explained, 'it says "salaam", which in English means "peace". I am a Muslim and I carry it as a symbol of my faith and the faith of my people.' He had her undivided attention now. He could see she was waiting for him to go on. So he did. Tahir liked to spread the word of peace in these difficult times.

'I am from Lahore,' he said. 'My wife and I have lived in Australia for ten years, and our two children were born right here in Sydney. We have always led a peaceful existence in this country. There was no trouble in our lives until the bombing of America.' He shook his head sorrowfully. 'That terrible day when the world went mad. Since September last year the lives of all Australian Muslims have changed. For over twelve months now we have been seen as a threat and we continue to be regarded as such. These days when my wife walks down the street she feels hatred from those she passes. Asmi senses hatred even towards our children, and she cannot understand why. Often I too in this taxi feel hatred, which I know to be born of suspicion and fear, but this is not right. The men who perpetrated the Twin Towers bombing are not men of our faith. The Quran teaches that those who breach the peace are corrupt and sinful. In Islam the pursuit of peace is seen as a Godly act.'

Tahir concluded his speech, which was in fact the longer version, the one he directed only to those whose attention he knew he had captured. Much as he loved to pass on the message of peace, he had no wish to irritate, for there were no tips to be had from irritated passengers. But he had known from the outset that the young woman whose eyes had remained so fiercely focused upon his in the rear-vision mirror had been captive to his story.

'This is why I carry my symbol,' he said, caressing the silver charm dangling from its chain. 'These ancient Islamic characters spell one simple word that sends a message to people of all races. *"Salaam"*, it says: "Peace".'

'I see,' Jess replied after a moment's pause. How fortuitous I insisted on catching a taxi to the airport, she thought. Another piece of the mystery is slowly unravelling.

When they arrived at the terminal she paid in cash, Tahir instantly jumping from the driver's seat to lift her case from the boot before she'd even alighted.

'What is your name?' she asked.

'Tahir,' he said, 'I am called Tahir.'

'Thank you for telling me your story, Tahir.'

'It was my pleasure,' he replied, smiling happily and offering a courteous bow; she had tipped him most handsomely. '*As-salamu alaykum*,' he said, 'peace be upon you.'

لسلام

1880

Mustafa and Abdullah are brothers from the ancient city of Ghazni in Afghanistan. They are cameleers who were brought out to Australia, along with many others, by the wealthy pastoral-ist and business entrepreneur Sir Thomas Elder. At thirty-three Mustafa is the older by five years and holds himself responsible at all times for his younger brother. He is the leader of the two, as his name dictates he should be, at least so he main-tains, for 'Mustafa' means 'chosen of Mohammad' and 'Abdullah' means 'servant of God'. Mustafa has always pretended to take these translations literally.

'Our parents chose our names with great care,' he told Abdullah on many an occasion throughout their childhood, 'for I am not only the older, I am the superior in every way.'

They are both aware he is making a joke about their names, but there is nonetheless some truth in what he says, for as time passes and they grow to manhood Mustafa proves an intelligent man with an astute eye for business while his brother, devoid of all ambition, is a dreamer who would happily flow wherever the tide of life takes him.

As if to prove his superiority Mustafa has also acquired an excellent command of the English language. This is due to the three years he served as a cameleer with the British Army in India. He is proud of these years and still wears his service medal pinned at all times to his turban. The medal was a personal gift from the regiment's commanding officer, but Mustafa has always declared it to be an official award from Queen Victoria herself. This is the only lie he has ever told, and he has told it so many times he now believes it to be the truth, as does his brother, who implicitly believes everything Mustafa tells him. There is no reason why Abdullah would do otherwise. Throughout their lives Mustafa has always been the dominant one. Mustafa is very bossy.

Abdullah does not in the least mind Mustafa's bossiness. To the contrary, he enjoys having his decisions made for him and is quite happy for his older brother to take control of his life. Abdullah is not lazy, he is willing to work physically hard, but he has no desire to assert command himself, for at heart he is a romantic. Besides, he knows Mustafa is only being protective, that despite their differences they love each other deeply, as brothers should.

After serving with Elder, Smith & Co for six years, Mustafa made the decision they must leave and form their own business and for four years now the brothers have been contracted by the South Australian Government. They and their string of eight camels transport supplies to the Overland Telegraph Line's repeater stations that are dotted across the lands of the central desert.

Their modest team of eight is a vastly different affair from the mighty camel trains of a hundred or more beasts to which they were accustomed when working with Elder, Smith & Co. But they are happy. Mustafa very much enjoys being his own master and Abdullah is content alone in the desert with his brother and the animals, who are family to him. It is true he misses his recently acquired young wife, an Aboriginal girl of the Arunta people called Nardji, but the long months of their separation only serve to make their reunions all the more sweet. He awaits his next return to camp with particular eagerness for by then Nardji will have given birth to their child. Abdullah looks forward to his new role as father and prays to Allah that his wife will bear him a son in order to maintain the proud family tradition, a son who will become a cameleer like his father, and his father's father before him. But should the child prove a daughter Abdullah will still love her. There will be sons to follow. Nardji is young and strong.

The brothers' permanent camp is at Hookey's Waterhole, roughly three hundred miles south of the Central Mount Stuart Repeater Station. This is the place they call home, where they have built their shelters and erected the corrals for their camels. They are rarely without company, as other camel-eers from time to time set up camp at Hookey's and Aboriginal people travel great distances from their tribal lands to gather at the waterhole for ceremonial occasions or simply to socialise and conduct trade. This is how Abdullah had met Nardji. Those of the Arunta people call this place, where in the midst of the most arid of lands there exists a reliable source of water, 'Utnadata', which in their tongue means 'mulga blossom'.

Mustafa and Abdullah have set out on their latest journey and are already some way from home, having just the previous day made their delivery to the telegraph station at Stuart. But distance and time mean little to the brothers. They have been travelling for barely more than a fortnight and there will be months to go yet as they follow the telegraph line across the desert. The long trek has only just begun.

The operator at Stuart had given them a keen welcome upon their arrival, as most telegraphists do in these remote outposts they have discovered. Such receptions differ from those they receive when negotiating with government representatives, who always patronise, and are at even greater variance from those they had encountered while working for Elder Smith & Co. During their days with the mighty camel trains when they had transported building equipment and furnishings, at one time even a piano, to the properties of wealthy pastoralists, the response they had met with had been redolent with hostility and fear. They and their fellow Afghan and Pakistani cameleers had clearly been considered not only inferior, but barely human.

As a result Mustafa remains, even now, cynical about the welcome offered by the telegraphists. 'It is the loneliness of these telegraph men,' he remarks dismissively, 'they long for the sight of another human creature, even a human creature such as us.' He smiles as he says it, but his smile lacks any trace of humour. 'There is no true pleasure for them in our meeting.'

Abdullah does not agree with his brother. He feels genuine pleasure in the greetings from the telegraphists, but as always he does not voice his opinion.

In this particular instance, however, Abdullah is right. Mustafa's observation of the racial bias that exists is certainly correct, the white settlers are suspicious and fearful of races alien to them, but

Mustafa underestimates the personal effect he and Abdullah have upon the telegraph operators who have come to know them.

Living lonely lives in remote huts with no human contact but the occasional company of a linesman, these men do indeed embrace the arrival of the camels, which are affectionately known as 'the ships of the desert'. These beasts of burden whose pack saddles bear the long-awaited supplies that will ease the harshness of their existence, including mail from loved ones, are always a welcome sight. But so too are the brothers. Tall and lean, bearded and turbaned, the brothers, too have become a welcome sight. Stern-faced Mustafa with his excellent command of English is a fine conversationalist and Abdullah with his ready smile is good-natured and likeable. The two prove a pleasurable distraction from the loneliness and monotony of a telegraph operator's life. The distraction, however, is all too rare in occurrence and when it does take place all too fleeting.

The telegraphist at Stuart the previous day had been plainly loath to say goodbye to the brothers even after they'd sat drinking tea with him for over two hours. In fact he'd all but begged them to stay longer. But they had prised themselves from him and left in the late afternoon, allowing time to make camp before dusk, travelling only several miles from the station and then settling down for the night.

The next day they are up at dawn to continue their trek north. Mustafa is at the head of the team, riding Aqela as always. She is the lead camel and most aptly named for Aqela means 'wise and of ripe years'.

Aqela was a personal gift from Sir Thomas Elder, supposedly in recognition of Mustafa's six years of impeccable and loyal service as a chief cameleer and to assist him and his brother in their new enterprise. It is possible however that Sir Thomas might have been informed no-one else would be able to work with Aqela. She had always proved stubborn and ill-tempered with her previous handlers, but after barely a year under Mustafa's care the two had bonded to such a degree that, docile and obedient, Aqela would do anything he bid her. Separated from him, the animal would be bound to pine and revert to her ways of old.

Aqela is of immense value to the brothers. As her name denotes, she is wise and, although of 'ripe years', at thirty-eight has much life left in her yet. Under the tender care of Mustafa it is most likely she will live to fifty years, perhaps even longer. An assertive animal and born leader, the other camels respect Aqela and willingly follow her example. Aqela herself, having recognised from the outset similar qualities of leadership and authority in her new master, had accepted unquestioningly Mustafa's command. The relationship the two have come to share over the years is one of mutual trust and respect mingled with the deepest affection.

The other camels of the team recognise the special bond between Mustafa and Aqela and happily accept the show of favouritism she is accorded, for their bond is with Abdullah. Abdullah has no favourite among the camels, who are all his family. At least if he does he never allows any show of preference. Abdullah is an excellent cameleer: it is his true vocation. He knows every idiosyn-crasy each animal possesses and there are many, for each of the seven has a distinctive personality. He soothes and caresses them equally, even those given to occasional displays of irritability, and each responds with a love that matches his. He is as much family to his camels as they are to him.

After their dawn start, the brothers continue northwards, following the Line towards their next port of call, the repeater station at Barrow Creek. The team maintains a steady speed, but Mustafa does not push the beasts. They are making good time and there is no hurry.

It is late afternoon when they reach the site where they intend to make camp. Mustafa has been deliberately heading the team in this specific direction for he knows the place well; they have camped here a number of times in the past. The clearing with the two hillocks has a creek nearby that at this time of year usually holds water. The site is obviously known to the local Aboriginal people as is often evidenced by the remnants of their cooking fires. It is true the camels do not need water at this stage, but Mustafa nonetheless likes to make camp near a water source whenever possible, and the clearing is sandy and comfortable.

But as they approach the site they are met by a grisly spectacle. Up ahead they can see bodies strewn about the clearing, eyes staring blindly skywards, flies gathered in clusters upon pools of congealed blood. Death in its most violent form is the spectacle that greets them.

Mustafa gives the order to Aqela, who halts, the other camels following suit. A further order and Aqela kneels on her forelegs then lowers herself to the ground. Abdullah gives a similar order to the rest of the team.

The brothers dismount and walk towards the clearing to examine the fearful scene. They are experienced travellers and read the situation with ease. A family has made camp here. They have shared an evening meal. Several parcels of meat are tied to the limbs of an acacia tree to be preserved for the following day. The family was never to see that day. They were taken by surprise and systematically slaughtered. Two men, one older, one of middle years, are slumped back on the ground where they had been resting not far from the cooking fire. Nearby is a woman who had apparently been digging potatoes and yams from the coals – the vegetables are still resting in the sand next to her. And there is another woman, younger, also by the fire's remnants, her arm encircling the dead body of her child. To complete the grim picture, in the midst of the slaughter lies a woman older in years and twenty yards away a young man, spear still in hand: the only person it appears who had time or the presence of mind to attempt any form of defence.

Mustafa and Abdullah are silent as they wander to and fro examining the bodies: there are seven in all. The story is so gruesomely vivid that words fail them, but they are both thinking the same thing. White men did this. Police or settlers, who could tell, but what difference did it make? White men have slaughtered an entire family who were innocently going about their business; white men who consider those with black skin little more than vermin.

Mustafa finally breaks the silence and he does so without comment upon the horror itself, merely stating the facts that are obvious.

'There is no decomposition or mutilation,' he says, 'the mild spring weather and the cold nights have preserved them and the animals have not yet ravaged the bodies.'

Abdullah simply nods.

'This happened only two, or possibly three, days ago,' Mustafa concludes.

But now the silence has been broken Abdullah has no wish to dwell upon the facts to hand, he wants action. They cannot avoid the responsibilities inherent with their discovery.

'We must report this massacre,' he says, 'these people must be buried with respect –'

'And to whom do we report murders such as this, little brother?' Mustafa interrupts, his response scathing. 'To the white men?'

Abdullah is once again silenced: he has no reply.

'We both know it is white men who have done this.' Mustafa gazes about at the carnage surrounding them. 'Just as we both know that in the eyes of the white men we are no better than these poor black heathens, we are nothing but scum, the lot of us. If we were to report this massacre we would be made to suffer, you can rest assured of that.'

Abdullah nods. As usual his brother has all the correct answers.

'But you are right nonetheless.' Mustafa's further response takes Abdullah by surprise. 'These people must be buried. And they must be buried with respect. It is our duty as men of faith.'

Fetching their axes and picks and shovels, standard equipment for use when weather conditions demand the construction of a sturdy camp, they set about their grim task with deliberation.

They carry the bodies to the edge of the clearing, respectfully, even tenderly, placing them there with care. Then they mark out a rectangular area they believe will be sufficient for a mass burial site, an area roughly six yards in width by two yards in length.

For some unknown reason Mustafa consults his Qibla compass while marking out the direction and dimensions of the grave. He carries this modified

compass with him at all times, for it points specifically
to the direction of Kaaba in Mecca and ensures he
and Abdullah always face the way of Qibla during
the performance of their ritual prayers. Now he uses
it to ensure the bodies, too, will be facing Mecca. He
does not know why he does this, as those they are
burying are not Muslim, but it seems somehow an
added gesture of respect on his part.

They start to dig, Mustafa on one side of the
rectangle and Abdullah on the other, working
their way towards each other as they go. A mass
grave in the centre of the clearing, a grave that will
accommodate seven bodies: this is a task that
will take time.

It is Abdullah who makes the discovery. As he
digs he comes upon loosened soil – others have been
digging here. Then he finds her. There is another
body already buried in this place. It is that of a
young white woman. They dig around the corpse
with care, disinterring her and laying her beside the
others at the edge of the clearing. The girl too has
been brutally murdered, shot through the chest. This
is a matter demanding of discussion.

They agree that the girl has been part of the
same massacre, for her body, like the others, as yet
displays no signs of decomposition, she has been
dead for only two or three days. They are at first
shocked by her nakedness, but they deduce from
this and from the pubic covering she wears that she
was living with the Aboriginal family as one of them.

'The killers must have buried her for fear of
reprisals,' Mustafa says. 'Perhaps they killed her
by mistake. Perhaps when they slaughtered the
blacks for sport they did not know there was a white
girl among them. They then buried her out of fear
and left the others to rot.'

Abdullah is in agreement: the scenario does seem a likely one. Then he comes up with a deduction of his own.

'The white baby at Stuart,' he says.'The telegraph man told us she had been there two days, that he had discovered her on his doorstep at dawn, remember?'

'Of course.' Mustafa is surprised that Abdullah has made the connection before he did himself, he is normally the quicker of the two, but he always gives credit where credit is due. 'You are right, little brother,' he says, 'the child is linked with these murders, there can be no doubt.'

They recall both of them only too vividly the dilemma of the telegraphist. The man had talked of little else throughout their entire time with him

'She was on my doorstep two days ago at dawn,' he had said, 'wrapped in emu feathers, calling out to be fed like I was her mother. Just as well I had powdered milk, and just as well you've arrived with a fresh supply.' The man had appeared quite frantic with worry. 'I've been telegraphing south for two days now. Someone has to come and get her, she can't stay here, I can't look after her.'

Abdullah had sat on the floor playing with the child, delighting in her antics as she gurgled and wobbled unsteadily on her little baby legs, while Mustafa and the telegraph operator had discussed the strange turn of events. Where had the child come from? Who had left her here and why? It was likely she had black blood in her, they agreed, but she looked so completely white.

'Perhaps she was left here by Aborigines,' Mustafa suggests. 'Perhaps one of their women slept with a white man . . .' He deliberately avoids saying 'was defiled by a white man' given the fact that it is a white man to whom he is speaking, but he firmly believes the latter would have been the case. 'And perhaps they wished to rid themselves of the evidence, which they would see as shameful.'

'Yes, yes, of course.' The telegraphist is quick to agree. This is what I like about Mustafa, he thinks, the man is so damn clever! 'No "perhaps" about it, my friend, that's what happened, I'd put my last penny on it.'

Two hours later when the brothers had taken their leave, the telegraph operator had still been bemoaning the situation. 'I'll just have to wait until they send someone up from Adelaide to collect her,' he'd said, 'and God only knows when that will happen.'

'She will be good company for you until then,' Abdullah had suggested brightly. He does not speak much as a rule. Although comfortable enough with the English language, he is not the conversationalist his brother is. 'She is a very nice baby.'

The telegraph operator had appeared highly dubious.

'They will come for her in time.' Mustafa had offered the man reassurance. 'She is so white that someone will wish to adopt her.'

'Yes, there is that.' The telegraphist had eagerly grabbed at the notion. 'I shall let them know she is white and someone is bound to adopt her.'

Now, as the brothers contemplate the dead bodies before them, Mustafa makes his fresh deductions. Clearly it was not the Aborigines who had delivered the child to the station.

'The killers buried the young white woman to cover their crime then left her baby to be discovered at the telegraph station,' he says thoughtfully. 'I am surprised, I admit, that they did not kill the child along with the others.'

'They did not kill her because she did not look black,' Abdullah is quick to counter. 'They would suffer great guilt killing a white child, and she did look white, Mustafa. That baby did not look black at all.'

'No, once again you are right, little brother. She did not look black, and that fact would certainly have played upon their consciences.'

Abdullah, pleased to be acknowledged as right, and several times in a row furthermore, studies the bodies in order to make his next deduction. Which of the three men fathered the white girl's child, he is wondering.

'The young man who died with the spear in his hand,' he says.

'What is this you are saying?' The comment puzzles Mustafa.

'He,' Abdullah points at the corpse of the young man, 'he was the father of the child.'

'Why do you say that?'

'He is young. They are both young. They had a child together and they would have loved each other. We must bury them side by side.'

Even in the grimness of their surrounds, Mustafa cannot help but smile. His brother is such a romantic. He does not remind Abdullah that Aboriginal men take wives many years their junior. For all they knew the white girl might have been the wife of the elderly man. But Abdullah is fully aware of these facts anyway, Mustafa thinks, so there is nothing to be gained in pointing them out. Abdullah, as always, chooses to view life from his own rosy perspective.

'Very well,' he agrees, humouring his brother, 'we will bury the young pair side by side.'

Once again they set to digging and their labour is hard, intense, for they wish to bury the bodies before night falls.

Upon completion, the grave proves perfectly adequate in its dimensions. Its depth will ensure the corpses do not fall prey to keen-scented animals and its breadth will comfortably house the bodies so that they lie in alignment facing Mecca.

The brothers are selective in their placement. The older man and woman are placed together at the head of the line in the assumption they are the family elders and the rest of the family follows in order of seniority. The younger woman is buried with her infant in her arms, and the last bodies to be placed in the grave are those of the young man and the white girl. At Abdullah's insistence, the white girl is laid to rest at the end of the line with her arm draped over the waist of the young man, as if they lie together in sleep.

'They are now reunited in death,' he says solemnly.

Looking down at the bodies so neatly laid out and so apparently at peace, Mustafa does not scorn his brother, believing after all that Abdullah may be right.

By the time they have filled in the grave and all is in place, dusk is falling.

Mustafa returns to where the camels sit, quietly dozing off for the most part. He gathers wood and starts building a fire amongst the scrub well distant from the clearing. They will not stay in this place ever again, but they must set about the practicalities of making camp nonetheless.

But Abdullah has one final thing to do. Selecting a sharp piece of quartz from the loose rocks that abound, he climbs the larger of the two hillocks and halfway to the top he carves a sign. The sign is in Arabic. It says *Peace*.

CHAPTER THIRTEEN

'I know what the sign means.'

They were the words that greeted him as soon as he arrived at her flat. He hadn't even stepped inside the door. He stared at her blankly.

'The sign at the site,' she said with a touch of impatience, as if he were a schoolboy who hadn't been paying attention, 'the sign on the rock.'

'Ah, that sign.'

'Come in. The fans are on and the beer's freezing.'

Matt followed her into the living room where both the ceiling fan and the fan on her desk were whirring away at top speed. Jess's flat didn't boast air-conditioning and the afternoon was a scorcher, with the temperature hovering just above forty, not unusual for Alice in January.

She fetched two icy cans of beer, which they drank from stubby-holders as they sat at the dining table.

'I thought you said the sign was probably just some old graffiti left by workers on the Overland Telegraph Line,' he said.

'I did. I was wrong.'

He could tell she was excited, but then she'd sounded excited when she'd rung several days earlier asking him to call around on Saturday. By choice he was staying at the Heavitree Gap Hotel full-time these days; he and his team now working closer to town than to the donga camp.

'So I take it the sign does have some Aboriginal significance after all,' he queried.

'No, none whatsoever, I was right about that part.'

'I see.' A brief pause ... 'Well, are you going to let me
in on the secret?'

'It's an Arabic word,' she said with a ring of triumph. 'It
says *Salaam*, which means peace.'

'Right.' He nodded, still somewhat in the dark. 'And
what does that tell us?'

'Judging by the age of the sign it tells us that it was most
probably left by a Muslim cameleer.' Following her return
from Sydney the previous week Jess had done a little
homework. 'The man could have been either an Afghan
or a Pakistani,' she went on. 'Both races worked on the
camel trains that transported materials for the Overland
Telegraph Line and nearly all of them were Muslim. Many
of these men were brought out to Australia by the government, along with hundreds of camels for the specific
purpose of constructing the Line.'

'Right,' he repeated, fully aware of the history himself,
but no less in the dark as to its relevance, 'and what
exactly does all this mean?'

'It means our cameleer knew of the site's importance to
the ancestors,' she said, 'of course' inherent in her tone.
'That's what led him to leave a sign saying peace,' she
added, and again Matt registered he was supposed to have
grasped this fact.

'I can't help but feel there's a certain degree of supposition
at play here,' he replied drily. 'You do realise, don't you,
that there might be absolutely no connection whatsoever.'

'Oh but there has to be,' Jess said in all earnestness, 'it's
far too much of a coincidence to be anything other than a
deliberate comment. I mean why else would he have left
the sign?'

Any number of reasons sprang instantly to Matt's mind.
A religious man perhaps, intent upon spreading the word

of Islam; a man wishing to state his presence in a new world; or perhaps as she'd suggested right from the start a form of graffiti, a man who had simply carved a word he knew in order to leave his mark. Matt rather favoured the latter himself, but didn't say so, knowing that if he were to offer any one of his suggestions it would lead to a lengthy and futile discussion. Instead, he got straight to the point.

'And where exactly does this discovery of yours lead us, Jess?' he asked. 'What exactly does it tell us about the site and its Aboriginal history?'

She was stumped. She'd been so excited by the discovery itself she hadn't given thought to the practical answers it might offer up. Which were what? she now asked herself. Forced to acknowledge defeat she gave in with good grace.

'Nothing,' she admitted, 'it tells us absolutely nothing and it leads us absolutely nowhere.' True to form she refused to be daunted however: 'But isn't it wonderful, Matt! How extraordinary to be so transported to the past. Wouldn't you just love to have been there? Wouldn't you just love to know what happened at that place?'

Her enthusiasm, infectious at the best of times, made its customary impact. 'Yes,' he said, 'yes, I would.'

A month later, on 7 February 2003, a path was blasted through the rock cuttings that formed an imposing barrier just under seven kilometres north of Alice Springs.

Matt invited Jess along to the blasting as an 'official observer', although she was really there at his personal invitation.

'I thought you might be interested in seeing it,' he said, 'should be pretty spectacular.'

'I'm most certainly interested,' she replied.

'To keep the contractors happy I told them you'll be present in an official capacity,' he explained, 'I said you'll be able to reassure the locals if there's concern raised after the blasting.'

'As there may well be,' she responded archly, 'and as would be perfectly justifiable.' Jess was critical of the decision to keep the news of the blasting from the local population. She understood the reason behind the decision being the wish to avoid panic, but this was their land after all – surely they had a right to be informed.

The event proved every bit as spectacular as Matt had promised – indeed even more so, certainly to Jess.

Standing beside him in the safe area along with the other spectators, she looked out at the vista of ancient rocks that had stood from time immemorial, a scene of rugged splendour. It's a pity, she thought, to destroy something so beautiful.

A sense of expectation rippled through the gathering as the moment approached. Then a series of detonations rent the air and before their very eyes it seemed the whole world exploded. Audible gasps sounded from many as the earth erupted sending angry towers of grey smoke billowing ever upwards into a cloudless sky. Huge boulders were hurtled high into the air, rocks and stones whizzed in every direction, lethal missiles and shrapnel all. The landscape looked like a battlefield.

As she watched, Jess was glad the local people were not there to witness the magnitude of the destruction. She could just picture the horror on the faces of the aunties at such wanton defilement of this land of their ancestors.

She found the sight strangely unsettling herself, although she told herself she mustn't. The blasting was necessary in the name of progress. No sacred sites were being affected and the creation of this path through the northern cuttings to Alice Springs was essential to the Ghan. But much as she reasoned with herself, Jess found it unnerving to see the earth so desecrated.

'What did I tell you?' Back on familiar ground at their window table in the tavern, toasting the event's success over a beer, Matt was pleased that the blasting hadn't disappointed. 'Spectacular, wasn't it?'

'Oh yes,' she said, 'it was certainly spectacular.' She decided not to share with him her personal reaction to the blasting. What would be the point? Besides, there was another item on the agenda that demanded discussion.

'The rail corridor to Alice is completed now, isn't it?' she queried in seeming innocence.

'More or less. There's the earthwork that'll follow the blasting of course, and there are major overpasses and road works to be constructed, but the actual path of the corridor is completed, yes.'

'So when do we go?' she asked. She'd dropped the innocent act. 'You said we'd visit the site when the corridor was completed. Actually,' she corrected herself, 'you said we'd go after the rock blasting. You were quite specific.'

'Yes, I was.' He'd known exactly where she was heading. 'And yes, we will visit the site.'

'Good. It's important we do, or rather that *you* do.'

'Why?' He was intrigued. 'Why is it important, Jess?'

'I have no idea,' she admitted with one of those smiles that always disarmed him, 'but I do know I'm right. Just as I know when we get there you'll find out for yourself. They'll tell you, Matt. They'll make their presence known.'

They, he thought, *the ancestors.* 'Right you are then.' He stood. 'Ready for another beer?'

'When?' she demanded. 'When do we go?'

'What's wrong with tomorrow?'

'Fine. Settled. Yes, I'd love another beer.'

The drive out to the site the following morning was pleasant. He picked her up in the Land Rover at nine. Even at that hour the day was turning into a scorcher, but as neither of them minded the heat they didn't turn the air-conditioning on, preferring to travel with the windows down and the desert air whipping about them.

They didn't talk much as they went, there didn't seem to be the need, although Jess initially wondered whether he might be feeling some trepidation at the prospect of what lay ahead. He'd certainly been wary on their last visit, she recalled. A quick glance told her that this time he wasn't.

After turning off the Stuart Highway into one of the newly created access roads that led directly to the rail corridor it wasn't long before they reached what had previously been the old surveyor's track.

'Wow,' she said as they turned right, back-tracking a short way south in the direction of Alice Springs, 'bit of a difference.'

The surveyor's track was no longer just a track, but had been widened to form a service road; and beside it, stretching north and south across the desert as far as the eye could see, was the wide, red path of the rail corridor.

'Yep, pretty impressive,' he agreed. 'All ready for the track-laying phase now and that's a much speedier process. The Ghan'll be finished way ahead of schedule.'

Before long the two rocky hillocks came into view up ahead. They were to the right on the other side of the corridor, with its attendant service roads either side.

'There they are,' Matt said as if sighting old friends.

He appeared equally relaxed five minutes or so later when he pulled up the vehicle and climbed from the driver's side. Jess was keeping a close eye on him by now, waiting for any signs of change. She expected that at some stage there would be.

They crossed the rail corridor and the service road on the other side and walked towards the site. But when they arrived at the edge of the clearing he halted. She came to a halt herself, not saying anything, just watching him.

'I'm trying to make out the sign,' he said by way of explanation, squinting up at the larger of the outcrops and feeling suddenly self-conscious. Why was he hesitant? He'd experienced no adverse effects when he'd visited the site with Bisley, the engineer. Perhaps it was simply being here in Jess's company. She was obviously intent upon invoking some form of supernatural phenomenon.

'You can't see it from here,' she said. Then, giving him time to adjust to his apparent wave of insecurity, she turned and looked at the rail corridor behind them.

She pictured the mighty Ghan passing by. She could see it now roaring across the flood plains and red spinifex country, people peering from its windows out at the wilderness, city people who had never witnessed the beauty of the desert. They'll be able to see the site, she thought, but they won't be able to see the sign. She was thankful for the fact. If discovered, the cameleer's sign, as a relic from the past and a link with the Overland Telegraph Line, could well become a tourist attraction drawing visitors to the site. It mustn't, Jess thought. The sign must remain undiscovered and the site simply an unremarkable spot in the middle of the desert.

She turned back to Matt. 'You can only see the sign from the centre of the clearing,' she said. 'Come on,' and she took his hand.

He allowed himself to be led, following her without question. But he didn't need her guidance anyway. Something other than Jess was already leading him.

When they reached the centre of the clearing she pointed to the sign where it sat half way up the hillock. 'See,' she said, 'there it is.' Then she realised that he wasn't looking. He was somewhere else altogether.

She felt similarly distracted and, letting go of his hand, they stood side by side in silence, both aware of a presence other than their own.

Jess embraced the familiar sensation, knowing she was being welcomed. The restlessness she'd felt emanating from the land on her last visit had gone. The spirits are content now, she thought, this is a peaceful place.

'You can feel it, can't you?' she whispered, knowing that he could. 'You can feel it, Matt: they're welcoming us.'

Matt wasn't sure what it was he felt, and he wasn't sure he liked it. The sensation was altogether too weird. Some strange energy seemed to surround him like an electric field, making his skin tingle. He recalled the first time he'd met Jess, how when they shook hands he'd felt an electric current run through her fingers into his. This was similar, but it was happening to his whole body and he couldn't control it. If he was being welcomed then he wasn't at all sure he wanted to be.

Beside him, Jess sensed his resistance. 'Don't be alarmed,' she said, 'there's nothing to be afraid of here. This is a beautiful place, a peaceful place.'

She could see immediately that her reassurance had made no impression whatsoever, so she went on, telling him what he needed to hear, and Matt found himself compelled to listen.

'Our people believe that we come from the land and that we go back to the land, Matt,' she said. 'We believe we are part of Apmere, which was created by the Ancestral Beings. Apmere is the Arunta word for land, but it really means so very much more. We belong to Apmere and Apmere belongs to us, we are part of the rocks and the earth and the creek beds and trees. Apmere is who we are, this is what our people believe.'

She smiled, breaking the solemnity of the moment. 'Now I don't know why,' she continued, 'but for some reason this particular piece of land where we're standing right now is of great personal significance to the ancestors who contacted you.' She stopped herself saying 'your ancestors', much as she wanted to. 'You saved this site for the ancestors, Matt, and they're grateful. Don't resist. Be polite. Give yourself to them and accept their thanks.'

He nodded obediently. It seemed he had no option other than to obey, but it also seemed right he should place his trust in her as he had before. 'Same as last time, I take it?'

She nodded in return. 'Same as last time,' she said and she watched as he closed his eyes and breathed in deeply, preparing himself. She closed her eyes and did the same.

But Matt could never have prepared himself for what happened next: he could never have believed such connection possible. Hands were touching him, lightly, softly, unseen hands. The tingling sensation he'd experienced had now become the gentlest caress, an all-encompassing presence, embracing him in its warmth, the faintest breeze of its breath fanning his face. The sensation was eerily physical, yet there was no-one there. Obeying her instruction, he stopped resisting and surrendered his will to the force that surrounded him.

Beside him Jess did the same, giving herself wholeheartedly to the spiritual presence that enveloped her.

Neither knew exactly when the embrace became real, when the hands became their hands and the breath their breath. A delicate transition had taken place. The touch was now physical, no longer an unearthly phenomenon and no longer unseen, this was flesh and blood. Drawn to each other by a power not their own, the embrace had become their embrace, and looking into each other's eyes they saw no surprise there. Both knew this was destined to happen.

They kissed, becoming one with each other and also with the presence that had willed this to happen. All were fused, timeless, existing on some other plane.

Then the moment slowly faded. The presence was no longer with them. They were just a couple alone in the desert. It was only then, when they had returned to reality, that Jess spoke.

'Perhaps this is why you were brought here, Matt,' she said, 'perhaps this is what your ancestors intended all along.' It was now right that she refer personally to his ancestors, she thought. Given the warmth of the reception they'd received and the resulting outcome it was only polite that she should.

'Perhaps,' he replied. Despite the experience, which he'd found overwhelming, Matt's tone remained as ever doubtful.

Jess laughed lightly. 'You still don't believe they are your ancestors, do you?'

'I don't know what I believe, Jess. I'm certainly aware that something extraordinary just happened, something quite inexplicable, but I honestly don't know what I believe.' He didn't, it was true, but he wasn't trying very hard. He didn't know or care about anything at this stage. He was unreasonably happy, joyous in an exquisite way he'd never have believed possible. Tears pricked his eyelids, he could have wept unashamedly. Nothing else mattered.

They sat in the centre of the dusty clearing for some time, talking endlessly about everything and nothing, kissing intermittently and making up for lost time, both wondering all the while how this hadn't happened sooner.

Then when they returned to Alice Springs he didn't drop her off at her flat. He stayed and they made love throughout the afternoon.

Everything changed from that day on. They were in love, certainly, but more than that they felt they'd known each other for the whole of their lives. 'Perhaps from a previous life too,' Jess said, and he knew she wasn't joking. For Matt, the ghost of Angie was finally laid to rest, a beautiful image forever young that belonged to his past. The rest of his life now belonged to Jess, just as hers belonged to him.

*

Several weeks later they flew to Adelaide for the weekend. Lilian had been nagging Matt for some time now, aware that his work was no longer as demanding as it had been.

'You don't mind Mum knowing about us, do you?' Matt asked. 'I haven't said a word to her yet and I won't if you don't want me to, but she's bound to guess.'

'Of course I don't mind,' Jess said. 'I adore your mother, you know that.'

'Jess darling, how lovely . . .'

A kaleidoscope of purple and pink greeted them at the front door and after the customary effusive hug Lilian swanned on ahead into the living room, where Dave was pouring the coffee.

'I've prepared the studio for you, dear,' she said pointedly, looking from one to the other as they settled into their armchairs.

'No need, Mum,' Matt interjected, 'Jess'll be staying in the flat with me.'

'Oh good. About time.' Lilian had known they were lovers the moment she'd opened the front door, but she'd wondered if they were going to try and disguise the fact. She was so glad they'd decided not to.

'So what finally brought things to fruition?' she asked, beaming broadly and ignoring Dave's warning glance. She didn't care in the least if she was overstepping the bounds of common decency, as he obviously thought she was. These two had been dillydallying for so long she had a right to know.

Had his mother been just a little more tactful Matt might have launched straight into their story, but as was so often the case Lilian's bluntness grated annoyingly. He gave one of his dagger-like glares and was about to tell her to mind her own bloody business when Jess leapt to the rescue.

'Actually, Lilian, that's a very interesting question.' She flashed him a quick smile that had an instant calming effect. They intended to share their story in any event, and Lilian's forthrightness was only expediting matters.

'We returned to the sacred site,' she said, 'the place that Matt was led to all those months ago, remember? The place where he had his blackout?'

She looked from Lilian to Dave, who both nodded. Then her eyes remained on Dave as she made her announcement, his reaction being the one that most interested her.

'And while we were there,' she said, 'we were visited by a presence. Both of us,' she added meaningfully.

'Oh how thrilling!' Lilian clapped her hands together like a ten-year-old promised fairy-floss. Dave remained silent.

Jess went on to recount her version of events briefly, succinctly, saying that she believed it was Matt's ancestors who had brought them together. 'As may well have been their intention – or at least part of their intention – right from the start,' she concluded.

Matt followed up with his own description of the incident, which was far more complex, far more passionate and surprisingly out of character.

'The experience was amazing, Dad,' he said, addressing his father, aware that Lilian was already enthralled and that Dave was the one who would take some convincing. 'The presence was palpable. I could swear I was being touched, I could feel something breathing, but there was no-one there. And when Jess and I were drawn together the sensation was exquisite, indescribable. It brought tears to my eyes, I swear. I could have cried right there in the middle of the desert for the sheer beauty of that moment . . .'

Lilian remained utterly spellbound throughout, but Dave, watching his son so uncharacteristically animated,

couldn't help wondering at the change. What a turna-
round, he thought. Does Matt really believe all this?
Many people feel a spiritual presence in the desert.
Crikey, the number of times I've felt it myself – but
direct contact with one's ancestors? Even if they're black,
as Jess believes them to be, this is stretching things a
bit, surely.

Dave's incredulity was so readable, that Jess decided
to save the poor man further turmoil. 'Don't worry,
Dave,' she said lightly, 'Matt's not a convert, I can
assure you.'

Dave felt guilty at having been so caught out. He liked
the girl a great deal and had no wish to trivialise her beliefs
or those of her people.

'I'm sorry ...' He started to apologise, but to Jess no
apology was necessary.

She went on to explain. 'Matt genuinely believes he was
visited by some force,' she said, 'but he doesn't for one
minute believe the contact was made by his own ancestors.
I doubt he ever will.'

Lilian's voice cut through the discussion bringing them
all to a halt.

'Well there's one way to solve at least part of the
mystery, isn't there?' she said.

No-one uttered a word as they waited for her to go on.

'DNA testing, of course.'

Father and son exchanged a glance.

'Yes, there is that,' Dave agreed, wondering why on
earth the thought hadn't occurred to him. 'There is certainly that.'

'And just think of the glorious babies you'll have.' Lilian
was already convinced the tests would prove Jess's theory.
'Not only physically beautiful, but you'll be re-injecting
black blood to the line –'

'Give it a rest, Mum.' Matt issued a final warning. 'One
thing at a time.'

But Lilian ignored him altogether. 'The re-introduction of black blood to the family line,' she said, turning to Jess. 'Mr Neville's "biological absorption" in reverse: a most responsible thing to do in my opinion.' She beamed, delighted that she'd had the final word. 'And now let's open a magnificent red wine.'

ACKNOWLEDGEMENTS

Love and thanks, as always, to my husband, Bruce Venables, who continues to be a constant source of inspiration and laughter.

Thanks also to those ever-supportive friends who offer not only encouragement but on so many occasions assistance of the most practical kind: Dr Meredith Burgmann, Michael Roberts, Colin Julin, James Laurie, Sue Greaves and Susan Mackie-Hookway.

A special thanks to two close family members who were always on hand and whose highly skilled areas of expertise provided invaluable research material: big brother Rob Nunn and cousin Max Brown. Max was ably assisted by his friends Jock Henderson and Colin Schipp, so thanks to them too.

The expertise of another close mate was of untold value. I speak of the inimitable Bill Leak, whose passionate discourse on art is always riveting. Thanks, Bill, for allowing me to quote you directly, giving colourful voice and views to one of my favourite characters, 'Lilian'.

Thanks again to my publisher, Beverley Cousins; my editors, Brandon VanOver and Kate O'Donnell; my publicist, Jessica Malpass, and the entire hard-working team at Random House.

There are many people in Alice Springs to whom I am most grateful: June Noble for the provision of contacts and material, and also for sharing her personal knowledge of the area; Liz Martin OAM and Kel Davis of The National Road Transport Hall of Fame and The Old Ghan Train Railway Museum for the encouragement they offered and the wealth of information I gained from their wonderful museum; Dr Patricia Miller AO, Deputy to the Administrator NT for providing information about traditional Indigenous rituals; Jenny and Alan Dietrich for sharing with me their knowledge of local Indigenous art, language and practices; Kathryn Bailey, Special Collections Librarian at Alice Springs Library for the provision of archival material; Charlie Poole for responding to my phone calls regarding added detail about the building of the Ghan; and Susan, Helen and Deb of Tourism Central Australia.

Thanks to other mates Peter Hiland and Wayne Anthoney for supplying contacts and research material, and also to David Kightley of the Adabco Hotel in Adelaide.

Special thanks must go to Hugh Warden of Gundooee Contemporary Indigenous Art for not only sharing with me his knowledge of central desert peoples, but for supplying me with a copy of *People of the Western Desert*, filmed in 1965 and 1967 by the Australian Commonwealth Film Unit for the Australian Institute of Aboriginal studies. This remarkable footage provides an excellent insight into the traditional daily life of the nomadic desert peoples of this country.

Among my other research sources I would like to recognise the following:

A Vision Fulfilled, David Hancock
Alice on the Line, Doris Blackwell, Douglas Lockwood, Rigby Ltd, Adelaide, 1965
The Surveyors, Margaret Goyder Kerr, Rigby Ltd, 1971
The Territory, Ernestine Hill, Angus & Robertson Ltd, 1951
Travels in a Foreign Land, Wayne Anthoney, 2010
Understanding Aboriginal Culture, Cyril Havecker, edited and foreword by Yvonne Malykke, Cosmos Periodicals, 1987

Iwenhe Tyerrtye – What it Means to be an Aboriginal Person, Margaret Kemarre Turner, IAD Press, Alice Springs, 2010

Western Arrarnta Picture Dictionary, IAD Press, 2006

The Red Centre, Jenny Stanton, photography by Barry Skipsey, Australian Geographic Pty Ltd, 1995

Bush Foods: Arrernte Foods from Central Australia, Margaret Kemarre Turner with John Henderson, IAD Press, Alice Springs, 1996

JUDY NUNN

Sanctuary

'They'd seen virtually nothing for days . . . sky and sea had merged into one all-consuming blur.'

On a barren island off the coast of Western Australia, a rickety wooden dinghy runs aground. Aboard are nine people who have no idea where they are. Strangers before the violent storm that tore their vessel apart, the instinct to survive has seen them bond during their days adrift on a vast and merciless ocean.

Fate has cast them ashore with only one thing in common . . . fear. Rassen the doctor, Massoud the student, the child Hamid and the others all fear for their lives. But in their midst is Jalila, who appears to fear nothing. The beautiful young Yazidi woman is a mystery to them all.

While they remain undiscovered on the deserted island, they dare to dream of a new life . . .

But forty kilometres away on the mainland lies the tiny fishing port of Shoalhaven. Here everyone knows everyone, and everyone has their place. In Shoalhaven things never change.

Until now . . .

A no.1 bestseller, *Sanctuary* is a compelling novel, where compassion meets bigotry, hatred meets love, and ultimately despair meets hope on the windswept shores of Australia.

CHAPTER ONE

The island appeared out of nowhere. One minute they were relentlessly adrift in a rickety wooden dinghy with nothing in sight but the horrifying blue of the Indian Ocean, then the next they had run aground. On what? Land? A submerged reef? Both it seemed. A rocky barren island with low-lying shrubs, little more than a scrub-covered reef. Why hadn't they seen it earlier? But then they'd seen virtually nothing for days as sky and sea had merged into one all-consuming blur. Even before the storm, which had wrecked their vessel and taken the lives of so many, they'd stopped looking for land. Their minds had been wandering in and out of consciousness for some time now, all nine of them, including the child, who was somehow still miraculously alive.

They couldn't tell how long they'd been adrift in the dinghy. Was it a day? A day and a night? Yes, there'd definitely been a night, a night of unbearable cold that had cut through their drenched clothes and their bones to the very marrow of their being. Was it two days? Perhaps three? They didn't know, and in their state of exhaustion were beyond caring. Even Rassen, the doctor who had taken on the role of leader and in whom the survivors had placed their trust, even Rassen had resigned himself to the inevitability of his death. He, too, had stopped looking out for land. Like the others, he'd stopped trying to even guess in which direction it might lie. And now there it was right before his very eyes.

The dinghy lurched drunkenly to one side and settled itself in the rocky shallows, as if like its occupants in a state of exhaustion and nearing the end of its life, which indeed it was.

No one made a move. Several of the survivors remained in a semi-conscious condition and were unaware of the extraordinary event that had taken place, while others stared dumbly, uncomprehendingly, their minds unable to absorb what they saw.

Rassen squinted through the morning's wintry glare, hardly daring to believe he could be right, for the light of the sun reflecting off the water's surface played tricks with a person's mind. Is this a mirage? he wondered. Surely my eyes deceive me. There are huts on this island. There are huts and there are jetties projecting into the sea. Where there are huts and jetties there are people. We are saved.

'We are saved,' he heard himself croak in a voice that wasn't his, a voice parched and by now so unused as to seem quite foreign. He addressed the words to his wife, Hala, who sat beside him, also unable to believe the vision before her.

'We are saved,' he repeated, but this time to the survivors in general and this time in a voice that, although weakened, held an edge of authority. Someone must lead them. His tone proved effective, bringing the others to their senses, rousing them from the lethargy of their surrender. 'Massoud,' he said to the young Iranian who throughout the ordeal had become his second-in-command, 'help me get everyone ashore. We must find water.'

Both men struggled to their feet, unsteady on limbs unaccustomed to action.

In stepping out of the dinghy, Massoud misjudged the water's depth, which was well above knee-height, and fell clumsily face-first into the sea. His immersion had an instantaneous effect. Suddenly he was revitalised, alert with a giddy form of madness, although he had the distinct feeling his elation was due not so much to a dunking, but rather the knowledge he was not going to die after all. Not yet anyway. As he stood, he let out a strange bark, which in actual fact was a laugh.

'All ashore everyone,' he said, beckoning emphatically for the benefit of those amongst them who did not speak English. He didn't know why he chose to address them in English at all, perhaps simply because the doctor had.

Rassen lowered himself carefully into the water, then assisted Hala, taking her full weight as he lifted her over the side of the dinghy.

'I can manage,' she said firmly when she was standing beside him, although she felt she might fall at any moment. 'Help the others.'

'Give me the child,' Rassen said in Arabic, and held his arms out to the young father.

The father passed the unconscious infant to him before alighting from the dinghy himself and tending to his wife. She, too, was barely conscious and moaned as she was lifted by her husband and cradled in his arms.

The other couple, Egyptians, a man and woman in their early forties, managed to climb out unassisted, albeit shakily. Then the man turned back to offer his hand to the girl. But she appeared not to notice the gesture, making no acknowledgement as she wordlessly slid her body over the dinghy's side, an action that even in her weakened condition was graceful.

The girl, whom they presumed to be around nineteen years of age, was a mystery to them all. She never spoke, but they knew she was not a mute for they had witnessed the occasional whispered response to her companion in the early days of their journey, before the storm and the capsizing of the vessel, when hopes were still high. Perhaps it had been her companion's gruesome death that had rendered her ongoing silence. At least that's what Rassen had first thought, but he'd come to doubt it, recalling how, even as she'd watched the man's blood swirl in the water, even as she'd heard his screams and witnessed the ferocity of the shark's attack, her reaction had been minimal: little more than resignation. The girl remained the same mystery to them all that she had been from the very outset. Her innate grace matched a beauty that was flawless, even now, sun-damaged and exhausted as she was. Eyes constantly downcast, she seemed unaware not only of herself, but of everything around her, as if she had removed herself to another place altogether. The others, who had bonded in the interest of survival, did not even know her name.

When everyone had alighted, they made their way slowly and gingerly across the twenty or so metres of rocky shallows to the shore, the young father carrying his wife, Rassen the child, and Massoud pulling behind him the dinghy, which minus its human cargo was now afloat.

Beneath bare feet, the feel of rough coral sand brought overwhelming relief, and those with footwear pulled off their sandals and shoes, relishing the sensation. Some offered prayers in the form of wordless thoughts giving thanks to their God, while some muttered through parched lips.

Massoud secured the dinghy's anchor in the rocks of the shoreline while Rassen led the way to the nearest hut, which, like its neighbours, was crudely constructed of corrugated iron attached to a timber frame. The hut was incongruously painted bright yellow and its tin roof, supported by roughly hewn wooden pillars, extended over a verandah floored with paving stones, a timber bench beside the front door completing an effect that, although ramshackle, was homely.

The young father, whose name was Karim, settled his wife gently on the bench. She had fully regained consciousness, but once again moaned, putting a hand to her ribs, the movement obviously causing her pain.

'We are safe, Azra,' Karim whispered in Hazaragi, the Persian dialect of his people. He knelt beside her. 'We are safe,' he repeated. Karim did not know if they were safe at all, but for the moment they were free of the relentless ocean and of the sharks and of all the other terrors he knew beset her. Given her intense fear of the sea, Azra had been terrified from the moment they had stepped aboard the vessel. He had deeply admired the strength she had displayed in undertaking such a journey.

Rassen passed the infant to Hala.

'Tend to the child,' he said, although they both knew there was little to be done. The child, a boy of barely three, was now conscious, his eyelids flickering open, his small chest rising with each shallow hard-won breath, but he was close to death. It was really only a matter of time.

Rassen knocked on the front door of the hut. There was no answer. Another knock, with a little more force this time: still no answer. Then he tried the handle and the door swung open to reveal an empty room.

'Hello?' he called. He peered into a roughly furnished living room with shelves and pots and pans to one side, but, through another open door that led to the rear of the hut, he could make out no activity. The place was clearly deserted. He stepped back, closing the door behind him.

'Do what you can for the others,' he instructed Hala, aware that if anyone could help ease their fear and uncertainty it was his wife. Hala was an experienced and highly competent nurse and, like many of her kind, had a way of instilling confidence during times of crisis. 'Massoud and I will make ourselves known to the island's inhabitants,' he said, although gazing about Rassen had the strangest feeling that something was wrong. Where *were* the inhabitants? Why had they not shown themselves?

Surely our arrival cannot have gone unnoticed, he thought. It is mid-morning – surely someone must have seen us. Do they fear our presence? Will they prove friend or foe? Perhaps they are in hiding, or perhaps at this very moment they are preparing to attack.

Then, scanning the line of huts for any sign of life, his eyes hit upon the most welcome of sights. A water tank. In fact more than one water tank. At least they had to be water tanks, his confused and exhausted mind told him, they simply had to be.

Beside several of the huts stood large round tanks with a height at rooftop and guttering level, presumably for drainage. They could be nothing other than a water supply, Rassen thought. He could even make out a tap on the side of the nearest one.

Rassen was not alone in noticing the tanks. Massoud, too, had seen them. And so had Hany, the Egyptian. Glances were exchanged between the three men and they set off with purpose, the renewed will to survive having lent them fresh strength, each praying desperately the tanks were not dry.

Behind them, Hala, obeying her husband's instruction, did the best she could to comfort the others, although without Rassen's medical kit and supplies, which had been lost along with everything else during the storm, there was little practical assistance she could offer.

'Hold little Hamid for me, will you please?' She could have passed the infant to his father, or to Hany's wife, the Egyptian woman, Sanaa, who appeared to have strength enough left to assist, but she deliberately chose the girl. Time to break through the barriers, she thought. 'I need to examine Azra,' she said when the girl hesitated. 'Azra is in pain and needs attention. Please take the child.' Hala spoke Arabic, the language in which they could all communicate, albeit in varying dialects, and in the case of Azra and Karim only to a limited degree. Her general manner and her tone were pleasant enough, but her request was really more a command.

The girl obeyed, taking the little boy in her arms, and

Hala sat on the bench beside Azra. She opened the young woman's rough woollen coat and, pulling back her own shoulder-length hair, now stiff and matted with salt, leant down to press her ear against Azra's chest. Without a stethoscope her ear would have to do, although she was confident she knew what the problem was. Azra had suffered rib damage during the storm and ensuing capsize. To what extent Hala could not be certain, but she was quite sure a broken rib had not punctured the lungs. If it had, by now the woman would no doubt be dead.

'Breathe in,' she said, and Azra obeyed, wincing as she did. 'Yes, I know,' Hala said sympathetically, 'it is painful to breathe deeply, yes?'

Azra nodded.

'And painful to cough also, am I right?' she asked, raising her head. During the past days she'd noticed the young woman holding her ribs and stemming a desire to cough.

Again Azra nodded.

'But if you feel the need to cough, do not stop yourself,' Hala said firmly. 'If you were to do so, it might invite a chest infection. And we would not want that, would we?' She spoke slowly, aware Azra's knowledge of Arabic was limited, but she'd apparently made her meaning quite clear.

'No,' Azra shook her head obediently, 'no, we would not.'

Azra would do whatever was asked of her for Nurse Hala had been sent by the angels, the messengers of God. Before the terrible storm, when the sickness had spread about the boat, they had all benefitted from the ministrations of Nurse Hala. She had saved little Hamid's life. At that time Azra had even thought that perhaps Nurse Hala herself was an angel, sent by Allah to cure their illnesses, as angels were bounden to do. And Nurse Hala's appearance, so different from them all with her fair hair and fair skin and her motherly English-looking face, might well have been that of an angel. Everyone knew that angels came in many guises. Azra recognised now that Nurse Hala was merely a woman, but one of such strength and goodness that it was surely true she had been sent by the angels.

'Do not be alarmed now, Azra, I am going to examine you.'

Hala lifted the young woman's blouse, enough to expose the ribcage, but not the breasts, aware that modesty was of paramount importance to a woman of Azra's devout faith. She examined the midsection with care – some bruising, but all appeared to be in order – then cupping the lower ribs of each side in her hands she gave a slight squeeze.

Azra cried out involuntarily.

'I'm sorry,' Hala said, 'I know I hurt you, but it was necessary.' Good, she thought. Things were just as she'd expected – there was elasticity in the ribs and the damage was fractures only, which would heal in time. 'There is no need for concern, Karim,' she added, having noted the husband's consternation at his wife's cry of pain. 'Azra has a fractured rib, perhaps two, I can't be sure, and they are painful, certainly . . .' she looked back at Azra and smiled '. . . but they will mend. Azra may be small,' she added encouragingly, 'but she is strong.'

Hala spoke as a mother might to a child. The young woman, in her early twenties, petite, pretty, hijab framing a doll-like face, was so disarmingly ingenuous it was difficult not to view her as a child.

They were child-like the pair of them, she thought as she stood and gestured for the bearded young man with the earnest eyes to sit beside his wife. They were a devoutly religious and simple young peasant couple, obviously very much in love, and she wondered what had driven them to take the drastic course of action they had. She wondered also how they would react to the death of their infant son. It was evident they did not realise the seriousness of little Hamid's condition.

While Karim sat on the bench, his arm comfortingly around his wife, Hala turned her attention to the girl, so unfathomable to them all. The Egyptian woman, Sanaa, was seated on the paving stones leaning against one of the wooden pillars, eyes trained on the men in the distance, which gave Hala ample opportunity to study the girl unobserved.

It appeared, for the very first time, that she might be showing something approaching a glimmer of interest as she looked down at the child in her arms. She was displaying no emotion certainly, but Hala noted she had drawn the end of the light shawl, which was draped over her head as it always was, about the child. Such a gesture was surely evidence of compassion.

Hala indicated they should move away from the bench and the child's parents, and the girl allowed herself to be led from the verandah around to the shaded side of the hut, where they stood in silence for a moment or so, the girl's eyes still focused upon the child.

'He is suffering from malnutrition,' Hala said, 'and most importantly dehydration.' Well of course, we all are, she thought, feeling stupid for stating the obvious.

The girl gave the slightest of nods.

'The degree of deprivation we have suffered affects a child far more severely,' Hala explained. 'To be quite honest, I'm surprised he's still alive.' She wondered why she was being so brutally truthful, presumably to shock the girl into some form of reaction.

Once again, the girl gave a slight nod, but her eyes remained on the child.

Hala waited for a moment, then . . . 'What is your name?' she asked.

There was no reply, no reaction whatsoever.

'We must have a name,' Hala insisted. 'In order to survive we must form a bond and work together. This is where our strength lies. What is your name?'

Still no reply, and still the girl did not meet Hala's eyes.

'Give me the child,' Hala said. No point in pushing any further, she told herself, although she felt a flash of annoyance, which she knew was quite irrational. The girl's condition was obviously a result of some trauma that was no fault of her own. But we've all suffered trauma, haven't we? Hala thought. Why else are we here? She was suddenly so very, very weary that she felt she might collapse. But she didn't, straightening her back instead and holding her arms out for the child.

The girl, with her customary grace, drew the end of her shawl aside as if parting a curtain in order to reveal something precious, and in doing so she exposed the little face looking up and the eyes that had been fixed upon her all the while. Then without a word, and with no obvious show of reluctance, she transferred the child into Hala's waiting arms.

Hala steeled herself, determined to remain unmoved; the girl's problems were her own. She took the child and turned away, her intention being to return the boy to his parents – she did not relish their queries about his condition – but she was barely a pace from the girl when . . .

'Jalila.'

She turned back. Silence. Then . . .

'My name is Jalila.' Little more than a whisper.

Their eyes locked and Hala was so startled it was all she could do to suppress an involuntary gasp. The girl's eyes, not unsurprisingly, were beautiful, heavy-lashed, hazel-green and arresting in the olive-skinned perfection of her face. But it was not the beauty of the eyes that so startled Hala – it was the lack of life she saw there. The girl held her gaze unwaveringly, yet appeared to see nothing. The girl was staring through eyes that were dead. Or else she's looking into somewhere else, Hala thought, some other place, some other time, I doubt she's seeing me at all. Hala was mesmerised; the girl's eyes engulfed her.

But whether she sees me or not, the offer of her name means something, Hala told herself, contact has been made. I must engage her. I must further the connection.

'Jalila,' she said gently, to which the girl gave another barely perceptible nod. 'What a pretty name.'

Any hope of more conversation, however, was quickly dashed as the girl broke eye contact and again focused upon the child.

'He needs water,' Hala said, looking down at the infant, once more stating the obvious, but determined to maintain the girl's interest. If the child was the only way to do so, then she would talk about the child. 'He needs water above all else. It is dehydration that is killing little Hamid. If we can get water into him, Jalila, then there is just a chance . . .' She turned her gaze upon the girl and left the sentence hanging.

The girl's nod this time was more positive and, as she raised her eyes, Hala was sure she saw a flicker of something there. A flicker of what, she wondered. Hope?

Then as if on cue the men arrived, Massoud and Hany carrying a bucket of water each, Rassen with a miscellany of tin mugs and cups.

'The tanks are full,' Rassen announced triumphantly, 'and we took these from one of the houses – no one was there. Come, come,' he urged, 'we must drink together.'

As he led the way around to the front of the hut, the others following, Hala glanced at the girl, receiving no reaction, which did not surprise her. Eyes downcast, the girl had once more retreated into her other world. But the girl now had a name. Jalila. And that was a start.

Hala returned the boy to his father, and the group gathered in a circle on the paving stones of the verandah, the buckets in the centre, Rassen handing out the mugs and cups.

'We washed them in sea water, the buckets as well,' he said in an aside to Hala, 'it's the best we could do.'

Hala smiled at the irony of the comment. They had survived typhoid aboard the vessel before the storm broke, they had survived death by drowning following the capsizing of the vessel and they had just now come very close to dying of thirst, so the sanitary requirements of the medical profession seemed somewhat superfluous.

Rassen returned the smile, aware of her thoughts. 'Drink my dear, drink,' he urged, handing her a cup of water. He took the child from Karim. 'I'll look after the boy, Karim,' he said, 'you must drink.'

Rassen, Massoud and Hany had slaked their thirst at the water tank and already looked stronger. The others now followed suit, feeling the dizziness lift, feeling their bodies re-energise.

'Be careful,' Rassen warned, 'do not drink too quickly.'

Then he started, very, very slowly, to feed the child, cup to tiny lips, parched and cracked, pausing carefully between each sip. Aware the boy would likely be unable to swallow, Rassen expected any minute that the water would be coughed back up. But the boy did not cough back the water. The boy was able to swallow. And he did so slowly and steadily, matching Rassen's timing with every single sip. Little Hamid, it seemed, was as intent upon survival as the rest of them.

Rassen and Hala shared a look of understanding: this was a very good sign. Hala's eyes darted to Jalila, hoping to share a look with her also, but none was forthcoming. No matter, she thought, as she watched the girl watching the child. The child is a strong enough link for the moment – given time Jalila will bond with the rest of us. Hala certainly hoped so anyway.

A half an hour later, it was decided to explore the island, or at least the huts, in an effort to find the inhabitants and hopefully food.

Rassen said nothing of his earlier misgivings and, preparing to set off once again with Massoud and Hany, he suggested Karim stay in the shade of the verandah and look after Azra and little Hamid.

'The women too,' he added, 'look after the women for me, Karim.' He did not wish the young man to feel emasculated.

But Hala had something to say about that.

'The women may wish to accompany you, Rassen.' She looked to Sanaa, who returned a vigorous nod. 'And we will no doubt be of great value in negotiating with the locals. We are, as you well know, my dear, far more skilled than you men in matters of diplomacy.'

Rassen acquiesced with a wry smile, considering it an extremely healthy sign that even under their current circumstances his feisty wife, a social activist and confirmed feminist, should behave so true to form.

'Jalila may wish to stay, however,' Hala said, noting the girl's continued lack of interest in anything but the child.

'Ah. Yes, of course.'

Rassen was not the only one taken aback by the comment. So the girl finally has a name, they all thought. But Hala's blatantly casual manner in announcing the fact signalled no response should be forthcoming, so no one uttered a word.

'Well let's be off then, shall we?' Rassen said as heartily as possible, although he continued to have a strange sense of foreboding. 'All those who are coming, join me.'

The others followed as he led the way along the path, Hala by his side.

'I gather you've had a bit of a breakthrough,' he muttered in English.

'Just a bit,' Hala replied. 'Not much, but it's a start.'

There were eight huts in all, each crudely constructed of wood and corrugated iron, but in good condition, brightly painted, homely and each, it was discovered, with a water tank of its own, some at the back and some at the side, dependent on the shape of the hut's roof. The overall effect was that of an attractively colourful miniature village. Freestanding cottages, some with verandahs, some without, yellow and blue, green and red, one even a bizarre shade of magenta, all in a line facing out to sea, a well-worn path of crushed coral running along the front linking them in neighbourly fashion.

Four sturdy wooden jetties projected forty metres or so from the rocky shore, each in excellent condition, ready to receive the vessels they had been built for. But where were the vessels? Apart from the survivors' own shabby dinghy anchored in the shallows there was not a boat in sight.

Equally strange, several hundred metres from the huts were a number of roughly hewn benches; was this a popular gathering place for the inhabitants? Certainly at dawn or dusk there would be no impediment to the view of a fine sunrise or sunset across the ocean. But where were the people who enjoyed this spectacle? A door knock had revealed each hut unlocked, but not one occupant. Apart from themselves, it would appear there was not a soul on the island.

'Well we have water and shelter,' Massoud said optimistically, although like the others he was fully aware that, in this desolate place and without assistance, they now faced the threat of starvation.

'You are right, my friend, it is an excellent start.' Rassen was grateful for his young ally's assistance in buoying their spirits. They had survived so much together; they must not give way to despair. 'We will scour the huts for food and provisions, we're bound to find something.'

Once again they progressed methodically from hut to hut, this time exploring each one in detail and, as they did, marvelling at every new discovery.

Many of the unruly, overgrown gardens at the rear of the houses bore produce. A healthy potato patch here, runner beans gone wild there, carrots, turnips, herbs.

Inside the houses, each kitchen was provided with a basic supply of cooking utensils, crockery and cutlery; and the bedrooms, although devoid of linen, revealed comfortable bedsteads with mattresses and pillows, together with cupboards housing an ample supply of blankets. Each hut even had its own outhouse with septic tank. Here indeed was luxury.

Further exploration of storage sheds revealed tools also, and, most important of all, fishing tackle: rods, hand lines, casting nets, scoop nets, apparently home-made three-pronged spears with broom-like wooden handles . . . The list went on.

A self-sufficient village all of our own, Rassen thought, barely able to believe their good fortune. A tiny ghost town with everything set up for instant tenancy as if we are being invited to move in. He didn't even pause to wonder about who had lived here, or where they were now or why they had left. Here on this seemingly barren island was everything they could possibly need in order to survive.

The group returned to the others to impart their findings and share their elation.

'We are most certainly saved,' Rassen declared.

Some once again gave thanks to God, and in their own way, through unspoken prayer or muttered words, but as they looked at each other one common thought was mirrored in their eyes. We have cheated death.

It was only Jalila who appeared not to care.

Khaki Town

**It seems to have happened overnight, Val thought.
How extraordinary. We've become a khaki town.**

It's March 1942. Singapore has fallen. Darwin has been
bombed. Australia is on the brink of being invaded
by the Imperial Japanese Forces. And Val Callahan,
publican of The Brown's Bar in Townsville, could
not be happier as she contemplates the fortune she's
making from lonely, thirsty soldiers.

Overnight the small Queensland city is transformed into
the transport hub for 70,000 American and Australian
soldiers destined for combat in the South Pacific. Barbed
wire and gun emplacements cover the beaches. Historic
buildings are commandeered. And the dance halls are in
full swing with jazz, jitterbug and jive.

The Australian troops begrudge the confident, well-fed
'Yanks' who have taken over their town and their
women. There's growing conflict, too, within the
American ranks, because black GIs are enjoying the
absence of segregation. And the white GIs don't like it.

As racial violence explodes through the ranks of the
military, a young United States Congressman, Lyndon
Baines Johnson, is sent to Townsville by his president
to investigate. 'Keep a goddamned lid on it, Lyndon,'
he is told, 'lest it explode in our faces . . .'

**Judy Nunn's no.1 bestseller was inspired by a
true wartime story that remained a well-kept
secret for over seventy years.**

Araluen

A spell-binding, multi-generational novel, set in the ruthless world of movie-making.

On a blistering hot day in 1850, George and Richard Ross take their first steps on Australian soil after three long months at sea. All they have is each other, and a quarterly remittance from their irate father who has banished them to the Colonies.

A decade on, and the brothers are the owners of successful vineyard, Araluen, nestled in a beautiful green valley not far from Adelaide. Now a successful businessman, George has laid down the roots of his own Ross dynasty, born of the New World. But building a family empire – at any cost – can have a shattering effect on the generations to come . . .

From the South Australian vineyards of the 1850s to the opulence and corruption of Hollywood's golden age . . . From the relentless loneliness of the outback to mega-budget movie-making in modern-day New York . . . Judy Nunn weaves an intricate web of characters and locations in this spellbinding saga of the Ross family and its inescapable legacy of greed and power.

Kal

In a story as sweeping as the land itself, bestselling author Judy Nunn brings Kal magically to life.

Kalgoorlie. It grew out of the red dust of the desert over the world's richest vein of gold. People were drawn there from all over the world, to start afresh or to seek their fortunes.

People like Giovanni Gianni, fleeing his part in a family tragedy. Or Maudie Gaskill, one of the first women to arrive at the goldfields, and now owner of the most popular pub in town. Or Caterina Panuzzi, banished to the other side of the world to protect her family's honour.

The burgeoning town could reward you or it could destroy you, but it would never let you go.

From the heady early days of the gold rush to the horrors of the First World War, to the shame and confrontation of the post-war riots, *Kal* tells the story of Australia itself and the people who forged a nation out of a harsh and unforgiving land.

Beneath the Southern Cross

A riveting novel that tells the story of Sydney and the people who shaped its character, its skyline and its heart.

In 1788, Thomas Kendall, a naïve nineteen-year-old sentenced to transportation for burglary, finds himself bound for Sydney Town and a new life in the wild and lawless land beneath the Southern Cross.

Thomas fathers a dynasty that will last more than two hundred years. His descendants play their part in the forging of a nation, but greed and prejudice see an irreparable rift in the family which will echo through the generations.

It is only at the dawn of the new Millennium – as an old journal lays bear a terrible secret – that the family can finally reclaim its honour . . .

Beneath the Southern Cross is as much a story of a city as it is a family chronicle. Bringing history to life, Judy Nunn traces the fortunes of Kendall's descendants through good times and bad, wars and social revolutions to the present day, vividly drawing the events, characters and issues that have made the city of Sydney and the nation of Australia what they are today.

Territory

**A breathtaking story of disaster, courage and passion
and that Top End spirit that never says die.**

Territory is the story of Henrietta Southern, a young
Englishwoman who trades her war-torn homeland for a
place of wild tropical storms and searing heat, crocodile-
infested rivers and barren red wilderness. Six months
after the bombing of Darwin, she joins her new husband,
Spitfire pilot Terence Galloway, for a new life on his
Northern Territory cattle station.

It is also the story of their sons. Of Malcolm and Kit,
two brothers who grow up in the harsh but beautiful
environment, and share a baptism of fire as young men
in the jungles of Vietnam.

And what of the Dutch East Indies treasure ship which
foundered off Western Australia in 1629? How is the
Galloway family's destiny linked with *Batavia*'s horrific
tale of mutiny and murder . . .?

**From the blazing inferno that was Darwin on 19
February 1942 to the devastation of Cyclone Tracy, from
the red desert to the tropical shore, *Territory* is a mile-a-
minute read from one of Australia's best loved writers.**

Pacific

An epic story of love, sacrifice and revenge swept along on the winds of war.

Australian actress Samantha Lindsay is thrilled when she scores her first lead movie role in the Hollywood epic *Torpedo Junction*, playing a character based on World War II heroine 'Mamma Tack'.

But as filming begins in Vanuatu, uncanny parallels between history and fiction emerge. Just who was the real Mamma Tack? And what mysterious forces are at play? The answers reveal not only bygone secrets but Sam's own destiny.

In another era, Jane Thackeray travels from England to the far distant islands of the New Hebrides. Ensnared in the turmoil of war, Jane witnesses the devastating effect human conflict has upon an innocent race of people. There she meets Charles 'Wolf' Baker, a charismatic fighter pilot, and Jean-Francois Marat, a powerful plantation owner – and soon their lives are entwined in a maelstrom of love and hate . . .

From the dark days of Dunkirk to the vicious fighting that was Guadalcanal, from the sedate beauty of the English Channel ports to a tropical paradise, *Pacific* is Judy Nunn at her enthralling best.

Heritage

They came to change the course of a river. And changed
the course of their lives . . .

In a time when desperate people were seizing with both
hands the chance for freedom, refugees from more than
seventy nations gathered beneath the Southern Cross to
forge a new national identity. They came from all over
wartorn Europe to the mountains of Australia to help
realise one man's dream: the mighty Snowy Mountains
Hydro-Electric Scheme, one of the greatest engineering
feats of the 20th century.

People of all races and creeds tunnelled through a
mountain range to turn the course of a majestic river,
trying to put to rest ghosts from the inferno of history:
buried memories, unimaginable pain and deadly secrets.

From the ruins of Berlin to the birth of Israel, from the
Italian Alps to the Australian high country, *Heritage*
is a passionate and fast-paced tale of rebirth, struggle,
sacrifice and redemption, and a tribute to those who
gave meaning to the Australian spirit.

Floodtide

Four men. One unbreakable friendship. Forged in the mighty Iron Ore State.

Floodtide is the story of Mike, Spud, Pembo and Murray, and the friendship that binds them over four memorable decades in Western Australia.

The prosperous 1950s when childhood is idyllic in the small city of Perth . . . The turbulent 60s of free love and war . . . The avaricious 70s when WA's mineral boom breeds a new kind of entrepreneur . . . The corrupt 80s, when greedy politicians and powerful businessmen bring the state to its knees . . .

Each of the four has a story to tell. An environmentalist fights to save the beautiful Pilbara coast from the mining conglomerates; a Vietnam veteran rises above crippling injuries to discover an extraordinary talent; and an ambitious geologist joins a hard-core businessman to lead the growth of Perth from a sleepy town to a glittering citadel of skyscrapers.

But, as the 1990s ushers in a new age, all four are caught up in the irreversible tides of change – and actions must be answered for . . .

Maralinga

Judy Nunn's gripping and thought-provoking bestseller. During the darkest days of the Cold War, in a remote SA desert, the future of a nation is being decided . . .

Maralinga is the story of British Lieutenant Daniel Gardiner, who accepts a twelve-month posting to the wilds of South Australia on a promise of rapid promotion; Harold Dartleigh, Deputy Director of MI6 and his undercover operative Gideon Melbray; Australian Army Colonel Nick Stratton and the enigmatic Petraeus Mitchell, bushman and anthropologist. They all find themselves in a violent and unforgiving landscape, infected with the unique madness and excitement that only nuclear testing creates.

Maralinga is also a story of love; a love so strong that it draws the adventurous young English journalist Elizabeth Hoffmann halfway around the world in search of the truth.

And *Maralinga* is a story of heartbreak; heartbreak brought to the innocent First Australians who had walked their land unhindered for 40,000 years . . .

Tiger Men

Set in Tasmania, *Tiger Men* is another brilliant work of historical fiction from master storyteller Judy Nunn.

Van Diemen's Land was an island of stark contrasts: a harsh penal colony, an English idyll for its gentry, and an island so rich in natural resources it was a profiteer's paradise.

Its capital, Hobart Town, had its contrasts too: the wealthy elite in their sandstone mansions, the exploited poor in the notorious Wapping slum, and the criminals who haunted the dockside taverns. Hobart Town was no place for the meek.

Tiger Men is the story of Silas Stanford, a wealthy Englishman; Mick O'Callaghan, an Irishman on the run; and Jefferson Powell, an idealistic American political prisoner. It is also the story of the strong, proud women who loved them, and of the children they bore who rose to power in the cutthroat world of international trade.

From the pen of master storyteller Judy Nunn comes a sweeping saga of three families who lived through Tasmania's golden era and the birth of Federation and then watched with pride as their sons marched off to fight for King and Country.

Elianne

Judy Nunn has sold over one million books worldwide. *Elianne*, her no.1 bestseller, is a sweeping story of wealth, power, privilege and betrayal, set on a grand sugar cane plantation in Queensland.

In 1881 'Big Jim' Durham ruthlessly creates for Elianne Desmarais, his young French wife, the finest of the great sugar mills of the Southern Queensland cane fields, and names it in her honour.

The massive estate becomes a self-sufficient fortress and home to hundreds of workers, but 'Elianne' and the Durham Family have dark and distant secrets; secrets that surface in the wildest of times, the 1960s.

For Kate Durham and her brothers Neil and Alan, freedom is the catchword of the decade. Rock 'n' roll, the Pill, the Vietnam War, the rise of Feminism, Asian immigration and the Freedom Ride join forces to rattle the chains of traditional values.

The workers leave the great sugar estates as mechanisation lessens the need for labour – and the Durham family, its secrets exposed, begins its fall from grace . . .

Elianne is a story of honour – family honour among hard men in a hard environment. But when honour is lost so too is love, and without love, what becomes of the family?

The Glitter Game

Edwina Dawling is the golden girl of Australian television. The former pop singer is now the country's most popular actress, an international star thanks to the hit TV soap *The Glitter Game*. But behind the seductive glamour of television is a cutthroat world where careers are made or destroyed with a word in the right ear . . . or a night in the right bed.

The *Glitter Game* is a delicious exposé of the world of television, a scandalous behind-the-scenes look at what goes on when the cameras stop rolling.

Centre Stage

Alex Rainford has it all. He's sexy, charismatic and adored by fans the world over. But he is not all he seems. What spectre from the past is driving him? And who will fall under his spell? Madeleine Frances, beautiful stage and screen actress? Susannah Wright, the finest classical actress of her generation? Or Imogen McLaughlin, the promising young actress whose biggest career break could be her greatest downfall?

Centre Stage is a tantalising glimpse into the world of theatre and what goes on when the spotlight dims and the curtain falls.